Private Listing

Tease Me

C.S. Berry

Author Note

Dear Reader,

Welcome back! If you haven't read Private Listing: Watch Me, Bind Me, and Boss Me, please be aware that this is the last book in the serial. There is no recap and if you haven't read the previous books, you will likely be lost unless you're looking for just the spicy stuff, which there is plenty.

This is it! The final book to complete the Private Listing series. No more cliffhangers. All will be revealed. When I wrote this serial on Vella, I loved every minute of it and revisiting this story, adding to it, and making it even better has been a treat.

PRIVATE LISTING is very much about consensual play.

While I tried to be conscious of proper play within the BDSM community, please remember this is a fantasy. It does not follow all the rules. While everything might be possible, always go to a more trusted source for information than my books.

I love that part of this experience is building a community of readers. You can join me on my Facebook group, C.S. Berry's Spicy Executive Suite. You can also follow me on Instagram, but I generally post about the stories that are ongoing on Kindle Vella (which may contain spoilers for future books).

If you aren't ready for the journey to be over, don't worry. We'll revisit Madison and her guys a little in Obsession, currently available on Kindle Vella. It will be published soon. Join my newsletter to get the details when they are available.

For a list of content warnings or to join my newsletter, please visit my website csberry.com.

Thank you for joining me on this journey and enjoy!!

XOXOXO,
C.S. Berry

Chapter 127

Future Incentives

Madison

While I've been setting up the conference room for the meeting, I've also been texting back and forth with Sara and Hope. Meeting Deidre Byrne, Dee, is fresh in my mind and I want to share with my friends. I need time with my friends. I love my guys, but I need to develop friendships because this is new to me too.

The girls and I decided tomorrow night would be better to hang out. Not just in my room, but out. At a bar. Now I just have to convince the guys to give me a little freedom.

I don't need to go alone, I just want to go. This is what I wanted from life after college. Friends.

I head into the break room to get the water pitcher. As I fill it with filtered water, I let my mind wander. These past few weeks have felt like a dream. Even though some parts have been nightmares, it's been the best time of my life, living with the guys.

The meeting with Dee has me considering all the possibilities again. That I could be someone like her. Own my own business. Head my own empire. It's a reminder that this is an essential stepping stone, but a stepping stone all the same.

"Deep thoughts, tiger?" Blake's voice startles me. Turning, I smile, holding the pitcher of water in front of me. He makes his way over to the dishwasher with his coffee mug.

"Just thinking about where I came from and how I got here." My heart squeezes when I meet his green eyes. If I tell him I love him, will he say it back? How bad would it hurt if he didn't? Seth, Noah, and Coop have admitted they love me, even in front of Blake.

How greedy am I to want all of their love? To want his?

"You've been through a lot." Blake closes the dishwasher and gestures for me to precede him.

It *has* been a lot. My mind skims over the assault by Val and Jeff. The sexual harassment from Hunter. Being attacked by Jimi.

The stalker.

A shiver creeps down my spine. The stalker looms like a shadow over my life that I can't get out from under. But since Jimi's arrest, we haven't heard anything from the stalker.

Maybe they've given up on me. Maybe I'm not worth their time anymore. A girl could hope.

"Do you need any help setting up?" Blake asks.

Glancing over my shoulder at him, I hold up the water pitcher. "No. This is the last thing. But thanks for offering."

Blake nods as he turns toward his office. "I'll be there in a few minutes. I need to make a phone call."

In the conference room, I set the water down and stare out the window. The whole city lies spread out before me. All those possibilities out there just waiting to be discovered.

Where do I want to be in five years? Dee's words keep coming back to haunt me. I don't want to *just* be the guys' assistant and they all know that. But what we have right now works.

What happens when I have to go to my job and can't see them as often? When I have to work late nights? When they get tied up at the office?

When all we have are stolen moments in bed at night? When

there are no more weekly meetings that end with me naked on the conference table? My fingers drift over the wooden surface.

As hands wrap around my waist and draw me back into a hard chest, I jerk. The scent of a fresh breeze, trees, and sunshine wraps around me, soothing me.

"Shh, kitten." Noah kisses my nape and I relax into his arms. "Tense?"

I rest my hands over his and lean against him. "Not particularly. Just on edge, I guess."

"You're safe with us." He kisses up my neck to my jaw. Sparks linger behind his kisses, lighting the fire within. "We've got you."

A soft breath falls from my lips. His arms are safe. This tower feels safe. It feels like home. I don't have to worry about my future right now. I'm building it. Gaining invaluable experience and enjoying the perks of the company.

Noah's hand massages my hip, adding fuel to the raging fire. I hold up the ring sparkling on my finger. The symbol of my fake future. I rest my head back on his shoulder.

"Are we going to talk about the future, Noah?" I ask softly, like it might break the spell if spoken too loudly. I'm not sure I could ask the others yet, but Noah and I, we have something unbreakable. It might bend a little, but it could never break.

He rubs a circle over my hip. His deep voice rumbles through me. "Do you want a future with us, kitten?"

The curiosity in his voice makes me turn to face him. His blond hair falls over his dark eyes as he studies my face. If I could stay in his arms forever, I would.

"I can't imagine a version of my life without you guys in it anymore." Pushing my hand through his hair, I press in close against him. "I love you."

He dips his head down, hovering over my lips, making me catch my breath in anticipation of his kiss. My body flows against his like water. We fit together perfectly. His hard lines and my soft curves.

"I don't want to let you go, Madison." His arms tighten around me.

"Then don't, Noah." I press up, closing the distance between our lips. The sparking touch of his lips against mine makes me gasp in a tiny breath. He claims me and my kiss, crowding me back until I'm trapped between him and the wall.

"Kitten, I want to fuck you until you scream my name." He lifts me, guiding my legs around his waist. His hard cock grinds against my aching pussy through our clothes. I love never having to worry about hiding what we have here.

Out in the real world, I belong to Cooper Graham and only Coop, but here . . . Here I'm Coop's and Seth's and Blake's and Noah's.

My breath rushes out of me against his lips. I open my eyes to search his brown ones. He's not being playful right now but possessive. It opens a craving deep inside me that longs to be possessed by him. To have him take all of me.

"Can I play rough with you, kitten?" He lifts his fingers to rub over my lips before caressing my jaw.

A thrill shoots through me. "Yes. Please, Noah."

His eyes flare with heat. His fingers trail down my neck, making my insides burst into flames. I try to lean forward to capture his lips, but his hand goes around my throat and holds me against the wall. A moment of panic surges through me as I get locked in the nightmare, but he's not squeezing, just holding me.

He stays perfectly still as he searches my eyes. His forehead touches mine and I close my eyes, feeling Noah against me, surrounding me. I breathe out and open my eyes. His hand starts to move away.

"Green," I whisper.

He smiles against my lips as his hand wraps around my throat again, holding me against the wall with his body. His mouth captures mine as I clutch at his shirt, trying to get closer, needing to feel him, all of him. His other hand sweeps up my dress. When he grabs my panties and rips them off, I gasp into his mouth at how wet that makes me.

He thrusts three fingers deep into my pussy, making me moan. It's a lot to take at once, but I'm already dripping wet for him.

"Take my cock out, kitten." His voice is rough against my lips.

I slide my hands down his shirt.

"Now," he commands, thrusting his fingers in deep. Sparks ignite everywhere at his tone. Need makes me tremble.

I reach for his belt and tug it loose while his fingers thrust in and out of me, the fire raging into an inferno until it threatens to consume me. Fuck, I want to burn with him. Burn for him.

His fingers leave me empty and pulsing, needy. He knocks my hands away and finishes freeing his cock. Grabbing my wrists, he brings them over my head, holding them with one hand.

His breath is harsh against my lips as he buries his cock inside me in one thrust.

A gasp leaves me. He presses me against the wall and pushes deeper into me. So deep it feels like he's trying to become part of me. Fuck, I want that. I need that from him.

"Tighten your legs around my waist, kitten," he murmurs against my lips.

When I do as he asks, he returns his hand to my neck. My arms stretch above me in his other hand.

"I want to pump you so full of my cum that it leaks out of you." He rubs his nose against mine. His lips brush my lips, making me long for him to move inside me. To stir that fire. To burn me to cinders for him.

He kisses along my cheek until his breath is hot on my ear. "Do you know what you do to me, kitten?"

Each word from his lips scorches into my soul.

"You make me burn for you. I've thought about fucking you all day. While I'm supposed to be concentrating, all I can think about is how tight your pussy is around my cock. You're so fucking wet for me. You're dripping all over me."

I breathe out in a rush as he thrusts deep. My eyes close and I'm falling into his voice and his body against mine, his cock buried inside me, his hands holding me captive, stretching me and bracing me.

"I love your tight cunt and how you take me so deep," he breathes out against my ear and shivers ripple through me. He slides almost all the way out of my pussy before punching back in. The friction makes me moan.

"That's it, kitten, purr for me."

My pussy clings to his cock as he draws it out before thrusting deep.

"Noah," I gasp, needing more.

"You like that, kitten? My cock buried deep inside you while you drip all over it? I want my cum running down your thighs during the meeting so you remember who you belong to." Every sentence he punctuates with a lingering slide out followed by a quick thrust in.

His words are for me alone. His desire is for me alone. I will always belong to him.

"Fuck, kitten, squeeze me any tighter and I'm going to lose it." He kisses beside my ear as he thrusts again. "You want me to fill up your sweet cunt?"

His hand tightens a little around my throat as he sucks on my earlobe.

"Noah." All I can do is feel him everywhere. It's overwhelming, like being surrounded by them. But it's all him right now.

"You want to come, kitten? You want to drench my cock in your essence?" His cheek brushes against mine as he draws his head back. "Look at me."

I open my eyes and Noah is right there. His dark eyes search mine while he thrusts in and out, filling me with his cock. My walls tremble, shaking with the need for release.

"Tell me how much you want my cum, kitten. Beg me for it." He leans in and licks at my lower lip.

"Please." The word falls from my lips. I can't think, all I can do is feel him. "Oh, fuck, Noah."

My eyes try to shut. When he squeezes gently around my throat, they open. "Nah, kitten. Keep those eyes on me. I want to see the moment you shatter for me. You're mine."

He thrusts faster and harder as our gazes remain locked. The inferno rages inside me until it explodes. Heat floods me as I scream his name. My vision clouds until all I can see are his satisfied eyes, smiling in triumph.

His lips touch my ear again. "I love the way you wrap around me when you come, kitten. So fucking tight."

His cock thrusts in deep and jerks as he comes with a groan, sending wave after wave of aftershocks through me.

"Noah," I sigh as I drift back to myself.

His thumb smooths over the pulse in my throat, gently. "We belong to each other, kitten. Never forget that."

"I love you," I whisper in his ear, still feeling breathless.

He kisses me softly, in sharp contrast to the way he just took my body. His hand slips around to the back of my neck, holding me to him as he explores my mouth like it's the first time we kissed all over again.

A throat clears behind Noah. He presses his forehead against mine as we breathe each other in. Neither of us moves.

"Not to be an ass, but we have a meeting." There's a tinge of laughter in Coop's voice.

When Noah's cock slips out of me, a piece of me shudders at the loss. I feel whole with him inside me. I put my feet on the floor but my knees tremble, not quite ready to hold me. My skirt falls around my legs.

"You good?" Noah's eyes search mine as he holds me upright. I lean back against the wall.

Smiling, I release my breath. "So good."

He presses a kiss to my lips before stepping away. I glance around the room at the others sitting in their seats, waiting to begin the meeting. If I could have this forever, I could be happy.

But I want more. I want to have my own business. My own accomplishments. But for now, I want this. These men. This company. This life. And I'm willing to fight to keep it.

Chapter 128

Blue Sky Thinking

Madison

"We have new information," Blake says. The meeting is almost over. We've discussed all the items on Seth's agenda.

Anticipation for what happens next has me squirming in my chair. I sit back and give Blake my full attention.

Blake meets my gaze. "Jeff approached me after lunch."

It takes my mind a second to place Jeff in business circles. But when Blake just looks at me, waiting, it clicks. Oh. My shaking hand goes to my throat as I swallow. He was there? I didn't know he was there.

A chill runs through me. Coop takes my other hand, rubbing it between his, and then holds it in his lap, warming it.

"A guy gave Val cameras to put in your apartment and Jeff installed them, but—"

"Cameras? As in more than one?" My pulse skips. Val knew my stalker. She helped him. The camera in the bathroom was bad enough. Where else could they have hidden them? What other private moments did they capture for some unknown person?

"Where?" I ask quietly, not sure I want to know but needing to.

"Living room, kitchen, and your bedroom."

Blake takes a breath and meets my gaze. "Breathe, love. Only the bathroom one was still working when we went in."

Even if they weren't *still* working, at some point this monster had access to my whole life. My stomach roils, but I choke down the rising panic.

"Breathe, princess." Seth nods to Coop.

I force a breath into my lungs and try to calm my racing heart. Standing, Coop lifts me from my seat before sliding beneath me, wrapping his arms around me as he holds me in his lap. He kisses my shoulder and a little shiver runs through me. The tightness inside loosens a little. His warmth draws me in. I lean my head against his heart, listening to the steady beat beneath my ear.

I'm safe with Coop and the others. They were with me at the restaurant. Jeff didn't find me alone and helpless this time.

"I'm going tomorrow to see if I can find the cameras. He also mentioned a phone the man gave Val to take pics of you with."

"Oh, god." I cover my mouth. The shaky video of me in the bathroom and all those pics of me around campus. I didn't even know she was following me. She was never around the apartment that much. At least not that I saw. How could I not have seen her?

"He said she called it her insurance plan. There may be a photo of the stalker on it," Blake finishes and rests his arms on the table before him. "The stalker can't get to you here, love. We won't leave you alone until we figure out who it is and he's behind bars."

Coop squeezes me and I release my breath. I'm safe here. For now.

Seth leans forward. "We called the police and gave them Jeff's last known location. Hopefully, they'll find him or he'll leave town. Either way, I don't think he'll be a problem for you anymore."

That's one more problem gone. Val is dead. Hunter may still be an issue, but he doesn't have access to me. But the specter of my stalker is still always right in the corner of my eye. Just out of sight. Just out of reach. Always watching. Always waiting.

"This may be over if we can find the phone," Blake assures me.

"I hope so. But your men have been through that apartment. Was there a phone in her room?" I entangle my fingers with Coop's.

"She probably wouldn't have left it out. Jeff said she hid it. We'll have to get inventive." Blake puts his hands behind his head.

"I want to go with you." That apartment still holds its own ghosts that I need to deal with.

"If that's what you want, tiger." Blake's green eyes search mine, but I'm determined to put this behind me. I want what's here in this room. These men with me and the freedom to live without the fear of my stalker.

There's another phantom lurking, unfortunately. Elizabeth made her play for Seth last night. If he's truly mine, we need to work past this.

"Should we talk about what happened at the restaurant?" I meet Seth's eyes reluctantly. While I forgive him, the pain is still a fresh wound that hasn't had a chance to heal.

"Did you find anything to hold over Elizabitch?" Coop rubs his fingers over mine.

"Elizabitch? Really? That's a little juvenile, don't you think?" Blake raises his eyebrow.

"If the broom fits." Coop maneuvers me on his lap so my back is to his front. My legs fall to either side of his, making me aware of my lack of panties and my thighs wet from Noah's cum.

I glance at Noah and his possessive gaze trails down my body to pause between my legs. My pussy throbs in response. I will always belong to him. I squirm on Coop's lap to get more comfortable.

Seth sighs. "We haven't found anything yet. She has the money to keep her track record clean, but there's always someone not happy with what they received. It's not like she's a decent person."

"That doesn't mean you have to continue with her." Coop's hands rest on my lap. His fingers stroke my inner thighs through my dress. His touch is soothing. "We can take the hit. I say we just tell everyone we're all fucking and let the cards fall where they will."

"It's not that easy." Seth runs a hand over his hair. "Even the rumor of Andrea cost us clients. It's what the corporate spy is counting on. We have to be unanimous on this, because once we put that out into the world, we won't be able to take it back."

"We're already the best at what we do." Noah steeples his fingers in front of his lips. His dark eyes fix on Seth. "We can't live our lives to please everyone. Yes, some clients might leave, but fuck them. What right do they have to dictate our personal lives?"

My insides churn with the arguments. I don't know how to help or what to do. What's right? Being free to live as we like as long as we're happy and not hurting anyone else? Or conforming to society for the sake of their business and my future?

"What if this doesn't last?" The words slip from me. My pulse skitters through my veins. I look at the three of them, surprised I let that out at all. Coop's hands tighten on my thighs. But we really haven't talked about our relationship beyond the contract. Beyond just sex. "I mean, shouldn't we figure out what we are before we decide whether it makes sense to go public?"

Blake's gaze captures mine. "You have the most to lose from this. Will we suffer a little if this comes to light? Probably, but even though someone is pushing away new clients, maybe we weren't the right fit for those clients. But you . . ."

He runs a hand through his hair as he pins me with those green eyes.

"You're just starting out. Things like this can cling to you and keep you from what you want to do. They can close doors that could help you." He stops and closes his eyes. His hand clenches into a fist on the table. "Fuck, Madison. They'll call you a lot of unpleasant things. Maybe you could stand it. Maybe you could turn the other cheek. But I couldn't."

"Blake—"

"It's one thing for Coop to call you a whore, but if someone else called you that in front of me, I couldn't let that stand." Blake scrubs a hand over his face. "You can't tell me that any of you guys would stay cool and collected if someone called her a whore. For saying that she got to where she is by sleeping with us and not on her own merit."

Noah and Seth both look at me. The truth is in their eyes. They wouldn't be able to handle it. Could I live with it? What would my family think? I could grow a business, do everything right, and they'd still question my start. Question my abilities because I slept with my bosses.

"You're ours." Seth leans forward on the table. "And we're yours. Nothing is going to change that."

My gaze flicks to Blake. He's never said I love you, but he's claimed me time and time again. That should be enough. It can be enough.

"We don't have to go public, but we don't have to prove anything either." Noah's words draw my attention to him. "We don't have to date anyone else. We don't have to claim she's only dating Coop. If people are confused about our relationship status, let them be. Maybe it's time we just live our lives and fuck the haters."

"So you just want me to tell Elizabeth to go fuck herself and live with whatever consequences come our way?" Seth rocks back in his chair. His face thoughtful. He rubs his lips as those blue eyes study me.

"What's the worst she can say?" Coop leans forward, pressing his body into mine. "That you want to fuck my fiancée?"

Coop's hands go to my zipper and ease it down. A shiver runs down my spine. He parts my dress and pushes it down my arms to rest on my lap. My breathing hitches at the heat in Seth's eyes as he takes in the pale blue bra he dressed me in.

Seth begins, "Coop—"

"No. Fuck that, Seth. Elizabitch thinks she can control all of us." Coop undoes my bra and slides it off me, leaving me naked from the waist up. "She believes she can control you, Seth, force you to do what she wants."

Coop draws me back against him. His hand curves around my

stomach before sliding down below the waist of my dress and between my legs. His touch makes me want more.

"Do you want to give Elizabitch that power? Do you want her to keep you away from us? Or do you want to fuck my girl? Our girl?" His fingers skate over my clit, circling it. I draw in a sharp breath. "Because if you don't fuck Madison, I will."

He slides his fingers into me and my breath catches.

"Coop, we haven't really finished this discussion." Seth loosens his tie as his gaze drops to my breasts. They grow heavy beneath the weight of his stare as my nipples tighten. Longing spirals through me.

Coop latches onto the spot where my neck meets my shoulder. I arch at the sizzle running through my veins. My eyes close as he thrusts his fingers in and out of my pussy. His other hand wraps around my breast, squeezing it gently and sliding his thumb over my hardened tip.

"I've been hard since I watched Noah fuck her against the wall." Coop licks my shoulder. A shudder runs through me. "Just be glad I waited this long before I fucked her."

He curls his fingers inside me. My lips part, but no sound comes out as I tip over the edge into free fall. He lifts me and lays me on my stomach on the cool table. My dress falls around my ankles, leaving me nearly naked in my garter belt and stockings.

Coop's belt clangs as he opens it and draws it out of his pants. He tosses Noah his belt and runs his hand down my spine. "Bind her hands above her head. I want her to feel as helpless as we do."

Noah stands and I reach my hands toward him in offering. My shoes arch my hips up against the table. I spread my legs wide for Coop, needing his cock buried inside me.

Noah lifts my knuckles to his lips and kisses them before he binds my wrists together. The sound of Coop's zipper is the only warning I have before his cock thrusts into my pussy.

I cry out as he fills me.

"You're ours, sweetheart."

My breath rushes out of me. He thrusts in deep a few times before he pulls out. I whimper at the loss. It wasn't enough, but then Seth's cock replaces Coop's, driving into my pussy all the way. Tingles race through me as he fucks in and out of me a few times before he also pulls out. Blake thrusts inside, thicker, stretching me, fucking me hard.

I glance up, but Noah is no longer near my hands. I lay my cheek against the solid surface. A slave to the pleasure they give me and withhold from me. Blake draws out before I get close to the edge and then Noah is inside me. His cock slides against my walls. I squeeze around him, wanting to hold him in.

My nipples ache and rub against the table as the guys continue to take turns fucking me, never enough to push me over the edge, keeping me clinging right there, so close, needing just that much more to get me there.

Their heavy breathing is the only sound in the room as they each claim me, take me, fuck me. It's primal. I'm stripped nearly naked, down to just my garters, stockings, and shoes. They have their cocks out of their pants, still dressed in their business clothes.

I lose track of who's in me, who's fucking me. My pussy aches, throbbing with the need for release. But they continue to slide their cocks into me, thrusting a few times and then pulling out. The closer I get, the slower they go.

Taking a shuddering breath in, I wait for the next cock to fill me, to make me whole. I'm limp on the table, theirs to do with as they please. Hands touch my ass, parting my cheeks. A cock fills my pussy and a breath escapes me.

Finally.

He pumps his cock in and out a few times and pulls out. The wet head presses against my asshole with steady pressure until it passes through the tight ring of muscles to fill my ass. My legs part on their own, easing the way as he pulls out. Another cock fills my pussy before slipping back to my puckered hole and easing inside.

They each follow the example before they take turns fucking my ass. Each pushes me higher and higher. Only to let me slide away from the edge while they change places.

"Please," I whimper, so fucking close to going over.

"Do you need us, tiger?"

Hands slide over me, so many hands. On my back, my sides, my ass cheeks, my thighs. It's torture and pleasure, but my pussy aches with the need for release.

"Yes, I need you."

I'm lifted up. My back presses against a naked chest. Heat pools in my center at the sensation of skin against skin.

"I've got you, baby." Coop's voice is in my ear. His cock rests against my ass as he holds me upright. "We've been holding off so we can all come with you. Are you ready for us?"

I whimper as Noah closes in on my front. My breasts slide against his bare chest. His lips claim mine, my bound arms lower over his head as I fall into the kiss.

Coop steps away from my back as Noah rests his forehead against mine. His hands slide over my hips.

"You still with us, princess?"

I turn to look at Seth. Naked and all hard muscle, he strokes his cock as he watches me.

"Yes, sir." I rub my thighs together, needing friction.

Seth nods. "Lower her."

Noah ducks out from my arms and turns me around. My gaze falls on Blake already lying on the floor. Noah helps me straddle Blake's waist and lower down over him. Blake guides the tip of his cock to my entrance and I sink down. Shivers flutter through me.

Before I can rise back up, Blake holds my hips steady. "Not so fast, tiger."

Coop kneels behind me and runs his hands down my sides to my hips. He parts my ass cheeks and his cock slides into my ass. My bound hands rest on Blake's stomach as I close my eyes at the overwhelming feeling of them both inside me.

Noah tips my chin his way. He runs his fingers over my lower lip, parting my lips. I open for him and he groans before sliding the tip of his cock into my mouth. My pussy throbs around Blake's cock.

My eyes search for Seth, needing him to be a part of this. He sits behind Blake's head with his cock in his hand. I hold his eyes as I press forward, taking Noah's cock deep into my throat.

As one, they move. Noah takes my hair and slides my mouth over his cock while he thrusts his hips. Coop lifts me on Blake's cock while sliding his own out of my ass before he lowers me and thrusts back in, filling me with both of them.

Blake palms my breast while his other hand circles my clit. I'm full of them, but my eyes remain locked with Seth's captivating blue eyes as he watches us move and strokes his cock, never releasing my eyes.

I'm so primed that the slow gentle moves set off the sparks that ignite me. I hollow out my cheeks while I suck hard on Noah's cock as my pussy and ass clamp down on Blake's and Coop's cocks, coming hard around them.

Their groans fill the conference room as they fill me with their cum. I swallow Noah's cum as he slips from my lips. Seth walks to my mouth.

"Open, princess."

I do as he asks and he slides his cock into my mouth. Closing my lips, I suck on him while still holding his eyes. He pushes in deep and I swallow around the tip of his cock. While he comes down my throat, aftershocks pulse through me around Coop and Blake.

Seth withdraws and rubs his thumb over my lips as he holds my chin to meet his eyes. "We belong to each other. No one else. When you ask if we have a future together, princess, all I see is this. You with us. That picture gets clearer every day. We can wait to announce our intentions, but I'm done playing. No more dates that aren't with you."

Chapter 129

Collusion

Seth

I hold my hands down to Madison and she lets me help her up. After leading her into the bathroom, I close the door on the others, wanting to care for her myself. Needing these moments alone with her.

"Do you mean it?" she asks as I turn on the sink and get the water warm.

Inhaling, I turn to her. "I'm sorry I hurt you. I never want to hurt you again. It doesn't matter what people say. We can take anything as long as you're in our lives."

Drawing her into my arms, I capture her lips. Our bodies fit together like they were built for each other. Her lips mold to mine. My cock hardens with every brush of skin. I pull away so we can both take in a breath.

"I don't need to show you off like the others, but I need to know you're mine. There's no one else for me, princess." I grab a washcloth and get it wet. I clean her and me up before lifting her onto the counter and shutting off the water.

I lean back against the wall across from her, taking in her beautiful nearly naked body. Her shoes were left behind, but she still has on her garters and stockings. "I love undressing you almost as much as I love dressing you."

She smiles and leans back against the mirror. "What do you want me to do, sir?"

Reaching down, I stroke my hand over my cock lazily. Her lips part and her tongue flicks out to wet them. "I don't deserve you, princess."

She laughs softly and shakes her head. She drags her finger down from her neck to her belly button. "It doesn't matter what we deserve, boss. We belong to each other. I belong to all of you. I belong to you. Play with me, Seth."

So much love pours through me for this woman. I hold her blue eyes with mine. "I love you, Madison."

"I love you."

My heart fills to overflowing. I lean back, remembering how open we had her. All of us taking turns filling her cunt and then filling her ass with our cocks. Never enough to push her over the edge. Never enough to reach satisfaction. But fuck, did she look beautiful spread before us. Ours to use. Ours to love.

"Feet up on the counter. Spread that pussy wide for me." I stroke down my cock. It throbs in my hand as she does as I ask.

"Like this, sir?" Her legs are wide, and with her leaning back, with her hips tilted just so, I can see all of her. Her pink pussy is spread out before me, showing me her beautiful cunt and her pretty puckered hole. All mine to play with.

"Yes, princess." I release my cock and cross my arms over my chest. My fingers stroke my chin as I study her. Her arousal causes a flush to creep up her chest to her neck. So many things I want to do to her. "Circle your nipple with your fingertip."

"Like this?" She drags her finger around her tightened nipple.

"Lick your finger."

She brings her finger to her lips and sucks it in, like she did my cock. She pulls her finger out and rubs her nipple with her saliva. A small, satisfied sound parts her lips and her breath quickens. "Please, sir."

"Open your pussy with your fingers, princess. Show me your clit."

Her other hand slides over her trembling stomach to her pussy lips. She spreads them out more, showing me those hidden parts of her perfect pussy.

"Press on your clit."

"Here, sir?" She presses her finger against her clit and she grows wetter.

"Drag your finger down to your cunt and circle it."

Still holding herself open, she does as I ask, circling her entrance.

"Slower."

"Seth, please." Her blue eyes are dark with need. Her lips part. My cock throbs, wanting to bury myself inside her, but I want to do more before I lose myself in her. I want to push her limits and see her fall apart at my command.

"Slide one finger inside your cunt."

She buries it deep inside but doesn't fuck herself with it because I didn't tell her to. I can't help but smile. She's perfect for me. Her breasts rise and fall with every breath.

"Add a finger."

She slides in another. So fucking beautiful.

"One more, princess." I rub my lower lip as she slides in a third finger, stretching herself, holding her pussy open for me. "Slowly fuck them in and out of yourself. I want to hear how dripping wet you are for me."

Her cunt clings to her fingers as she pulls out and pushes back in. Every time, her fingers get a little wetter and the sounds her cunt makes fill the room, making me want to fuck into her with my cock and feel that exquisite cunt tighten around me, milk me, make me hers. But not yet.

"Slide your fingers out and push them all into your puckered hole." I meet her startled eyes and raise an eyebrow at her confused expression.

"What?" Her fingers stay in her cunt.

"Have you never played with your own ass, princess?" I come off the wall and take a step closer. The smell of her musk fills the room, making my cock ache.

She shakes her head. She'll tell me if she doesn't want to do this, but I know she does. Her darkened eyes meet mine. I smirk at her and step closer.

"I'll help." I take her wrist and pull her fingers from her cunt. "So fucking wet. I want to taste it, but I won't. Yet. I need this wetness to fuck your ass."

She whimpers with need. I take her hand and lower it until her fingers brush her puckered hole. Slowly, I ease her fingers into her ass. They slide in easily with all her slick coating them.

She moans as I make her bury them deep and stretch herself out.

I lean in until my lips touch her ear. "You should know what it feels like to be buried inside your warm wet holes, princess. How it feels for us to be inside you. How hard you clench around us when you come."

I draw her fingers out before thrusting them back in. Her breath pushes against my ear as I fuck her ass with her fingers. I pause.

"Hold them still. Take your other hand and thrust three fingers into your needy cunt." I suck on her ear as I feel her shift to do as I ask. She gasps. I wrap my other hand around her wrist and back away to watch.

I pull her fingers out of her holes almost all the way before sliding them back in together.

"Oh, fuck. Oh, Seth." She's breathing hard as she tips her head down to watch me do it again and again.

"I want to watch the videos tonight, princess. I want you to see what I see when I watch them take you. While we watch, I want to fuck this tight little pussy until you scream." I fuck her hands in and out faster until she's moaning.

I press my thumb against her clit and rub, pushing her over the edge. She thrusts in deep and I watch her holes contract around her fingers.

"Feel how good that feels, princess?"

"So good," she murmurs. I draw her hands away and hold them down on the counter, pressing my cock into her cunt inch by agonizing inch while we both watch.

"You feel so good around my cock. So wet and warm and tight." I'm done holding back. I keep her hands to her sides as I fuck her pussy hard. Thrusting in deep before dragging back out. Watching my cock slide in and out, getting wetter and wetter from her arousal.

She shatters after seconds of me being inside her. Her walls convulse around me, dragging me in deeper, pulling me into my climax.

"Tell me how it feels," I whisper in her ear as I keep fucking her through my release before burying myself deep inside her and letting go.

"I can feel your cock as it pumps me full of your warm seed. I can feel you making me yours. It feels like home." She breathes out against my ear and I shudder against her.

I kiss my way to her lips, releasing her hands to hold her head. I pull back and look into her satisfied blue eyes, and I see my forever in them. "You feel like home to me."

Madison

We head down to the apartment. Noah put together some meat, cheese, vegetable, and fruit boards for dinner, all finger foods, and has them set up in the living room by the time I come out of my bedroom in a silky negligee and panties.

I don't know why I bother with the panties, but I guess the guys like taking them off. Blake drags me down onto his lap when I try to sit next to him. The guys are all in boxers. The amount of muscle and beautifully toned man surrounding me is almost overwhelming.

Noah hands me a cracker with meat and cheese on it. I smile as I eat it.

Coop gives me a glass of wine before pressing his lips against mine. The conversation is loose and easy as we dig into our food. I'm surrounded by men who love me. Maybe Blake hasn't said it, but he wants me, and that should be enough.

Seth holds a piece of fruit in front of my mouth and I take it from him, licking and sucking the juice from his fingers. His eyes darken as he watches me.

"Tonight, we sleep together," Blake says and smooths his hands over my silky negligee. "Tomorrow night, I'll take my night. With us watching the videos, I don't think anyone will want to go to bed alone."

I feel heat lick up my ears and cheeks. I didn't want to say anything, but I'm glad Blake did.

He leans in and whispers in my ear, "I'm still going to fuck you, tiger."

A shiver works through me. "Yes, please."

Noah and Coop take the empty trays into the kitchen while Seth works on setting up the TV. Noah passes out wipes for our hands.

"Before we turn on the movies." I pause and blush, aware that we're about to watch ourselves have sex. I've never done anything like this. Have they? I could ask, but do I want to know?

"Yes, kitten?" Noah runs a hand up the back of my negligee, teasing my skin and making me want to forget everything.

"Tomorrow night, I want to go to the bar to hang out with Hope and Sara," I blurt out before someone else touches me and I end up fucking someone.

"Too dangerous." Seth leans back on the couch and shakes his head. "You have a stalker. Public locations like dark, crowded bars on a busy night make it too easy for them to get to you."

"But I'll be with friends. You guys could come and watch over me." I want to go alone but I'm willing to negotiate.

Coop's already shaking his head.

"I'll go with you," Blake says, and I turn to meet his green eyes.

"You will?"

He pushes my hair behind my ear. "Of course I will, love. You're right. We can't keep you locked up here indefinitely. And I know it's important for you to have friends."

Twisting my body and digging my fingers into his dark hair, I kiss him. He deepens the kiss, threading his fingers into my hair. His tongue slides against mine and heat floods me. I'm half a second from turning and straddling his lap.

"I think it's important you have friends too," Coop tries to say sternly but laughs. "My lips are right here, baby."

I draw away from Blake. Our eyes lock. "Thank you."

When my gaze finds Coop, I lift an eyebrow.

"I mean, if you don't want to suck face, I have something else you can—" A pillow smacks Coop upside his head, cutting him off.

"You're welcome, kitten." Noah winks as he sets the pillow down. "If you need us to go with you, we'll be there."

I take a breath and rub the ends of Blake's hair between my fingers. "I just want to be normal again. To go out with my friends to a bar and worry about the normal things. Like creepy guys hitting on me. Or guys asking to buy me a drink."

Blake clears his throat. "I don't think you're effectively pleading your case, tiger."

The guys all have frowns on.

"I doubt that will happen with this rock on." The engagement ring is still on my hand. I've actually gotten used to wearing it. "Are we going to announce this is off?"

Coop grabs a grape and gives me a curious look. "Why would we do that, sweetheart?"

"Because we aren't engaged?" I ask him like he's a crazy person, because ever since we started "dating" he's been possessive.

"Yes, we are." Coop pops the grape into his mouth, followed by another.

"Coop," I say.

He glances around at the others. "Hey, it's not my fault you guys didn't fuck her in the file room and then kiss her in front of Hope. Then when you took her to the benefit, you didn't tell your ex that you two were engaged. And then tell an old friend you're engaged. And an ex-lover. And then your mom didn't find out."

"Coop." Seth shakes his head. "What's the point of being engaged now, if we aren't going to hide our relationship?"

"Besides making my mom shit a brick?" Coop grins and leans back. His fingertips tease the nape of my neck, sending little flutters through me. "I like it."

"You like it?" Noah sits forward on the couch to look at Coop around me and Blake. "What if I decide to marry Madison?"

"Oh, sorry, dude. Current law says one hubby." Coop points to himself. "I put a ring on it and you guys didn't. Sorry, that's just the way things go. Don't worry, I still support your relationships with her."

"You never technically asked me to marry you, Coop," I point out.

"Ah, but you're wearing the ring and you love me, so . . ." He waves his hand as if it's magic. "You're my dirty little whore. Pretty sure I can get you to walk down the aisle with me. Then I'm going to knock you up first."

"You live in a fantasy land." Noah shakes his head.

"Don't worry. I'll let you knock her up too." Coop winks at Noah.

My mouth is still open at the knocking me up part. Coop takes a grape and pushes it into my open mouth. I chew it while I glare at him.

"Madison and I are still engaged for all intents and purposes." Coop points at the TV. "Can we watch ourselves fuck her now? Or is there something else we need to discuss?"

Blake lifts me against him.

"Wha—" I lean back to stabilize myself.

"Hold still, tiger." Blake shifts my panties to the side. His cock presses against my entrance before he impales me on it.

"Fuck." So fucking full.

"Who do you belong to, love?" Blake's voice in my ear makes heat work its way through me. That, and his cock filling my pussy.

"You, Blake," I sigh and lean back against him, feeling his thick cock stretching me out.

"That's unfair." Coop points out before taking my hand and sliding it inside his boxers.

Meeting his light blue eyes, I smirk. My fingers brush over the smooth skin of his hard cock. I wrap my hand around him and squeeze slightly.

"Fuck, I love it when you're rough with me." He grabs the back of my neck and kisses me. I tighten around Blake's cock as Coop explores my mouth.

I pull back and squeeze Coop's cock again. "Behave."

His eyes glow. "I already told you I'm a brat."

Seth slides down to sit on the floor between Blake's and my legs. He glances up at me and smiles. Fuck, I love his smiles. I run my fingers through his hair and he tips his head back, leaning into my touch.

Noah cups my breast and rubs the satin over my hardened nipple. I bite my lip at the pleasure racing through my body.

Seth turns on the TV and past-Coop prowls toward past-me. It's fascinating to watch them manhandle me on the screen. My insides burn with need, I rock against Blake's cock, craving friction. I stroke over Coop's cock and tug at Seth's hair.

Seeing my men hot and naked for me on TV and feeling them surrounding me makes me want them so fucking bad. I'm not sure how much of the show I'm actually going to get to watch.

Chapter 130

Dirty Business

Madison

I've watched porn before, but watching myself get railed by four guys is something new entirely. When we're in the middle of it, I'm usually so wrapped up in the actual act that I don't notice all the nuances.

The battle onscreen between Coop and me is intense, and so fucking sexual. His expression as he hovered over me is delightfully wicked. When he pressed me back into the bench and fucked me, I remember that feeling of wanting to get him off, wanting to win, and admitting defeat as he pushed me over the edge.

It's turning me on more than I already was. Whimpering, I rock a little harder on Blake as my thumb smooths over the tip of Coop's cock.

Blake's tongue strokes up my neck, sending sparks cascading through me. "Put your hands on the boss's shoulders, love."

Reluctantly, I release Coop's cock and rest my hands on Seth's shoulders. The move angles me slightly differently on Blake's cock, so I'm taking him deeper. Coop and Noah both slide their hands beneath my negligee to massage my breasts and tease my nipples. My breath comes out in a rush, needing more, wanting more.

My eyes latch on to past-Coop fucking me onscreen before he pulled away. Past-Noah took his place. He fucked me slow and steady. His cock glistened with my slick as he thrust deep into me.

In the present, Blake lifts my hips and thrusts up into me. I moan at the feel of him filling me as I watch myself get slow-fucked by past-Noah. On the screen, Blake stepped behind Noah and his fingers slid into me with Noah's cock.

"How did that feel, tiger?" Blake says into my ear, slowly fucking up into my pussy. "My fingers stretching you around Noah's cock?"

"So good," I breathe out.

Noah's other hand slides between my legs and circles my clit. "You look so beautiful when you come, kitten."

I whimper, feeling that need building inside me. Coop's hand slides over my ass and teases my puckered hole.

"We had to get you nice and wet so you could take all of us." Coop's finger lingers there, not pressing in.

"She's so fucking wet right now." Blake fucks up into me faster. Noah's fingers work on my clit and breast. Coop rubs my breast and ass.

Onscreen, Noah slipped away and Blake took my breast into his mouth while Coop claimed my mouth. I writhed beneath them.

Moaning, I climax in real life, squeezing Seth's shoulders and dragging Blake into his release. My hips are lifted and Coop slides his cock deep inside me. He drags me back against him. Noah slides to the floor in front of Coop and lifts my negligee off.

My panties are slid to the side but riding a little up my butt. I squirm to try to right them.

"Let's take these off." Noah takes hold of the sides of my panties, and I grab his shoulders for support while Coop lifts me off his cock. As soon as my panties are over my hips, Coop slides back inside me, triggering aftershocks.

Noah presses me back against Coop and trails kisses down my

neck to my breast. Coop's cock throbs inside me as Noah sucks my nipple into his mouth.

Onscreen, Blake sucked on my clit while Coop's mouth was on my nipple and Noah kissed me. I can see the moment the overwhelm got to be too much and I started to slip into something like subspace.

I cried out onscreen, and they all moved away slowly until Seth came to me and lifted me onto his lap.

In real life, Coop lifts me and lowers me on his cock. He lifts me all the way off before sliding back to my asshole and easing me down over his cock, taking my ass. I moan as he stretches me.

Noah chuckles against my breast before lifting my knees and spreading me wide. His kisses trail down until his mouth is on my pubic bone. My breath catches in anticipation.

He pauses and looks up at me before slipping lower and sucking on my clit. Coop rocks his cock in my ass.

Onscreen, I gave Seth a blowjob while Blake fucked my pussy. The image combined with what they're doing to me currently throws me over the edge.

Arching, I shatter here and now. Noah pulls away, wiping his mouth. Coop stands with me and puts my hands on the ottoman before he grabs my hair to pull my head back so I can watch the movie while he thrusts deep into my ass before pulling out and slamming back in.

"Do you enjoy watching yourself get fucked, my little whore?" Coop's hand wraps around my waist and his fingers slide inside my pussy, curling to hit my G-spot.

"Yes," I whimper, knowing another climax is hovering just out of reach.

I watch myself onscreen, taking past-Seth's cock in my mouth while Blake's cock fucked my pussy. Coop slid his fingers into my ass while Noah pressed his fingers in with Blake's cock. It was too much.

I come onscreen and off as Coop slides his cock in and out of my ass. He curses as I clamp down on his cock. He thrusts in deep and groans as he fills me with his cum.

He drags me up against him. "Such a good little whore."

Noah steps in front of me and grabs my legs, lifting them wide as Coop holds me tight.

"More, kitten?"

"Always."

Coop's cock remains hard in my ass as Noah thrusts his cock into my pussy. I cry out at being filled. I tip my head back against Coop's shoulder. His skin hot against mine. My eyes are riveted to my onscreen self crawling to Noah and Coop. I took both their cocks into my mouth as Blake worked his fingers in my pussy.

"You should suck our cocks like that again." Coop holds me while Noah fucks me. My breath comes out in pants.

My whole body shuddered onscreen as I came again.

Noah watches his cock thrust in and out of my pussy, holding my legs spread. "You want us to ruin you again, kitten? You want to feel that stretch as we sink our cocks into your sweet, tight cunt?"

My onscreen self lowers onto Coop's and Noah's cocks. I know that I did that. I know it's me on the screen, but it still seems impossible that both their cocks fit inside me together. Feeling them rub against each other through the thin wall separating them now is almost too much for me.

"Or we can finally play," Coop whispers in my ear like it's a dirty little secret. "I like the idea of hunting for you and taking you when I find you."

I shiver at the thought. He captures my ear in his teeth before pulling out and thrusting deep into my ass. Noah's thrusts get harder and I fall over the edge again. Crying out, I come all around them.

Noah captures my lips as he groans his release deep inside me. I wrap myself around him as Coop fucks in and out of my ass, fully hard again, pushing me higher and higher.

"Do you think we could both fit in here, my little whore?" Coop presses up against my back. "You want two cocks in your ass, stretching you wide open?"

I bite down on Noah's shoulder as I come again on Coop's cock.

"Fuck," he mutters as his cum fills my ass. He kisses the nape of my neck. "Maybe, sweetheart."

He pulls out and Noah lowers me down to Seth's lap on the floor. He draws my back against his front. His hard cock is under me, but he relaxes with me like he's content just to have me in his lap. I tingle all over from coming.

Drawing in a breath, I take in the scene on the TV. I did that. All four of their cocks were inside my body at once. I watch each of them as they came. The beautiful contortion of their faces as they found that moment of ecstasy.

As I collapsed forward on Coop's chest onscreen, I said, "I love you."

Seth's fingers slip into mine, and he lifts my hand to press a kiss on it.

"I love you," he says softly, but it rings loudly in my heart.

"I love you, kitten." Noah's hand slides over my hair and I smile up at him.

"I love you, sweetheart." Coop winks at me.

My heart feels full, but it's missing a piece. I don't want Blake to feel put on the spot, so I say, "I love you all."

Blake's fingers trail down the side of my neck, sending waves of heat through me. "I belong to you, love."

The screen blanks for a moment. Then it's just the bondage horse. Past-Blake walked onto the screen, holding me before lowering me onto the horse. Past-Noah worked on tying me down.

I lean on Seth's upraised knee as I watch. I want to see this. When I go into subspace everything is heightened, but I'm not as aware. It doesn't matter whose cock is in me as long as I'm filled.

When past-Noah had me exactly how he wanted me, he took scissors and cut off my panties.

Seth's hand slides between my legs and skims along my clit. I suck in a breath at the slight touch. He toys with me while I watch.

The camera is angled so you can see my pussy and ass on display. Onscreen, Noah slid his fingers into my ass and into my pussy.

Seth's finger slides into my pussy and glides in and out, making my breath catch.

Past-Noah stepped offscreen. When he returned, he grabbed my hair and fucked deep into my mouth. Blake stepped up and spanked me before he thrust his fingers into my ass.

Fuck. My lips part and my breath shudders in and out. Seth toys with my pussy now as I watch myself being used on the screen. I'm keyed up as past-Noah came in my mouth and Coop stepped into his place. Noah spanked my ass before he smacked my pussy.

My hips rock with Seth's hand. My insides burn. He draws me back against him. "Do you want me inside you, princess?"

Fuck, is that even a question? I throb with the need to come. I bite my lip. "Yes."

When I kneel before Seth with my arms on the ottoman, he lifts my hips and his cock presses against my entrance. The room fills with the sound of past-Coop groaning onscreen. I watch as Seth stepped in front of me while handing Noah a butt plug.

As onscreen Seth slid his cock into my mouth, Seth thrusts into my pussy. I clench my hands as he falls into rhythm with himself and Noah onscreen. My pussy throbs as I watch myself come on them. Blake stepped into Seth's place and Noah set the plug to the side so he could fill my ass with his cock.

My skin is flushed onscreen, but I watch their faces. How they worshipped my body as they took me. Sliding their hands over me. Taking turns drawing pleasure from me.

"Do you see what I see, princess?" Seth whispers in my ear as he thrusts deep into me. "Do you see how they crave you? How they have to have you? Do you see how enthralled with you we all are?"

They surrounded me onscreen. It's captivating. I gave myself into their hands, trusted them to care for me while they used my body.

They moved around me, using my mouth, using my pussy, using my ass, but at the same time, they made me come over and over again. It was a beautiful dance that makes me shatter around Seth's cock in the present.

Chapter 131

Revisit

Blake

I hold the umbrella over the car door as I offer Madison my hand. She joins me under the umbrella and we make our way to her apartment building's door. Her fingers tremble against mine as we step into the lobby.

Folding it and shaking it off, I study her. Her eyes are wide as she looks around the old building. It's dingy and has a musty smell. Someone broke a lock on the mailboxes and the little brass door hangs open. Junk mail covers the counter beneath.

She walks to the mailboxes and sorts through her keys. Her blond hair is pulled into a tight bun. She has on jeans and a t-shirt that I'm sure Seth didn't pick out but were hers before us. She looks like a college student as she reaches in and takes the few envelopes out.

Young.

Last night, we were all insatiable. We didn't fall asleep until the sun started to rise, collapsing on her bed and not getting up until late. It's after noon now.

She turns so I can see her profile as she sifts through the mail. She's not wearing makeup, but she's effortlessly beautiful. Her long lashes brush her cheeks. I'm captivated by her. After a few seconds, she glances over at me.

"Sorry." She gives me a self-conscious smile. "Should we?"

When I reach out my hand to her, she slides her fingers through mine and holds on tight as we make our way to the stairs. It seems like forever ago that I carried her down these stairs, worry fueling my every step. A smile kicks at my lips when I remember the last time we were here. We fucked in her apartment to wash away the bad memories. When we left, I threw her over my shoulder to hurry her along.

I clear my throat. "I had the apartment cleaned. Val's things are packed but still in her room. We're waiting for her family to let us know what they want us to do with her belongings."

"I still can't believe she's gone." Madison rounds the landing with me. Her blue eyes meet mine. "We were the same age. I wanted her to go to jail, not end up dead."

We reach her floor and I glance at the doors. My gaze pauses on Robert's, half expecting him to pop out. I don't like that he worries Madison. Her body language when he gave her back the bracelet spoke volumes. It frustrated me that I was several floors away when it happened.

"Hopefully, Valerie left us a clue." I don't tell her Jeff's theory that someone killed her. Maybe Valerie tried to blackmail the stalker. If the stalker could kill Valerie, the lengths he'd go to get to Madison frighten me.

I also kept from her the fact that he wanted her panties. Just the thought of someone watching her in her private moments freaked her out. If she knew they had her personal things, I'm not sure how she'd react. I don't want her to retreat into herself or be afraid to go out. That's not healthy.

When I open her door, Madison steps into the apartment, flicking on the lights. The gloom from outside clings in the corners of the room. It's dull and lifeless. Everything that happened here seems so long ago.

My insides churn at the memory of Madison collapsing on the ground. I clench my fists, reminding myself I got here in time.

"Do we want to split up to look?" Madison glances at me over her shoulder. Her hand tightens slightly on mine and I almost smile. She doesn't want to split up. I draw her into my arms and hold her against me.

"Let's stick together this time, tiger." I kiss the top of her head and draw in her soft floral scent. Her arms wrap around me as I take in her apartment. There's not much left. I have a storage company coming on Monday to empty it. Her month is almost over and Madison won't be returning here. Ever.

I don't know what the future holds for us, but like Seth, I can't see a future without her in it. I release her and she smiles. She makes it easy to believe that this could all work out. There's still a part of me that questions when everything is good. That waits to see when the shit will hit the fan. But I'm not letting that part rule me right now.

"Where should we look first?" Her gaze roams the room.

Reaching into my pocket, I pull out two multi-tools. I gesture to a register near the base of the wall. "You start with the registers and I'll check the light switches and plugs."

Her eyebrows lift as she takes the tool. "This is going to take some time, isn't it?"

My heart squeezes in my chest with what I feel for this woman. She told us she loves us last night, but I didn't want to tell her in that moment. Our first kiss was after I almost lost her to Val and Jeff. When I tell her I love her, I want it to be special. I want it to be right.

She opens the tools and finds the Phillips-head screwdriver before glancing at me.

She's mine. She belongs to me, with me. I'll find the right time to tell her, but I know she can feel that I love her. How could she not know?

"Yeah, love. It'll take time." The way she lights up every time I call her *love* is enough. Like she knows it means something, because it does. I've never felt for anyone the way I feel about Madison.

She grins and goes to the register, sitting on the floor. Shaking those thoughts out of my head, I go to the light switch and get to work.

The living room camera was in one of the registers. Madison's squeal of joy when she discovered it startled me. But it wasn't as bad as the shriek when she found a dead mouse.

"I touched it," she cries. Tears run down her cheeks as she scrubs her hands in the sink. She's rubbing too hard, like she can scrub off the feeling.

Coming up behind her, I wrap my arms around her to keep her from rubbing her hands raw. "You're fine, love."

Gently, I wash each of her hands before drying them. She leans back into me.

"It squished," she whispers in horror.

Chuckling, I turn her in my arms and tip her chin up. Using my thumbs, I brush away the tears remaining on her cheeks. "I'll clean it out. Are you good to keep going?"

She draws in a breath. "Yes, I'm sorry. I don't know why I'm so emotional."

Her forehead rests on my chest and my heart thumps. Her hands clutch at my t-shirt. I glance around the dimly lit room. This place is haunting her even now. We've barely made it through the living space. We still need to go through her bedroom and Val's.

Maybe questions will help her not think of the stalker and what we're really looking for here: evidence of this person who's been terrorizing Madison.

"How long did you live here?"

She steps away and grabs the multi-tool. "I moved in here my third year at school. I lived on campus the first couple years, but it was so expensive. Even living in a triple."

I crouch in front of the open register and use a paper towel to fish out the little pile of fur left and slide it into a trash bag. "You said you did internships every summer?"

Her gaze flicks to me as I screw on the register cover. She shakes her head and takes off the cover on the vent. Using a paper towel this time, she reaches into the opening. I quickly wash my hands.

"I did. The first year is when I worked for the Becks. I babysat a lot during high school, so it made sense to take on the nanny position. The kids were great. Anna and Patrick were nice, but they were definitely involved in their own careers." She puts the register back on and screws it tight. "Anna would sometimes vent to me about her husband and how much he works. Other times she'd talk about the dinners they had out. It was always surface stuff though. The kids were really fun ages. I spent most my time there with them."

"You like kids?" I move to the electrical outlet and loosen the screws holding the plate.

She arches her eyebrow. "You don't have to do this. I'm over being squicked out from feeling up the dead mouse."

"Maybe I'm curious." I lift the plate off and check around the box. A small bag of weed is the only thing I've found so far, which might have been from previous tenants since it's legal now.

"If I like kids?" She laughs. "Yeah, I guess I do. I've never really thought about having kids though. Or even what life looks like after I achieve my dream. It's all kind of just waiting in the background. Until I figure out how to do that."

Standing, she dusts off her bottom before moving into the kitchen. There's a register up high above the cabinets. She glances around and walks over to grab a chair from the table. When her fingers close on it, she freezes and her eyes widen. I'm not even sure she's breathing.

"Madison?" I say, hoping to pull her out of whatever nightmare has her in its grip.

Her shoulders shake as she looks at the ground. "I couldn't stop thinking there was no hope. That they could do anything to me and no one would know. No one would come looking for me. No one expected me until Monday morning. It was Friday night. They could have tortured me all weekend. They could have killed me and I would have been just another statistic."

I stand during her speech and move behind her, but I don't touch her. Her knuckles are white around the chairback.

"They didn't care about me. They just wanted money. They wanted to use me." Anger strains her voice, but tears drop on the chair. "They let someone into my life. Gave them pieces of me without me knowing. They knew my patterns and used them against me." She lifts the chair and slams it down on the floor.

I rest my hand on her shoulder gently, giving her my strength.

"Someone wants to use me. They know things about me. Personal things that they took. Someone wants me." She turns and grabs my shirt. Her eyes are wide and tears float in them. "Someone wants to take me away from you."

"I'll never let them."

She stares at my chest with her brows scrunched together. "I have more to lose now. Before, I would have lost the potential of something more. Now I'll lose you guys and my career and my friends."

I run my hand over her hair and grab the back of her neck, lowering my forehead to rest against hers. "I would never let anyone take you away from me. I will always find you. I will always save you. I can't lose you, love."

Madison

"Why does this person want me, Blake?" I fist his shirt as I try to make it make sense in my mind. "What did I do to make them think I want this? That I want them to watch me? To know me when I don't know them? What do they want from me?"

He releases a breath and tightens his grip on the back of my neck. "I know why I want you. You're beautiful. Intelligent. Sexy as hell. Willing to do whatever crazy thing we throw your way without batting an eyelash."

I lift my gaze to his beautiful green eyes. They smile down at me as his thumb smooths over my jaw. My heart swells in my chest at the look in his eyes. It speaks directly to my heart.

"You're soft and caring. You work hard and submit so beautifully. You're perfect in every way. Any man would be a fool not to keep you for himself." He breathes out and smiles. "You're one in a million, love. We would have been fools if we hadn't seen it and kept you for ours."

My heart trips over itself, falling a little harder for this man.

"Now." He smirks at me. "Do you want to break this chair, or were you going to search that grate in the kitchen? Because if you want to break it, you're definitely going to have to hit it harder than you just did."

I glance at the chair. A few minutes ago, I remembered it saved me, but now I know *he* did. *They* did. They gave me something to fight for. Something I wanted more than I thought. I need them.

Drawing in a breath, I blow it out and release his shirt along with those demons that tried to drag me under. I want to shake off the bad vibes this place gives me. I want to enjoy this man who belongs to me.

"I'm good now." I run my hand over his jaw. He didn't shave this morning, so the dark scruff teases my skin.

He turns and presses a kiss into my palm. "Good."

"What about you?"

His brow furrows. "Me?"

"Do you like kids?" I brush the wrinkles out of his shirt and step toward the chair, lifting it to carry it into the kitchen. "Do you want to be a dad someday?"

I set the chair down and then smirk back at him. "Or are you happy just being a daddy?"

His eyebrow arches. He carefully sets his tools on the table before brushing his hands off on his jeans. His heated eyes meet mine and a thrill shoots through me. I'm so going to be punished, and I can't wait.

"What was that?" He takes a step in my direction and I back toward my bedroom door. Bursts of lust spark through me like falling fireworks.

"What was what?" I try to keep my grin from growing. I'm not sure why I like tormenting him with this. "You mean Daddy?"

His playful growl sends a bolt of lust through me as I giggle and turn and run for my bedroom. My hand is on the doorknob when his arm wraps around my waist and lifts me off my feet.

"Ah, do I say uncle here?" I push open the bedroom door with my foot and glance over my shoulder up into his green eyes. "Or just *Please, Daddy, don't spank me?*"

"You're a spoiled little brat who needs a lesson." Blake carries me into the bedroom and drops me on my bed.

"Oh, Daddy's going to teach me a lesson." Winking at him, I scramble toward the other side of the bed. He grabs my ankle and tugs me back toward him. I give a little shriek and laughter spills out of me.

As he drags me across the bed, I pull my foot back weakly without really trying to get away.

"When did you become a brat, tiger?" Blake arches an eyebrow and gives my leg a quick yank, making me shriek again, before coming down over me, caging me in with his body. "Is Coop a bad influence?"

"Maybe I like ruffling your feathers." I sink my fingers into his hair.

His green eyes flare with heat. "Then I'll have to teach you not to."

My pulse jumps as he stands and jerks me to my feet. Before I can get my balance, he spins me and pushes my chest down on the bed.

"Fuck," I breathe out, but before I push up, he grabs my jeans and has them down around my ankles. "If you wanted me to strip, all you had to do was ask, Daddy."

His hand comes down on my panty-covered ass, filling the room with the smacking sound.

I hiss at the pain. "That wasn't very nice, Daddy."

I swear I giggle internally every time. He might not be an actual Daddy Dom, but his cock gets hard when I call him that.

"Stand up, brat." There's his dom voice that makes my pussy buzz with need.

I push back against him as I stand, feeling his denim-covered erection press into my back.

"Take everything off like a good girl," he whispers in my ear as he undoes his belt.

"Yes, Daddy." My voice is a little breathless as I feel him undressing right behind me. Last night, Blake and I were supposed to play, but we all fell into bed together. Each of them fucked me again and again before we finally passed out.

He smacks my ass and a moan breaks free from my throat.

"I'm going to have to come up with a punishment that doesn't get you off." His voice is low in my ear and sends shivers coursing through me.

I lift my shirt over my head. "Not possible."

"Maybe I'll make you count rice."

I straighten. "Wait? What?"

He smacks my ass. "Did I say stop undressing?"

I undo my bra and kick off my shoes and jeans and panties. Fully naked, I turn to face him.

"Count rice?" My mouth goes dry at his naked body. He's built thick and hard, all over. Broad shoulders, lean waist, and his cock . . . I get wet just seeing it.

"Menial tasks designed to make you aware of what you did wrong." Blake nods his head toward the bed. "Ass up, head down."

I smirk. "You're a kinky daddy, aren't you?"

He turns me and smacks my ass. "Now, brat."

Chapter 132

Bond

Before I climb on the bed, my mind locks on something. I pause and look around the room. "Yellow."

Blake closes in on my back, pressing his warm body against mine. "What is it, love?"

"The camera?" I look at the vent registers and the light above.

"It's not on. I had them do a sweep when they came to clean and before when they packed Valerie's belongings. The cameras never came on. They aren't transmitting, but if you want to postpone . . ." His hands skim my hips.

I really want to find out what punishment Blake has in store for me. I bite my lip and lean back into him. "If they're watching, we should give them one hell of a show."

His chuckle goes straight to my pussy. Fuck.

"Are we green?" he asks.

"Green." I tip my head back on his shoulder. Looking into his green eyes, I smirk. "Daddy."

He lifts me and tosses me face down on the bed, then follows after. Before I can get my legs under myself to scramble away, he grips my hips and pulls them up. He takes my arms behind my back and holds them with one hand.

I'm completely under his control and it's freeing.

"Some subs hate anal or getting their face fucked, but we both know you get wet for that." Blake slides his hand over my ass cheek and I brace myself for the smack, craving it.

"That causes a dilemma, doesn't it?" I huff out a breath. This isn't the most comfortable position. I definitely can't do much, which is probably the point. "You could just fuck me, Daddy."

His chuckle should have warned me. "You're right. But we can't take forever, we still have stuff to do." Leaning over me, he says in my ear, "Stay put or I won't fuck you."

He releases my hands and backs off the bed. I can hear him get something out of his jeans. His cell phone drops next to me on the bed. A timer counts down thirty minutes. I don't need that long to get off.

He kneels behind me and takes my hands in one of his, holding my arms behind my back. His other hand slides over the curve of my ass. Sparks follow his touch like moths to a flame.

His hand comes down with a crack on my ass cheek twice. I draw in a breath and release it.

"What do you think, love?" He rubs my ass cheek, bleeding the pain into pleasure. "Should I spank you for the whole thirty minutes?"

"No, Daddy." I can't seem to help myself, and his growl just turns me on more instead of deterring me.

He smacks my other ass cheek twice. Fuck, that feels oddly good. He rubs my sore cheek.

"Maybe I'll just come on your pussy and ass." His hand leaves me and I wiggle my bottom.

I can't see him from this angle, but the motion of the bed and the sounds tell me he's stroking his cock. My pussy aches with the need to be touched. He holds my hands tight. My eyes go to the timer.

Seconds tick away with me just bent over in front of him, naked, exposed.

My pussy is wet and I want to get fucked. The tip of his cock brushes against me. A whimper flows out of me. That one little touch felt so fucking good.

"Want to help me out, tiger?"

I sigh with relief. "Yes."

He rubs my pussy before his fingers dip inside. I press back against him but he takes his hand away. He slides it down his cock, rubbing my slick on himself.

"Thank you, love." His words are a little breathy, like he's close.

I'm glad one of us is enjoying this. The time ticks by as his breathing gets heavy, and the motion of the bed is the only action I'm getting.

All I can think about is his thick cock buried inside me, thrusting, making me come. How good it feels. How full he makes me.

"What do you call me, tiger?"

Fuck. If I say Daddy, pretty sure this is all the excitement I'll be getting. Part of me really wants to push my luck and call him Daddy anyway, but most of me just wants to feel that cock inside me. To have his cum fill me and not just spill over my ass and pussy.

"This isn't complicated, love."

I let out a disgruntled noise. "Easy for you to say. You get to come either way."

He runs the tip of his cock from my clit to my entrance and back. I gasp at the touch, needing so much more. He draws back again.

"Tease," I mutter.

"Let's try this another way. Why do you want to call me Daddy?"

I smile. "Because it makes you smile and playful and growly."

He grunts. "And?"

I blow out a breath. "It makes you want to punish me, which feels exquisite. Normally. This really sucks, by the way."

He chuckles. "You don't like being used as a visual aid?"

"Maybe if I got to watch, but this is just me in an uncomfortable position knowing you're getting off, but I'm getting nothing out of it."

"Are you learning your lesson?"

"Maybe?" The time ticks down.

"Does it feel like a punishment, love?" Blake's voice is tight like he's about to come.

"Yes, Blake. It feels like punishment." I exhale. "I've been a very naughty girl. Will you please come on my ass . . . Daddy?"

I need something to enjoy about this experience.

Blake groans. His cum lands on my ass and pussy, covering me in the thick substance. He makes tsking noises.

"Is this going to be an every time thing?" His fingers trail through the cooling cum, smearing it over my ass.

"Fuck, I hope not. I don't mind being punished, but this would suck if it was all we did."

His fingers trail close to my pussy, and those parts of me that were already burning for him flame even hotter. He smears his cum over my entrance and down to my clit.

"Next time, we'll do it in the mirror so you can watch." With his fingers, he shoves his cum into my pussy and I cry out at how good it feels.

"Pretty sure that will just encourage bad behavior," I admit, pressing back to take his fingers deep, but he holds them just inside me. I let out a frustrated noise.

He pulls his fingers out and draws through more of the cool cum on my skin. "You should see how pretty your skin looks with my cum on it."

My pussy throbs. The timer keeps counting down. If this is all the time I have to get off, I'm fucked—or rather, not fucked. Especially if he's just going to tease me.

"Blake?"

"Yes, love." He thrusts his fingers deep into me.

I bite my lip and wait for him to do more. "Please make me come."

"Are you going to call me Daddy again?" He draws his fingers almost all the way out.

"Maybe?" I don't want to lie to him.

He takes his fingers out of me and I sigh, disheartened. He releases my hands but I don't move them. The timer is ticking down. Soon there'll be no time to play.

"At least you're honest about it." His hand strokes over my ass cheek. "I don't mind you being a brat sometimes, but I love when you submit to me. When you open yourself up to the possibilities. When you don't fight the pleasure or pain."

When he says things like that, my heart feels like it's going to burst if I don't say something.

"I love you, Blake." I can't hold it back any longer. I squeeze my eyes shut because I know he won't say it. "It doesn't matter if you don't love me back. I understand if you don't, but I need you to know that I do. I love you."

"Fuck, Madison." His harsh laugh isn't what I expected.

He eases me out of the position. He sits cross-legged on the bed with his thick, hard cock. "Come here, love."

He helps me straddle him. My hands rest on his shoulders.

"May I?" I ask, looking into his green eyes.

"Yes."

Tingles rush through me as I lower my pussy over his cock, taking him deep inside. My breasts rub against his chest. Fuck, it all feels so good. I breathe out.

Tipping my face up to his, he lowers his mouth to taste mine gently, thoroughly. Even if he doesn't love me, the way he makes me feel is very much like love. He rests his head against mine.

"I wanted to make it special. I needed for it to mean something. Do you realize the first time I kissed you was after you passed out in this apartment?" His hands cradle my head. "I'd fucked your mouth and had my fingers in your pussy, but I hadn't kissed you."

"I didn't know." I never thought about it.

"I definitely didn't want to tell you as an afterthought to the others." Blake shifts me on his lap and I sigh at the slight movement. "You and I have been connected since the beginning. This apartment."

He looks around the mostly bare room. It's dull and functional. Every piece of me that made it home is gone. Except this bed and Blake.

"This apartment is where I knew I loved you." Blake presses his lips to mine and breathes me in. "When I realized I could have lost you, I knew I had to keep you. I fought against it. It's difficult to trust again after the others. But seeing you frightened of the place where you should have felt safe made me need to protect you. I couldn't help falling in love with you even more."

A tear slips out of my eye and his thumb catches it.

"I guess it makes sense that this is where I tell you I love you for the first time. This final time in your apartment. I love you, Madison. I can't and won't lose you. You walked in and my heart couldn't help falling for you."

"Blake, I—" The timer goes off. I jerk my gaze to it. "I hate your phone."

He laughs and presses the stop button.

"I love you. You're a piece of my soul." I take a breath. "Could you please fuck me now?"

He kisses me and my chest explodes with love. I rock my hips over his cock. I don't want to release him to get more friction. Our hips rock together as we stare into each other's eyes. His thumb slides over my clit, winding me tighter.

My lips part as I build toward my release. His green eyes are filled with so much love. This speed bump in my life with the stalker, I can't wait for it to be over so I can spend all of my future with these guys.

The wave of my orgasm is soft and flows through me, drawing me deeper into his eyes.

"You belong to me, love, and I belong to you." He kisses me and lays me back on the bed before thrusting in deep.

I grab his jaw and hold him to me, breathing his breath as he pushes me over the edge again. I cry out as he pounds into me until he finds his release and fills me.

He collapses over me, and suddenly, I don't want to leave this apartment. I don't want to leave this feeling of being complete. Of having his love and knowing this place helped make it happen.

His lips claim mine and the world slips away again. Everything is falling into place.

Chapter 133

Forward Momentum

Madison

Time got away from us before we finally made it back to the kitchen. After having sex again, we checked Val's room and mine. The camera in my room was in the light fixture and had shorted out at some point. So maybe Jeff did me a favor by installing it wrong.

When I get to the chair, I blush as my gaze meets Blake's. He keeps smiling at me and it makes me so fucking warm inside. It's ridiculous, but I can't believe he loves me. It's amazing.

I climb up. While I'm unscrewing the register, I can't help but think, *What if it's not here?*

"Blake?"

He keeps unscrewing the light switch plate. "Yes, love?"

A brief happy glow fills me at the deeper meaning that word now holds. "What if we can't find the phone?"

"He'll screw up." His voice is gruff.

"But—"

"Guys like him always screw up. They show their hand in little ways. He may have already screwed up and we just haven't caught it yet." He turns and holds me with those determined green eyes. "We will get through this."

I press my lips together. I want to say, *But what if he doesn't? What if something happens, and whatever his end goal is, he achieves it before any of us realizes he's already ahead of us?*

With one last screw, the register comes off. I'm wearing an old set of plastic gloves I found underneath the sink, from when I dyed some of my hair pink during spring break. After the mouse incident, I'm glad to have protection.

The register is still above my head so I tentatively put my hand in and feel around. My heart pounds when I find something smooth. As I grip it, it feels like a phone and I hope it is. I need a win.

I lift it out and stare down at the black phone with a majorly cracked screen.

"Blake." My voice shakes.

He comes up and takes it out of my hand. I rip off the gloves, and using his shoulder for support, step off the chair. My eyes never leave the phone.

"It's not charged. It might require a passcode." He inspects it and then releases a breath. "As much as I want to do this ourselves, I told Bill I'd let him know if we found anything. If we fuck this up, we could destroy the one piece of evidence they have."

I swallow. "You're right."

The police can handle this part. Them coming and looking for a phone that may or may not exist wouldn't happen, but they should be able to take this and find the evidence for us.

He wraps his arm around my shoulders and pulls me into his chest. He kisses the top of my head. "See? He already screwed up."

I hope Blake's right.

Blake holds my hand as we approach the bar. It took me twenty extra minutes to get ready since my first outfit, a short black dress, was vetoed. Followed by another veto of skinny jeans and an off-the-shoulder shirt. Finally, Seth pulled an outfit that suited going out with the girls without showing off too much of the goods.

A soft-as-sin white sweater with black jeans and a pair of calf-high boots. I left my hair down and it falls in soft waves around my shoulders. I squeeze Blake's hand when we get to the door.

I'm so excited.

Girlfriends! At a bar on a Saturday night. This is what I wanted from my new life.

The guys are a bonus that I wouldn't trade for the world, but right now, I'm on such a high. Blake follows me through the doors. Music plays beneath the din of voices. The fairy lights over the bar are on, and there's a soft glow to everything here that was missing last weekend when Hope's brother, Jason, was passed out.

"Madison!" Hope calls from the bar. Her dark hair hangs in a single braid down her back. She's wearing a black shirt and blue jeans.

Sara turns next to her. She has her red hair pulled to one side. Her blouse is white and her black leather pencil skirt is to die for.

They both smile as I approach, and Hope hugs me. "Thank you so much for last weekend."

I hug her back, inhaling her vanilla perfume. "I'm glad your brother's okay."

We separate and I turn to Sara.

"I'm so glad you could make it," I say.

Sara tugs me into a hug. For a second, I'm startled and breathe in her citrus-scented perfume. I didn't know we were this close already. But I return the hug.

"Are you feeling better?" she says in my ear.

Heat fills my cheeks as I remember what the guys told her on Thursday at dinner to explain why we had to leave our double date suddenly.

"Much better. Thank you." I smile, and her green eyes crinkle with her own.

Blake touches my back. I spin to him and kind of want to hug him too. It's a total mood. Instead, I smile.

He leans in close. "I'll be over there."

He brushes my hair behind my ear before gesturing with his head to a less crowded spot down the bar.

Our eyes meet and I really want to press up and kiss him, but we agreed, until the stalker is caught, we should keep public displays of affection to a minimum. To which Coop laughed.

Blake's fingers caress my jaw as he pulls away. I let out a happy sigh.

Thankfully, both Sara and Hope were getting Jason's attention. I take the bar stool in the middle and look up at the big guy. He gives me a nod.

"Drinks are on me." Jason places a strawberry daiquiri in front of me.

"Thank you. I'm glad you're doing better."

He gives me a smile and a nod before he's pulled away.

I draw in a deep breath and almost squeal with joy. It's a Saturday night and I'm out with the girls. I still can't believe it.

"How's work been?" Hope asks as we get settled.

"Great. I met Deidre Byrne on Friday. She gave me her card." I can't help sharing. The guys wouldn't get it. "She said I could call her anytime. She's amazing."

"She spoke at our sorority last month." Sara draws my attention. "She'd be an amazing mentor. She's done everything. Built her company on her own."

"I've always wanted to meet her," Hope says, taking a drink. "She has this program that only takes a few women each year, but I've been too chickenshit to apply. Besides the fact I love my job at Morrigan Technology and don't really want to leave."

"I love that everything in their company is about female pleasure." Sara toys with her straw. "I have a few of her products and they're the best."

My face feels warm as I remember Coop and Noah showing me her products. "They're very good."

"Have you two made any arrangements for your wedding?" Hope grins and lifts my hand to see my ring better. "That's gorgeous."

I sigh. This is the part I don't like. I can't tell my friends about everything that's happening in my life, and I have to keep straight who knows what. "We haven't talked wedding details. It's all so new still."

"I can't believe he actually asked you to marry him." Hope shakes her head. "Not that you aren't great, but Cooper Graham was a player before you showed up."

"Yeah, even in my circles, women talk about the unattainable Cooper Graham." Sara leans over to say, "I mean, you could have him, but you couldn't keep him. His reputation made him desirable. I'm not surprised you landed him though."

"Really?" Honestly, if I'd known Coop's reputation, I would have been surprised that he wanted to fuck me and only me. That he fell in love with me is amazing. When this stalker thing is over though, we'll have to have a long talk about this "engagement."

"Oh, yeah. You're gorgeous and intelligent. If I were a dude, I'd be all over you." Sara laughs.

The two guys I've seen that she's into are tall and intimidating. They're also both gorgeous.

"How are you going to land that guy? Wyatt?" I'm curious how she's going to go about it, since jealousy doesn't seem to be a factor. She went to the benefit with Noah and then dinner out, and it doesn't seem to have made a dent in the guy.

"Wait, I thought she was dating Noah," Hope says.

"We're just . . ." Sara's eyes meet mine and I give her a little shake of my head to let her know Hope doesn't know about Noah and me. "Friends. Our mothers are hell-bent on setting us up with people, so we're just going out to make this guy I like jealous. Though it doesn't seem to be working."

"That sucks. Noah's such a nice guy." Hope sighs. "I know he's the youngest of the bosses, but I gotta admit, he's got that shy guy thing going for him."

I'm sure my cheeks are pink because Noah might seem shy, but the things he does to me . . . I press my thighs together. He's neither shy nor nice in bed.

"Yeah, I was pleasantly surprised." Sara laughs. "So many times my mom sets me up with rejects, but Noah's a genuinely nice guy. It's kind of a shame he's already taken."

My eyes widen. Fuck. Sara's eyes widen as she realizes her slipup. She mouths *Sorry* to me.

"I didn't know Noah was dating anyone." Hope looks at me. "Did you know?"

I take a drink of my daiquiri and shake my head. I hate this. I hate having to lie to my friends. But this part of it will be over soon. As soon as we know who the stalker is. Bill took the phone in and said they'd work on it. Then we can just live our lives.

When Blake asked how long, Bill couldn't give us a straight answer. Too much backlog.

"Weird. It's always the quiet ones." Hope shakes her head.

Sara takes pity on me and talks about a show she just watched. Apparently Hope watches it too. For a second, I feel like an outsider again. The guys take up a lot of my time, but I have had some moments to read or watch TV.

I'm just not used to it yet.

"Madison has barely watched anything for years, so almost everything is new to her." Hope brings me back into the conversation. "We should totally do a movie night."

"That sounds amazing. I could use a break from my little sister. We watch Barbie movies or Disney. She randomly belts out songs from *Frozen*. Caitlyn cannot carry a tune in a bucket. I swear if I hear 'Let It Go' one more time, I'm going to scream." Sara laughs.

"I'm in." More time getting to know these women seems like an easy decision.

We drink and laugh about all sorts of things. My phone buzzes and I glance at Blake, who's talking with Jason. As if he senses me watching him, he turns. Our eyes meet and my heart swells.

I pull out my phone, expecting it to be one of the guys. It's an unknown number. My heart beats hard in my ears as I stare at the notification. I could ignore it. Deal with it later. I don't have to let my stalker have control over my life.

The notification is a picture, so if I don't open it, I won't know what it is. Another notification comes in, followed by another.

"I need to use the bathroom." Hope smiles at me before she leaves and I register it, but part of me can't help thinking, *What did he send me now?*

"I'm sorry about Noah. It just slipped out." Sara takes a drink and her eyes search my face. "Are you okay?"

I release my breath. It could just be some sales thing. I'm being ridiculous.

"Just a message on my phone. I'm sure it can wait." Setting it down, I turn back to Sara. "I'm sorry, you were saying?"

She smiles. "I'm the one who's sorry. I didn't mean to out Noah. He's just such a great guy and I can see why you'd want him."

Warmth fills me. "Noah is great. We've connected since the beginning."

"I wish Wyatt saw me as someone other than his best friend's little sister." She grins. "Maybe I'll actually start dating someone for real and just let the whole Wyatt thing go."

"There's that group of guys over there that have been watching you." I gesture with my head. The guys are around our age, in jeans and Henley shirts with their hair perfectly styled. When both Sara and I look at them, one of them cocks an eyebrow and gives us a flirty smile.

Giggling, Sara and I turn back to the bar.

"I'm not sure where I'll find a guy. Probably not a bar. Maybe I'll wait until I have my internship lined up for the fall and go for the boss like you did." Sara bumps her shoulder into mine.

I laugh and take a drink. She doesn't know about the contract. Which involves all my bosses.

Hope slides up next to me on her bar stool. "What's funny?"

Sara jerks her head in the direction of the guys. "Madison was helpfully pointing out the table of guys checking us out."

"I said checking *you* out. I've got a man." Grinning, I love that I can say that. I can't wait for the day I can claim all of them. My gaze darts to Blake.

"Well, I don't." Hope turns and winks at the guy who gave us the flirty smile.

He grins and stands from his table.

"Oh, shit." Sara giggles and takes another drink. "I'm too buzzed to be cool about this. I'm so sorry in advance."

Hope leans back on the bar and never takes her eyes off the guy. "I bet you he doesn't even come over here."

I turn to watch him. "He's obviously heading over here."

She shakes her head. "Oh, he'll start to but . . ."

The guy turns with a cocky smile and heads our way. His gaze takes in each of us from head to toe. He's got dark hair and dark eyes. He's fit and tall but not as gorgeous as my guys. I'm curious what will happen.

The guy's gaze lifts and his eyes widen. His step falters. He just stops and then, giving us an apologetic look, he turns and heads back to his table.

"That was weird." I turn around on the bar stool and Jason stands behind Hope, cracking his knuckles. I laugh. Jason winks at me before he picks up the bar rag to wipe down the counter.

"Fuck. And I thought my brother was bad." Sara shakes her head. "That guy totally would have hit on all three of us, but one look at your brother and he slunk back to his sad corner."

My phone buzzes again, and I turn it over.

UNKNOWN:
You aren't curious, little one?

Chapter 134

Go Back and Sharpen Your Pencils

Madison

Fuck. Am I curious? Yes. Do I want to ruin my evening with whatever game my stalker is playing now? Not really.

Sara and Hope are comparing notes about their brothers. As an only child, I really have nothing to contribute.

What's the worst my stalker could send me? He's already sent pictures of me around town. Me naked and masturbating in my shower. An old dress. I can't think of anything worse that he can send me on my phone.

I don't even have a bunny he can boil.

Fuck it.

I unlock my screen and click on the message. A picture of Blake and me walking to the bar opens. It's definitely from tonight. The second is an audio recording I'll have to listen to later when it's not so noisy, and most likely with the guys. And another picture of me at the bar with Sara.

As I'm looking, another picture arrives. It's me at the bar looking at my phone with Sara and Hope still talking.

My insides go cold.

He's here.

He's right here.

I can't turn around. I copy the photo and send it to Blake. My gaze finds him and I wait until he looks at his phone. His face goes stony as he stands and scans the bar. Jason leans over to ask him something. Blake shows him the phone. Jason looks around the room.

My heart thuds in my ears, heavy. I don't want to look. I don't want to know.

"You okay?"

I lift my head to tell Hope I'm fine, but it would just be another lie. Both her and Sara are concerned. I hold out my phone so they can see the picture.

"Fuck," Hope breathes and turns to check out behind us.

"Stalker?" Sara takes my hand. I squeeze her hand back. It's good to know I'm not alone.

I nod and swallow. I still haven't turned around, but if anyone should recognize him, it would be me. This person has made it his mission to follow me and catch me unaware, but at some point, he had to be part of my life. I must have seen or talked to him at least once. Right?

Otherwise, why?

Taking a breath, I turn and face the direction the picture was taken from. The bar is dimly lit and there are tons of people moving about. No one looks familiar. No one appears to be looking my way.

"That's it." Blake's voice is in my ear as his hand captures my elbow. I almost sag with relief at his warmth surrounding me. "We're getting out of here. A car is waiting. Tell your friends. We aren't leaving anyone behind."

I turn to Hope and Sara. "We have a car outside. We should go."

Hope bites her lip and looks at her brother. He makes a shooing motion.

As we make our way to the doors, Hope and Sara lead the way. Blake wraps his arm around my waist and holds me tight against him as we maneuver through the thick crowd. We move slowly to stay together.

The doors open and we walk out into the cool night air. Blake keeps us moving until we get to the car. He holds the door open as we climb in before he gets in the passenger seat.

"Was that all they sent?" Sara asks. Her hand shakes as she brushes her hair behind her ear.

"No. They sent a picture while Hope was in the bathroom. And one of me and Blake arriving." I glance at my phone but there aren't any new notifications. "There's also an audio file I haven't listened to."

"Let me see your phone." Blake puts his hand out and I pass it to him.

I tip my head back on the car seat and close my eyes as we head back to the tower. It's been over a week since we heard anything from the stalker. While it's terrifying how close he was and how unaware I was, it's almost a relief to get something finally.

"Are you going to be okay?" Hope asks.

I open my eyes and her blue eyes watch me. Blowing out my breath, I straighten.

"It feels like we're getting close to who it is, but then something like this happens." I shake my head. "For years apparently, this person watched and took pictures, but now they want me to know I'm being watched. But they haven't done anything to me, even when they had the chance. It doesn't make sense."

Blake meets my gaze in the rearview mirror. He's trying to give me his strength, but I didn't want to see who it was at the bar. I don't want to face this nightmare. I just want it to disappear. But I'm going to have to face it.

"Do you want to come up and have a glass of wine with me?" I ask Sara and Hope. I want to pretend a little longer that I'm just me and that the only men interested in me are the four who hold my heart.

Even if I don't deserve them, they love me.

"Yeah, I could use a drink." Sara shakes her head. "We can watch an episode of *The Great British Bake Off*."

"Oh, yes, that always helps calm me down." Hope smiles and holds my arm. "You're going to love it."

"That sounds good." Anything to take my mind off this person. He doesn't deserve to occupy my thoughts.

Blake

It's almost midnight before we call the driver to take Sara and Hope home. Madison is a little tipsy as she walks them to the door. I sit at the island with her phone, waiting.

"We have to do this again." She hugs Hope and then turns to hug Sara. "I need this."

Hope laughs. "I agree."

"Hopefully, we took your mind off things for a while," Sara says and squeezes Madison's hand. "Oh, next week, Kayla comes in. We all need to get together. You too, Hope."

"You're going to love Kayla." Madison points at me. "She's Blake's sister."

She's smiling, but I know that underneath that brave face, she's crumbling. Noah comes out of the library.

"I'll take them downstairs," he offers. As he passes Madison, he draws her in for a hug. Sara makes this *aw* face.

"See? He's such a good guy." Hope sighs. "See you Monday."

Once everyone says their goodbyes, the door closes, leaving Madison on this side of it.

"Can I pretend there isn't more?" she says to the ceiling. Her hands cover her forehead.

Coop comes out of his room at that moment. He doesn't hesitate to go to her and wrap his arms around her from behind. She turns and clings to him. Her eyes open and meet mine.

"We'll wait for the boss and Noah." I tap her phone on the island. "We all need to hear this."

Coop puts his arm around Madison and leads her to me. She sits beside me at the island and rests her head on my shoulder.

"Thank you for letting me go out tonight," she says softly. Her hand slides into mine and our fingers lock together.

"I'm sorry your night out got interrupted." I kiss the top of her head. Her hand is small and delicate. So fucking fragile, but so strong at the same time. This woman gets under my skin, makes me long to protect her. Makes me need to love her.

This was never supposed to be part of the deal. Falling in love with her? The contract between us was only for sex, but we didn't factor in how much she would become a part of us.

None of the other women ever came close to making me feel what we all feel for Madison. They don't hold a candle to her.

Coop leans on the island next to her. He brushes a strand of her golden hair behind her ear. "We'll keep you safe, sweetheart."

Her smile is a little sloppy. I'm glad she and I had our time alone already because I have a feeling the others won't want her out of their sight after they hear this. I'm not sure any of us will sleep alone anytime soon.

Seth comes out of his room in a pair of pajama pants with no shirt and no socks on. He goes straight to Madison and kisses her softly on the temple before moving to the other side of the kitchen to start a pot of coffee.

"Decaf?" Madison asks.

"Of course, princess."

We all watch as he prepares the coffee maker. The front door rattles and Noah comes in.

"I guess I'm the last." He puts his hands in his pockets and walks to the island. He takes the chair on my other side. "Is it as fucked-up as I think it is?"

"Before I play this, it's important you know that I've swept the whole apartment for listening devices." Her hand tightens in mine and I meet her wide blue eyes. "There aren't any currently transmitting."

"Why does that not reassure me?" Coop groans and goes over to help Seth with the coffee cups.

When everyone settles with their coffee, I look to Seth. We listened to the audio and we've both been processing. I'm not sure how the others will react.

"Just play it, Blake." He shakes his head. There's no way to prepare them.

I press the audio file Play button. Coop's voice fills the room.

"Bind her hands above her head. I want her to feel as helpless as we do."

The sounds are hauntingly familiar. Madison clings to my hand with her eyes closed. Our moans, her pants, the sound of us fucking, it's all there. It goes on and on. Crystal fucking clear.

"Please." It ends with Madison's plea.

"Fuck." Coop slams his hand down on the island. Madison flinches. He paces angrily back and forth with his hands buried in his hair. "What the fuck? The conference room? How the fuck did anyone bug our fucking conference room?"

"It's not currently transmitting, but we'll have a team go in tomorrow and find it." Seth's focus is on Madison. It's another invasion into her life. Another piece of her stolen. A piece of us someone else took.

"We can't be sure how much the stalker has, but it's safe to assume he has recordings back to when the fire alarm got triggered." I set the phone away from me. "Madison saw someone go behind the building. We know it wasn't a coincidence that the alarms went off. Someone triggered them. It would make sense that they could have gotten in during that time and planted it."

"The other option is that someone who has access planted it." Noah runs a hand through his hair and shoves off the stool. He strides to Madison and takes her in his arms.

She releases a sob as she turns to hold him. He curls around her like she's a part of him he wants to take inside himself to keep safe. Her shoulders shake.

"Who all has access?" I rub my jaw. "The cleaning crew. Whoever got in that night. The security team. Patrick Beck. Fuck, we've had clients including Hunter Adams in there. It really doesn't narrow down the suspect pool much."

"We can't forget the corporate spy might have planted it and the stalker either gained access, or they're working together," Seth says. "There are access cards that are supposed to be kept under lock and key, but it wouldn't be hard to work around that. There's a possibility that they know about our honey trap idea."

Seth stays calm. This is why we excel at business. We remain cool under pressure even if it feels like the pressure is going to explode out the top of our heads.

To have a moment of joy sullied by this asshole's need to control our woman is infuriating. This all needs to stop. We can't deal with this on our own. The police are doing what they can, but their hands are tied. Stalking is important, but we don't have a suspect to point them to. And while he's sent shit like this, the stalker hasn't done anything directly to Madison.

"We go forward with our scheme to interview the fake client." Seth rubs his chin. "We need to go on as if nothing happened. He'll expect us to find the bug or he wouldn't have sent the audio."

"I've already called Patrick." Coop leans against the refrigerator with his hands on his head. "He's coming in to help us with the corporate spy. He's setting up the honey trap for us and making sure everything we do to catch the spy will hold up in court."

The spy that's been contacting new customers and warning them about our "questionable morals." We narrowed down which types of clients they're contacting to set a trap. The only problem is Patrick.

"Are we sure the stalker isn't Patrick?" I ask, because someone has to. "He knew Madison before."

"He has a family." Coop shakes his head. "He talks about his kids all the time. Shows me pictures. He barely remembers the current nanny's name. I'm not surprised he doesn't remember Madison. He's at a benefit for work tonight so he couldn't have been at the bar."

Coop holds up a picture of Anna and Patrick Beck at a function.

I nod. It's an alibi for tonight. If it was the stalker at the bar and not someone he hired like Valerie. Fuck. "I've called Bill. They're going to check into the texts. But tonight we need to go to bed. It's late."

Seth nods. His gaze falls on Noah and Madison. "We can go to a hotel tonight. The team will do a sweep of the apartment tomorrow, just to make sure there aren't any recording devices up here, but we can't say for sure whether someone got into our suite during the false alarm."

"If you think it's safe, we can stay." She turns her cheek to rest on Noah's chest while she faces the rest of us. "I don't want him to win. Obviously, he doesn't want us to feel safe in our home."

Standing, I step toward her. Her haunted eyes meet mine. I want to find that guy tonight and drag him through the same hell she's been through. "Do you want to stay in my room or yours tonight?"

She sighs and releases Noah to come into my arms, wrapping her arms around my waist.

"We'll all be more comfortable on your bed, but we can make mine work. For all of us." I brush my hand over her hair and kiss the top of her head.

Her gaze lifts to mine. "We don't have to—"

"If it were just you and me, love, yeah, but we're all gutted." I meet all of their eyes, Seth's, Coop's, and Noah's. These are my brothers and we won't let our woman down. "We're all together and we're all here for you."

Chapter 135

Goodwill

Madison

"I'll be fine," I assure Noah as we walk through the restaurant where I'm meeting Anna Beck for lunch. He wanted me to cancel, but I refuse to let the stalker control my life. A restaurant in the middle of the day should be safe.

The guys only agreed if one of them came with me.

"And I'll be right here in case anything goes wrong." His hand is on the small of my back. I'd prefer to be holding it, but while the stalker is on the loose, I'm Coop's fiancée. Period.

Noah walks me all the way to the table where Anna stands, waiting. Her auburn hair is pulled into a loose bun with ringlets falling around her face. Her brown eyes smile at me. She's wearing a pair of wide-leg pants that flow like a skirt to swirl around her nude high heels. Her matching wrap top is both stylish and simple. Diamonds flash at her ears and wrist and finger.

She looks effortlessly elegant. The first time I met her, I was in awe. She has a corporate job, a gorgeous home, a high-powered husband, and two adorable children. She's living the dream.

"I'm so glad you could meet with me." Anna grabs my arms and leans in to air-kiss next to my cheeks. She's polite and a little cold, but I expect that. Her gaze flicks to Noah. "I didn't know we'd have a plus-one."

I glance at Noah and smile. "He isn't staying."

"Let me know when you're ready to go." He nods when I know he'd kiss me if he could. But we need to tackle one thing at a time. "Good seeing you again, Anna."

"You too, Noah." She smiles at his retreating form. "Bodyguard?"

"My bosses are a little protective right now since I was attacked." I take the chair opposite her. "I was actually surprised you called so soon."

It surprised me she called at all, but I don't know what kind of agenda Anna might have. She was friendly enough when I worked for her, but we definitely weren't lunch buddies back then. We rarely talked. I just watched her kids and did laundry and dishes when I could. I was the hired help. Maybe this is because of Coop?

She lifts her glass of white wine and swirls the liquid. "When I found out what happened at the benefit, I had to make sure you were okay. To be attacked by someone you used to know." She shudders delicately and pouts at me. "I'm just glad my Patrick was there to save you."

"Me too." The memory of it isn't as powerful as the incident with Jeff, but it still lingers. It was sudden and unexpected. If Patrick hadn't shown up, I don't know what I would have done. "You'll have to thank him again for me. I'm just glad he was there before anything worse happened."

"You'll have a chance to thank him yourself when he's in your office on Monday." She sips her wine while observing me.

"I guess I'll do that." I'm not sure what she's looking for or expecting from me. Taking a drink from my water glass, I glance around for the waiter. We don't have menus, so I'm not sure if we're just having a drink or lunch.

I could have sworn she said lunch. This whole thing feels off, but she was so insistent I come. And I did love her children. Maybe it's just awkward because it's awkward.

"How is your new job working out?" She sets down her glass, crosses her legs, and leans back in the chair. "You didn't tell me at the benefit that you and Cooper were engaged. That happened fast, didn't it?"

"Uh, yes, he decided quickly." It didn't happen at all. Coop just proclaimed it so. "My job is amazing. It's just what I was looking for. I get to learn all the parts of the business and what it takes to run an organization as large as Morrigan Technology." Not to mention the benefit of fucking my bosses. Definitely not mentioning that.

"Fascinating. Even though they're young, they definitely have a well-oiled machine of a company. They've certainly made a name for themselves." She leans forward and holds her hand out to me. "Is that one of the Graham family diamond rings?"

"I believe so." I place my hand in hers and let her draw it across the table to examine the ring. Her eyes widen as she looks over the setting. I tell her, "It matches the diamonds I wore to the benefit."

"It's gorgeous. I've heard there's a vault of diamonds just waiting for his fiancée." Her gaze lifts to mine with a question in them.

I draw my hand back and look at the ring. That day he gave it to me, he told me it reminded him of me. "I wouldn't know. Coop said he wanted me to wear this one."

"Of course, Cooper would. He's always been a collector of pretty things. Nothing but the best." She gives me this smile that doesn't quite reach her eyes. She lifts her finger, and the waiter appears with two menus. "I shouldn't be surprised you're the one that ended up with the prize everyone wanted. You always attracted so much attention."

She lifts her menu and I do the same just to keep from gaping at her. *Always?* I'm not sure what's going on in her mind right now, but something seems off. Is she jealous of Coop and me? And me attracting attention? What's that supposed to mean?

There weren't any problems that I was aware of while nannying for Anna. Maybe I misread the situation.

I find something to order on the menu and set it down. It's a good time to change the subject.

"How are Lily and Elijah?" I ask softly.

When Anna puts down the menu, she smiles. "They're lovely. They love their new nanny. But no one really replaced you. They loved you so much. We all thought so highly of you, and look at how far you've come."

She smiles like she's proud of me. I don't understand what's going on. I can't shake the feeling that something is off. But after the waiter comes by and takes our order, Anna starts telling me gossip about people I don't know.

I nod like I'm following her story about Lexi Stratford, but I have no clue who any of the people are. When our meals arrive, Anna snaps her fingers.

"Your CEO is dating Elizabeth Hartfield, right?" She takes a delicate bite of her salad.

I swallow the lump in my throat, thinking of Elizabeth with Seth. "I believe so."

Anna's eyes light up like they did when she talked about Lexi. "They went to the benefit together, but my friend saw her duck into the special exhibits area. When she came out, she'd obviously been with someone back there. Do you think it was Seth?"

I freeze. She did? "I wouldn't know."

What if this is what we need to get Elizabeth to back off? What if she has a secret lover she doesn't want to get out?

Anna pouts. "We've been trying to figure it out all week. You didn't hear it from me, and I'll deny it, but Elizabeth can be a bitch. I'd love to see her get what's coming to her."

I nod. She moves on to some woman named Rita Carlisle. My mind keeps going back to the benefit. Seth never left my sight except when the guys went to talk. Elizabeth was left alone. A lot.

It's possible she met with someone. If she's chasing so hard after

Seth, then the person isn't to her mother's standards. Or he's married. Or he could be a she.

The real question is, How do we use this knowledge to trap her?

"I'm so glad we could do this." Anna sits back and drinks the last of her wine. "I always liked you and hoped you'd go far."

"Thank you." I smile. "You were always so nice to me. I really appreciated having you and the kids the first year I was away from home. You made being away from my family bearable."

Anna puts her hand over her heart, and her eyes soften. "I only wish you'd become a professional nanny. Good help is hard to find."

When we stand, she gives me another air-kiss beside my cheek.

"We should do this more often." Her eyes search mine.

I smile, because what else am I supposed to do? It's just something people say, right? "Of course."

She squeezes my arms and releases me. "You have a ride?"

I glance over at the bar and see Noah watching me. My heart fills. "Yes, I do."

She pats my arm. "Don't be a stranger. We'll talk soon."

Somehow I doubt that. I'm not sure what she was looking for, but hopefully, she got it. Maybe she really did just want to catch up. Or maybe she was horrified that I was attacked at the benefit. I really don't know. I don't think I'll ever fit into the wealthy world.

Monday morning comes way too soon. I've put up the dishes and have a pot of coffee started in the break room. I lean back against the counter to wait for the coffee to brew. Yesterday was low-key. We worked in the morning. I had lunch with Anna. The guys and I spent the afternoon watching a couple movies before dinner and bed.

Seth was excited to know that Elizabeth was sneaking around the benefit. It definitely lent itself to a clandestine meeting of some kind. We discussed Elizabeth and how we might figure out who she's secretly seeing, but we didn't come up with any good ideas.

Everyone seemed lost in their own thoughts after Blake's team found the bug under the conference room table. It was almost obvious. The second one was not obvious. And, after a long talk, we left it where it was. It isn't currently transmitting, but with Theo's computer skills, we set up a trace protocol for when it activates.

Thankfully, our apartment is bug free as far as we know. The coffee finishes and I grab a cup for myself.

When I walk out of the break room area, someone clears their throat. My gaze flicks up to see Patrick Beck standing next to my desk.

"Sorry, I was getting coffee." I rush around my desk and set the cup down.

"I wasn't waiting long." His gaze sweeps over me dismissively. "I just need to know where you want me to set up."

"I'll get Coop." I turn and head to Coop's door. I knock and wait. He left bed before I woke this morning. I missed seeing him.

"Come in."

When I open his door, his brow furrows as he stares at a report. He gestures for me to enter the room and come closer.

"Patrick Beck wants to know where you want him to set up." I rest my hands on the chair opposite Coop.

He lifts his gaze and looks me over, doing a much more thorough job than Patrick did. Seth has me in a black pencil skirt with a high waist and a billowy red blouse. His lingerie selection is black panties, black demi bra, and garters with thigh-high stockings. The red high heels have a little bow on the back. I pulled my hair into a low bun with tendrils framing my face and put on a bold red lipstick with minimal makeup.

His heated eyes lift to mine, making my insides thrum.

"You're going to have to give me a minute, sweetheart." Coop quirks a smile. "Otherwise, my cock will lead the way."

I blush, realizing I left the door open and Patrick can probably hear Coop. At least we're still technically engaged, and Patrick knows

Coop and I are together. My face flashes hotter as I realize with horror: he's their lawyer.

Every paper I've signed probably goes through Patrick. I never thought about that. Didn't really think those documents left this office. I glance over my shoulder and hurry around Coop's desk to stand beside him.

"Does Patrick get all of your legal documents?" I whisper, not wanting Patrick to hear me. My heart pounds and my eyes widen as I think of the NDA, the consent forms, the contract. My voice goes high. "Like our contract?"

"Whoa, Madison." Coop draws me down to sit on his lap. "It's fine. Patrick has been with us since the beginning of Morrigan Technology Group. He helped us with the case against Andrea and the NDA with Rachel. His firm handles everything for us."

This isn't making me feel better. He rubs his hand over my back.

"We wanted to do it right this time. Yes, he helped us draft your contracts and NDA. We have the originals here in Seth's office, but Patrick has copies at his office. He deals with it directly, so he doesn't have his paralegal or anyone else in the office look over the forms." Coop takes my left hand with his ring still on it and threads our fingers together.

"He saw the checklist?" I never considered anyone, outside of Seth, Coop, Blake, and Noah, would see it. It's one thing for them to know my limits and all those things I marked as *maybe*. Heat swamps my face.

I can't face him again.

Coop smiles and shakes his head. "Not the checklist, but the contract we all signed."

I'm not relieved. I used to watch this guy's kids. What must he think of me now? I willingly agreed to a sex contract with four strangers. I took their money to sign consent forms.

My stomach roils. To someone outside of this arrangement, it could look like I took their money for sex.

"Hey." Coop tips my head so our eyes meet. "He's our lawyer.

He's not allowed to talk about it with anyone else. Not even his wife. Strictly confidential. He isn't here to judge us, just to protect us from lawsuits."

It still makes my insides churn uncomfortably. But I know the guys did it to protect themselves. What if it ever got leaked? The sex contract between all of us? It'd be an even bigger scandal than us trying to take our relationship public.

"Are we good, sweetheart?" He rubs his thumb along my jaw.

When he helps me stand, I run my hands over my skirt to straighten it. Standing behind me, he leans into my ear. "I can't wait to have you bent over my desk with that skirt bunched around your waist while I fuck your tight pussy."

My breath catches, and I sway back into his heat before remembering we have someone waiting. Fuck.

I give him a glare with a small smile to lessen the impact before heading back out to my desk. Back out to face the guy who knows I sleep with my four bosses. I'm a professional assistant and I can behave as such in this case.

Taking my seat, I meet Patrick's brown eyes for a second before he lifts them to Coop.

"Patrick, we figured we'd set you up in the conference room, but there's a slight problem with a bug infestation." Coop claps Patrick on the shoulder and moves him toward the break room. "For now, we have you set up in the break room until we can verify that the bug situation is under control."

I glance toward the conference room and see Blake and a few others doing a sweep. There's a device set on the conference table that's designed to trigger when the bug transmits. It should light up. It's possible for the device to record some in its buffer before sending. Blake explained it to me yesterday, but it was a lot of things I didn't understand.

All I know is, it isn't safe in the conference room for now. It's hard to feel safe even in the apartment, but Blake assured me we are.

I trust him. I trust all of them.

Chapter 136

Discrepancy

Blake

"We have an issue." I walk into the break room to find Seth working with Patrick.

Seth straightens. "What is it?"

Patrick lifts his gaze from his laptop and looks at me expectantly. I'm hesitant to say this in front of him, but fuck it, he's our lawyer. Maybe he'll be useful in this instance.

"Security caught Robert Addler trying to get in the fire door for our apartment." Madison's old neighbor decided to try his luck at our back door. The door that leads to the staircase into her bedroom.

"Was he trying to break in?" Seth leans back.

"He tried the door and then waited for security to come for him." It doesn't make sense. We've ruled him out as the stalker time after time, but what if we were just wrong? What if he's been planning this all along and we're walking into his trap?

"Are you sure he wasn't invited?" Patrick taps his pen on the table. "It wouldn't be the first time one of your assistants had a man up to her apartment."

That makes no sense. It's daytime. Madison is working. She's ours.

When we were working on our case against Andrea, we told him she had people up to the apartment. Technically, we weren't exclusive, but everything seemed relevant to tell our attorney at that time. Rachel also had guests up occasionally. There was nothing wrong with that.

"Madison wouldn't do that." Seth meets my eyes and I know we're on the same page.

Patrick holds up his hands as if in surrender. "I didn't want to stir the pot, but it's not like Ms. Harris is known for her discretion. We used to worry she had boyfriends over after the kids were in bed."

Maybe back then. She's been with other people before, but not now. Andrea had a few guys up to the apartment. Rachel probably did too. But usually they came in through the front door. We only found out about Andrea's visitors by the emergency exit when she told us. I don't know what Patrick is trying to imply, but I trust Madison.

"Robert says he'll only talk to Madison," I say.

"We can't call the police, right?" Seth turns to Patrick.

"He tried the door and didn't get in. There's nothing illegal about that." Patrick rubs his chin. "I'd be concerned that it was a miscommunication between the two of them. Otherwise, why would he want to talk to her and only her?"

"She was always polite to him. He was her neighbor." The words fall out of my mouth without a second thought. Maybe when she shouldn't have been. I can't forget how nervous she looked when he kept stepping closer to her in the lobby. But then, she knew I was watching . . . I rub a hand over my face. Fuck, what am I even thinking?

Patrick gives me a knowing look. "Girls like her are always bound to attract the wrong attention."

Girls like her? What the fuck is that supposed to mean?

"Do you mind if I borrow Seth?" I step back as I take in Patrick.

He's relaxed. Not tense at all. This could just be how he thinks. He's paid to protect us.

Seth stands. "We're finished."

Patrick nods and pulls over his laptop. Something isn't sitting right, and I'm not sure what as I lead Seth past Madison's empty desk and into his office. It's grocery day so she must be putting away groceries. Which puts her in the apartment around the time Robert tried to get in.

Fuck. What if she was meeting with him in secret? What would she have to hide from us?

"How do you want to approach this?" Seth sits behind his desk and leans back.

"Do you think it's possible?" I can't help asking because I need a check on myself. I trusted Andrea and I was wrong. Madison isn't anything like Andrea, but . . .

His brows furrow. "What's possible?"

I can't believe I'm even going to ask this. "That she asked him to—"

"No." Seth doesn't add any inflection.

I rub my jaw with my hand. "Okay, but what if we can find out for sure?"

Madison

The day flew by. Lunch was a working lunch. Coop worked with Patrick most of the day.

I just returned to my desk from putting away the groceries when Blake comes out of his office. "We need you in Seth's office."

I grab my tablet and follow Blake in. Usually it's work related, but not always, so it's best to be prepared. Blake closes the door behind me. Seth's concerned eyes lift to mine. My insides sink.

What now?

"They caught your neighbor Robert trying to access the back door a half hour ago. He's being detained downstairs." Seth's hands are folded on his desk in front of him.

My brow furrows. This doesn't make sense. "Robert?"

"We don't know what he hoped to do. He said he wouldn't talk to anyone but you." Seth's dark blue eyes hold mine as I take in that information. "He won't leave until he's talked to you."

When my legs feel like they won't hold me, I sink down into the chair, setting my tablet on Seth's desk. "Robert?"

"Yes, princess." Seth's worried gaze lifts to Blake's.

Blake sits in the chair next to me and takes my hand. "Any information he can give you will be useful. We don't know why he was outside. While security can escort him off the premises, we can't press charges because he didn't do anything illegal."

"How does he know about the back door?" My mind churns trying to think of everything the stalker had access to and what Robert might have access to. I've wondered if he was the stalker before, but every time, I find a reason to absolve him. Am I letting him off because he was nice to me?

Because he seems like the most likely suspect and not at the same time? Is my sense of people that far off?

"We don't know." Seth's tired voice draws my attention. Darkness lingers under his eyes. A pang of worry squeezes my chest. Did he sleep at all last night?

We talked a lot about Elizabeth and got nowhere. Just trying to figure out who she might have met at the benefit is a long list.

The function was well attended. No one really watched Elizabeth that night. And once I was attacked, the guys were with me.

"If you don't want to talk to him, we understand, tiger." Blake squeezes my hand, bringing me back to the present. "But he came here looking for you. Whatever he wants to tell you, he feels strongly enough about it to break in."

Fuck, I don't know what they want from me. Am I supposed to sit across from someone who may be my stalker? Who saw me at my most vulnerable? And what?

I meet Blake's green eyes and sigh. "How? Do I have to talk to him alone? What if he tries to grab me?"

Blake glances at Seth. Something passes between them. "We'll be close and monitoring the situation. We have video in the conference room on the sixth floor but no sound. If he makes one move toward you, get to the door. I'll be there."

"You won't be able to hear us?" I don't know if that's smart. What if he says something that proves he's my stalker?

"We'll both be down there with you. Can you do this, princess?" Seth searches my eyes.

I want to be strong for them, but all those videos and audio clips . . . If Robert is the stalker, he would have heard and seen all those things. That anyone heard and saw those private moments makes me cringe and want to hide forever. Not confront them.

It was easy with Hunter because I was positive he wasn't the stalker but needed to rule him out. Robert, though? They want me to talk to him and find out why he's here. What if that reason is me?

"Wait, the stalker got in the building using an old employee security card." I perk up. Robert wouldn't have that kind of access. So, he couldn't be the stalker.

"That we shut off after that weekend, love." Blake stands and pulls me up. "I don't believe he's the stalker, but we have to behave as if he is. Just to be safe."

I nod. I can't make heads or tails of whether Robert is the stalker. He's always been kind and a little aggressive about being friendly, but he's never tried anything. He never even asked me out before. But maybe he wanted to and didn't think I'd say yes.

I draw in a breath and step into Blake's arms, wrapping my arm around his waist and blowing out my breath as his arms come around me. I just need a little of his strength and I'll be good to go.

When I release him and nod, we all three make our way down to the sixth floor. A couple of guys stand outside the door like Robert's being held prisoner. One opens the door for me as I approach.

When I turn back, both Blake and Seth give me encouraging

looks. Seth goes to the security room on this floor to watch the monitor.

"I'll be right here." Blake leans against the wall opposite the door.

I want another hug, but this floor is busy with employees. People glance over as they work, trying to figure out what's going on. If I hugged the boss, word would spread like wildfire.

Someone here might be working with the stalker. They have to be to get the kind of access the stalker has. Which means we need to be extra cautious about giving up too much information.

Taking one more hit of Blake's green eyes, I turn and enter the conference room. Robert stands looking out the window. His hands are clasped behind his back. He looks like a normal guy.

It takes him a moment to realize I'm in the room. When his intense gaze finds me, my nerves get the better of me. Flinching, I back against the wall.

"Madison, thank goodness you're all right." Robert rounds the table.

"Stay there, please." I hold my shaking hand up to stop him.

He gives me a wounded look. "I'm not here to hurt you."

"Why are you here?" I wrap my arms around my waist and stand against the wall next to the door, knowing if I pull it open, Blake is right there on the other side. He has me.

"The woman I told you about before. The one that tried to get into your apartment?" Robert's eyes are a little wild and he gestures as he speaks.

"The brunette." I nod to encourage him to get to the point.

"Yes, she stopped at my place instead."

I step closer. "What did she look like?"

"Pretty. Brown hair. Blue eyes."

Like Hope. Or like Courtney. Or any number of women. She may not even be someone I know.

"She said you were in trouble and I should help you." He puts his hands on the table between us. "She stressed you needed to escape."

My brows furrow. "In trouble how?"

"Your bosses. She said they're using you and you need help to get away from them. She told me about the back door that leads to your place. It's not safe for you here." Robert's voice gets more passionate as he continues, "You'll get hurt if you stay."

What the fuck is going on? This woman thinks the guys are holding me hostage? Or is this a plan to get me away from their safety, so the stalker can get to me easier?

Who is this woman, and what's her game?

"Was she as tall as me or shorter?" I need to get specific here.

"As tall, but she had on heels." He blows out a breath and holds his hand out to me. "Just come back to your apartment where you'll be safe. I can keep you safe."

It could be Courtney or some other woman we haven't even considered.

"I'm safe here, Robert." I back up against the wall again. "My apartment wasn't safe. It never was."

I didn't know it at the time. My roommate had taken money to spy on me, to let some creep into the intimate moments of my life.

"Is it because of that guy Blake?" Robert straightens. His voice is a little rougher. "I heard you two in your apartment on Saturday. It sounded like he hit you. I heard you crying. You don't have to stay with someone like that."

My face heats. Not something I wanted anyone to hear. But that seems to be my life right now. "Someone is stalking me. They may be working with someone here, but they can get to me easily in the apartment building. They already did."

"Then stay with me. I have a couch, and you can take the bed. I don't want you to be in danger." Robert steps closer again. "I can keep you safe."

I wrap my arms around my waist, but I don't reach for the door. Something's not right. I can't figure it out yet, but something is definitely off.

Why? Why did this woman approach Robert? What did that gain her?

"Why did the woman tell you about the back door?" I ask, thinking out loud, not really expecting an answer.

"She said I'd never get in any other way. The guys would stop me from getting to you." He glances toward the door. "If they're hurting you, I can help you get away. I'm not afraid of them."

"They aren't hurting me." I breathe in and drop my arms. "My bosses are protecting me. I don't know what that woman wants, but it's probably not in my best interest. For all I know, she's working with the stalker, and they want me out so he can get to me easier."

"She swore they were hurting you. That I should do anything to get to you. Even pick the lock and take you, whether or not you wanted to go. But I know you're reasonable, and if I could just talk to you, I could make you come with me."

Take me?

I gasp. "She wanted you to get in trouble." My mind whirls around the possibilities. "What if she wanted us to think you were the stalker? What if she tried to set up Jimi as the stalker, too, but that didn't work? So she moved on to you. The guy who's been a little too forward sometimes but who actually cares about me."

His cheeks get a little red. "I just don't want anything bad to happen to you."

"And I appreciate that, but my bosses will take care of me, so you don't have to worry about me anymore." I step forward as I say this, trying to reassure him.

"You'll call me if you need me?" His dark eyes search mine.

I nod, knowing I won't, but if times get dark, it doesn't hurt to have a friend.

"Good." He steps back from the table. "I didn't scare you, did I?"

The door opens before I can figure out a reply. Blake comes in and the tension releases out of my body.

"We need to talk about the woman you talked to." Blake doesn't look my way.

My brow furrows. I thought they couldn't hear what we were saying. Why would they tell me they couldn't hear me? It would have made me less fearful knowing they were listening to every word. So why not reassure me?

The guy was trying to get into our apartment and take me.

Unless they don't trust me? Did they think I set this up? My hand goes over my mouth to hide my hurt.

But the ache is deep in my heart. Seth and Blake didn't trust that I'd tell them what Robert said. Did they think I was involved with him too? My stomach churns. Robert's brown eyes flick to me.

"I'd recognize the woman if I saw her. I'm good with faces."

Blake glances at me briefly. His expression is blank. My throat thickens and I'm pretty sure I'm going to cry or throw up or both. What happened to "We need to trust each other for this to work"?

"Take a walk with me." Blake gestures with his head to Robert. He pauses next to me. When he reaches out to touch my arm, I flinch away. I can't.

He releases a breath. His green eyes capture mine. His mouth presses into a thin line. "Wait here for Seth."

I cross my arms and look away.

Robert stops beside me. He glances at Blake's tense back and then to me. "If you need me . . ."

I force a smile like my heart isn't breaking a little. "I'm fine. Thank you."

I just know where I stand now. They may claim to love me, but they don't trust me.

Chapter 137

Personal Responsibility

Blake

Seth warned me it was a bad idea, but fuck, I can't help if I don't trust anyone. Another man is after Madison. Maybe Robert isn't the stalker, but he could be something else. Something more to her.

Madison's watery eyes tore at me before she took them away entirely. The way she flinched from me. The hurt and pain on her face made my insides crumble. I'm the one she turned to for comfort and I've pushed her away. But I can't focus on that right now.

Right now, I have to follow this clue. We need any lead we can get on Madison's stalker.

"I'm going to show you around the office." Stopping a few feet from the conference room with Robert, I glance back but the door is still open. She's hurting and there's nothing I can do about it. At least not right now. Fuck. I turn to Robert. "I want you to see if the woman you talked to is here."

"Anything to help Madison." He doesn't meet my eyes, but he's already looking around the office.

I don't want to be correct about this, but I lead him to Hope's desk. Hope lifts her head and gives me a smile before turning to look at Robert. There's no spark of recognition in her eyes. She gives him a curious once-over before turning back to me.

"Do you need my help, Mr. Wagner?"

When I glance at Robert for confirmation, he shakes his head. Some of the tension leaves me. If it had been Hope, it would devastate Madison. She trusts Hope, and I know they've gotten close.

"No, not right now." I blow out a breath. "But maybe check in with Madison today."

Hope tips her head to the side. "Is she okay?"

"She might be having a rough day." I leave it at that. I can't tell Hope that I fucked up. That I didn't do the one thing Madison needs me to do. Trust her. Because I'm fucking broken.

Hope frowns and picks up her phone. "I'll text her. Thanks for the heads-up."

I lead Robert through the hallways. We stop by every office with a dark-haired woman, but no one seems to catch his attention. My mind keeps drifting back to Madison's face. How she looked at me. I never should have doubted her.

I'm an asshole.

Courtney's office door is closed, so I knock and wait. When she doesn't answer, I hold up a finger to Robert to wait. I call the receptionist.

"Is Courtney Miller in today?"

"No, sir, she called in sick." The receptionist is polite, but curt.

"Thank you." I hang up and pull out my keys. Unlocking the door, I push it open and lead Robert inside.

Courtney's office is small but neat. Pictures of her and friends fill her shelves.

Robert tugs on my sleeve. "That's her."

He points to a picture with a group of women in it. I lift it off the shelf and hold it in front of us.

"Which one?"

When he points, my stomach turns.

Fuck. I wasn't expecting that.

Seth

When I reach the conference room, it's empty. I glance at Matt who guards the door.

"Where is she?"

"She needed to use the restroom, sir." Matt gestures toward the bathrooms.

"Why didn't one of you go with her?" I can feel the tension headache starting behind my brow. My chest squeezes. We played a stupid game. One we knew we could end up losing. I just hope she gives us a chance to explain.

Matt glances at Alex and they both look at me. "We were told to stay here."

I release a breath. "You can return to work now."

I check the bathrooms on this floor, but they're unoccupied. Blake told her to wait for me, but it took a few minutes in the control booth before I could come get her. I refuse to panic as I ride the executive elevator to our office and check to see if she's there.

Her desk chair is empty. The bathroom is unoccupied. A thick, choking pressure builds in my chest.

When I open Noah's door, he lifts his head from his work. "What's up?"

I glance at his empty couch.

"Have you seen Madison?" I run a hand through my hair.

Blake's plan wasn't necessary. I felt it in my bones, but that little voice warned me, *What if I can't trust her? What if this whole thing is moving too fast? What if she fits too well? What if this is a setup?*

Even in the video, I could see the hurt on her face when Blake came in. All this time she gave us her trust, bending beautifully to our will, and then we pull this shit. She's right to be angry and upset.

Now, I'm afraid she's left us, and it would be all my fault.

"No, but I've been working." He stands. "Everything okay?"

"I just wanted to check in with her."

I'll have to come clean to the others about what Blake and I did, but first, I need to find Madison. Honestly, I don't know how they'll take it. I'm not sure what I would do if one of them abused her trust in us.

"I'll text her." Noah lifts his phone and I nod. I should have done that, but there's this pressure in my chest that I can't seem to shake. The fear that I drove her away. That she wouldn't answer me if I messaged her.

Coop isn't in his office, so I go to the break room, checking the file room on the way. It's late in the day, almost time to quit.

"If the spy contacts the pretend client, do we need to let the spy know they're being recorded?" Coop's voice greets me as I enter the room.

He and Patrick raise their gazes to me. It's obvious Madison isn't in here. That sinking feeling grabs onto my heart and pulls down.

"Do you need something?" Coop leans back in his chair. His light blue eyes focus on me.

This definitely isn't something I want to share with our lawyer. Especially since he fed into our fears. As always, Patrick looks unworried and a bit bored.

"No."

Coop lifts an eyebrow, but I give him a subtle head shake. I'll tell him later because that's how you build trust. You share your concerns with the people you love. Which is exactly what Madison has always done with us.

I'm the asshole.

One last place to check.

The elevator to the apartment takes forever. I walk into the foyer and the apartment lights are all out, only the lowering sunlight from the windows spills into the space. Hurrying to Madison's door, I knock and turn the knob. Nothing.

For a second, I'm completely dumbfounded that the door didn't open and try the knob again. When I realize it's locked, I try the number on the keypad and still nothing.

Fuck. She locked it and put in a new code. I knock, but still don't get any response. Fuck.

"Madison?" I yell at the door. "Are you in there?"

I blow out a frustrated breath and take my phone out of my pocket. I just want to make sure she didn't leave. That she's safe. That she didn't make herself a target because of me.

> **ME:**
> Are you okay?

This door hasn't been locked the entire time she's been with us. She doesn't want to see me, but I need to know if she's okay. I need to know she's still here. After a minute with no reply, I open a text to Blake.

> **ME:**
> Robert still with you?

> **BLAKE:**
> I'm seeing him out right now. Problem?

My gaze lingers on the closed door.

> **ME:**
> Maybe.

> **BLAKE:**
> Where?

> **ME:**
> Apartment. Her door is locked.

He doesn't respond, but I don't expect him to. He knows what this means. I take in a breath and slide down the wall next to her door. I open a text to Noah.

> **ME:**
> Have you heard from her?

NOAH:

Not yet.

My head hangs as I try to think how I'd feel if she didn't trust me. The only time I gave her any doubt was when I kissed Elizabeth, and she was right to feel betrayed. I betrayed what we were growing, and she forgave me, but this . . .

ME:

Princess, please.

ME:

Just let one of us know you're okay.

ME:

It was Blake's and my decision.

ME:

Don't punish Coop and Noah for our stupidity.

I can take yelling, even throwing things, but this silence and not knowing is killing me. My phone buzzes and I glance at the screen.

NOAH:

She's fine.

Fuck, that hurts more than anything else. She knows I'm here. She knows I want to see her.

NOAH:

Why isn't she telling you this?

ME:

I'll explain later.

I pull up my one-sided text conversation with her.

ME:

I'm sorry.

The door to the apartment opens, and after a moment, Blake rounds the corner. He stalls as he looks at her door, now a barrier between us and her. One that we erected.

Standing, I brush off my pants and join him at the kitchen island. "Did you find out anything?"

"I'll update everyone when we're together." Blake grimaces as he glances at the door again. "Has she spoken to you?"

I shake my head. "Noah texted. She told him she's fine."

Blake inhales and releases his breath, sitting on a stool and running his hands through his hair. "I fucked this up."

"We both did." I join him and place my phone on the island, hoping she'll text me, knowing she won't. That weight settles in my stomach, so fucking heavy.

"How do we fix this?" Blake turns and his green eyes are solemn.

"I don't know." The words make my chest ache. Maybe the Elizabeth issue was easier to deal with because I never wanted Elizabeth. Madison knew I had to play like I liked her. But after all the times I stressed trust in this arrangement, to throw that away because of something other women have done in the past is potentially unforgivable. I shrug. "Maybe we're too broken to love."

Blake grunts in acknowledgment. "Want a drink?"

"Yeah." I can't do anything else until she's ready to talk.

Madison

After managing to keep my lunch down and texting Noah to say

I'm fine just not feeling well, I climb onto my huge bed that smells like each of their colognes and close my eyes. Usually their scents help soothe me, but not this time.

I don't know what I did wrong. What gave them the idea they couldn't trust me? Have they ever trusted me? Or was it all a ruse?

After hearing Seth call out to me, I leave the door between my bedroom and my private living room open. I can't face him yet. Not after the conference room.

What did they think they'd find out? I take a while to sort it out in my head, but all I can come up with is they didn't think I would tell them the truth. That I had something to hide. Do they think so little of me that they thought I set this up?

I received and read all Seth's texts, but I can't answer him. Not yet. Not until I figure out where my head is. And what I want to do.

Open and honest communication. That was supposed to be our mantra. So what the fuck was that with the conference room? I've been outside that door while a meeting was going on. Blake couldn't hear through the door.

Isn't it bad enough that I have someone else recording my life and finding my faults without my own guys doing the same? Did they really believe something might be going on between me and Robert or that I wouldn't tell them exactly what he said?

The ache grows within me, spreading like a virus.

My phone has been silent for a while. Hope texted to see if I needed anything. I wrote her back that I'm fine. And I am. My heart's a little tattered right now, but if Seth is to be believed, they feel bad about what they did.

The problem I have now is whether I can trust them not to do this again.

The door to the apartment slams, jolting me upright.

"What the fuck did you two do now?" Coop's voice rings through the apartment. My door only muffles it slightly.

Jumping to my feet, I rush through my living room without thinking. I stop before opening the door, choosing to listen instead. I don't know that I can trust them. Not if they don't trust me.

Blake grumbles something I can't hear.

"This isn't just about you." Noah's voice is firm. "We're all a part of this relationship."

"You didn't hear—"

"What, Blake?" Coop demands. "What did you hear that made you forget what you know to be true?"

Blake doesn't answer.

"We fucked up." Seth sounds miserable.

I put my hand and head against the door. His pain and the brokenness of his voice makes me want to cry for him.

I still love them. I still want them. But if they can't trust me, what do we really have?

Chapter 138

Foot the Bill

Coop

Blake and Seth look miserable with a bottle between them they've barely touched. Fuck. The door to Madison's suite remains closed, which is a bad fucking sign.

Noah's dark eyes meet mine and he nods. We don't know what these two did, but it must have blown up in their faces.

We need all of us for this discussion. Noah and I both know it.

"Get takeout," I order Seth, something I never do. But he grabs his phone and gets to work.

Running a hand over the back of my neck and gritting my teeth, I head to that fucking door in our way. Noah walks with me. We're together in this. I don't know what the others did to fuck this up, but we're going to figure it out and make it right.

Knocking lightly on the door, I take a breath. "Madison, could you join us, please?"

The lock disengages, and the tension eases from my shoulders. She opens the door and lifts her red-rimmed eyes to us. They fucking made her cry. I open my arms and she steps into them, giving me all her weight and resting her head over my beating heart.

Noah rubs her back. "We all need to talk through this. But if you need a break at any point, you let us know."

She nods her head against my chest but doesn't release her hold on me.

Noah's gaze lifts to mine and I can feel his fury inside me. Whatever the others did won't be solved over dinner, but we'll do what we can to mend whatever they broke. We have to.

This relationship isn't just between Madison, Noah, and me. It's all of us.

I smooth my hand over her bound hair. "Seth ordered us dinner and we're all going to sit and talk. Is that okay, sweetheart?"

Her arms tighten around me before she lifts her blue eyes to mine. "Yes."

I cup her jaw and see in her eyes her love for me and the hurt the others caused reflected there. If we were younger, I would have decked both guys as soon as I made it to the apartment. They both would've been nursing bruises, and deserved them.

But I'm old enough to have self-control. I'm not guaranteeing no one will get punched, but at least I didn't react without talking about it first.

Seth and Blake move to the table as Noah and I lead Madison over. She sits between us and away from the others. Noah goes into the kitchen and gets everyone drinks before sitting beside Madison and taking her hand.

"Who's going to start?" I glare at Seth and Blake.

Blake starts, "Robert—"

"Madison's old neighbor?" Noah asks.

"Yes. Robert tried to get in through the back door to Madison's apartment while she was putting away groceries." Blake leans back and runs his hand through his hair. "When security brought him inside, Robert insisted he'd only speak to Madison and no one else."

"Okay, so what happened?" I ask. So far nothing is really bad except this guy trying to get into Madison's apartment, but that doesn't seem like something to get torn up over. More like call the police on his ass and let them sort it out.

"We put Robert in the conference room on the sixth floor and brought Madison into my office to tell her." Seth takes a drink of his water. "We told her he wanted to speak to her alone and we wouldn't be able to hear her."

"You fucking tested her?" Noah surges to his feet. "What the fuck were you thinking? That she wanted Robert to come upstairs? That she was involved with him?"

Madison's hand trembles in mine, and I weave my fingers through hers.

"No, I didn't want to think that. But she could have been hiding something from us. I wanted to be sure." Blake doesn't take his gaze off Noah, like he's afraid to look at Madison.

"I didn't think we needed to." Seth puts his elbows on the table. His gaze never leaves Madison. His blue eyes reflect his misery. "I trust her, but after Patrick said—"

"Wait." I straighten in my chair. "Patrick? Our lawyer? What does he have to do with this?"

Madison leans against me as Noah takes his seat again.

Blake blows out a breath. "He reminded us that both Andrea and Rachel had guys up to the apartment."

"And you automatically thought Madison was doing the same?" I laugh. "You do know she's not Andrea and Rachel, right? She's not Elizabitch or Leighton either."

"Patrick didn't stop there. He said they worried Madison had guys over when she watched the kids." Seth shakes his head like he knows what he's saying is bullshit.

Which it is. Complete and utter bullshit.

"And you lost your damn mind?" I ask.

"I never had anyone to their house." Madison's brows furrow. "Why would he say that? He acts like he doesn't even remember me."

The benefit comes to mind. When Patrick acted like he didn't know who Madison was even though their firm put through the background check. Maybe Madison didn't list Patrick and Anna as previous employers, but he still should have recognized her name.

"Andrea was my push." Blake's voice draws me out of my memories. "I thought she'd be perfect for us. I trusted her. Convinced you guys that this could work. With her. And then she backstabbed all of us."

"That's your baggage." I squeeze Madison's hand. "I get it. We've had a lot of issues. Andrea. Rachel. Elizabeth. Leighton." I glance at Noah. "Beth."

Noah pushes out a breath. We don't talk about Beth much, but we all knew the toll it took on Noah when she tried to make him choose us or her. Madison's gaze grows curious as she looks at Noah.

He lifts her knuckles to his lips and presses a kiss to them. "College girlfriend. Thought I spent too much time with the guys. Made me choose. I chose them."

She brushes his hair out of his eyes and leans her forehead against his. I don't have jealousy about a lot of things, but that connection between them seems so easy. I wish things could be that easy in my world.

"No one should make you choose," she whispers.

And none of us would insist she choose just one of us. We all want her and love her. She loves and wants us.

At least she did until Blake and Seth made waves.

"What made you decide to test Madison's loyalty?" I meet Blake's eyes head on.

He sighs and finally looks at Madison as she lifts her eyes to meet his. "Everything works with you. Everything. You fit us. All of us. No one has ever been that for us before."

She rests her head against my shoulder and warmth fills me. He's not wrong.

"At first, we were all attracted to you. Your body. Your looks. Your mind. But then you were here with us and we needed to be more, craved more. We protect you. We fuck you. We talk to you. We love you. And it's so effortless."

He stands abruptly and paces away before coming back. Resting his hands on the table, he blows out his breath. "It's fucking terrifying. It's like someone looked into our brains and created a woman built just for us. This shit doesn't happen. We don't find someone who wants all of us the way we want her.

"Coop would fuck anyone, but connect with a woman on an emotional level? And Noah. Fuck, we all knew how the other women felt about him. He's too smart, too distant, too introverted for them, but not for you. You two connected that first day, and fuck, did that make me jealous. Not jealous of Noah but of what you had with him, because I knew I couldn't be that easy to love.

"Seth and I were burned hard. We set this whole contract up so our emotions wouldn't get tangled in it. We wanted you, but we didn't think we'd need you. We definitely didn't plan to love you, but we do. We didn't love the others and they nearly destroyed us. And that's scary shit."

Blake runs his hand over his head and straightens.

"Seth didn't want to test you. I planted the doubt. I stoked his fear the same way Patrick stoked mine. Don't punish Seth for being a fool for you and letting his fear drive him."

Madison straightens, but before she says anything, Seth's phone buzzes.

"The food." He gestures to the phone and takes the call, heading toward the door. Rising, Noah kisses Madison on her head and joins Seth as they head out of the apartment.

She leans back on the chair and presses her lips together. The silence is daunting.

"There's something off about Patrick." I rub my chin. It keeps churning through my head.

Blake lowers into his chair. "You noticed too?"

She looks between us but says nothing.

"Why wouldn't he recognize her name from the background search? She was his children's nanny. Surely he ran a background check on her. It was only four years ago."

"Three," she says.

"What?"

She clears her throat. "I hadn't seen Anna or Patrick for three years. I worked for them my entire freshman year and the summer after. So it's been three years since they last saw me. But it wouldn't surprise me if he didn't even know the new nanny's name. Anna always took care of the household."

"Maybe." Maybe the guy doesn't look at other women since he's married. Madison is a beautiful woman, but she would have been young for him at eighteen. He's older than me by a few years at least. I'm not sure I've really noticed other women since Madison. But I know my employees. "But you were with them for a year. That has to be significant."

"I interacted with him maybe a handful of times. Only when Anna had to work late and I needed a ride to the dorm." Madison shrugs. "I didn't matter to him. I was the help."

I can't imagine anyone feeling that way about Madison. But I know a lot of people in my circle who don't look twice at those they consider the hired help.

"Did Robert find the woman?" Madison's voice is even as she looks at Blake like he's just her employer. That shit has to hurt.

"Maybe." Blake rubs a hand over his face. "I want to make sure. We're best when we're all together."

Her eyes narrow. "Did you want me to leave when the others get back?"

"No." Blake's brows furrow as he leans forward. "Fuck no. You're part of us. You make us better."

The door to the apartment opens. Noah and Seth walk in with the bags. They glance at the mulish expressions on Blake's and Madison's faces as they sort the food. When they look at me, I just shrug.

When everyone sits down, Madison plays with her food with her fork before setting it carefully on the table.

"I'm not perfect." She holds up her hand and keeps talking. "I'm flawed, but I will never be a cheater. I'm terrified of this stalker because he does things I can't imagine doing. Conniving, manipulative things."

She takes a breath. "Like the women you've been with before. I know they abused the trust you gave them, and I wish they hadn't. But I haven't. I've trusted you from the beginning, and maybe that makes me naive, but what I feel for you is too big sometimes."

She plucks at the shirt she has on. "These clothes, this apartment, this job, all of you. It's like I'm living in a dream that I never want to wake up from. But then there's this darkness lingering outside of us, trying to tear us apart.

"They pick at the pieces of us that are most vulnerable and poke and poke until we don't trust what we've always known about each other.

"In what world would I get not one amazing guy but four? Is it messy and will we have growing pains? Yes, but it will hurt less if we all stick together. I know you trust each other, and I hope you trust me."

She leans back and meets Blake's eyes. "I'm not them. I'm not Andrea. I'm not Elizabeth. I'm not Rachel. I don't want to tear you apart. I want to be the glue that helps hold you together. I want to be the one you turn to when you need help making the right and moral decision. If I'm being honest . . ."

She swallows and puts her hands on the edge of the table. "I want this to work long-term. When my employment ends, I don't want this to end. I don't want us to end. I don't want another assistant to take my place *here*. In this apartment. In your beds. In your hearts. Because that's where I belong."

She picks up her fork and points it at Blake and Seth. "You hurt me today. I can understand your why, but I can't forgive it right away. I love you both, but I need to know I can trust you to trust me. To know me like I know you at your core being. To protect my heart the way you protect my body."

"Anything, princess." Seth lowers his head. "Anything you need me to do, I'll do it for you."

"Time, boss. I need time to heal. Time to trust you again." She turns to Blake. "I put my trust in your hands every day. I accept your protection of me and the things you do to me. Those women hurt you. Not me. I put all my love and faith in you from the beginning, Blake. You saved me in more ways than just physical. I just wish you could trust me too."

"I do, tiger. I trust you. I don't trust myself or my judgment. I don't want to let my friends down again. But I let you down and I'm willing to pay the price. I will earn your trust back, love, because I can't see a future without you in it."

Their eyes hold for a moment, and then she nods.

When she begins to eat, we all dig in. Things aren't going back to the way they were, but hopefully we'll grow from this. Maybe even stronger.

Blake clears his throat after a few minutes. "Robert saw a picture of who he thinks the woman was."

Madison's eyes widen. "A picture?"

"In Courtney's office." Blake meets all of our gazes and says the one name I hate more than Elizabeth. "Andrea."

Chapter 139

Ah-Ha Moment

Madison

Andrea! The woman who blackmailed the guys and started the rumors about them.

To me, she's a ghost. A ghost with brown hair and blue eyes now, but a ghost all the same. She still haunts each of my guys. The things she broke affect *our* relationship.

"We need to figure out how she fits into the puzzle." Seth leans back in his chair. His gaze meets mine, but the hurt is too fresh for me to hold his.

"I'll check in with Theo tomorrow." Coop rests his upturned hand on my thigh and I slide mine into it. I'm grateful for the warmth of him and Noah. That they didn't lose faith in me. "He's been at Cliodhna this week to see if the spy might contact Deidre."

I turn to him. "I thought Patrick was here to help set up the honey trap?"

Coop's eyes smile when he catches mine. "He is, but Cliodhna is an almost perfect match for the other companies the spy contacted. Why waste the perfect opportunity? Besides, it will give us a trial run if nothing else."

Blake stands and starts clearing the table. He keeps his eyes down when he says, "You shouldn't sleep in your room tonight. We don't know why Andrea wanted Robert to come after you, but we can't be sure she won't send someone else. Someone who might not be so respectful."

I didn't even think that my room might not be safe. My chest warms. Blake is still protecting me. I watch his back as he goes into the kitchen. What did I do that made him think he couldn't trust me? Was it really all about the women in the past?

"We can sleep in my room." Noah draws my attention his way. His dark eyes hold mine.

We've all been sharing my bed, but I can't see all of us fitting on Noah's bed. It's also too soon for me to forgive Seth and Blake.

Coop squeezes my hand, breaking me out of my thoughts.

Nodding, I turn to Coop. "Both of you."

I avoid the others' eyes. It's too soon. I need time but I need comfort too. Coop and Noah will provide that.

"Of course, sweetheart." Coop lifts my hand and grazes my knuckles with his lips. Warmth settles in my stomach.

"You guys go." Seth stands and picks up some trash to throw away. "Blake and I will clean up out here before retiring to bed."

My chest tightens at the resignation in his voice. I don't want to shut them out. Not completely.

Noah pulls my chair out. When I stand, I can't help stopping and watching Seth and Blake. They work seamlessly to clean the kitchen. I don't want to be like this, but the hurt still aches in my chest. I'm not those women. I will never be those women.

Hopefully, they realize that.

When Noah offers me his hand, I hold mine up to him and walk into the kitchen. Seth pauses and I step into his arms and hug him around the waist, pressing my cheek against his steady heartbeat.

"Good night, princess," he whispers into my hair as his arms close around me.

I breathe in deep, because this man is still mine and I'm still his. "Good night."

When I step back, Blake drops his gaze from us and turns to load the dishwasher. Releasing my breath, I close the distance between us. "Blake?"

He doesn't turn around. "Yeah?"

"I love you." My words are soft.

He turns and sweeps me into his arms. His heartbeat drums in my ear as he holds me tight. "I love you, tiger."

Tears well in my eyes. We're not completely torn apart, but we're definitely shaken from their lack of trust.

When I pull away, he cups my cheek and lifts my face to look at him. His green eyes shine. "I know you aren't like them, love. I feel it in my soul, but I've been wrong before and let everyone down."

Exhaling, I cover his hand with mine. "We can't go forward if you can't let go of the past. Those weren't lessons for the future. They were warnings about those women."

"I know." He blows out a breath and slips his hand from my face. "I don't know why I let it get to me."

I step closer to him and slide my hand over his rough jaw. "You don't have to worry about me with another guy. At least not outside of this group. I love each of you and would never hurt or betray you in that way. I'm yours and you're mine. End of story."

He turns his head to press a kiss against my palm. "You need rest. Good night, tiger."

"Good night."

I put on comfy pajamas and climb into Noah's bed. My bones are tired, but my mind still races. Nothing makes sense right now. Andrea doesn't know me. Why would she try to get into my apartment and tell Robert to save me from the guys?

Does she want them back? Is she trying to punish them? Is she behind the stalking?

"You okay, sweetheart?" Coop climbs into bed next to me and runs his hand over my stomach.

"I just can't understand how Andrea would know about my stalker or why she would target me." I turn my head on the pillow to stare into Coop's light blue eyes. "She was working here when I was in school, and my stalker is a man. That's what Jeff said. And how would she know my stalker?"

"She might not know your stalker, but she might know you have one and want to fuck with our lives." Coop's fingers stroke under my tank top, grazing my skin. "She didn't exactly leave on happy terms. And she always was a vindictive bitch."

I blow out a breath. Noah slides into the bed on my other side.

"I just need for all this to make sense." My brain spins in a hundred different directions. "I mean, Courtney could be feeding her information. Hope said they were friends, and Robert saw Andrea's picture in Courtney's office."

"That's true." Noah strokes his fingers down my neck before running them under the strap of my tank top. Heat builds under their gentle touches, but my brain won't stop.

"Andrea would know Patrick from work and the legal action we took against her." Coop's fingers trace the elastic waist of my shorts. "Though I'm not sure why Andrea would work with Patrick."

My brow furrows. "Patrick can't be my stalker. He's happily married to Anna. He barely remembers me and barely tolerated my presence. Sure, he gave me a ride every now and then and gave me sweets, but he always claimed he was trying to watch his sugar intake and I was doing him a favor by taking them."

"He's our attorney." Coop strokes his fingers across my stomach absent-mindedly. "He'd be risking his marriage and his career. His license. It doesn't make sense."

"The police have the phone." Noah leans down and kisses my

shoulder. "All we can hope is Valerie took a picture of whoever gave her the phone or something as proof."

Valerie. Fuck. She's dead. It's still weird to think about.

"Do you want to be bound, sweetheart?" Coop whispers in my ear as his fingers slide beneath my panties.

I grab his hand to stop him from melting my brain. His words triggered a memory. It's faint. "Wait. What were we discussing before we had the sex the stalker recorded and sent to us?"

"How we should all be together and fuck the haters?" Noah draws my shirt down and kisses my hardened nipple.

I bite my lip at the desire coursing through my veins. "Before that."

"Blake told us about Jeff." Coop kisses my other shoulder, making shivers rush through me.

"Jeff told us about the phone, which means the stalker would know that Val hid the phone in the apartment." I struggle to stay focused as Coop's hand slips from mine and delves between my legs.

"Keep going, sweetheart." Coop grins wickedly at me as he tugs off my shorts and panties. "We'll help inspire you. You might be onto something."

He kisses my stomach before lifting my knees and lowering between my legs, worshipping my pussy with his tongue and mouth. My brain fogs as Noah sucks my nipple into his mouth.

"The phone was shattered when we found it." I squirm beneath them. Everything blurs as they keep pushing me higher. "The stalker knew we'd find the phone and when we'd go looking for it."

"Blake changed the lock." Noah rises so his face is above mine. "The stalker couldn't get in unless he picked the lock."

"We don't know what resources he has." My hips lift as Coop thrusts his fingers inside me and sucks on my clit. I cry out as I tip over the edge. It's quick and throbs through me. I cling to Noah's dark eyes as I come down from my high, gasping in little breaths.

His fingers trail over my breasts, lighting sparks in their wake.

"But it's possible he could have destroyed the phone intentionally," I breathe out.

"If he got to it before us, yes. But then, why leave it at all?" Noah brushes my hair out of my face and cups the back of my head. "We won't know until the police look it over."

I dig my hands into Noah's hair and pull his mouth to mine. Focusing is impossible when they touch me like this. I'm done talking for now.

Coop drags my top up. Noah and I break apart so he can peel it off me. When Noah's hands go to his shorts, I keep my hands in his hair, waiting until we can kiss again.

"On your side, goddess." Coop pushes my hip until I'm facing Noah.

Our eyes lock as Coop's hands trail over my side. Noah leans in and captures my mouth again, taking everything I have to give. Our warm bodies press flush against each other, and I whimper at the touch.

Coop presses against my back and trails kisses along my neck, stopping to suck and bite my skin. His hands slide over my hips, trapping me between the two of them. But being surrounded by them frees me.

The stress of today doesn't belong in this bed. Not when I have two gods of my own worshipping my body. I love them so much.

Noah lifts my leg and places it over his hip. He leans his forehead against mine and we lock eyes. "I love you, kitten."

His cock sinks into my pussy achingly slow. Every inch stretches me out and brings us closer to completion. Coop slides his wet fingers between my ass cheeks and coats my asshole in lube before pressing his fingers inside me.

I gasp as Noah fills me completely. Coop thrusts his fingers into my puckered hole.

"I love you, Noah." I kiss him before turning my head to look at Coop. "Please. I need you."

Coop smirks as he draws his fingers out of me and lines his cock up against my ass. "I always aim to please, sweetheart."

He sinks in just as slowly, like we have all night to make love.

When he's fully inside me, we all hold still, connected. This is what I need. I need them. I want the others too. But for now, this is enough.

"Together?" Noah looks over my shoulder at Coop.

"What do you want, goddess? Together or alternating? What's your pleasure tonight?" Coop's words make me clench around them.

"Kiss me first."

Coop leans up and captures my mouth in a scorching-hot kiss. He gives me a little thrust of his hips and I moan into his mouth. He chuckles. "I love you."

I look into his light blue eyes. "I love you, Coop."

That wonder fills his eyes, like he still can't believe I love him. I'll tell him every day for the rest of our lives to make him believe.

"Together," Coop says.

They begin to slowly torture me, dragging their cocks out of my body before easing back in at the same pace. Our bodies remain flush against each other. Their hands locked on my hips and mine in Noah's hair.

As one, they gradually pick up the pace until I'm a mess between them, hovering on the edge of something so spectacular I'm barely breathing.

"Come for us, kitten." Noah thrusts hard into me at the same time Coop does, so in sync it's like they're one.

My orgasm flows over me, taking me under as they hold me through it, still buried deep inside me, making me feel every inch of them. I rest my head against Coop's shoulder as I start to come down, pulsing around their cocks.

"We're not done yet, goddess," Coop says in my ear, his voice dark. He withdraws from me and Noah rolls onto his back, dragging me with him.

My legs fall to either side of Noah's as he thrusts up into me. Moving behind me, Coop draws me up against him before thrusting his cock into my ass again. I moan as tremors work their way through me.

Coop's hands slide over my breasts, and his mouth caresses my ear. "We're going to fuck you until you come so hard you pass out, my little whore."

Noah reaches between my legs to pinch my clit. I suck in a breath at the pain and pleasure that pulse through me. "So fucking wet for us."

"Fuck, I love you." I press my hands to Noah's chest as he gives me an evil grin.

Coop pinches my nipples when they thrust into me. Noah continues to play with my clit. I'm already so sensitive that another orgasm builds, swelling inside me.

"Stop," Noah says, and they both pause.

Our harsh breaths fill the room. I groan and try to shift between them, but they have a firm hold on me.

My orgasm slips out of reach. They withdraw and thrust in short bursts, staggering them so I can't build any momentum.

Coop chuckles in my ear. "We could keep this up all night. Couldn't we, Noah?"

Noah's dark eyes capture mine. "Definitely."

When my nails dig into Noah's chest, he hisses slightly but grins at me.

"What do you want, my pretty slut?" Noah flicks my clit, making a wave crash over me, not enough to get me there though.

"I want to come," I whimper, too far gone to care about whatever game they're playing.

Coop grabs my hair tight and pulls my head back. He sucks so hard on my neck I know it will leave a mark. I love it when they mark me as theirs. "Good little whores get to come. Are you a good little whore?"

"Yes, Coop. I'm your good little whore."

Noah chuckles darkly as he gently strokes my clit. "Play with your tits for us."

Coop moves his hands down to my ribs as he sucks on another spot on my neck, biting, licking, sucking. I lift my hands to my breasts and cup them for Noah.

"Pinch your nipples."

I do as he asks, moaning with the flood of wetness that coats his cock.

"Ride my cock, take what you want from me, and Coop will fuck your ass."

When I start to lower my hands, he makes a negative noise. "Don't stop touching yourself, kitten."

I move awkwardly at first over his cock, but then I find my rhythm while I roll my hips and bursts of pleasure spiral through me. Pinching my nipples, I meet Noah's glazed eyes.

Coop draws out before punching back in deep inside me. My moan fills the room. Noah reaches between my legs again and strokes my clit. While I rock on his cock, Coop fucks my ass hard. This time the orgasm that builds combusts, fast and hot.

It bears down on me with all the force of a freight train. I couldn't hold it back if I tried. A scream rips from my throat as I ride Noah, coming on him and Coop. My insides clench around their cocks hard, trying to draw them deeper.

Groaning, Noah releases inside me, followed by Coop, thrusting a few more times to fill me with his cum. I collapse on Noah and Coop follows me, pressing me between them.

"I love you." Coop presses a kiss to my neck before climbing off me.

"I love you." Noah kisses my head.

I sigh happily. "I love you both."

My heart twinges a little, knowing we have to wait to be all together again. The five of us. I want Blake and Seth here in the bed with us. I want to be dominated by them. When I bury my face into

Noah's neck, he wraps his arms around me like he knows what I need.

"They love you too, kitten."

Chapter 140

Back in Business

Seth

"What do you have for me?" My impatience and lack of sleep bleeds through in my tone on the phone. It's Thursday morning. The past three nights I slept alone, not well and not by choice. I don't know how long Madison will need before she can forgive me or what I can do to prove I trust her.

We've talked over what we need to do about the stalker and spy, but this week has been busy with actual work. There's a lot we still need to do. We need to talk with Andrea to see what she knows. Courtney has been out most of the week. Family emergency.

Patrick and Coop almost have a plan in place for our honey trap setup for tomorrow. Cliodhna hasn't heard from the spy. No more contact from the stalker. While not everything is locked down, the pieces are falling into place.

Except for one.

"We've been following her for a week. Got a few pictures for you to review," the deep voice says. Sebastian Cross is the head of security for Heath Duncan. His team is one of the best we know of. He's a slick bastard, but if Elizabeth is seeing someone on the down-low, he'll find out who.

"When can you come in?" I glance up as Madison walks by my office door. She doesn't look in. That's the worst part of this. I miss her smiles, her coy looks, and when she would get caught up while looking into my eyes. I'm ready for this part to be over, but that's not my decision.

"An hour. Meet on the sixth floor?" Sebastian sounds a little distracted.

"See you then." I set my phone down and walk to my door. My mind can't settle either. Madison is at her desk. She still wears the clothes I pick for her every day.

Her hair is pulled up and leaves her neck bare, showing marks Coop or Noah left the nights before. But underneath that silky blouse and pencil skirt, she should be wearing a skimpy pair of pink panties with a matching lace bra that I chose.

The temptation to leave her bare keeps rearing its head, but it would only distract me more from work. I'm just happy she hasn't shut Blake and me out completely. Every night she gives us both a hug before going to bed in Noah's room with him and Coop.

The muffled sounds of her pleasure through the door fill the apartment and make me wish I could be there with them. I crave her.

As if sensing me watching her, she turns in her desk chair.

"Can I help you, boss?" She lifts an eyebrow and gives me a cheeky grin that makes my heart race and my cock throb.

I clear my throat. "I have a meeting on the sixth floor in an hour. Can you reserve the conference room?"

Her smile softens. "Of course."

She turns to her computer to make the arrangements. Without her eyes on me, I let my gaze trail over every inch of her. All the way down to her black high heels with the flash of red on the bottom.

After a minute, she turns to me again. "Did you need something else, boss?"

You.

It pulses through me, the need, the desire, the craving. The total lack of control over my base desires surges through me. She's it for me now. I can't find relief anywhere else and I don't want to.

Biting on her lip, Madison glances at her computer and phone. She stands and walks over to me. She's so close her floral scent washes over me. My dick is hard as a rock for her, but I know I haven't proven myself yet.

Her fingers drag down my tie. Her gaze follows the path before looking at my cock.

When she licks her lips, her darkened eyes lift to mine.

"Having trouble concentrating, boss?" She puts her hand on my chest and pushes me back into my office. When we're both in, she closes the door and leans back against it.

"You distract me," I admit.

"Does that bother you?" She tips her head to the side.

"When I can't fuck you when I want to." I shrug. "I can deal with it."

"What if I want to help you?"

Fuck, my cock is about to burst. "How would you do that?"

"Trust me, boss." Her eyes hold mine, and for a minute, I'm content just to be in this moment here with her. I also know this is a test that I hope to fuck I pass.

"I trust you."

"We're going to go fast because you have things to do." Her fingers reach up to touch her lips. "Is that okay?"

I nod, mesmerized by her beautiful lips and remembering how good they feel wrapped around my cock. "Whatever you want."

She smiles. "Bring a chair over."

I grab a chair from my desk and set it in front of her.

"Closer. Almost. Right there." She urges me to set it directly in front of her. "Sit."

I do as she asks, willing to play her pawn for a change. Giving in to her orders might not be what I'm used to, but for her, I'll do anything. When I told her that, I meant it.

She's it for me.

When I sit, she lifts her high-heeled foot and puts it between my legs on the chair. "Good. Now take out your cock and put your hands on your knees."

As I release my straining cock, relief floods me. When she licks her lips, precum wells on my tip as a pulse of lust flows through me. Anticipation buzzes through my veins like the sweetest drug.

"Have you gotten off since Sunday?" She cocks her head to the side.

"No." My gaze follows the length of her leg up to where it disappears beneath her straining skirt. I long to touch her silky skin but know that won't likely happen. I need to maintain my control for her.

She frowns but recovers. Her fingers tease her shirt's button. "Do you want to see how well you dress me?"

"Always, princess." My hands tighten on my thighs.

She unbuttons her shirt, opening it enough to reveal her breasts perfectly held in the cups of her bra, just as I imagined they would be. Then she leans over and draws her skirt up so I can see her panties. My insides twist with need.

Her eyes lift to mine. "Do you want to touch yourself, boss?"

Unable to resist, my hand grips my cock and I stroke myself, taking in this gorgeous woman. "Fuck, princess, I miss you."

She leans back against the door and drags her finger between her breasts. "How do you miss me?"

"I miss smelling your perfume on my pillow on nights you don't sleep with me." I'm not going to last as I watch her drag her finger down. "I miss the way your eyes widen when you come for me. The feel of you in my arms at night, soft and warm. I miss the smile you give me like we share a secret only the two of us know."

Her lips part and I want them on my cock. Her mouth is divine. When her hand trails down to her thigh, all my attention focuses there and how good it feels to sink deep inside her warm, welcoming cunt.

"I miss the way you follow my every command. I miss you

looking at me like I'm the most wonderful man you've met, and I hate that I'm the one who took it all away." Squeezing my cock a little harder, I say, "We were good and I fucked that up."

"You did." She licks her lips as she watches me fist my cock. "But you also take care of me. You set limits when I want to blow past them even when it's for my own good."

She lowers her foot to the ground. After kicking her shoes off, she steps forward to stand straddling me on the chair. "I miss you and your control of me. Stop touching yourself, boss."

I do as she asks. The heat of her body calls to me, making me want to touch her. But I resist, knowing this is her show.

Her hand cups my jaw and tips it up so that we look into each other's eyes. That connection is still there. I didn't break it fully.

"Tell me what you want, princess," I whisper. "Anything."

"Pull my panties to the side," she whispers too, like any loud noise will break this between us.

Even though I want to do more, I do exactly as she asks and let my gaze fall to her wet, swollen pussy. Saliva fills my mouth and I long for a taste of her. All the things I want to do to her, but I stay in control.

Her hand wraps around my cock, and she lowers herself until the tip notches at her entrance. Her hands return to hold my face and our eyes remain locked.

"I miss you too," she whispers before she sinks down onto my cock. We both groan at the feel of coming together. It's only been days, but it feels like forever.

"Seth," she breathes out against my lips. It's a question, a plea.

"What do you need, Madison?" My lips brush hers as I speak. Neither of us moves, locked together.

She tips her head down and stares into my eyes. "Fuck me, sir. Make me come."

All my pent-up control shatters. I grab her hips and rise, pressing her back against the door. My cock pistons in and out of her sweet, tight cunt, so fucking glad to be where I belong.

"Harder, sir."

Our open lips hover together, touching but not kissing as I pick up the pace, driving into her as if my soul depends on it. I press my chest against hers and slip one of my hands between us, teasing her clit with gentle strokes while I thrust deep and hard into her.

"Oh, fuck," she cries out as her cunt pulses around me, drawing me deeper, squeezing me so fucking tight that I have no choice but to give in. I keep thrusting through our release and then bury myself deep inside her.

I've missed this. Missed her. I rest my head against her forehead as we breathe raggedly together.

"I love you, princess. Trust is part of that. I'm sorry I failed you. I swear to you I'll trust my own judgment when it comes to you. Always."

She blows out a breath. "I need all of you. My heart feels tattered and torn when we aren't all together. I need you, Seth. I need you."

"I'm yours." I claim her lips, tasting her for the first time in days, diving into the soft warm heat of her as she surrenders to my kiss so beautifully. Taking my time, I explore her mouth, teasing, tasting, until I grow hard inside her again.

She moans into my mouth as I slowly pull out and ease back in. It's slower this time. We never stop kissing. Minutes pass and I don't have a care in the world except this woman in my arms. The business could fall around me, and as long as she's here, I'm good. Everything feels bright and beautiful with her. When she shatters around me, I swallow her moan as I come deep inside her.

I lift my mouth from her swollen lips. Her blue eyes open and search mine as little aftershocks clutch at my cock. I love this woman.

Her fingers smooth over the back of my head. "Can I sleep in your bed tonight?"

I'm still grinning as I ride the elevator down to the sixth floor. For the first time in days, my steps are light and my chest feels like it will burst from the happiness welling inside. She's mine tonight.

Possibly Coop's and Noah's too, but mine.

I stride through the office and into the conference room.

"Afternoon, boss." Sebastian Cross leans back in the chair with his feet crossed on the conference table. His voice is low and dark. His dark hair falls over his green eyes. While I rarely think of men as pretty, Sebastian is almost as pretty as Coop and probably just as wealthy.

But he chooses to work for Heath and others. Whatever they want, usually the stuff they don't want to get their hands dirty with. Maybe it's his way of sticking it to his old man. I don't know him well enough to ask. All I know is he's good at what he does.

"Cross." I take a seat at the table. "What do you have for me?"

He slides a manila envelope across the table. "Your pretty little bird is aware of her surroundings at all times."

Fuck.

"But she still fucks up." Cross shakes his head like everyone eventually fucks up for him.

Taking the envelope and opening it, I spill the contents onto the table. I take my time sorting through it. Pictures of Elizabeth going about her day. Shopping. Working. Having dinner out.

Then there are the photos through a window of her in her negligee, drawing a man down on top of her. Quite a few pictures of them in various positions and states of undress.

"If you'd like a copy of the video, I can send it to you." Cross smirks. He flicks his hand at the pictures. "The guy is Drew Young. He's mostly been dating Leighton Porter, but apparently, he's been fucking Elizabeth."

I sigh. I'd hoped for someone married or someone her mother wouldn't approve of, but this guy should get the stamp of approval. "Why doesn't she just have a relationship with Drew if he's part of their world?"

Cross laughs. "Young is new money. Leighton's family needs it, but Elizabeth's doesn't. Word has it that Gloria is pushing Elizabeth to find the cream of the crop."

"So why is she sniffing around me?" After all, I'm new money too. I glance over the pictures. They do nothing for me.

Cross chuckles darkly and lifts an eyebrow. "Who do you know who's old money?"

Fuck, this shit again. "Thank you, Cross."

"Any time. Your job was easy. I like easy."

My eyes skim over the pictures. We've seen a lot of pictures like this lately. Maybe once Valerie was out of the way, the stalker used someone like Cross to get the job done. "Do you know of any jobs concerning Madison Harris?"

"What's it worth to you?" Cross grins and puts his feet on the ground. "I don't usually discuss other jobs."

"I'm willing to pay to know. Someone's been stalking her and their old accomplice met an untimely end." I lean back in my seat. "It would be helpful to know if someone even asked about a job."

A timid knock sounds on the door, and it pushes open. Hope appears in the doorway.

"I don't mean to interrupt." Her gaze skates over Sebastian before she looks back at me. "Madison says you have a meeting in a few minutes and that you haven't replied to her texts."

I pat my empty pocket. "Forgot my phone. Tell her I'll be up in a few."

"Of course." Hope backs out with her eyes on the floor.

When I turn back to Sebastian, his gaze lingers on the door with a contemplative look.

This back-and-forth game could go on for a while, but I need to get results. "How much for what you know?"

Chapter 141

Breakthrough

Coop

Madison walks into the break room and over to the coffee. My gaze doesn't follow her though. I keep it trained on Patrick. All week I've been watching him, looking for hints that he might have more than a passing interest in our girl.

Noah told us at the benefit Patrick was in the hallway to meet some woman when Madison was attacked. He seems happily married to Anna, but we don't know the inner workings of their relationship. It isn't hard to imagine someone having an affair. After all, I've been to plenty of those parties where guests disappear with someone other than their significant other.

Could Patrick want Madison?

When Patrick doesn't turn to look at her but keeps working, I rise and go over to Madison. Maybe he doesn't. Maybe he knows she's mine and is being respectful.

The stalker is smart and rich, but Patrick doesn't seem to be passionate about anything. Him being the stalker could be a stretch.

When I touch Madison's back, her startled blue eyes dart to me before she relaxes.

"Coop," she says quietly. Her gaze flicks over to Patrick. His head is bent over his laptop as his fingers click on the keyboard.

"How are you today?" I reach out and tuck a tendril behind her ear. Her eyes darken before she fills her coffee cup. I can't decide if I like her being mad at the other two or not. After all, that means she's been all mine and Noah's the past few nights.

"I'm good." Her eyes twinkle when they meet mine.

Smirking, I lower my head until my lips brush her ear. "Have you been a naughty little whore?"

She places a hand on my shoulder, holding me back. "Later, Coop."

I straighten and look over at Patrick. Fuck. If he weren't here, I'd lift her onto the counter and spread her legs. I'd fuck her with my fingers to find out if someone came inside her before adding my own to the mix.

I blow out a frustrated breath. Tomorrow, we go to lunch with the honey trap. Hopefully, that will solve one of our problems. And Patrick won't be in our offices anymore after next week. Allowing me full access to my assistant again.

Madison rises on her toes and kisses my jawline. "See you later."

I turn as she leaves. Her hips sway and I want to follow her, drag her into my office, and spend an hour doing naughty things to her.

My phone buzzes on the table. I take my seat and look at the text.

THEO:

We have a live one.

"Will you excuse me, Patrick? I need to take a call in my office."

Patrick waves his hand at me briefly, not even bothering to lift his eyes from his work. He's always consumed by his work. When I walk into the main office area, Madison sits at her desk. She lifts her gaze to me and I give her a smile as I pass her.

Once in my office, I shut my door and call Theo.

"What's happening?" Sitting behind my desk, I stare at the door. I'm eager to put this all behind us.

"The receptionist just put through a call to Deidre. She's talking to the spy now." Theo pauses.

"Tracking?" Let this work. We need a win.

"I'm closing in on it."

I blow out a breath. This unfortunately won't hold up in court, but at least we'll know the players. That's more than we know at the moment. Except for Andrea.

It would make sense if she were a player trying to take down our business. She's a bitter bitch.

"Let me know when it's done."

"Will do," Theo says.

I end the call. What if all roads lead to our major fuckup? What if Andrea is playing us so perfectly that we can't even tell right from wrong?

She saw behind the curtain. She knows us on a level few do. Madison is closer to all of us, but Andrea was with us for a while. Unlike Madison, she never demanded monogamy, and I was happy to find others to fuck. There were times though that convenience won out, or Seth wanted to watch. I'm always happy to be watched.

The whole situation wasn't ideal. The way she treated Noah made me furious. She fucked him, but she treated him like a job. Just something she needed to do to get paid. Not that we paid her for sex, but she obviously had a major boner for Blake.

Or at least we thought she did until she blackmailed us.

A gentle knock sounds on my door.

"Come in."

The door opens and Madison stands uncertain in the doorframe. I gesture her in.

"Lock the door behind you."

Her eyes widen but she does as I ask.

"Are you okay?" she asks as she approaches my desk.

I lean back and gesture to a chair opposite me. She sinks into the seat.

"Theo might have something on the corporate spy."

She smiles. "That's great."

"It won't hold up since we didn't involve the authorities, but it means we might narrow down the suspect pool." I run my finger over my bottom lip. "Did you need something?"

She glances at the door and runs her hands over her skirt. Her gaze drops to her lap. "I didn't want you to think I was blowing you off in the break room. I just don't feel comfortable around Patrick. Maybe because I used to babysit his kids and now he knows I'm a whore for you guys."

"You're not a whore." I stand and come around the desk. I drop to one knee before her and take her cold hands into mine, rubbing them to warm them up.

She looks at me with those pretty blue eyes, so uncertain. "I agreed to have sex with my bosses after meeting them once."

"That doesn't make you a whore." I squeeze her hands. "I might enjoy calling you that as part of a game, but I don't believe for one second you're a whore."

She blows out a breath. "But what if he thinks—"

"You think I give a damn what he thinks? What anyone thinks?" Pulling her against me, I drag her onto my lap as I sit on the floor. I brush a piece of her hair off her face. "I love you, and that's a lot coming from me. If anyone's a whore, it was me before I met you. I don't care about what other people think. I was raised to act a certain way and behave a certain way or else, but fuck that noise. You and me and the guys have something most people would kill for."

She cups my jaw and searches my eyes. "I love you, Coop. You're not a whore either."

Smirking, I lean my forehead against hers. "I don't know," I tease. "I'm pretty sure most people think I'm a whore."

She leans in and kisses me sweetly. Before I can draw her closer and deepen the kiss, my phone rings.

"Hold that thought." I answer my phone with my hand around her back, keeping her against me. "This is Cooper."

"We've got the number and I've got a trace locked on the phone."

Theo's voice is filled with pride. "We recorded the call and I'm forwarding it to you now. It'll take a little work to get access to the phone records and location."

"Great work, Theo." I brush my thumb over Madison's back. "Let me know if you find out anything concrete."

"Yes, sir." Theo ends the call.

I set my phone on the chair and glance down at Madison's full lips. "Now, where were we?"

Madison

I laugh as Coop leans in, but we both stop at a rap on the door. Our heads swivel to the door.

"Cooper Jamison Graham, open this door now." A slightly muffled, authoritative feminine voice sounds in his office.

He stiffens beneath me and whispers, "Fuck."

Before I can ask him anything, he lifts me off his lap and rises to his feet. He reaches his hand down and helps me stand.

Pressing his lips to my forehead, he whispers, "I'm so sorry, sweetheart."

My heart stalls in my chest as he walks to the door and unlocks it. When he opens it, a petite older woman stands there giving him an impatient look. Her gray hair is pulled back into a severe bun and her clothes scream wealth. Her light blue eyes match Coop's perfectly.

"Mother," Coop says without inflection.

My heart thumps heavy in my chest. This is Coop's mother. The one he wanted to love him. She hasn't spotted me though.

"I had lunch with Leighton and she had a lot to say about your *fiancée*." She takes two steps into Coop's office and spots me. Her eyes widen as she takes me in from head to toe.

Swallowing hard, I resist the urge to check every inch of my body for imperfections.

Coop steps forward and takes his mother's elbow.

"Why don't we have a seat and talk?" He guides her to a set of comfortable chairs he has off to the side. "Madison?"

His resigned eyes meet mine. He didn't want me to meet his mother. Even after he told everyone we were engaged. Are we going to continue this farce? It's not like we're actually getting married, but every time someone brings up ending the charade, Coop shoots it down. Especially with the stalker still on the loose.

He holds his hand out to me as his mother lowers into the chair.

My heart beats like a hummingbird's wings as I take his hand and let him help me into a chair beside him.

"Mother, this is Madison Harris. Madison, this is my mother, Victoria Graham."

I fold my hands in my lap. "It's a pleasure to meet you."

Victoria's perfectly painted lips press into a fine line as she looks me over again. Her gaze lingers on the ring on my finger. I try not to fidget under her scrutiny.

Coop slides his hand under mine and entangles our fingers. "To what do I owe this honor? You usually don't mix with the common folk."

Victoria's sharp blue eyes go to Coop, letting me breathe for a moment.

"How else am I supposed to find out what my only child is up to?" Victoria sits properly in the chair. I almost expect her to clap her hands for the staff to bring her tea. I'm afraid I might be "the staff" in her mind.

"My phone still works." Coop's hand tightens on mine.

I glance over and see the strain around his lips. I want to draw his head to mine and give him my strength. Instead, I squeeze his hand to let him know I'm here for whatever he needs.

"Yes, and you know exactly how to avoid me on it. No, Cooper, you will explain yourself this minute. If you'd like your"—her eyes sweep over me briefly—"companion to excuse us, that would probably be for the best."

I tense to rise, but Coop presses our hands down on my thigh.

"No, if you have something to say, you can say it to us both."

My breath catches, and I want to say thanks but no thanks, but it's not really an option. Instead, I squeeze Coop's hand back to let him know he has my support.

Victoria presses her lips into a fine line again before resting her hands on her knee. "Fine. As I was saying, Leighton and I were having lunch—"

"Because you were always such great friends," Coop says sarcastically.

"Don't be rude, Cooper." She glares at him. "Leighton's done some digging on your fiancée."

My already skyrocketing pulse shoots higher, even though there's nothing to find. I'm no one.

"She has no connections, no money, and barely any future." Victoria brushes imaginary lint off her skirt before lifting her icy gaze to Coop. "She's unacceptable and you need to end this engagement at once."

A laugh bursts out of me. I cover my mouth, but I can't help it. She sounds like a mother in a period drama. And even with everything else that has happened to me since starting here, this has to be the most ludicrous.

Coop's eyes dance with laughter as he looks at me.

"Pardon me?" Victoria huffs out. "I don't see what's funny."

Maybe if the engagement were real, I'd feel crushed by her rejection. Instead, it's just silly. Coop doesn't deserve a mother like her.

I wipe a tear from my eye as I get myself under control.

"She's obviously after your money and power." Victoria gestures at me.

I shake my head. This woman has it so wrong.

"I don't care about his money or power. I don't care who you are or what you're worth." My smile softens as I look over at Coop. "I love him. He's smart and sexy. He cares for me like no one else does, but he's also playful. When everyone takes things too seriously, he pulls us back. I can't imagine a day without Coop in my life."

His thumb brushes over the back of my hand.

Drawing in a breath, I settle and feel his love for me. "If Coop wants to marry me, I'd be stupid to say no to him. Not for his money. Not for his power. But for the way he loves me back."

He lifts my hand to his lips and kisses my knuckles. I remember being afraid to love him for fear he wouldn't love me in return. But he's so easy to love, it would have been impossible not to fall.

"While I appreciate your concern, Mother, for once I'm letting my happiness outweigh what you think is proper." Coop's words take my breath away. "I'd marry Madison every day for the rest of my life if she'd let me."

"Cooper Jamison, you know what's expected of you, and being a fool for love only makes our family look weak." Victoria straightens even more if possible. "End this before it goes too far, or I'll bring it to your father's attention. He knows what needs to be done. You're lucky Leighton will still have you after this fiasco."

"Enough." Coop stands and looks down his nose at his mother. "You have insulted me and my future wife. Leighton isn't an option. She never was. She was me placating you when I still cared enough to try. But let's be honest, Mother, no one will ever be 'good enough' for the Graham line."

"Cooper—"

"No, I'm done. You didn't even try to meet Madison or learn anything about her before you attacked her. She's intelligent and caring. She loves me with all her heart. And for the first time in my life, I feel loved. If you don't think that's worth more than a fancy name and a family history of prohibition smuggling, then I don't think we have anything more to discuss. Goodbye, Mother."

Chapter 142

Olive Branch

Coop

My mother purses her lips like she's tasted something sour. I wouldn't be surprised if the next words out of her mouth were *well, I never* as she clutched her pearls.

Instead, she rises and glares at Madison for a second before she turns on her heel. I escort her to the elevator. Her nose is in the air and her shoulders are stiff as she enters.

As soon as the elevator closes, she turns to me.

"Cooper, you need to rethink this." Her voice is firm. "You can't possibly marry that woman."

I lean against the back wall of the elevator and cross my ankles. "Why not? Just because you settled for a loveless marriage doesn't mean I have to."

Her lips press into a thin line. "I suppose you think you love this woman and that will be enough? You are a Graham. It's bad enough that you started this company with those friends of yours, but to honestly think marrying a woman you barely know is a good idea? Your father will—"

"Will what, Mother?" I straighten as we reach the first floor.

"Will be disappointed in me? Will cut me off? Will leave his entire fortune to some organization that will spend it? What are you going to threaten me with?"

She tips her chin up but says nothing as the doors open.

"I have a trust fund from my grandfather that is plenty large enough to keep me in the lifestyle I'm accustomed to. Plus, I own a business and make good money of my own. I don't need the wealth and prestige you and my father have. You've barely been a parent to me. So if you feel the need to cut me off, that's your prerogative. But if she'll have me, I'll marry Madison Harris with or without my family present."

For a second, she almost looks stunned. Before her forehead smooths out and she brushes her hand over her skirt. "Your father will be in touch."

She walks away without a backward glance. That woman gave birth to me, but she never was a mother to me. I got more affection from the cook than her. Even so, my heart still aches at the dismissal.

The receptionist glances my way but turns away when she sees me looking her direction. Mother couldn't have gotten upstairs on her own. She doesn't have access.

"Excuse me, Yvonne." I stop behind her.

She turns, batting her eyelashes, and smiles. "Yes, Mr. Graham? How may I help you?"

"Did you send my mother upstairs without announcing her?" I have enough to deal with without our receptionist going rogue.

Her smile almost drops, but she keeps it. "She insisted on going up. I texted your assistant."

I nod. Madison was in my office. If her phone was on her, I didn't hear it go off. I can confirm with her later if she even got a message.

"Why didn't you wait until Madison let you know if I was available?"

There goes that flirty smile. *Yeah, you fucked up.*

"It was your mother."

"You know the protocol, Ms. Diaz."

She stiffens at my use of her last name. I've always been pleasant to her, but she didn't do her job this time.

"No one is to ride up the elevator unannounced." This isn't a hard job. "We have a protocol for a reason."

Yvonne's lips tighten and she has the decency to look a little shaken. "Of course, Mr. Graham."

The phone rings and she turns to answer it. I have all this pent-up energy. I want to tear her a new one, but that's not a great idea. Drawing in a breath, I return to the elevator.

My mother always riles me up, but I need to let it go this time. Yes, Yvonne didn't do her job. I'll make sure she's written up, but I don't have to tear into her for it.

When the doors open, Madison looks at me from her computer. Our eyes lock and something settles in me. Some of the rage seeps away.

She's mine.

That's all that matters.

"Patrick was looking for you," she says as I approach. As I round her desk, her mouth drops open like she's going to say more.

I lean over and, holding her chin, take her mouth with mine. Pressing up into me, she parts her lips as her hand grabs hold of my wrist. She's the air I need to breathe.

A throat clears behind me. I lift my mouth from Madison's and wait for her blue eyes to open. When I see the love reflected there, I breathe a little easier. This is all I need. She's all I need.

Straightening, I turn to find Patrick standing opposite Madison's desk.

"Don't mean to interrupt, but I need to clear one more thing before the meeting tomorrow at lunch." Patrick's eyes never leave me. He doesn't even glance at Madison.

Is that weird? Is he avoiding looking at her? Does he avoid looking at her because he wants to look at her? Or does she just not matter to him? He doesn't have to work with her. If he needs something from her, we get it for him.

"Sure." I glance down at Madison. She's turned back to her work. Her cheeks are flushed pink as she types on her computer. Unable to resist, I brush her hair behind her ear. Her lips tip up into an almost smile even though she doesn't look at me.

My heart settles. This is what family looks like. What the guys and I have and what Madison and I have.

I follow Patrick back to the break room with none of the anger my mother's visit triggered.

Madison

My mind still spins hours later when I'm helping Seth make dinner. Coop stood up to his mother for me. He walked her out and spoke to the receptionist about letting her up without announcing her.

He chose me.

Coop went down to work out in the gym before dinner. Noah sits at the island, working on his laptop.

I haven't seen Blake except in passing today. Every time I see him, my heart aches. I fell for him first and trusted him, but he didn't trust me. I don't know how we come back from that or what he can do to make it okay.

Seth isn't completely forgiven, but he let Blake convince him to not trust me. That's not as bad as being the one doing the convincing. I blow out a breath, and Noah lifts his dark eyes to mine.

"You good, kitten?"

Seth glances at me from the stove where he's stirring a pot. His eyes aren't as tense, knowing we're going to sleep together tonight. It's a move in the right direction. A move I needed to make.

Because I don't feel complete. I feel unbalanced. But I don't want the others to worry about it. Blake and I need to figure this out. I don't know what he can do to make me believe he trusts me.

"I'm good." I give Noah a smile as I pick up the bowl of salad to put on the table.

"You don't have to do that." Noah shuts his laptop and follows me. "You don't have to keep it to yourself if you're hurting."

I set the bowl on the table and release my breath. "What am I supposed to say? That I don't know what to do? That I don't know how to fix this? That I miss having all of you with me and that feeling of being whole?"

Noah's arms wrap around my waist and draw me back against his warm body. "We can work through it, kitten. You don't have to figure this out on your own."

I rest my head against his shoulder as I stare out the windows into the night. The city lights sparkle around our tower. We're untouchable up here. At least that's how I felt. But now I'm shaken.

The foundation of what we've built is a little rotten, and I'm not sure we can fix it without tearing everything apart and rebuilding.

I sink into Noah's warmth as he presses his lips to my temple and holds me.

Seth walks over and puts dinner on the table. He stands next to me, close enough to touch, but he doesn't. I hate that he still hesitates, but I'm also not willing to give him control so soon.

"We've always been a little broken, princess." Seth's voice is low and soothing. He reaches out his fingers and brushes them over mine. A little sizzle of awareness buzzes through me. "We'll find a way back to each other."

I turn my head to meet Seth's mesmerizing eyes as I link my fingers with his. "I hope so."

"Time for dinner?" Coop walks out of his room. His damp hair hangs around his shoulders. His smile is easy and carefree again.

"Everything's ready," Seth says.

Noah pulls away from me. Seth squeezes my hand before releasing it. I inhale and turn to the table, taking my seat.

Coop sits across from me. "You were brilliant today, goddess."

My cheeks flush at his praise. "I don't know if I'd go that far. I shouldn't have been rude to your mother."

"You met Victoria?" Noah seems surprised.

"Mother came to tell me in person that Madison is the wrong person for me." Coop drapes a napkin over his lap.

"Did she have a correct woman in mind?" Noah arches his eyebrow.

Coop laughs. "Leighton."

"That reminds me—" Seth stops himself. "Where's Blake?"

"He was still downstairs working out when I came up." Coop loads up his plate.

"I'll call him." Seth reaches for his phone.

Drawing in a breath, I shake my head. "No, I'll go get him."

"Are you sure?" Noah searches my eyes.

Nodding, I stand. "I should really get a look at the gym, and I need to talk to him about self-defense training."

"We'll wait for you." Seth sits back. His eyes track me as I pick up my phone and head to the door.

"Start without us. It'll only be a few minutes."

I get in the elevator and press the button for the executive gym. It's actually the back half of the corporate gym, but it's partitioned off and only used by my guys. And me, if I want to.

I need to use it.

Too many times, I've felt helpless and trapped and needed someone to rescue me. I need to help myself. While I hope the guys are around to protect me, the stalker isn't likely to attack me when everyone is around.

The elevator opens on the gym floor and I walk to the door, pressing my card against the reader to gain access. When I step into the workout room, Blake is in the corner with the free weights. Music fills the room with a hard, driving rhythm.

He's abandoned his shirt, so his chest is on full display, all those lovely rippling muscles. His arm curls with a weight in his hand.

Attraction isn't our problem. Trust is. While Seth will relinquish control to me, I doubt Blake would do the same.

I clear my throat. "It's dinnertime."

His green eyes lift to mine as he returns the weight to the rack and turns off the music. "Thank you."

He grabs a towel and swipes it over his face.

"When can I learn self-defense?" I lean against the door while he tidies up the area.

"I've been too preoccupied to hire you a trainer." It's stated as fact and I believe him. Things have been hectic this week. "If you want, we can go through a few moves after dinner tonight."

When his eyes return to me, my breath catches. I want to spend time with him and avoid him all in the same breath. I love him, and right now, it hurts too much to be with him but not be with him.

"That would be nice." I need to learn, and he'll make sure I at least get the basics down.

He grabs his shirt and drapes it over his shoulders before walking to me.

That hint of spice blends with his natural scent to make my panties damp. My body misses him almost as much as I miss him.

"Let's go." He gestures to the door.

I blush, realizing I'm in the way. Stepping aside, I open the door and walk to the elevator. It opens right away and we both get on. After I press the button, the silence is almost stifling.

My phone buzzes. It's probably one of the guys wondering what's taking so long. I glance down at my phone. *Unknown.*

Fuck. My heart races. I don't want to know. I want to bury my head in the sand and forget this is happening to me.

"What is it?" Blake's eyes narrow on me.

I take a breath and look at the text.

UNKNOWN:

Do you enjoy being his whore?

The next message comes in. A picture of Coop and me kissing in the lobby from a while ago.

UNKNOWN:

It's not like you're the first or the last to fall for the playboy.

A video is attached.

"I can't." It's too much. Every time he sends audio or video, it's me being exposed in an intimate moment and it takes another piece of me.

Closing my eyes, I hold out my phone to Blake. He takes it.

"Coop." My voice comes from my phone.

"*Open your eyes, goddess. See what I see.*" Coop's voice follows, but both of our voices are whispers. The night of the benefit. When Coop led me off after Seth arrived with Elizabeth.

Blake shuts it off. I glance at him. His fist clenches and opens.

"He's fucking irresponsible." The elevator doors open, and Blake storms out and into the apartment.

I hurry after him in time to see him drop my phone in front of Coop.

"You fucking asshole. We never should have let you take her to the benefit." Blake barely contains his anger.

Coop lifts my phone and I see us on the screen over his shoulder. His hand is beneath my gold dress and I'm pressed against him in front of the mirror.

My breath catches and I grab the back of a chair before I go down completely. Blake's hand grabs my elbow to steady me. He helps me sit in the chair.

It's one more thing. One more piece of me stolen by the stalker. It's too much. This whole thing is too much.

A notification pops up.

UNKNOWN:

Soon, little one.

Chapter 143

Risk Management

Madison

Words buzz around me. But I'm not present anymore. Physically, I'm at this table. Dinner sits mostly untouched before us. But mentally, I'm trying to search my memories to recall if I saw anyone at the benefit when we were in that hallway. Was I so wrapped up in Coop that I didn't see someone filming us?

His words. His touch. It's easy to get caught up in any of my guys.

I'm aware of the guys watching the video and blaming Coop for his exhibitionist tendencies. For being caught fucking with me not once but twice at the benefit. I can't focus on it though, because I'm lost.

Whoever the stalker is, this person has access to me. He filmed me in my apartment. Had my roommate take pictures of me. He even got past security in this building at least twice and bugged our conference room. He has the money to get to me no matter where I am.

The urge to run pulses through me like an adrenaline rush. How far would I have to run though? Where could I hide from someone if I don't even know who I'm hiding from?

Even if I could run away, would he just follow me? Or would I have to run forever? Keep running to stay one step ahead?

It doesn't matter though because I couldn't leave Seth, Noah, Coop, or Blake behind.

I can't get away from this person. We need to figure out who it is. Otherwise, at some point, he'll pounce and I won't be ready. I don't even really understand what he wants from me.

"Princess?" Seth's voice cuts through the fog and I turn to him. His furrowed brow makes me focus on him.

"Yes?" I lift my trembling hands onto the table. I stare at them. When did that start? The shaking is weird.

Noah takes my hand between his and rubs it. Am I cold? Blake's hand squeezes my shoulder. Awareness blankets me. As I slam back to the here and now, I suck in a breath.

"You still with us?" Seth leans forward.

"Yes, I'm here." I shut all the fear and confusion in a box in my mind. I'm giving the stalker what he wants. He wants me to feel his presence everywhere. He's not here though. Not when I'm with these men. They're my safety. I need to focus on them. "What are we talking about?"

My gaze flits to each of their concerned looks. I squeeze Noah's hand.

"This isn't the first time he's mentioned Coop." Seth blows out an exhausted breath.

What? My eyes widen as I meet Coop's light blue eyes. Did the stalker threaten him? When?

"The bottom of the dress box had that exact picture of us with a note on it." Coop runs his fingers through his hair. "Something about 'don't play with the boys.'"

What if the stalker goes after Coop? What if all of them are in danger too? What if he already knows about our arrangement?

"Does he know about us?" I swallow. "All of us?"

Only my and Coop's voices were on the audio recording the stalker sent when I was at the bar, but we don't know how much more he heard in the conference room audio, and there's obviously more than one man in that recording when they were all fucking me.

"It's possible the stalker knows everything." Seth takes a deep breath. "He's got someone new taking pictures for him now."

Blake settles into a chair. "What do you mean?"

"Talked with Cross today about Elizabeth. She *is* fucking someone. But I also asked him if someone offered a contract on Madison or if anyone approached him about it." Seth picks up his fork, looking at his food like he isn't really seeing it. "He didn't take the job, but it exists. Whoever wanted those pictures will pay a lot of money for them."

"So the person taking the pictures is hired like Val and might never have had any previous contact with Madison." Noah shakes his head. "This is fucked-up. He could be anyone. The man Val interacted with might not even be the stalker, but someone the stalker hired. It could be a woman or multiple people. We basically know nothing."

I squeeze Noah's hand. But he's right. If this person is hiring people to follow me, I'll never know who they are.

"Who's Elizabitch sleeping with?" Coop sets my phone to the side and leans his elbows on the table.

"Drew Young."

Coop laughs harshly. "Fuck, that's precious."

"Who's Drew Young?" I'm just grateful to steer the conversation away from the stalker. I could use something else to focus on, and getting rid of Elizabeth's hold on Seth is a high priority.

"Leighton's benefit date. Wonder if Elizabeth's doing it intentionally to get back at Leighton? But honestly, Leighton didn't seem that into the guy." Coop shakes his head and drops his gaze to the table. His fists clench. "Leighton's been fucking up my life with my mother. That's why Victoria came to see me today. I vote we fuck up both Leighton's and Elizabeth's lives."

"What do you have in mind?" Seth sets his fork down.

"A casual get-together." Coop's smile turns wicked. "Just a few couples having dinner out on the town."

"I could bring Sara to round things out." Noah draws me into his side. I sink into his warmth. Sara's a good idea. I could use a friend when facing down the two women who held my men's hearts.

I don't need to worry about Noah. Not with Sara, not with anyone else. Noah is my home, my center.

"We'll plan for Saturday night. It shouldn't be a problem getting Elizabeth to go. She's been calling and texting me all week." Seth's stony gaze meets mine. "If you're okay with it, princess?"

"If this works to make those women leave us alone, I'm all for it." I reach for my water, wishing it was something stronger. My insides feel all tangled up. I don't know if I'm ready to confront their exes any more than I'm prepared to confront my stalker.

The text comes back to me. *Soon, little one.*

What does that mean? He texted it before. Does it mean he's going to escalate? Is he going to contact me more directly?

My gaze lifts to Blake. His green eyes meet mine. While the others talk logistics about restaurants and how to get everyone there, I fall into his eyes and forget about the stalker for a moment.

I miss Blake. So fucking much. I don't know what will fix this broken trust. He's just as fiercely protective as he's always been. But now regret lingers in his eyes.

"Eat, tiger. You'll need your strength if we're going to train tonight." He gestures to the plate of food in front of me.

"Self-defense?" Noah looks between the two of us.

"Yes. Do you want to come down and help?" I hope my face doesn't look too desperate. I don't want to be alone with Blake. Not yet. My body doesn't know why we're mad at him or why he upset us. It just wants to fall into his arms and let him take away the bad.

To submit to him. To love him. To trust him.

But he doesn't trust me. He put me in the same category as those other women who played games. I have enough to worry about. I'm not ready to deal with this.

"Of course, kitten." Noah takes my hand on the table. I give him a warm smile.

When I glance at Blake, disappointment flashes in his eyes before it's gone.

———

After eating some dinner, I slip into my room to change into something more suitable for working out. I don't think anything of it when Coop comes in and sits on the bench in my closet while I pick through the clothes. It shouldn't matter what I wear, but somehow it does.

Maybe Seth's meticulous dressing of me every day is rubbing off on me. Maybe I just need armor to help me not want to submit to Blake.

"I'm sorry." Coop's words reverberate through the small room. I pause and my heart thumps. What did he do?

I set the clothes down and turn to face Coop. "For what?"

"For being irresponsible." His blue eyes lift to mine. "For taking advantage of having you on my arm that night. For being selfish and thinking that no one could touch us there. That somehow we would be immune."

His gaze drops to his hands in his lap. His loose dark hair falls in a curtain around his face. My heartbeat quickens. This is easy.

Drawing in a breath, I unzip my skirt, letting it slip to the floor before I cross to Coop. My skirt would prevent me from being close to him and I need to change, anyway. His eyes darken when he glances at my panties. I straddle his lap and cup his face with my palms. Our eyes lock.

The torment in his makes me lean in and press a soft kiss to his lips.

"You were only trying to help me, Coop." I brush my thumb along his jaw.

His hands cup my hips and draw me in closer. His head

lowers to rest against my heart. "I love fucking you, but I shouldn't have done it out in the open while you have a stalker."

"You were helping me cope." I run my fingers through his hair and draw in a breath. "This wouldn't be happening—"

"Yes, it would." He lifts his head to meet my gaze again. His hands cup my face as he searches my eyes. "I'm not like the others. I'm not anonymous, especially at an event like that."

My brow furrows. I haven't been out with the guys much. The benefit was all about being seen.

"Everything I've done since I was born has been under harsh scrutiny. I didn't grow up unaware of what people think of me. I'm a Graham. Everyone I've ever come into contact with knows who I am. Maybe not at first, but they learn."

He presses his forehead against mine, and I wrap my hands around the back of his neck. I want to protect him the way these guys protect me.

"People use me. For wealth, for fame, for infamy. I don't give a fuck anymore about that shit, but I should have thought about you. I should have protected you."

"You do protect me. When things went wrong, you also reassured me. You didn't force me to do anything I didn't want to do. I knew the risks, but I didn't think about the stalker either." Breathing in his crisp scent, I blow out my breath. "I love you, and I love the way you love me."

"Even if we end up getting caught every time?" His finger trails along my jaw, making me conscious of the physical intimacy of our position.

"Maybe we can try a little harder to be discreet?" Lifting my head, I search his eyes. "I'm not sorry about what we did. I'm freaked out about the stalker, but I wouldn't have let you take things that far if I didn't want to."

"Fuck, Madison. I love you so fucking much." His lips take mine as his words fill my heart. I'd give him my heart all over again without hesitation because I feel his love with his every touch and word. He's mine. And I'm his.

Coop trails kisses to my ear before whispering, "I wanted to fuck you in the break room today. I wished Patrick wasn't there. Or that it didn't matter. I would have lifted you onto that counter and fucked you until you came on my cock."

My breath escapes me, remembering him hovering close. And then in his office before his mother came in. The potential for more had been right there. He stood up for me. He chose me.

"Sweetheart, want to pretend with me?" He kisses my throbbing pulse as his hand sweeps over my ass.

"I don't have a lot of time."

He pulls back a little disappointed. His blue eyes search mine. "It's okay. I'll let you get ready."

I arch an eyebrow and glance over my shoulder at the door like I'm worried. "My boss expects me back at work. You'll get me in trouble if you keep me too long."

His smile grows. "We wouldn't want you to get in trouble."

I grind my pussy against his erection through my panties and his sweatpants. "I could get fired."

"We wouldn't want that either." He lifts my shirt off over my head. "Don't worry. I can get us there."

When he tries to take off my bra, I hold it and try to look fearful. "Sir? Anyone could walk into the break room and see us."

Coop's chuckle burns through me like a heat wave. He moves my arms. "Let them see you, sweetheart. They can watch as I make you come so hard."

He drops my bra behind the bench and slides his hand into the front of my panties. I suck in a breath.

"So fucking wet. You wanted me to come after you, didn't you? Wanted me to find you all alone in this room so I could fuck you." Coop thrusts his fingers into my pussy.

I cling to his shoulders as he fucks his fingers up into me.

"You wanted to be my dirty little whore, didn't you?" Coop nips and sucks at my jawline as he pushes me higher and higher with every thrust of his fingers.

"Yes, Coop," I whimper as need spirals through me. "I want to be your whore."

I'm so close when he pulls his fingers out. "What?"

He smirks. "On your knees."

I slide off his lap to kneel between his knees, shaking with the need to come.

"Take out my cock and show me how much you appreciate being mine." Coop grabs his shirt in the back with one hand and pulls it off. Fuck, my mouth drools at his gorgeous, sculpted body.

I push his pants down and draw his cock out. He leans back on his hands and watches me with hooded eyes. "No one will know, sweetheart. I'll keep it our secret."

I purposely glance at the door and nibble on my lip. "What if my boss comes in?"

His gaze flows over my tightened nipples. My breasts grow heavy, aching to be touched. All I have on are my panties and they're soaked as I stroke my hand over the smooth skin of his cock.

"Maybe if you're lucky, he'll watch. Or join in." Coop's smile is devious.

I glance at the door again. Fuck, I kind of want someone else to come in and find us. To watch me take Coop's cock and then fuck him.

"Does that make you nervous?" He caresses my jaw and brushes his thumb over my bottom lip. "Or hot?"

Our eyes meet and the heat in his melts my insides.

I wet my lips, brushing the tip of his thumb with my tongue. "Needy."

Coop's other hand swipes over his phone. I arch an eyebrow at him, but he winks at me.

"Suck me off like a good little whore."

I lean forward and swipe my tongue through his slit, gathering his precum and taking it into my mouth.

"Better make it quick. The boss is waiting. You wouldn't want to be punished." Coop chuckles.

I cock an eyebrow but take his cock into my mouth, pushing past my gag reflex to swallow around him.

"Fuck, I love when you do that." His hand threads into my hair and pushes me a little farther onto his cock. I practically choke on him. "I could come right now. You're such a good little whore."

He releases me and I come up and gasp in a breath. I suck on his cock as I slide my mouth up and down over him. The click of the doorknob sends a rush of pleasure through me.

"Ms. Harris, I needed you in my office." Seth's voice is like the sweetest drug sweeping through my system. I thought for sure it would be Noah, but Seth is good.

Before I can lift my head, Coop holds me on his cock. "She needs a little incentive, boss. She wants to be watched."

The door remains open. I do my best to look toward Seth. He leans in the doorway with a smile. "Better hurry, Ms. Harris if you want to fulfill your duties."

My pussy aches with the need to be fucked. Seth and I are still figuring this out, but I love that he's watching me and Coop. Seth isn't running this show.

"Do the work, sweetheart." Coop releases my head and I work my mouth over his hard, thick cock. Coop says, in the most conversational tone ever, "She's got the sweetest pussy I've ever tasted."

"Wet too." Seth sounds like he's discussing developing a new product. "Tight."

"Mmm. Her ass is tight too. Squeezing around my cock so fucking hard when she comes, and she does. Often." Coop strokes his hand over my hair. "Are you two good?"

I pause and suck, waiting for Seth's answer.

"We're getting there." Seth walks into the room and sits next to Coop on the bench. His eyes flow over my mostly naked body. The fabric of his pants brushes against my side, sending tingles of anticipation through me.

I whimper at how much I ache for them.

Coop grabs my hair and lifts my mouth from his cock. "Take off your panties and fuck me, sweetheart."

I rise before them. Eager and willing.

"Such a firm body." Coop brushes his fingers over my trembling stomach as I lower my panties and step out of them. "You should feel how tight her cunt is."

My eyes dart to Seth's. He smiles. "I fucked her earlier today. Took her hard up against the door of my office until she shattered all over my cock."

I straddle Coop's lap and guide his cock to my entrance. Coop grabs my hip with one hand to stop me from taking him inside.

"My eyes, sweetheart. When you fuck me, look into my eyes." He raises his eyebrow like I'm going to argue with him.

Meeting his eyes, I tighten my hands on his shoulders as I sink down onto his cock, impaling myself. My lips part at the stretch and fullness. Fuck, that feels so fucking good. Coop's eyes are still hooded as he meets mine.

"Does having the boss watch you fuck me get you wet?" Coop brushes the back of his fingers across my breast, gliding his fingers down.

"Yes," I whisper.

Seth shifts next to us and his thigh brushes my calf, sending heat through me. The back of his hand grazes my thigh as I rise and fall over Coop's cock.

"I love showing you off, sweetheart. Making the others want what you have to offer." Coop slides his fingers over my clit. "But taking it for myself."

I moan as he brushes the sensitive flesh. I roll my hips over his cock.

"You're stunning in your pleasure and only a fool wouldn't watch you fuck someone." Coop touches his lips against mine as he presses on my clit. "I'm going to enjoy watching you shatter for me in public, knowing none of them will ever see you like this. And I'm going to make my friends watch as I fuck you, knowing they're the only ones who understand how sweet it is to fuck this cunt."

I explode, throwing my head back as I ride his cock through the waves of my climax. My breasts slide against Coop's chest.

"So fucking beautiful," Seth whispers. His hand glides up my side to cup my breast.

Coop thrusts up hard into me, suspending me in ecstasy. "We will always crave you, sweetheart."

I lower my head to look into Coop's eyes as he fucks me. "I will always need you, Coop."

I cup his cheeks as I pulse around his cock, milking him, and he roars his release. Thrusting in deep and spilling his warm cum inside as he captures my mouth and holds me tight against him.

Seth stands and I draw away from Coop's lips. Our foreheads rest against each other as we come down. I'm aware of Seth moving around, but he doesn't close in on me. Doesn't take my hair to fuck my mouth or slide behind me to fuck my ass.

He sets some clothes next to us and touches my hair softly, hesitantly, like he's not sure it's okay. Fuck.

"Get dressed, princess. They're waiting for you."

I want to ask what about him, but he smiles.

"I look forward to sleeping with you tonight," he says as he walks out the door, leaving it open.

Coop chuckles. "You like the idea of having the boss to yourself tonight, don't you, my little whore?"

I tug on Coop's hair. "I love spending time with all of you."

His cock is still hard inside me. "This one's for me."

He lifts me and backs me against the wall before fucking me hard and fast. I cling to him as my body strains against his. It won't take much for him to make me come.

"I love you," I whisper in his ear as I shatter.

Blake

Madison went to change about a half hour ago. Coop followed her into her room, so I'm not surprised she isn't down in the gym yet. I figured it was safe to come set up since Noah is waiting for her upstairs.

I want to find this stalker now and be done with it. I left a message with Bill to see if they have an update on the phone and to let him know she's received new messages. The desire to delete the video before giving the phone to him almost wins out. It's evidence for the police, but I don't want anyone to see Madison like that.

It's a punishment from the stalker to all of us.

The door opens, and Noah and Madison come in.

"Alone," she says emphatically. She's gorgeous and youthful with her hair pulled up in a high ponytail. Her face is scrubbed clean. Her black yoga pants cling to her long legs. A black sports bra covered by a sheer white tank top holds her full breasts together, showing off her cleavage.

Noah shakes his head. "It's not like he isn't used to sharing."

They both find me on the mats I've spread out in an open area.

"Who's used to sharing?" I don't know why I ask. All of us are used to sharing Madison. At least we were before I fucked things up.

"Seth." Noah links his hand with Madison's and draws her to me. "Madison is sleeping in his bed tonight."

"Good." I'm glad for my friend. He followed my lead with the testing. He kept saying we should trust her. But my fear led him astray.

Madison studies me while I put the last mat down.

Clearing my throat, I straighten. "We'll do some basics tonight. Find the vulnerable spots and work on targeting them. Tomorrow we'll work on breaking out of holds."

"I definitely need to know how to get out of a choke hold." Madison's face is pale but determined. "Twice it's been used against me."

"We'll get you there, tiger." I want to help her focus. I want to feel her submit to me like she does. Hell, I'd be willing to let her be a brat and call me Daddy if it meant she'd treat me the way she did before I shattered what we were building.

"What do you need me to do?" Noah steps forward. He's doing what he can to make this situation easier for both of us, but I wish we didn't need a buffer.

"You can be my dummy." I gesture for him to stand next to me, then lift my gaze to Madison. "If you want to sit on the bench, you can."

She lowers onto the bench and crosses her legs. Leaning in, she pays close attention.

"Besides the obvious knee to the groin. Pressure points will help give you means to escape." I point to each on Noah. "The sciatic nerve above the knee. The biceps. Brachial plexus above the armpit. The thumb webbing. The shin. The lymph node behind the ear."

Her eyes take in everything.

"If you get a shot at hitting him where he's vulnerable, palm to the jaw, thumbs in the eyes, palm to the nose, and knee to the groin."

"Can we not actually injure the groin?" Noah flinches as I gesture to that area.

"We'll just work on pressure points tonight." I hold my hand out to Madison without a thought.

She stands and walks toward me but doesn't take my hand. I release the breath I didn't know I was holding and let go of the tension in my shoulders. It's too soon. She trusts me to train her, but she thinks I don't trust her.

She may have given leeway to Seth, but she's not there with me. Her eyes at dinner told me that, but we'll get there. We have to.

I'll do whatever it takes to win her back.

Chapter 144

Business Relations

Madison

By the time we get on the elevator to head upstairs, I'm a little worse for wear. Noah's limping from an overenthusiastic kick to the shin. Blake watches me like he's proud of me, which makes my heart pound.

My ponytail is loose and I definitely need a shower, but I feel more confident in my ability to fight someone off. I'll feel even better when we work on holds more.

"Put some ice on your shoulder, tiger." Blake's green eyes look me over, making my blood heat.

When he grabbed my wrist one time, I jerked my arm away hard and hurt my shoulder. His fingers were tender as he checked it for me. The attraction between us sizzles in the air every time we get close. As much as I want to give in to it, I can't.

"Okay." Before, I would have maybe made a joke or implied something else he could do with ice, but his distrust still burns inside me.

"I'll ice my shin too." Noah leans against the side of the elevator. "But thanks for your concern, Blake."

Blake chuckles softly. "Want Madison to kiss it and make it better?"

Noah lifts his dark gaze to me and my breath catches at the heat there. "She could definitely kiss me better."

I raise an eyebrow. "Tonight, I'm sleeping."

The elevator doors open and we all head to the main door. When we get to the kitchen, Blake goes to the freezer and grabs two ice packs.

"Heads up." He tosses one to Noah, who grumbles when he catches it.

Blake walks the other one over and hands it to me. "Fifteen minutes."

He reaches up and tucks my hair behind my ear. This is the closest we've been this week, not including training tonight. My heart races as I search his eyes. I want to forgive him and get back to where we were, but at what cost?

How often will he need to test me? Why should I be the only one giving my trust to this relationship fully?

"You did well, love." His words are soft as his gaze drops. He backs away.

I want to reach out for him and draw him into my arms. I want to forgive him, but how do I know he won't doubt me on something bigger? How do I expose my deepest darkest parts to someone who doesn't believe in me?

My gaze follows Blake as he goes into his room. Noah watches me in silence. When the door shuts, I release my breath.

I bite my lip. It feels like I'm punishing him, but I'm not. That's not the point of the time I need. I want to resolve this. But I don't know how.

It hurts me just as much as it seems to hurt him. Testing me wasn't like cheating on me. But with as much as the guys say this is all about trust, it hurt that they didn't trust me to tell them the truth.

That they could even think I would go outside of these walls to find something more. That my love wasn't enough for them to believe in me.

"You okay, princess?"

I lift my gaze to Seth's gentle look. Barefoot, he's still wearing his shirt and pants from today. My heart skips for a different reason. I wasn't planning on having sex tonight. I hoped to have a conversation with Seth. But my blood thrums through my veins, hot after Blake and Noah manhandled me. And Seth watching me and Coop in the closet didn't exactly cool my jets. Maybe I need to reconsider.

Seth looks pointedly at the ice pack hanging in my hand, forgotten.

"Oh." I lift it and press it against my shoulder. "Things got a little rough."

Noah laughs and limps over to me. He catches my ponytail and drags my head back. "I can't wait to see your moves when we play again."

Before I can respond, his lips claim mine. Liquid heat floods me as he draws me into his arms. Our bodies press together like two broken halves of a whole. When he deepens the kiss, our tongues tangle.

The idea of fighting back appeals to me almost as much as submitting, especially with Noah and Coop together. I'd definitely be game to try that again.

Noah lifts his mouth from mine and smiles. "Good night, kitten. I love you."

"I love you, Noah." I rise on my toes to kiss him one more time.

Brushing his thumb over my cheek, he steps away and walks to his room.

"Do you want to shower in my room or yours?" Seth sits at the island casually. "I can grab your pajamas while you get ready."

"Thank you. I'll take my shower in your room, if that's okay." I glance up at him through my lashes, feeling a little awkward. We have a lot to talk about, but my hormones are all over the place.

"My door is unlocked. I'll bring you your things in five minutes."

He stands and heads to my bedroom. Since I haven't been sleeping in there, I've left the door unlocked after that first day when I needed space from Seth and Blake.

That Seth came after me, and Blake said he needed to be convinced, makes me think the trust issue isn't as deep for Seth. If Blake hadn't pushed, Seth might never have tested me. I need to repair the pieces of my heart and Seth is the easiest piece to fit back in.

When I walk into Seth's bedroom, sandalwood fills my nose. Fuck, I've missed him. My insides soften. I want to lie down on his sheets and just breathe him in. I'm trying to be strong with these men, but I love them and want their comfort. Even if they were the ones that hurt me.

Blowing out a breath, I head into the bathroom. It's odd to be in here alone, but it's still comfortable. Seth has always made this home for me. It's the little things like having spares of my toiletries in every bathroom, including underwear.

I turn the shower on and strip out of my clothes. In the mirror, I check on my shoulder, which doesn't seem swollen or discolored.

Both Noah and Blake were gentle with me for the most part. We did everything slowly so I could hit the right spots to get away. It's just going to take time and practice until it's my reaction to certain touches.

A knock sounds on the bathroom door. I appreciate Seth knocking, but it's not really necessary. A rush of desire flows through me. Seth knows what I need before I do. Today in his office . . . Fuck, that was exactly what I needed.

"Come in," I say loud enough to be heard over the shower.

Seth's eyes darken as he takes in my naked body from head to toe. My pulse quickens and my thighs rub together.

"I'll just set this . . ." He closes in on me and sets the clothes on the counter. He doesn't touch me, but his eyes make so many dark promises.

"Join me." The words slip out but I don't regret them. I want him, and why shouldn't I have him? We need to talk, but we can talk after. My body buzzes with need. My pussy aches the way it did earlier as I took him inside me.

He doesn't back up or drop his gaze from mine as he unbuttons his shirt. I lean against the counter as he slowly undresses for me. His shirt flutters to the ground and he takes his white undershirt off with one hand.

He's not as ripped as Blake, but Seth definitely keeps it tight. I can count each of his abs. He pulls his belt out of his pants and drops it onto his discarded clothes.

"I wanted you from the moment you shook my hand." Seth undoes his pants. "When you sucked in your breath, your eyes dilated. I saw that hunger in you."

I bite my lip as he slides his pants to the floor to stand before me in his boxers. His hard, thick cock is swollen beneath, making me throb in need.

"I trust you, princess." He lowers his boxers and steps out of them. We're both standing naked, bared to the other's gaze. "I didn't doubt you. But I should have never agreed to test you."

He steps closer, but still not close enough to touch me. His body heat warms me. My breath shudders in and out of me.

"You are the most spectacular woman I've known. Other women have abused our trust before, but that's not on you. Both Blake and I take the blame for bringing in women who tried to break us." He releases a breath and closes the distance.

His hard body molds to mine as his hand threads into my hair, cradling my head. He draws me into him with his other hand wrapped around my hip. His dark blue eyes search mine as his lips tip into a smile. Fuck, I love his smile.

"I love you, princess. I will do anything for you. And I mean that. You're it for me. The future without you looks bleak and uninteresting. I need you in my life. I will never let doubt cloud my mind again. If I even think about it, I'll confront you directly. Because I want you to do the same."

My hands wrap around his back. His skin slides against mine, making fire flood me. "I love you, boss. I don't need to test you. I just want you to trust me the way I trust you."

"I do. Anything, princess." His nose grazes mine.

I draw in a deep breath, so ready to be done with this part.

"I forgive you, Seth." No sooner do the words leave my mouth than he sweeps me into his arms. His mouth claims mine. This isn't controlled Seth. His kiss is hot and demanding, seeking my tongue with his.

He lifts me against him and my legs wrap around his waist. I hold on as he walks us into the shower. Water cascades over us, but he doesn't relinquish my lips. His cock throbs against my clit, but I don't want to shift to take him in yet.

All of my focus is on this kiss. The way his tongue slides against mine. The sparks coursing through me. His hunger. His need.

It only amplifies my own. I missed him so fucking much.

He presses me back against the tile and tilts my head to deepen our kiss. Every inch of me longs for more. I love this man.

My hands slide into his hair as his explore me. Rediscovering every inch while his mouth claims mine.

He breaks our kiss and groans. "I can't wait, princess."

"I don't want you to." I meet his eyes and shift my hips. "Fuck me, sir."

His cock brushes my entrance before he thrusts deep. I gasp at the stretch of him buried inside me. We both groan at the feel of being together again.

His forehead rests on mine. "Fuck, princess, you test my control every fucking day. I can't get enough of you."

I brush my thumb over the water on his cheek. "I can't get enough of you either."

Looking down between us, he slowly draws out of me before punching back in. I watch with him, loving seeing how wet I'm making his cock. Each stroke brings me closer to the edge.

I need this. I need to be claimed by him.

"I'm yours, princess."

Oh, fuck.

My pussy clenches around his cock as I come. I cry out, "I'm yours, boss."

He thrusts a few more times, wildly, out of control, before he follows me into oblivion, pressing in deep and spilling his warm cum inside me. His forehead rests on mine. Our breaths mingle as we come down from the high.

My heart presses against my chest like it's too full to stay within. This is what I've been missing. I need all of them. Without any one of them, I feel broken and lost. With Seth, I almost feel whole again, but I'm still missing part of me.

Seth cups my cheek and kisses me softly. "Are we good, princess?"

"Yes, Seth. We're good." I smile, but I'm still not whole yet.

He draws out of me. My feet lower to the shower floor, and he leads me back under the water. We're both quiet as we wash each other. After the frantic way we fucked, this is nice. Our hands rediscovering every part of the other. After Seth dries himself off, he takes my towel to dry me.

Then he helps me dress, piece by piece, putting us back together. His moves growing more confident.

He holds my hand on the way to his bed. Releasing me, he goes to his dresser to put on a fresh pair of boxers. Once we're in bed, he draws me in close. I rest my head over his heart, snuggling against him. I've missed this.

I've missed him.

Seth's fingers stroke through my damp hair.

"You've met Elizabeth." His words are soft, but they still burn into me. Just her name is acid on my tongue. But I don't need him to confess anything. I'm not sure I want to know.

"It's okay. You don't—" I start to rise, but he holds me in place.

"Madison, I want to tell you. I don't want you to worry about this again." He blows out a breath as I settle back into my spot. "We dated in college. She seemed so sophisticated and smart. We got hot and heavy pretty fast, and soon she was spending almost every night in our apartment."

I put my hands on his chest and rest my chin on them so I can see him. His thumb trails over my cheek. His eyes take on that faraway look.

"We spent all our time together. I fell in love with the girl she pretended to be. That girl never existed. The whole time she was with me, her actual goal was Coop. But he'd been with Leighton since his freshman year. Probably before then, honestly."

My brow furrows. What's that supposed to mean? Were Coop and Leighton childhood sweethearts?

His thumb smooths out my forehead. "Their parents arranged their relationship. Their families took trips together and they were pushed together at every turn. Coop didn't mind following his parents' directives back then. As long as they let him be friends with us and do what he wanted in college, he let them believe he was their little puppet."

"I can't imagine Coop following anyone's rules."

Seth chuckles. "His parents didn't care if Coop was playacting as long as he toed the line. So the only way to Coop Elizabeth had was through one of us. It should have made me suspicious that she had a class with each of us."

"Diabolical." The arranging that must have taken her.

He smiles softly and cups my cheek. "I fell for her trap hook, line, and sinker. Mom had died the summer before after a long battle with cancer. The guys helped me through it, but I was unmoored. Elizabeth was nice and sweet. I thought I'd found someone I could really have a life with."

"I'm sorry she played you, Seth." I want to tear her apart for taking advantage of him.

"She used me to get to Coop. One night, Leighton was gone and Elizabeth snuck out of my room and into Coop's. I woke to find her out of bed and went to look for her. I heard her begging him to fuck her."

His fingers on my hip clench down. I kiss his chest, wishing I could take away that pain.

"We kicked her out that night. After that, Leighton insisted Coop choose between us and her. It was a fucking mess. The next year, Noah's girlfriend told Noah he had to choose either us or her. Every time a girl tried to come between us, we dropped her."

"That's when you decided to share?" I draw a circle on his chest. The guys really are tight-knit. Some woman before me should have recognized that my guys are family. They could have had wives who understood their relationship and flourished in it. But I'm glad they didn't. Because they're mine.

"A woman couldn't come between us if we were all fucking her. I wasn't about to let my heart get drawn in again, so I was good with the arrangements." Seth's chest rises and falls. "We didn't continue with it after college. College seemed like a good place to experiment. After, we had enough to do to keep our business afloat at first.

"We found it difficult to maintain anything but business. We created this floor to make it easier on us and figured we could have our assistant live with us for exactly the reasons we first told you. We were working crazy hours. When Andrea came on, she reminded us of our college days and how easy it had been to share a woman. Andrea fucked us all over, but Blake was the one who had brought it up to us as an option. He feels responsible for her and her blackmail because he invited her in."

My heart squeezes. Blake has always been more closed off with me. Especially at the beginning.

"That's his story to tell." His thumb brushes my lower lip and my attention returns to him. "After Andrea, we didn't think we'd try it again."

"But then Rachel kissed you."

He nods. "I didn't want a woman to come between us again, so I sold the guys on the idea of sharing her."

"She didn't like that idea." The venom in her voice in the bathroom still rings in my ears. "Thankfully."

He chuckles and smiles. "I didn't think I'd be grateful to those women who came before, but they all led to you. I thought for sure you'd tell me to fuck off when I gave you our offer."

My heart beats a little faster. "I didn't know how I was going to get through the days without trying to fuck any or all of you. Pretty sure that would have been unprofessional."

"If there's one thing you aren't, princess, it's unprofessional. You would have worked with us just like you do now, but we would have all taken a lot of cold showers."

I rest my cheek against his beating heart, letting it lull me. "I don't want any secrets between us."

"No more secrets. Open and honest, but we also need to get to know each other better. Outside of sex."

I glance up at him and he winks.

"And work," I add. "We've done this all backward. Sex and love, but I don't know much about any of you outside of the women you guys have shared. I know that you all grew up together."

"I'm more than willing to divulge some of their secrets."

I move up so our heads are on the same pillow, face-to-face. "Spill."

Chapter 145

Deliverable

Coop

I pace my office, waiting for Theo to come in. He sent a text in the middle of the night saying he thought he had a lead on the corporate spy.

My mind is spinning with all the things. Today is our honey trap lunch. Our chance to catch the spy in a legitimate trap. What Theo found might just point us in the correct direction, even if it won't hold up in court.

I'm also waiting for the stalker to step up his game. He doesn't like me. He's made that obvious. It won't be long before he attacks me, but *how* is the problem. He hasn't gotten physical with Madison except to scare her.

But he wants her for some sick game, not to hurt her.

I'm in his way. He might have killed Valerie for getting in his way. If he wants a fight, he should consider me a worthy adversary.

A knock echoes through my office.

"Come in." I straighten my suit.

"Theo called to ask for an escort up." Madison stands in my doorframe. Her blond hair falls in soft waves around her shoulders. The dress she has on is a wrap dress, making my fingers itch to grab hold of the tie and unwrap her.

"You can bring him up." I focus on her red lipstick. Next time we play, I want her to wear that lipstick and smear it all over my cock.

"Be right back." She turns on her heels and leaves.

Fuck, she distracts me. She distracts all of us in the best possible way. She won't work as our assistant forever. At some point we'll have taken her as far as she can go in our business and she'll go off to a new adventure, but we'll still be with her. Madison is ours, and I'll do what it takes to keep her bound to us.

My phone buzzes.

MOTHER:

Saw the announcement. You need to call home. Your father and I need to talk to you.

Announcement? I turn to my computer and do a quick search on my name. My eyes widen as I read the article. My hand clenches tighter with each word. What the actual fuck?

"Theo to see you." Madison's voice penetrates my brain fog.

"Tell him to wait and come here." I don't take my attention off the announcement that I didn't send in. My phone rings. It's my publicist. Fuck.

Madison returns.

"Close the door." I hit Speaker on my phone. "I'm looking at it now, Grant. Tell me you didn't post this."

Madison comes around the desk to see what I'm looking at.

"No. We didn't even get notice before it was posted." Grant sounds harried. I'm sure my mom's already been on his case.

"What is this?" Madison's fingers cover her lips as she squints at the screen.

"Have it taken down, Grant. I'll call you in a few minutes." I disconnect the call and draw Madison down on my lap, needing her close.

"'Known Man Whore Cooper Graham Takes a Naive Farm Girl for His Bride'?" Madison shakes her head. "What is this?"

"We don't know." I rub my forehead and sigh. This is the last thing we need. "It must have just shown up because my mother and my publicist just contacted me."

Madison turns to look in my eyes. "Any idea who could have done this?"

I stroke my hand down her back. Her being close helps calm me down. "A spurned ex? Leighton comes to mind. Elizabitch? Your stalker? Some other jealous woman? Who knows?"

Madison's lips press into a fine line as she turns to read the rest of the article. "Do you really think it could be the stalker?"

The tremor in her voice makes me pause. The stalker is getting to her. She can't live her life in fear of his next move. I take a deep breath. "I don't know, sweetheart, but we'll find out. It's only on one site so far. My publicist should be able to get it taken down before it spreads."

She draws in a breath and lets it out slowly. I can almost feel her putting her shield back up.

"Should I go get Theo?"

I wrap my arms around her and hold her to me, breathing in her floral scent for a moment. I almost wish the stalker would come at me. Then I could fight back. That's the most frustrating part of this. He decides when to strike. He decides how to terrorize her. We have no way to protect her besides putting her in a tower. Which isn't fair to her.

When I release her, I help her to her feet. "Yes. Get Theo."

She turns and her blue eyes lock on mine. "I'm sorry—"

"This isn't on you, sweetheart. I'm just surprised it took someone this long to post something." I give her my best cocky smile to hide the anger simmering below the surface. "What can I say? Women love me. It's probably someone bitter that I didn't choose them. Don't think any more about it, sweetheart."

She gives me that soft smile that punches me right in the heart before going to get Theo.

My smile slips as soon as she leaves the room. I capture the article with a screenshot because Grant will get it taken down. That's why our family uses his firm. I attach it in an email to Seth, Blake, and Noah.

Just had this brought to my attention. An "engagement announcement" posted early this morning. Publicist is working to take it down. Madison is aware. Either some ex or stalker. Given the timing, I'm leaning toward the stalker.

The door opens, and I smile at Madison as Theo walks in with his computer bag over his shoulder. His usually crisp shirt is a little wrinkled and there are bags under his brown eyes. Madison closes the door.

"You okay?" I can't help but ask.

"Just a late night." Theo cracks a crooked smile. "I get a little obsessed when I catch a trail."

"Coffee?"

"That would be great." He pulls out his laptop while I message Madison to bring him coffee.

"You found something then?" Right now, I feel like we're on the losing team and I need a win. Something that will get us ahead in this war.

"The caller sounded male. He used a burner cell phone, bought with cash. But I traced the call to this apartment building. It has too many apartments for me to narrow it down." Theo hands over a paper with *641 Oakland Dr, Brooklyn* written on it. "Figured you might find out if an employee lives there."

The tightness in my chest eases. It's definitely a step in the right direction. "We'll cross reference. You did an amazing job, Theo."

"Thanks. That means a lot coming from you." He grins.

Madison comes in with two coffee cups and hands one to me and the other to Theo. "Do you need anything else?"

I shake my head. As she turns and walks away, I enjoy the view.

When I shift my attention to Theo, I notice he's enjoying the view too. When he turns back, his cheeks darken at my raised eyebrow.

"She's a gorgeous woman. You're a lucky man." Theo's words calm the jealous beat of my heart. He's right. She's gorgeous and she's mine.

"Thanks. I am lucky." I take a sip of my coffee. "Are you ready for today?"

"The dummy number is set up to come to my office. I'll be ready when they call again." Theo is key to the honey trap. With Cliodhna, we were off-the-books, but this time we have everything lined up to take the spy down legally.

"Patrick will be here all next week. As soon as you have something, notify us immediately."

"Will do." Theo takes a drink.

Patrick is also key as our lawyer, but I'm not sure how much I trust him right now.

Madison

"You're riding in our car, tiger."

Little sparks float through me at the roughness of Blake's voice. It's time for lunch with Coop's honey trap. It has to look like a legit lunch with a client. I gather my purse from my desk. Wait. I open the drawer again. I could have sworn I had a sweater in this drawer. Now it's empty.

Setting my purse on my desk, I open all my drawers. Maybe I just forgot which drawer I put it in, or maybe I wore it back to the apartment. I didn't think I was in that much of a daze. But after yesterday with the stalker and today with that weird announcement, I'm just off.

"You lose something?" Blake asks.

I blow out my breath and close the last drawer. "Maybe. I don't know anymore."

I'm so fucking tired of this cat and mouse game. I'm not sure if it's even possible to win. But losing means coming face-to-face with the stalker. I don't want that to happen either.

"We'll get through this."

My gaze lifts to his green eyes. It hurts to stand here and not step into his arms. To feel him holding me, protecting me. Every instinct tells me to just let it go and be with him, but this could blow up if we don't deal with his trust issues. A Band-Aid won't fix this.

"Have you heard anything from the police about the phone Valerie had?" I grab my purse and head to the elevator with Blake. Noah and Coop step out of their offices. Their voices are low as they speak to each other.

"No." Blake rakes a hand through his dark hair. "It's in the queue but it's not high priority. I'm sure they'll get to it soon."

He presses the button for the elevator and the others join us. I glance back at Seth's closed door.

"Is Seth coming?" I ask.

"He said he'd meet us at the restaurant. Call came in last minute." Blake rubs the back of his neck.

"Oh." Well, fuck. That means Blake and I will be alone in the car. A little nervous trill hums through me.

The elevator doors open and Blake waits for me to step on. Noah and Coop follow him.

"Did the announcement get taken down?" I need to focus on something, not Blake.

Coop nods. "Grant is looking into who posted it."

"It's not like you have a long list of women who might want to get back at you." Noah strokes his finger over his lips to hide his smile.

"It seems a little lowbrow for Leighton." Blake leans back against the wall of the elevator car. "I bet your mother loved that article though."

"I had to hear about it for an hour. Both her and my father." Coop rubs his temple. Does he have a headache? I take a step toward him.

"Pretty sure we're just going to have to pop out grandkids as quickly as possible, sweetheart, to appease them."

Excuse me? My mouth drops open. He gives me a wicked look. Oh, hell no. My mouth snaps shut and I cross my arms.

"I'm only twenty-two. There will be no popping out anything for a long time." I arch an eyebrow at him. I'm not a breeding factory.

Coop closes in on me, towering over me as I retreat until my back presses against the elevator wall. His hands go to either side of my head as he lowers his face to mine.

"Admit it, my little whore. You like the idea of me fucking you and filling you with my cum to make a baby."

My body softens under his heat as desire curls inside me.

The elevator comes to a stop. My passion-addled brain catches on to his words. I narrow my eyes and put my hands on his chest to push him back. He chuckles as he lets me move him away.

"No babies." I turn and walk into the garage.

"You know, one would probably soften the old bat," Coop calls after me. "Just think about it."

I shake my head as Tim holds the door open for me.

"Thank you." I slide into the seat, and Blake walks around to the other side to sit in the back with me.

I don't know what to say as the car rolls out of the garage. This isn't even a legit business meeting, but we're taking the "client" to lunch at our normal spot, hoping the corporate spy will contact them.

"I don't know what I can do to fix this, Madison."

My heart stops as I lift my gaze to meet Blake's green eyes. This is causing him emotional pain too. I wish it were as easy as a trip to my apartment, but his ghosts have a stranglehold on him. I don't know if we can get them to release him.

"I don't trust anyone but the guys. Because they've been there with me through it all. Whenever I've let someone in, they ended up hurting me—or worse, hurting Seth, Coop, or Noah."

"I don't know either," I admit, clasping my hands in my lap. This is the crux of our situation. How do I make him trust me without time? How does he get over hang-ups I didn't cause? "I would never intentionally hurt any of you, Blake. I would never betray you. Not without a damn good reason. You have to know that."

"I've always had to be the strong one. The one that protected the others. The one who stepped in and fought when the others didn't have the strength." He shuts his eyes, shutting me out. Coldness flows through me.

Is he too broken to get past this? Will he never trust me?

His eyes open and the warmth returns. "I love you, Madison. I'm trying to trust you. I'm trying to leave the past in the past. On some level, I do trust you, but then the doubts creep in. I don't know how to fight off those doubts."

Pain lingers in his eyes. I hold my hand out to him and he takes it in his. I can give him this connection. Because it still pulses like a live wire between us. I have to fix this.

"We're broken but not shattered, Blake. I love you so fucking much, and I miss you, but I can't settle for someone who doesn't trust me fully." I blow out a breath and squeeze his hand. "We'll find a way through this. We have to. Because without you, I'm not whole."

Chapter 146

The Honey Trap

Seth

The others are already heading out to lunch while my phone tries to connect to the number in the file. Coop filled us in about the apartment building and the announcement. If Coop had put the announcement in, Blake's jealousy would have gone through the roof, especially since he can't claim Madison right now. As it stands, it's one more thing to worry about.

We're healing, me and her. But it's still going to take time to rebuild the trust we lost. If I could help her and Blake get through this, I would.

"Glenco Apartment Management, how may I direct your call?"

"May I speak to your manager please?" I tap my pen on my desk. One more rabbit hole to go down. Hopefully this one won't be a dead end.

"Yes, sir. May I say who's calling?"

"Seth Hart from Morrigan Technology Group."

"Thank you. Please hold." The hold music comes on.

This day is odd. It's Friday, but we won't have our normal Friday meeting in the conference room because it's bugged. We can't discuss anything proprietary.

Patrick has been working here too. He's supposed to leave early this afternoon, though, which means we'll still meet, but there won't be anyone fucking Madison in the conference room anytime soon.

Even if we could have our normal meeting, it wouldn't be the same. Blake and Madison are still on the outs, and Madison and I just started to fix us. Maybe we'll skip it this week and do a recap at dinner. Though we have to behave normally so they don't realize we know about the second bug. Fuck, this is complicated.

"This is Parker Anderson." Her voice is low and commanding.

"I'm Seth Hart, CEO of Morrigan Technology Group. I just wanted to confirm that our employee still lives there." My pen taps against the desk.

"Name?"

"Peter Martin." One more piece to the puzzle. But not the only piece, we're positive. He doesn't have the access the spy needs.

"Yes, sir. This is still his address."

"Thank you." I disconnect the call and grab my suit jacket. I'm only a little late to lunch. Peter was on a lot of the development teams we sent out. There's also the weekend he tried to get in because he forgot something at his desk. Blake mentioned he seemed enamored with Courtney, which makes sense, because otherwise what would his motive be?

Courtney has motive. We've skipped her resume every time for our assistant. Her friendship with Andrea made us all wary. She may be qualified for the assistant position, but we definitely wouldn't feel comfortable letting her into our lives and never would have offered her the other arrangement.

When I close the door to my office, something moves in the corner of my eye. Patrick stops as he comes out of the break room.

"I thought you were all gone to lunch." He moves forward, heading to the elevator.

And I thought he'd already left. "Had a phone call to make. You heading out for the day?"

"Got to get back to the office." He presses the button and glances back at me. "How's everything going? I mean, besides the espionage and your assistant's stalker."

The elevator doors open and we both step on. He presses the ground level, and I press the garage button.

"Business is good. We've brought on a few new clients, despite the spy's attempts." I lean back against the wall and study him.

Patrick is a good-looking man. A little older than us. Settled, with a wife and kids. He flies under the radar. One of those guys that blends into the background. He's been our lawyer from the beginning. An up-and-coming star in his firm.

"That's good. It surprised me your assistant took the offer we drew up." Patrick holds his laptop bag in front of him with both hands on the handle. He seems like he's just making conversation. But could it be something more?

"She's an amazing assistant. We couldn't have found a more perfect fit for us."

His face remains placid as a lake. "Good. I know you've had issues in the past. I'm glad you've found someone who fits you."

Was there extra inflection on *fits* or am I imagining it?

His phone buzzes and he glances down at it. "Fuck."

"Is there a problem?" I ask. I don't think I've ever heard Patrick curse.

He sighs. "I've been getting these texts since the benefit. It's really ramped up since I've been here this week though."

"What kind of texts?"

He shakes his head and hands me his phone.

UNKNOWN:

Don't even look at the girl if you don't want me to come after yours.

That's the latest one. But there are about a half dozen other warnings like it.

"Did you show these to the police?" I ask.

Patrick nods and takes his phone back. "I'm sure it's just because I'm here every day. Is your assistant still receiving them?"

I sigh. "Yeah. She's ready for this to be over."

Patrick nods. "Understandable. Hopefully the police find the guy."

The elevator stops on the ground floor.

"Have a good weekend." Patrick steps off.

"You too." The doors close. There's something off about Patrick. I've never noticed it before, since most of our conversations are business related, but he doesn't really engage in small talk or nonbusiness conversations. Maybe he's just an introvert or neurodivergent.

I don't like that we left him alone in the office. But he's our lawyer so it shouldn't be an issue. He's been with us for years. But he's also known Madison for years. All these problems have me stressed and looking at all the relationships in our lives differently.

I'll bring it up to the others though. Especially since he's receiving texts too. Right now, we have no leads on the stalker, so maybe looking through everyone again would be a good idea.

Tim brought the car back to pick me up, and we immediately head to the restaurant. I walk into the dining room. We have a room in the back. The honey trap, as Coop keeps calling it, is a medium-sized, venture-capitalist-funded corporation called Astrum.

The main thing is to behave like this isn't all a setup because we don't know how our spy is getting their information. For all we know, it could be a server at this restaurant that informs the spy.

I texted with Sebastian Cross on the car ride over to dig up everything he can on Peter Martin. We need to know our enemy. Where are his weaknesses? Is that how he got involved in this?

I enter the room with a smile and shake hands with Andrew Faust.

"Great to finally meet you." Andrew shakes my hand vigorously.

He glances over to Madison. "Join us. Your team was just telling me all about Morrigan Technology Group."

Who is this guy? I lift an eyebrow at Blake, who shrugs. I sit in the chair next to Madison and explain how this entire process works to Andrew.

Madison's knee bounces under the table as Andrew glances her way once again. I rest my hand on her thigh and she stills beneath my touch. Her hand covers mine and I turn mine over to lace our fingers together. I'm not sure what has her nervous.

Lunch winds down and Andrew leans back in his chair, studying Madison. She keeps her gaze on her napkin in her lap. Something's not right here.

"Do you know our assistant?" I finally ask.

"Sure, Madison and I went to school together." His grin says they did more than just get an education together.

Madison rises from her chair. "Please excuse me."

She vanishes into the restaurant. Blake rises and doesn't give an excuse as he follows. I'm glad he's going after her. It's still not safe for her to be alone.

I smile at Andrew and fold my napkin, setting it beside my plate. "The last client that made our assistant uncomfortable we walked away from."

He shakes his head and looks at Noah, Coop, and me. "I don't mean any offense. It's just been a while since I last saw her. She's always been beautiful."

"Yes, *my fiancée* is beautiful. How do you know Patrick?" Coop leans forward intently, which stretches his shirt against his muscles. He practically cracks his knuckles.

Patrick is the one who suggested Andrew.

"My family and his are friends. We've gotten drunk at a few cookouts together." Andrew swallows. "I wasn't aware Madison would be at this meeting. So seeing her again was startling. I didn't mean to be offensive."

This could just be a coincidence. Patrick setting us up with someone who might have slept with Madison. It could be a coincidence . . . But there are a lot of coincidences lately with Patrick that are starting to add up. I'm going to need Cross to do a deep dive into Patrick too.

Maybe he doesn't fit the profile for the stalker, but he's definitely been present a lot more recently. Maybe he's as much a victim as we are in this. Maybe he didn't realize Andrew *knew* Madison. Maybe.

Madison

Fuck my life. I wash my hands in the sink, trying to waste time so I don't have to return to the table and sit across from Andrew Faust while he smirks at me. We fucked one time after a particularly hard final. I needed to blow off steam, and he was there.

That whole semester he tried to get into my pants. He always was an arrogant prick, and the sex was not worth it.

I'm so glad I'm done fucking random college guys. My guys at least make sure the deed is done right.

Drying my hands, I take in a deep breath. The bathroom door opens and Anna Beck steps inside. She startles slightly when she sees me.

"Madison, what are you doing here?"

"I'm at a business lunch." I should just leave. Lunch was so awkward with her. I don't want to end up with another invite.

"Is Patrick here with you?" She closes the distance between us.

My brow furrows. Why would Patrick be here? "No. We're at a client meeting."

"Oh, good." She looks relieved. Maybe she's seeing someone on the side and doesn't want to run into her husband. That would make sense. Is that what all married people do? Sleep around with other people? Or is that just Patrick and Anna's marriage?

"I should get back to my party." I move toward the door.

"Are you and Coop still together?" She doesn't appear tense, just seems to be making conversation.

"Yes." I hold up my left hand with the ring on it. "Still engaged and everything."

She smiles. "Good. You should hold on tight to that one. You never know when someone will try to steal your man out from under you."

Okay and now it's weird again. "It was good seeing you. I need to return . . ."

She waves me off and heads to the stalls. "I'm sure we'll run into each other again. Take care, Madison."

I exit the bathroom and Blake leans against the wall nearby. My heart slows down and the tension in my shoulders eases. Safety. He still protects me, and I still trust him to keep me safe.

"Everything okay?" he asks.

No. "Yes." Pretty sure Anna needs new meds, because whatever she's currently on makes my head spin.

"Do you want to go back to the lunch? Or would you prefer to go out to the car?"

I give him a questioning look.

"You looked uncomfortable in there. I assume Andrew is someone you know. We don't have to go back if you don't want to." Blake's green eyes never leave mine. Maybe there's a little jealousy there, but he's not letting it control him. Though I usually like the results of his jealous tendencies.

"I think I can handle it." I give him a smile and move to walk with him. With these guys beside me, I'm pretty sure I can handle anything. Even slightly crazy ex-employers and leering ex-lovers.

We walk into our room, and Andrew doesn't look at me this time. Coop looks cocky about something. Blake holds out my chair and I lower into it.

"We'll have more information sent to your email. Is there a time that would work for you for our development team to come out and access your current systems?" Seth appears to be all business, but his hand reaches for mine.

I slide my hand into his and he squeezes it. When I turn to look at Coop, he winks. I'm not sure what went down while I was in the bathroom, but Andrew is now purposely not looking my way. I take in a relieved breath.

"We can get started right away. Our conference room is yours when you need it." Andrew smiles and looks at everyone, but his eyes skip right over me. I've never been so happy to be ignored.

"It's been a pleasure getting to know you, Andrew." Seth shakes his hand. The server brings in the receipt and Noah signs it before passing it back to her. The guys all stand.

Blake pulls out my chair and offers me his hand. I glance into his eyes before taking it. He draws me into his side and maneuvers us around Noah and Coop as they shake Andrew's hand.

Seth joins us as we move through the dining room. My eyes catch Anna's auburn hair. There are two other women at the table with her. They both turn to look at Seth and Blake escorting me. They look somewhat familiar, like I've seen them before, maybe at the benefit, but not met them.

Seth holds open the door for me, and Blake's hand settles on my lower back to guide me out to the car. My breath catches at his nearness. The way Blake handles me during sex is unlike the others, and I long for that. His quiet control. His looming presence.

I sigh as I move to the middle of the back seat. Sex won't solve anything between us, but fuck, would it feel good. The guys join me and Tim rolls away from the curb.

"Princess, did you fuck Andrew Faust?" Seth runs a hand over his blond hair as his blue eyes lock on me.

"Once in college." No need to deny it. The guy had been mentally undressing me the first half of lunch. "Not my finest hour."

Blake grunts, but he doesn't look pissed off like he did in Taylor's offices. Maybe he trusts that what I had with those guys is in the past.

It's a move in the right direction. Blake, Seth, Noah, and Coop are my future.

"Did you guys say something to him?" I turn back to Seth. His lips tip into a smug smile.

"Coop let the guy know he's your fiancé." Seth's eyes go to Blake and his smile grows.

"Whatever you did, thank you." I lean back against the seat and close my eyes. "I ran into Anna Beck in the bathroom."

"What did she say?"

I open my eyes and meet Seth's. Interest flares in his.

"She asked if Patrick was with us and if Coop and I were still engaged." I shrug. "Most of the time I'm not sure what's going to come out of her mouth. For a minute, I thought she might be out on a date because she seemed so tense that Patrick was with us, but I saw her with two women when we left."

"How well do you know the Becks?" Seth's quiet intensity is intimidating.

"I watched their kids for a year. They had to give me rides to and from campus. Both of them were gone when I was with the children. The kids were adorable and I loved every minute of my time with them." I inhale and blow it out. "Honestly, I was a little shocked Anna approached me at the benefit. We weren't real friends. I was the hired help. She'd complain to me occasionally on the way back to my dorm. About work, the kids, Patrick, but overall, she seemed pretty happy with her life."

"What about when Patrick took you home?"

"He rarely did because he worked so late. But when he did, sometimes he'd give me a cookie or brownie or something that someone gave him at the office and he didn't want. I was a broke college student, so I took every sweet he gave me."

"Did he ever make a pass at you?"

I laugh before I look at Seth's completely straight face. "Oh, you're serious? No. The guy barely knew my name. Anna's the one that hired me. She paid me. She made sure I knew what they expected of me. Patrick was just along for the ride. She told me once he worked so hard to make partner early."

Seth rubs at his temples.

"Are you worried about Patrick?" I reach out and take one of his hands.

"Something just feels off." Seth's fingers tighten around mine.

"He's been there since the beginning." Blake draws my attention. "It lines up a little too neatly. Jeff said the guy told Val he wouldn't need her because he had a new way to access you when you started working for us. Patrick happens to be headed for a tryst in the museum when he stumbles on you and Jimi Alan. He was there the day you received the dress."

A chill races down my spine. "But he barely says anything to me. He dismisses me like I don't matter."

It doesn't make sense. No matter which way I turn it over in my head. He's not interested in me like that. He can't be. He's married with two kids. My stalker is this creepy guy who hides in the shadows and makes deals with my druggie roommate to take pictures of me.

He stalked me in the file room and sent me a video of me masturbating.

"No." I shake my head. "It doesn't make sense. Why? Why would he harass me like that?"

"I don't know, princess." Seth wraps his arm around me. "Maybe it's not him. He is receiving threats about you since he helped you and started working at our office. But there's still something off about him."

I think back to the interactions I've had with him, and everything in me says he's not the stalker. But in my mind, the stalker is this omniscient being that looms over every aspect of my life, not a real person.

"We need to remain vigilant," Blake says. "It's always possible that the person we least suspect is your stalker."

A shiver runs through me again as I lean into Seth's warmth. I reach out my hand and Blake takes it, threading his fingers through mine. I need all of my guys. We need to be together on this.

Chapter 147

An Amenable Deal

Madison

I set the table while Blake finishes dinner. He keeps drawing my gaze. Do I honestly think there is one thing Blake can do that will make me believe he trusts me? Or is this just something that will resolve itself over time?

I'm so torn about what to do with him, but I know we need to be a unit to deal with this stalker.

Seth's theory in the car has me out of sorts. I just can't imagine Patrick being the stalker. There's too much disconnect between the guy I've met and the terror the stalker makes me feel. Patrick doesn't act like he wants me or is even remotely interested in me.

But then again, I can't really put a face to the stalker. No one I've met gives me the same feeling he creates. It kept my mind spinning all afternoon.

It was hard to focus on work. My thoughts kept straying to Blake and how he can sharpen my focus and bring me into the present. But it wouldn't be fair to him because I'm not ready to forgive him fully. I'm not ready to put all my trust in his hands.

Blake lifts his head and catches me looking at him. He gives me a half smile that makes my heart beat a little faster. I can't give him all of my trust, but maybe I can give him some of it.

"We have a lot to discuss tonight." Seth comes from his room, freshly showered after working out with Coop.

Our conference room isn't safe to have confidential discussions in anymore. Not since we left the other bug in place, waiting and hoping whoever planted it activates it so we can catch them.

Our Friday meeting in the conference room was just the normal, run-of-the-mill, here's what happened this week in the world of Morrigan Technology sort of meeting.

No stripping me naked. No sitting on Coop's cock while everyone discusses business. No fucking me on the conference table until my legs shake from coming so much.

It was still necessary to give each other the information, but it wasn't nearly as exciting or fulfilling.

Coop comes out of his bedroom with his dark, wet hair slicked back. When his gaze finds me, he grins and stalks across the room for me. My pulse races in anticipation as he closes in on me and lifts me off my feet.

"What are you doing?" The words escape me in surprise.

He carries me over to the couch and drops me onto the cushions before following me down and kissing me like we haven't kissed in days. I fall into the kiss, needing our connection and the distraction.

"Dinner's ready." Blake's voice penetrates the sensual fog Coop's lips and tongue weave around me.

I push on Coop's shoulder, and he lifts his mouth from mine. He grinds his hard cock against my pussy, making me suck in a breath. Fuck, I miss playing with all of them.

"Do you know how much I've been wanting to fuck you in this dress, goddess?" Coop's pupils are dilated, and I'm sure mine are the same.

"The same amount as you usually want to fuck me?" I arch an eyebrow. It's not like Coop holds back, but with Patrick in our office this week, he had to.

180

"Coop, we need to have a discussion before you go all caveman on Madison." Seth's tone tells me he's exasperated, but Coop has that effect.

Coop's eyebrows wiggle. "You want me to go all caveman tonight, my little whore? Use you until you pass out?"

I bite my lip as my panties grow even wetter.

He smiles knowingly and leans down to whisper in my ear. "I know what you like, my little whore. Cock filling every hole. We can make that happen. I can make that happen."

He draws away and holds out his hand to help me off the couch. Swallowing hard against the aching need to draw him back down on top of me, I accept his help and he lifts me up against him. His thumb brushes over the corner of my lips.

"Eat up, sweetheart. You're going to need your energy." He draws away and swats my ass.

Shaking my head, I walk back to the table and take my seat. My gaze catches on Blake's green eyes. He's hungry for more than the food before us.

My core tightens. Fuck, I don't want to leave him out tonight. If this is going to take time, we're going to have to put in the work to make it happen. That means I can't just ignore him until he does something that makes me change my mind.

I want him, but the trust needs to be there for us to play alone. Trust on both sides. But if it's all of us, we aren't doing a power exchange between him and me. It could help us work toward healing. His eyebrow arches like he's not sure what I'm thinking.

Can he tell it's not just food I'm hungry for either?

I blow out a breath and focus on Noah as he sits beside me.

He kisses me softly. "Good evening, kitten."

"Noah," I breathe out against his lips.

He brushes his nose against mine. Butterflies float drunkenly in my stomach. His dark eyes draw me in before he brushes a kiss against my lips. So soft and fleeting, it makes me crave more. So much more.

Seth takes his seat and clears his throat, capturing our attention. "Tomorrow night is all set up."

We fill our plates while he continues. Thinking about tomorrow helps cool me down. I don't know whether to be nervous or excited about Saturday night. Both Leighton and Elizabeth are powerful women. It will definitely be entertaining.

"We have a reservation in a private room at an exclusive restaurant thanks to Deidre Byrne. It thrilled her to have Theo's undivided attention all week and she wanted to send her gratitude. We needed the right restaurant and the type of room that would make everyone want to come and be seen."

Coop sits across from me. "I've invited Leighton and Drew."

"Sara is excited to join us. She can't wait for the fireworks," Noah says.

My gaze stops on Blake. Once again, he'll be the odd man out.

"Are you going to come?" I ask him.

Blake's eyes widen in surprise. "No, tiger, but I'll be close in case anything happens."

Excluding Blake leaves him on the outside. But for this particular night, it wouldn't make sense for him to be there unless he had a date.

Blake has refused to find dates before. I'd trust him to remain true to me if he brought a date, but me trusting him isn't the larger issue.

"If seeing Drew doesn't get Elizabeth to crack, we have a plan B." Seth nods to Coop.

"I'll get Elizabeth alone so she can confess her actual plan." Coop's light blue eyes meet mine. "I can be very persuasive. Can't I, goddess?"

Coop does have a track record of getting his way, especially with me. Heat flares inside me.

"This is important, princess. You can't leave the table alone." Seth breathes out. His dark blue eyes lock on mine and I can feel his seriousness down to the center of my being. "Sara will escort you to the bathroom if you need to go, but you don't leave without one of us."

I nod. I'm not foolish enough to believe I'm invincible. My stalker could be there. Even if I can't picture him, he's a normal man. Well, normal and rich. He has the means to do a lot of things. It's likely he's in the same circles as Coop. Which doesn't make sense because when would I have run into a guy with that kind of money?

We all eat a little, lost in our own thoughts. Seth straightens and clears his throat.

"We need to discuss Patrick again." Seth rubs his jaw. "We've left him alone in our offices on more than one occasion. He's supposed to know our business, but does he seem too invested in Madison at times? He received texts, but anyone can send texts."

Coop blows out a breath. "I've thought about it, but I've also spent time with him. He doesn't actively seek Madison out. If she comes into the room, he doesn't stop what he's doing. He doesn't even acknowledge her. But while we've known him for years, do any of us really know him? He's not really the kind of guy you ask to have a drink after work. He gets the job done and goes home to his wife and kids."

Exactly.

"I wouldn't rule him out though." Blake puts his fork down and looks around the table. "He's known Madison longer than he let on. He didn't mention she worked for him when he ran the background check."

When I open my mouth, Blake shakes his head. "I know he doesn't run the household, but as a father, he should know who's being let into his home and who takes care of his children."

Okay, that's fair.

"He has access to us here. He knows our business. He knows that the four of us are in a relationship with Madison."

"Wouldn't the stalker want that to stop?" Noah leans in. "If Patrick is the stalker, then why didn't he try to interfere with Madison being hired? He knew we'd offer her the deal. He knew we wanted to fuck her. If he wants her to himself, why would he allow that to happen?"

Everyone is quiet and contemplative for a moment. I just can't connect the faceless terror in my life with Patrick. Robert would be more likely than Patrick. But it's not Robert.

"Does Patrick even have that kind of money?" I ask. "Yes, he's a lawyer, but why would he waste resources on me when he has a house, a wife, and kids to take care of?"

"Anna." Coop taps his finger on the table. "Anna is a Whitley. If she'd been a few years younger, my parents would have approached hers about arranging a match. But Anna fell in love with her college sweetheart. Her parents are a love match, so they wouldn't consider arranging a marriage over love."

Well, fuck. That means he would have access to wealth. "But they both work."

Coop nods. "And they have a huge trust fund to fall back on if they ever can't work. They work by choice, not necessity. If he left Anna, he'd be leaving her money. The stalker also doesn't like the fact I'm fucking Madison. Patrick knew about our offer."

"True, but we shouldn't discount Patrick just yet." Seth rests his elbows on the table. "That means his access to her and our areas needs to be limited. We also need to consider everyone in our lives as a potential suspect."

I poke at my food, suddenly not very hungry. They have to deal with this stalker because of me. So far it's just me he's been after, but if he's going after Coop, that means he could go after all of them.

That announcement sounded really bitter.

"Did your publicist figure out who put in the announcement?"

Coop's blue eyes meet mine as he shakes his head. "It was done through their website using a generic web payment. Whoever did it was not my fan."

"We'll need to update Bill and check on where they are on the phone." Blake watches me. "Maybe this might be the escalation we need to push it to a higher priority."

"Can we not talk about the stalker or the spy any more tonight?" I set my fork down and meet their concerned eyes. "It's like my head is full from all this. We have to put a leash on Elizabeth tomorrow, hope the spy falls for the honey trap, and wait for the stalker to mess up and reveal themselves."

Noah takes my hand on the table and it helps center me. There's one issue I can deal with tonight though.

I settle on Blake's green eyes. "We need to have a talk."

He straightens. "Okay."

"This isn't just about you and me. We're stronger together, and that means I need to know that you'll try to trust me." I squeeze Noah's hand, probably harder than I should, but if Blake can't try, we're irrevocably damaged. I don't know what that means for all of us, because I can't just wall off part of my heart.

"I can trust you, love. I know it on so many levels, but there's this nagging fear."

"So let's work on it together." I release my grip on Noah's hand. "We can spend time talking about everything. Our pasts. But I know my future includes you in it, so we need to work through this."

"I'm all in, Madison." Blake's gaze never falters.

"I can't play with you alone until we get our trust back." I swallow at his wince. "But that doesn't mean we can't play all together."

It's a concession I need to make because if I keep excluding him, it will only form a wedge between us. I don't want it to be us against him. I don't want him to be left out.

Blake's shoulders visibly relax.

"When I submit to you, I give you all my trust. If you aren't putting all your trust in me, I can't give you that." Tears press at the back of my eyes, but I swallow them down. "But I can put my trust in all of you to take care of me."

Blake nods and looks thoughtful as we all resume eating silently.

"We'll all sleep in my room tonight." I glance at Blake in time to see the smile tug at his lips. He has trouble sleeping when he needs to protect me and I'm not in his bed.

I glance at Seth. I love when he takes control, but we're still healing and need time.

"Noah can decide how tonight goes." I meet Seth's blue eyes, and he gives me a nod of approval. Some of the tension unwinds within me.

"As your fiancé, I should be the one directing how everyone takes you." Coop's heated gaze takes in every inch of me, making my breasts grow heavy and panties damp.

Noah laughs. "But she knows she can dominate you any time she wants."

My gaze collides with Blake's. He gives me a half smile and some part of me settles. This will be good for all of us.

Chapter 148

Compounding Interest

The dishes are done and we've tidied up the kitchen. Now we sit in the living room, waiting for Noah's plan. We could just fuck, but it feels like we need something to bring us back together.

While I enjoy being used and submitting, I want more than that tonight. Coop sits next to me on the couch with his fingers skating up and down the inside of my thigh. My skin buzzes with anticipation, and every stroke sets electricity zinging through my blood. Blake sits on the other couch, drinking a scotch. His heavy gaze never leaves me.

Seth walks over and sits on my other side, taking my hand. He weaves our fingers together, and I lean my head against his shoulder, grateful that we've reconciled. It's been about fifteen minutes since Noah disappeared into the play room.

"You know . . ." Coop slides his hand higher up my thigh beneath my skirt. "You don't want to ruin this pretty dress with whatever Noah is planning."

I bite my lip as his fingers graze my panties. I'm beyond ready to play with my guys.

"Stand, princess." Seth's commanding tone sends shivers down my back. I've missed this.

When I stand, I glance over my shoulder at Blake. He raises his glass to me before he takes a sip. He's willing to take a back seat on this because he thinks that's what I need. I hold my hand out to him. I need him to be part of us. We can sort through the mess later. He walks over to me and sets his drink down.

My front faces Seth and Coop on the couch, while Blake stands beside my arm. Blake reaches out and takes my chin, tipping my face up and toward him. Anticipation cascades through me like sparks raining down. For a second, we just search each other's eyes.

He lowers his mouth to mine, giving me plenty of time to say no or pull away, but I don't. Fuck, I want his kiss so badly. His lips touch mine briefly and heat rushes through me like a wildfire. Untamable and hungry.

Seth reaches out for the tie holding my dress closed and pulls. It slips free of the knot and falls open, revealing my pink satin bra and the edge of my pink panties. Coop slides my dress the rest of the way open to reach the tie on the inside. His fingers brush my overheated skin, igniting sparks. Blake's lips keep brushing over mine, a tease of a kiss.

The other knot releases, and Coop stands up next to me. As one, Blake and Coop draw my dress off my shoulders to slide down my arms like a gentle caress. Coop drapes it over the ottoman. Blake's lips never leave mine as he reaches behind me and undoes my bra.

They remove that too, leaving me standing between them in only my panties. My breath rushes in and out of my lungs in time with my pulse. Anticipation flutters through my veins.

"Much better, goddess." Coop tips my chin his way and slides his lips across mine. Blake brushes my hair over my shoulder and shivers race through me. He kisses my shoulder softly, then presses kisses along my arm. Everything within me hums, recognizing the pleasure these men can give me and knowing they'll take care of me.

Seth's fingers hook into the sides of my panties. My breath

catches, waiting. Blake turns my lips back to him as Seth lowers my panties. When Seth's lips graze above my pubic bone, I whimper at the aching need rising inside. Their lips are gentle as Blake brushes his lips across mine and Coop kisses my shoulder.

It's the sweetest torture. These soft brushes of their lips as I stand naked before them. When I try to reach out for them, needing to touch them, Blake and Coop take my hands, threading their fingers through mine and holding my arms out to the side.

Seth kisses lower and lower. Blake and Coop trail their kisses down my neck and over my clavicle before grazing the tops of my breasts. Everything moves so slowly, making me ache. I'm a mess of need and want.

When Seth lifts my leg over his shoulder, I'm ready for what's next. I want them to devour me, not just toy with my skin. Seth's lips tease around my pussy, kissing me softly everywhere but where I need him most.

The others finally reach my hardened nipples and kiss all around them. I'll die if they don't take me. My breasts ache.

I whimper in frustration.

"What's wrong, kitten?" Noah stands behind Seth. My eyes lock on his dark ones.

As one, the guys change from using their lips to using their tongues, licking my nipples. Seth's tongue slides through my folds. My skin feels like it's shimmering beneath their touch.

Each stroke winds me up, edging me closer and closer to free fall.

"Do you want to come, kitten?"

"Yes, please," I whisper, hanging on by a thread.

"We love it when you beg."

Blake and Coop take my nipples into their mouths and suck, while Seth sucks on my clit. Seth slides two fingers into my dripping wet pussy and I explode, crying out as they draw out my orgasm. Electricity flows over my skin, making me sensitive to even the air in the room.

Coop releases my breast and tips my chin toward him. I open my eyes and his light blue eyes search mine for a hot moment before his lips crash down, claiming me.

"Beautiful, goddess," he whispers, bringing my hand up to kiss my knuckles.

Blake turns my chin his way and takes my mouth in a kiss so heavy with desire that my pussy pulses around Seth's fingers as he draws them out. Seth kisses my hip, but I'm caught up in this need between Blake and me.

Want and need circle within me. I've missed his touch. The feel of his body against mine.

I turn my body into his. His clothes brush my skin. I drown in his spicy cologne.

"Take out his cock, kitten."

Blake moans into my mouth as my hands go to his waist, making quick work of his belt and pants before reaching in and freeing his cock. I can't help stroking it with my hand as he deepens our kiss, sliding his tongue along mine. I'm wet for him, aching to feel him inside.

"Take him, kitten. He's yours."

Fuck yes, I want that. I want him. When I give a little jump, Blake catches me and lifts me. My legs wrap around his waist as I guide his cock to my entrance.

He breaks the kiss. "You don't have to, tiger."

Holding his gaze, I take him inside me. Deep, so fucking deep. And the stretch, fuck have I missed him. Cupping his face, I sink into his green eyes. "I need you."

Stepping up behind me, Coop holds my hips, kissing my shoulders and the nape of my neck. He helps me move my hips up and down on Blake's cock, letting me take what I need from the man I love.

Our eyes remain locked and I see the love in his. The anguish at hurting me. The joy of rediscovering me. The need to make this right.

"We'll get there," I whisper before I bring his lips down on mine. He groans into my mouth, taking everything I have to give him. He takes over lifting me and fucking me until everything shatters into a thousand bursts of light as I come all around him. Groaning into my mouth, he releases deep inside my pussy.

Feeling his cock jerk inside me as he fills me makes an aftershock tremble through me.

When he breaks the kiss, I whisper, "I love you, Blake."

"No one else has made me feel what you do, Madison. I love you so much it terrifies me." He presses his forehead against mine and my love for him swells within.

I need this man, so fucking much.

"If we don't want him to fall, I've got to take you, goddess." Coop wraps his arms around me from behind. His bare skin touches my back and I tremble at how good it feels.

Blake's pants hang around his knees. He releases me and finishes taking off his pants and shirt.

Turning in Coop's arms, I wrap around him. My skin sparks at the warmth of his skin against it. While he carries me to the play room, my fingers toy with the ends of his hair.

"I like it when you wear your hair down." It's soft and silky between my fingers. I'm ready to play more.

"I like your hair down too." Coop smirks. "But tonight you might want to tie it back."

Coop puts me down on the bed and hands me a hair tie. Cuffs lie on the sheet toward the foot of the bed, anchored to the eyebolts on the sides of the bedframe, and a chain links the top cuffs to the headboard. Noah likes to tie me down. I'm not sure what his plan is tonight, but I usually like what he does to me. My thighs press together as need throbs between them.

I pull my hair back as Coop's gaze lowers to my breasts. Seth and Blake walk into the room naked and close the door behind them.

Sitting beside me, Coop cups my breast, teasing my already hardened nipple. I turn to watch his eyes as his other hand creeps up my thigh. Parting my legs, I lean back on my hands, giving him more access to do what he wants. With a cocky grin, he slides his fingers through my folds to push Blake's cum back inside me.

My breath quickens, the only sound in the quiet room besides the slide of Coop's fingers into my wet pussy.

Noah comes out of the bathroom naked with a wet washcloth and a bottle of lube. He scoops up a small stool as he makes his way over to the bed. Coop pulls his fingers out and brings them up to my lips, painting them with the mixture of Blake and me. I lick my lips and take Coop's fingers into my mouth.

Meeting Blake's darkened eyes, I moan at the taste of us as I lick Coop's fingers clean. Noah uses the washcloth to clean between my thighs before setting it aside.

"Feet up on the bed, kitten, but stay in that position." Noah puts the stool between my feet and sits down with his face between my legs. His breath is hot against my pussy. Heat floods my whole body as I wait for his touch.

I lift my feet onto the edge of the bed as Coop takes his fingers out of my mouth and slides them down my neck to my breast, circling my nipple. My lips part as I watch him tease me. He knows what I like.

Noah squirts lube onto his fingers and rubs it around my puckered hole.

Blake and Seth sit behind Noah, watching, waiting to be beckoned forward. Their eyes never leave me. I'm exposed and I love it. Coop's hair tickles my skin before his mouth closes over my nipple, sucking and tugging on it. Noah slips his fingers inside my ass and licks my pussy.

Fuck, I love when these two play with me. I'm already right on the edge again.

My head falls back between my arms as Coop sucks my breast and works my other nipple with his fingers while Noah licks my pussy, his fingers gently stretching my ass. Every touch burns into my skin and makes me need more. Just a little push to get over the edge.

My thighs tremble from holding myself in this position, but I don't move.

"She's beautiful." Seth's dark voice fills the room.

"Absolutely breathtaking," Blake says with a sense of awe in his voice.

"There's no one like her in this world."

"No one who fits us like she does."

Each word is another note in the musical being written with my body. Noah slides his other fingers into my pussy and thrusts in and out while he sucks on my clit. The fire burns hotter and hotter until I can't help but combust.

Coop pinches my nipple at the same time he bites gently on the other. My body arches as my release screams through me. Coop and Noah work me through my orgasm, making me cry out. It tightens like a bow before it releases.

"So fucking beautiful."

I tremble at the words as Noah eases out of me and Coop brings his mouth to my neck.

"She's a goddess," he whispers against my skin. I shudder as a ripple of desire strokes through me.

"Coop." Noah's tone makes Coop sit up.

"Nice."

I'm not sure what Coop is talking about, but I wasn't told to move, so I don't, knowing the other two have a perfect view of my pussy. Noah disappears and I hear the water run. I draw in a deep breath as anticipation tingles through my bloodstream.

Noah returns and picks up the stool to move it off to the side. "Coop, sit on the bed. Yes, on that side."

Coop sits down behind me on the other side of the bed and gives me a wink. I'm still propped up on my arms, waiting. Noah steps between my legs again. His cock presses flat against my clit and he holds his hands out.

"Take my hands, kitten."

As I take them, my still-sensitive pussy slides against his cock.

Fuck, that feels good. When I gasp, he smirks. I want more friction. I want to feel him buried inside me.

"Not yet. I'll make sure you're taken care of, kitten. You think you can be patient?"

Fuck, I can be patient this time. His dark eyes search mine with a tender smile on his lips.

"Yes."

"Good." He steps back and I almost whimper in disappointment, but I keep it to myself. "Stand."

My legs tremble like a newborn foal as I stand before Noah. He holds my elbows to help stabilize me. Our eyes lock. My breasts rub against his chest as his warmth draws me.

"Don't worry. You won't have to do much work." Noah leads me around the bed to the side Coop sits on. With his legs spread, he strokes his lubed-up cock with one hand.

"Hold my arms, kitten, and back that ass up to Coop."

Back that ass? My eyes widen as I meet Noah's. "What?"

"I get to fuck your ass, sweetheart." His hands grip my hips and pull me back toward him.

Noah rolls his eyes. "Patience, my love. It'll take a moment for everyone to get into position."

Position? I'm not sure what Noah has in mind, but I know whatever it is, he'll make sure I enjoy it. I blow out a breath and reposition my arms so I'm clasping Noah's forearms. Coop draws my hips down, but then can only guide with one, as he uses the other to position the head of his cock against my asshole.

"Slowly, sweetheart. Take me into you, like the first time."

Coop holds my ass cheeks apart as Noah keeps me balanced. I ease back, almost feeling like I'm falling, but my eyes focus on Noah's. I relax and Coop's cock slides through the tight ring of muscle.

"You feel good, goddess. So fucking tight around my cock."

Slowly, I inch back, taking more and more of him inside me until

I bump against him. I breathe out and Coop wraps his arm around my waist. I'm sitting on his lap with his cock buried in my ass.

"Good girl," he whispers in my ear. Warmth floods my veins at his words. There are times I enjoy being his good little whore, but I'm pretty sure I like being his good girl more.

"I'm going to lie down now." Coop brings me back with him. It feels odd to lie motionless on him.

Noah grabs a cuff. "Your arm."

I hold out my arm, and he latches the cuff around my wrist. He kneels on the bed between my and Coop's legs. It shifts Coop's cock inside me and I bite my lip against the sensation.

"Your other arm." When he lifts the cuff from the bed, it pulls my other arm up. He slips the cuff around my wrist and my arms are tied up. "Good, kitten?"

I check the cuffs, but if I pull on one it pulls my other arm. "Green."

Coop thrusts his hips, making a moan escape me. It's different from having a butt plug, even the vibrating kind. His warmth surrounds me. When he shifts below me, every move makes his cock shift inside me, lighting up all kinds of nerve endings and making me so wet.

Noah leaves the bed and grabs one of the other cuffs. He wraps it around my ankle and tightens it down before picking up the other and doing the same. My head rests on Coop's chest as I'm splayed spread eagle over him.

"Seth. Blake." Noah gestures for them to come over.

When they stop beside Noah, I turn my head toward them. All three of their cocks are hard and dripping with precum. My pussy throbs and Coop thrusts into me. I gasp in a quick breath. His hands slide up my sides until he cups both my breasts, pushing them together.

"What do you think they'll do to you like this, goddess?" Coop's voice is a dark note in my ear. "How do you want to be fucked?"

I release a shuddering breath as arousal floods my body. "I want to have you all."

Chapter 149

Asset Stabilization

Madison

Noah's gaze lifts to mine. "I know what you want, kitten."

Our eyes hold as one of Coop's hands brush down my trembling stomach. His fingers slip between my parted legs, sliding over my clit. I suck in my breath as I writhe on his cock, needing more.

"Seth, fuck her sweet cunt." Noah gestures like it's an afterthought. "Blake, you'll take her mouth."

Just thinking about them taking me makes me wetter. Noah watches the other men step into place. Seth kneels between Coop's and my legs. When Coop moves his hand back up to tease my breast, Seth slides his fingers into my pussy and pulses them against my G-spot.

I arch into Coop's hands, sliding his cock deeper into me as I gush around Seth's fingers.

"So fucking responsive." Seth eases his fingers out and licks my juices from them. My breath shudders in and out of my lungs as I wait for them to claim me. To make me theirs again.

Seth presses his cock's head against my entrance and lifts my hips, sliding my ass up Coop's cock. He thrusts into my pussy and presses my hips down on Coop, making both Coop and I groan. Both of them are buried deep inside me.

I love the feeling of fullness and that aching need to come.

"Tiger." Blake's voice makes me open my eyes to him standing before me. "I've missed your lips around my cock, love."

I lick my lips and part them in invitation. My current position makes it hard for me to move, but I'm just as eager to have him inside my mouth.

He kneels on one leg beside Coop's shoulder before he grasps my ponytail and guides his cock into my mouth. As his thick length slides along my tongue, Seth lifts my hips and eases his cock back.

When Blake pushes forward, so does Seth, thrusting in his cock and pushing my hips down on Coop's cock. The sensation is overwhelming as my insides light up. I moan around Blake's cock and he hisses out a breath.

"Fuck, love." He slides back so he's not so deep. I suck on his cock, hollowing out my cheeks. The smooth skin against my tongue arouses me. He slowly rocks within my mouth as Seth follows his pace, slowly rocking into my pussy and easing my ass up and down on Coop's cock.

The bed dips beside me and Coop's hands slide down to my hips. Noah's hands rub massage oil between my breasts and over my nipples, making me moan. I can't move my arms or legs, but the way the guys are gently fucking me, they make me feel safe as they push me toward the edge.

Blake pulls out of my mouth and turns my head so I can watch Noah. He has firm pillows on either side of Coop and there's a bar hanging from the bed's metal canopy frame. I noticed it before but didn't think anything of it. Seth holds still, buried inside me.

"Do you want us all, kitten?" Noah's dark eyes meet mine.

"Yes, please." My words are breathless, but I can't wait to have them all fucking me again. I need them to move, to take me, to make me theirs.

With one hand holding the bar overhead, Noah straddles me,

using the pillows for his knees. When he rests his cock on my breast-bone, Coop's hands skim up my sides to press my breasts around Noah's cock.

Noah's cock slides between my breasts, while his hand holds onto the swing to keep his weight off me and his other hand toys with my nipples. Blake lifts my head as Noah's tip emerges and I greedily lick the precum off his slit.

"Fuck, kitten. Are you ready?"

Beyond ready. My body feels restless with them inside me and on me, but not fucking me yet.

Blake turns my head back to face his cock. "Are you ready, love?"

I meet Blake's green eyes. "I'm ready."

He smiles as he waits for the others to pull out before he slides his cock against my lips. I open for him, keeping my eyes on him as they all thrust inside me, deep. I hum around Blake's cock at the feeling of being taken by all of them. Coop's hands keep my breasts wrapped around Noah's cock. His thumbs work my nipples along with Noah's free hand.

They all move slowly, building up to longer, deeper strokes. I'm locked in place, but I've never felt so free as they make love to me. Seth's finger rubs my clit as his cock rocks into my pussy. Blake fills my mouth, but he stays away from my throat, so I can use my tongue to stroke along the underside and suck on his cock. Our eyes remain on each other's.

With his hands pressing my breasts around Noah, Coop gives little lifts of his hips, staying buried deep in my ass and making me feel so full. Noah's cock glides between my breasts, making the skin sensitive. His and Coop's fingers work my nipples in time with his thrusts.

Their every move pushes me closer to the edge, but I never want this to stop. I want to stay in this moment, cocooned in their love as they find their pleasure while lifting me to mine. I'm bound to these men like no one else in my life.

They are my everything. My present. My future. My love.

"Come for us, kitten."

My eyes lock with Blake's and I spill over the edge, crashing into ecstasy as wave after wave of pleasure pulls me down. I moan as my entire body tenses around them, holding them to me as tight as I can, as if I'm afraid to let them go.

"That's it, love." Blake's voice makes me release the tension in my body, knowing he'll never let me go. That he'll always be there when I need him the most.

His eyes soften as he strokes my cheek. "Are you ready, love?"

His cock thickens in my mouth and I suck harder, eager to make him break. His eyes close as he groans, and his expression is pure bliss as he comes deep in my mouth. I swallow his cum greedily.

His green eyes open and I see all the love he feels for me. He draws out of my mouth and brushes his thumb over my lips.

"I love you, tiger."

"I love you." Another orgasm ripples through me as the others still fuck me.

I cry out and shudder between them. Noah's dark eyes capture mine. His hand wraps behind my head to lift it so I can watch his cock sliding between my breasts.

"Give me your mouth, kitten," he grits out.

I open my lips for him and he surges forward. The head of his cock barely passes my lips before his cum jets into my mouth. I close my lips around his head and suck on him through his release.

When he finishes, I lick his slit. He jolts above me before smiling and removing his cock from my mouth. He lifts off me and sits on the bed beside me and Coop. Seth holds his cock buried inside me, waiting for his turn.

Noah cups my cheek and turns me to face him. "No one has ever been what you are to me, kitten. You belong to me. I belong to you."

I turn to kiss his palm. "I love you, Noah."

He kisses me with such passion that I know I'll never meet anyone who can love me the way Noah does. I sigh when he pulls away to sit against the headboard.

Coop's hands slide over my stomach as Seth takes my hips in his hands. I bite my lip as I meet Seth's determined eyes, knowing he's going to make me come again.

I rest my head back against Coop's chest as his fingers slide over my clit. My breath catches, and I close my eyes, surrendering to what I know will be an amazing fuck because anything these men do to my body is amazing.

"Our turn, goddess." Coop's dark voice rumbles through my body.

Seth lifts my hips and thrusts inside me before pulling back and fucking me on Coop's cock. He builds a rhythm while Coop works my clit and his other hand tweaks my nipples until I'm writhing between them, held in place by the cuffs linked to the bed.

"Come on our cocks, princess, so we can fill you with our cum."

Seth's words drag me under. I arch against Coop, crying out as my body pulses around their cocks thrusting inside me. Coop's hands go to my hips so he can fuck my ass from below, while Seth thrusts in and out of my pussy and pulls at my nipples, prolonging my orgasm.

Seth groans as his cock jerks inside me, filling me with his cum.

He leans down to kiss me, whispering against my lips. "Love you, princess."

I search his dark blue eyes that are still as captivating to me as the first day we met.

"I love you, boss."

Seth pulls out and sits on the bed between our legs while Coop bucks up into me. I'm too sensitive. It's too much.

I scream as I come hard, clamping down around his cock.

He roars as his cock unloads inside my ass. We both collapse. Him on the bed and me on him, with his cock still semihard and buried inside me.

"Fuck, sweetheart. I think you may have worn me out." Coop slides his hand between my legs and pushes Seth's cum back into my pussy, holding it there.

An aftershock ripples around his fingers and cock. I release my breath and laugh. "You think you're worn out."

"You know I could fuck you all night, sweetheart. This isn't a competition."

I reach behind me to cup his face. "I love you, Coop."

"I love you, Madison." He kisses my palm before he turns his head toward Noah. "So am I sleeping like this? Because I have to say I might be into cock warming."

Blake

This feels familiar but different as I sit in Madison's closet while she gets ready to go out tonight. Unlike last time, I'm wearing a nice suit so I can drink at the bar while the others hand Elizabeth her walking papers. I have one of our guys holding the perfect two seats at the bar with lines of sight to the bathroom and the private dining room's door.

I'm not letting Madison's stalker get close enough to smell her perfume tonight.

Madison comes in with a towel wrapped around her naked body. She has her blond hair dried and pulled up with curls dangling down around her neck. "Here to keep me company?"

When she drops her towel, for a second, I just take in her beautiful form. It doesn't matter how many times I see her naked, she's stunning every time. Last night was fantastic, but if I want to win back her trust, it's going to take more than great sex.

Though great sex definitely helps.

"I thought you might like to talk while you get ready." I swallow because Madison bends over to pick up the panties Seth picked out, flashing me all her naughty bits. My already hard cock throbs.

"Just talk?" She glances over her shoulder like she knows exactly what she's doing.

"Yes, tiger."

She slips the panties on and lifts the matching strapless bra. "Okay."

"What do you want to know?" I clear the frog from my throat as she covers her perfect breasts.

"I guess we should discuss our history with previous lovers. Maybe that will help to figure out why it's so hard for you to trust me?" She walks over to the dress Seth picked out for tonight. It's red and tight and will make every man in the restaurant envious of Cooper Graham.

"I don't think it started with Andrea, but she certainly solidified my opinion of women. In college, women would seek us out knowing they could get close to Coop through us. Andrea wanted me, but she let me think she was okay with the setup. In reality, she thought she could get me by playing along." I rub my jaw. We still haven't tracked Andrea down to confront her about Robert. She knows something, but wherever she's hidden, we can't find her. It's frustrating.

"The woman blackmailed you after agreeing to the arrangement. Pretty sure that would turn me off from guys if it happened to me." Madison slides the dress up over her hips and holds it against her body. She glances over her shoulder at me. "Care to zip me up, Daddy?"

Chuckling, I shake my head as I walk over to her. "That's not playing fair, tiger. I can't exactly punish you."

"It still makes you smile." She ducks her head as I grab the zipper and ease it up. My fingers trail along her spine, making her tremble.

The zipper reaches the top, and I latch the little hook and eye before kissing her back right above it. A shiver works through her as I step back.

She smooths her hands over her dress and turns around. "What do you think?"

"Seth has a fucking death wish."

The dress seems like it covers more than the last dress he put on her to go out on a date, but it hugs her curves perfectly. She's elegant and sexy. It makes my fingers itch to grab her and hold her against me.

She closes the gap between us in her bare feet and straightens my tie, looking up at me with those wide blue eyes and a coy little pout. "You don't like my dress, Daddy?"

"That dress looks amazing on you, but I'm going to have to deck anyone that even thinks about you inappropriately. And trust me, any guy and potentially a handful of women will have inappropriate thoughts about you."

She shakes her head and grabs my lapels. "You overestimate my desirability."

"And you underestimate it." I lower my mouth to hover over hers. "Can I kiss you, tiger?"

Her eyes search mine for a second before she whispers, "Yes."

I close the distance and capture her lips. With a little sigh, she gives in, opens for me. Careful of her hair, I slide my hand behind her neck and my other hand around her hip to pull her closer.

She comes willingly, but this has never been our problem. The chemistry between us is off the charts and explosive, but she needs to know that emotionally I'm here and that I can trust her.

I end our kiss and smooth my thumb over her jaw as I lift my head.

"My past is a mess of users and women trying to get something from us. You shouldn't have to pay for their crimes. You and I are so much more than any of them." I release her neck and step away. "I knew that from the moment I met you."

Her hand catches mine. "We are more. But something about me must be triggering these responses. I'm pushing buttons I don't even know are there. That's why we need to revisit the past. Because they built those buttons. We just have to tear them out."

I hold her hand. "You'll get first row seats to two of the women who tried to destroy us tonight. We can talk about that part of my story later. You need to finish getting ready."

She smiles and releases my hand. "Are you going to stay and watch?"

"Absolutely."

Chapter 150

Low-Hanging Fruit

Coop

"I can't believe we're doing this," Sara says, walking with Madison ahead of Noah and me. The outside of this restaurant is a mess of flashing lights and security holding photographers back. It's the perfect place to make sure that when these women make a scene, it's everywhere by the time we leave.

"I promised Hope I'd tell her all about it," Madison says.

These women need to be taken down a notch. Elizabeth's a snake waiting to strike. Leighton's interference jeopardizes my relationship with Madison, which is unacceptable.

I draw Madison against me as we're shown into the private dining room. Her eyes smile up at me as I escort her to our chairs. My hand goes to the small of her back. She looks fucking edible in the outfit Seth put her in. If I thought I could get away with dragging her off somewhere to find out if she's wearing panties, I would.

But that's not on the program for tonight. Or at all in public until we find her stalker. Tonight, we spay two stray cats. Then I'll be free to mess Madison up with the others in celebration.

The table is set for eight and ready for the fireworks to begin.

After seating Madison, I take the chair next to her and bring her hand to my lips. "Be strong, goddess."

Her strength shines in her blue eyes. This woman makes me want things I've never imagined for myself. Lazy Sundays, hectic weeknights, even babies. She cups my jaw with her hand. "I love you."

"I don't know what I did to deserve you, but there are no take-backs now. You're mine, goddess. I love you." As much as my heart feels full, fear lingers beneath the love. That this can all be taken away from me so easily. That someone hovers in the shadows, waiting to rip her from my arms.

As if she can sense my fear, she kisses me softly and rests her forehead against mine. "I'm always yours, Coop."

"I didn't realize we were having a show along with dinner."

My gaze lifts at Elizabeth's snide tone and Madison straightens. With Noah beside Madison and Sara on his other side, we've manufactured the perfect situation. We know Leighton and Elizabeth won't want to sit next to each other. Leighton will choose to sit beside me, which will put Drew and Elizabeth together. We're hoping that's all it takes. But these women were raised to stay calm in any situation.

Fucking etiquette.

"We figured it's time to clear the air." Seth's smile doesn't reach his eyes as he holds out the chair for Elizabeth. She smiles at him like he's this devoted man who will do anything for her. I've only seen one woman Seth would do anything for, and she's beside me tonight.

"Of course." Elizabeth smiles indulgently at Madison like she's winning. "We should all get to be close friends since we'll be seeing each other more often."

Her gaze settles on me with interest. This bitch can't take no for an answer. Right now, I have to play along, so I give her a small acknowledging nod. Just in case I need to go with plan B.

Pretending to even like Elizabeth will be the performance of a lifetime, but I'm up for it.

"Sara, it's good to see you again. How's your mother?" Elizabeth places her hand over Seth's on the table.

He doesn't pull away, but he doesn't take it either. She's forced to drape her hand over his fist. Her smile has an edge to it.

"My mother is doing well." Sara glances at Noah with a smile before turning back to Elizabeth. "She's having lunch with your mother tomorrow."

"That's nice." Elizabeth really isn't interested. She just wants to get under Madison's skin by ignoring her. She won't be able to ignore our next guests. As if she's just now noticing the extra chairs, she turns to Seth. "Is Blake joining us? With an actual date this time? Or his sister again?"

The host opens the door and Leighton and Drew walk in. I couldn't have planned it better. When she turns to see the newcomers, Elizabeth stiffens. Her smile freezes, locked on her lips. Her face pales and her cheeks grow pink.

"Lovely of you to join us, Leighton." I stand and offer her the seat next to me. I nod to Drew. "Good to see you again, Drew."

Nodding to me, Drew pulls out Leighton's chair before sitting down next to Elizabeth.

"We thought it was time to clear *all* the air." Seth draws his hand out from under Elizabeth's and takes a drink of his water.

Before anyone can talk, the server comes in and fills everyone's wineglasses with a Chablis before the staff brings in a green salad and sets the plates before us.

"I hope no one minds, but I ordered ahead so we wouldn't waste one minute of our time together." I give them the smile I've perfected over years of training. It's beyond fake, but no one but those closest to me can tell.

Madison slides her hand over mine on my lap. I weave our fingers together, rubbing my thumb over the ring that states she's mine to the world. The guys and Madison think I did it for the fake engagement, but I would have never put it on her if I intended for her to take it off. After that night at the benefit, I knew she was my future, and I'll fight tooth and nail to keep her.

Putting a ring on it definitely doesn't hurt.

"How thoughtful of you." Leighton sits rigid in her chair as her eyes bounce around the table. "I was surprised to be invited, but maybe I shouldn't have been. What game are you playing now, Coop?"

"No game, Leighton." I take a sip of my wine. "We need to discuss a few things and make sure everyone understands exactly where they stand in my life."

She shrinks just a little, but not nearly as much as I want her to. She's been in my mother's ear. If anyone posted that engagement announcement, it would have been one of these two women. They're both bold enough to believe they could get away with it.

If it wasn't them, it could be a warning shot from the stalker. He doesn't like me claiming Madison. Well, fuck him. I want to end that fucker for putting Madison through his bullshit. At least I have the balls to claim her as my own. Not terrify her.

When the servers leave and shut the door, silence descends as we pick at our salads. I don't bother with my food as I study Leighton, Drew, and Elizabeth. Elizabeth makes sure there's plenty of distance between her and Drew. Leighton does the same.

Drew doesn't seem to care about either of them. Neither woman really claims him, but he doesn't appear bothered as he eats his salad and talks with Seth.

The women are nervous. They should be.

I don't need to use the Graham name to make their lives hell. Though it would be effective. I'm happy to do it in person, instead.

"Drew." I wait for him to lift his gaze. "We haven't actually had a chance to get to know each other."

"I don't believe we have." Drew's voice is smooth as he leans back in his chair. He doesn't have a care in the world, but he has two powerful women on his hook, and from the sounds of it, a fortune to back his future.

"How long have you and Leighton been an item?" I smile. I don't really give a shit, but we've got to get the ball rolling somehow.

"Leighton and I have been dating for the past year now." He

reaches over and takes her hand. She gives him a smile I've seen millions of times. It's her pleasant smile. She had the same training I did. How to always be on. How to make the right connections.

What's interesting is she has the name and lineage a family like his can only buy into, but Drew hasn't pulled the trigger on marriage yet. Or is Leighton dragging her feet?

And what's with fucking Elizabeth? Her family doesn't need the money, they want someone with my lineage.

"I'm surprised we haven't run into each other more often." I load my fork with salad but don't lift it to my mouth. "After all, Leighton is best friends with my mother, apparently."

"Family friends. My mother and Coop's are close, so occasionally I'll dine with them." Leighton smooths the bumps I'm trying to form. She can't let Drew go without the guarantee of someone else. The guarantee of me.

"Of course." I take a bite.

"You don't know our history, Drew." Seth leans back with his wineglass. "Coop and Leighton dated in college and I dated Elizabeth."

At the mention of Elizabeth, Drew's gaze falls on her. I'm not sure what the two have planned, but there's got to be a reason for them to bump uglies.

"Leighton mentioned that you two were once engaged," Drew says to me.

"Never engaged. Just promised to each other by our parents." I give him a knowing look. "See, families like ours—and by ours, I mean Leighton's and mine—with money going back generations, want to combine our power to make our families even more pretentious in the future. So it makes sense that she and my mother cling to this hope that maybe I'll still be available to marry her. But I already know who I want to marry."

My eyes meet Madison's and I lift her hand to kiss her knuckle. She blushes softly.

Drew smiles like nothing about this is new to him. I'm not

surprised. Leighton is strategic if nothing else. She would have laid out everything for him. It's the one reason she and I worked well together. She wasn't emotional about what we were doing. We weren't in love. We were a business decision.

"Sometimes new blood can be good for a family." Drew runs his finger down the stem of his wineglass. His words are calculated, but there's no heat beneath them. "Like Elizabeth and Seth. He's a nobody with a fortune like me. I'm surprised her mother allows it."

Elizabeth stiffens. "Mother prizes intellect above all else. Seth has proven that he's brilliant."

"But that's not what you need, is it?" Drew arches his eyebrow with a knowing smile.

The tension between the two is palpable. I need to figure out how to draw that out more.

"Of course, Coop's mother would prefer someone with good breeding." Leighton disrupts the almost beautiful blowup to bring it back to me. She never did like to play with her food. "Money isn't important to the Grahams, but a family that ticks all the right boxes is."

"Good thing I don't give a fuck what's important to my family and prefer to make decisions based on what I want and need."

Her blue eyes lock with mine, and I finally see the hate in them. Good. I've fucking hated her for years. She kept trying to get back with me, even when I'd pick the woman next to her to take home to fuck.

When I was young and naive enough to think my family might know what's best for me, I thought we could have something. I tried. But then Elizabeth happened and Leighton got worried, so she pressed me to decide.

Her or them.

Seth, Blake, and Noah. The only people who ever stood up for me because they fucking like me and not because of what I could do for them. There's a reason I'm not CEO or vice president. I didn't want it.

I didn't want people to think Morrigan Technology Group rose because of my family name.

We did it together. My name had nothing to do with it.

Seth is the reason we are as large and profitable as we are now. Noah's financial planning made us all wealthy men in our own rights. Blake kept us together and made the tough decisions when we couldn't. Together, we're indestructible.

Madison holds us together instead of trying to tear us apart.

And it's time these women finally realized that.

The door opens and the staff comes in to take the salads, refresh the wineglasses, and serve the fish course. The air is tense, but Madison holds up beautifully. Because she's confident in our love. These women are nothing to us and she knows that now.

I dip my head beside hers. "How are you doing, sweetheart?"

"Good." Her blue eyes lift to mine. "Do what you have to do."

I press my forehead against hers and close my eyes, thanking whatever power led her to me. To us. I breathe in her soft floral scent and let it settle in my lungs. This woman is my everything.

I rub my thumb over her jaw as I lift my head from hers. The staff finish and exit the room, leaving the eight of us to eat.

Everyone settles into eating their fish, talking about the flavor profile of the meal.

"When are you two going to get engaged?" I ask Drew.

Leighton coughs and blots her lips with her napkin. She glances at Drew. But he just relaxes and dabs his napkin at his mouth. His brown eyes meet mine with a smirk.

"What do you really want to know, Cooper?" Drew rests his elbows on the table and contemplates me. "I mean, this dinner is a fishing expedition if I ever saw one."

Drew smiles and looks around the table. His gaze settles on Sara and Noah. "Though I'm not sure what you two are doing here?"

Sara raises an eyebrow. "Entertainment. Of course."

Drew gives her a flirty wink. "I live to entertain."

His attention returns to me while Leighton tries to lean in to him to say something and Elizabeth looks like she swallowed a bone.

I think I'm going to like this guy. "If this is a society match between you and Leighton, why aren't you engaged?"

Leighton's eyes flick to me almost hopefully. Like the reason I'm asking is because I want her.

"My family is pushing the match, but Leighton confided in me she still wants to marry you." Drew's eyes sparkle. He's open and clearly eager to spark the fire that will burn these women to the ground.

"Drew." Leighton's got her serious voice on now.

"So you're just fucking her?" I arch an eyebrow.

"She's hot and good at what she does." Drew shrugs. "Who am I to say no to a beautiful woman?"

"And Elizabeth?" Seth's gaze meets Elizabeth's horrified one.

"Oh, she's good too." Drew smirks.

"You slept with her?" Leighton's voice is almost a shriek as she stands abruptly.

Drew rubs his finger beside his lip. "We didn't exactly sleep."

"How long?" Leighton's hands shake on her napkin as she tries to squeeze the life out of it.

"Since the benefit." Drew smirks. "She came on to me. Said she wanted to take something of yours, and that would be me. Of course, she doesn't want to marry someone like me, but fucking me behind your back makes her so fucking needy. Do you know the things you can make a woman do when she wants revenge?"

Elizabeth shakes her head. "You asshole."

"I don't mind being a bone you both want to fight over, but not when it's obvious you both actually want Cooper." Drew leans back. His gaze flicks between the two women before settling his gaze on Sara. "Personally, I wouldn't marry either of you, but I'm always down to fuck."

This is better than we could have imagined. Sara's shoulders shake as she tries to hold in her laughter. Madison's hand squeezes mine.

"Let's get one thing straight." I kiss Madison's hand before releasing it and standing. "I'm not available to either of you conniving bitches. If you don't want this all to end up as gossip, you'll stop thinking you can get to me by using my friends"—I glare at Elizabeth —"or my family." I shift my glare to Leighton.

"We have pictures of Elizabeth and Drew fucking." Seth wipes his hands and stands. "If you try to release information about us or publish any more fake announcements about Coop's engagement, we'll release those pictures. Both of you will look bad."

Elizabeth's lips press together tightly.

"See, now this is a good dinner party." Drew takes a drink of wine. "If you need any additional information, I'm more than willing to help. And ladies, I'm always available."

He winks at Sara, who releases a little laugh before containing it. He picks up his fork and digs into his food.

"I'm not staying here." Leighton picks up her clutch. Her gaze goes to me. "I'm so fucking done with all of this. I didn't put in an engagement notice. It would have been too humiliating if we got back together."

"Which is never happening." I make sure she understands that as I retake my seat.

"Whatever." She glares for a second before turning to Drew. "Oh, Drew?"

He turns his head and smirks.

She slaps him. "Lose my number."

"Gladly." He rubs his cheek.

Leighton storms out of the room. One down, one to go.

Elizabeth clears her throat and looks at her half-full wineglass. "I don't know what announcement you're talking about. I need those pictures to remain private."

"As long as nothing about me wanting Madison comes to light, your secret is safe with us." Seth leans back. "However, I need you to admit you were using me again."

Elizabeth blows out a very unladylike breath. She straightens and turns to Seth. "I didn't want to use you in college. I actually liked you. But Mother has plans for me. Plans that include the Graham family. When you reached out as a business, Mother wanted me to go for Coop, but I wanted a touch of revenge, especially after the benefit and how obvious it was that you wanted Madison."

She gives a bitter laugh. "I don't want any of you. But Leighton was relentless after I went after Coop. She made my life hell. Especially after Coop dumped her. When the opportunity to take something that was hers presented itself . . ."

"I'm always available for revenge sex," Drew says.

"You have my word, Seth. Not that it means anything to you. I won't go to the press or anyone else." Elizabeth stands and takes her clutch. "Thank you for an eye-opening dinner."

"I'll call you," Drew says. Elizabeth doesn't acknowledge him as she walks out.

"So, dessert?" Drew smirks at all of us.

Chapter 151

Escalation

Madison

Blake joins us after Elizabeth leaves. Coop holds my hand under the table while we all try to figure out why Drew is still here.

"Oh, good." Drew waves Blake over and pushes out the chair next to him. "Since we're all here now."

Blake's brow furrows as he looks around at all of us. Maybe he thinks we know what's happening, but we're just as clueless.

"Sit, Blake." Drew throws his napkin on his plate and leans back like a well-fed king holding court. "As fun as this has been, I've got something else you guys should know."

Blake sits. My hand goes for the simple necklace Coop draped around my neck earlier. My fingers caress the teardrop-shaped diamond. Butterflies flutter in my stomach as anxiety crawls up my spine. This doesn't feel like it will be pleasant.

"I assume it isn't anything to do with Leighton or Elizabeth," Coop says. Both women are gone. Thankfully.

"No, it isn't." Drew meets my gaze. I hold perfectly still as he says, "I heard a rumor you were attacked at the benefit. Is that true?"

The benefit. My throat closes as I nod.

Drew sighs. "I overheard some guys talking when I was on my way to meet up with Elizabeth."

"What did they say?" Blake leans in close to Drew. Always my protector.

"One guy was clearly drunk. He kept mentioning how grown-up Madison looked and that he lost his shot to get her when she was in school. How he should have fucked her on his desk. Sounded like a major creep."

Ice floods my veins. But I knew Professor Alan was a creep. It's why I stayed away from him while I was in college.

"The other guy told him maybe he hadn't lost his shot. Kept egging him on. 'She's here. You're here. Get her alone. Don't take no for an answer. Get what you deserve. What you're owed.'"

Blood rushes in my ears. My heart pounds heavy in my chest. Owed? I'm there in that hallway. Pressed against the wall. My head aching. I'm there in my apartment. Hands tightening on my neck, taking my life away second after second.

Trapped, hopeless, scared, alone.

My body is lifted and warmth surrounds me. The buzzing quiets as I focus on Coop murmuring little nothings to me. His voice draws me out and helps warm me. He cuddles me in his lap with my head tucked beneath his chin.

The room comes back into focus.

Seth and Blake talk to Drew, seeing if he has more information, but I can't focus on what they're saying. Noah rubs my hands. Locking on his worried brown eyes, I take in a breath.

I'm here.

I'm safe.

"It's going to be okay. Just breathe with me, sweetheart," Coop whispers against my hair. Another breath.

The tightness in my chest eases. Noah reaches out and strokes my jaw.

I turn to look at Drew. He's saying something important.

"I didn't recognize the guy's voice. Sorry. But he said if she was fucking four guys, what was one more?"

My eyes widen. Oh, shit. He knows. My stalker knows. He was there at the benefit, which the video of Coop and me made clear. Why would anyone else tell Professor Alan that?

Why involve Jimi Alan at all? Why not attack me himself when the opportunity presented itself? Maybe Jimi was the scapegoat for the stalker. Someone to pin his sins on. The stalker wanted Jimi to attack me.

We assumed the stalker only knew about Coop and me. But if he knows about all of them, are any of us safe?

My gaze goes to each of my guys. I can't lose any of them.

Then my gaze falls on Sara. Her hand covers her mouth as she meets my eyes. Well, this should be interesting.

* * *

It's three a.m. when I slip out of bed. I've been trying to sleep for an hour now. I grab a discarded dress shirt, and the scent of Coop's cologne surrounds me as I put it on and button it. I look at my guys sprawled naked with the sheet covering some of them.

Noah took Sara home. I promised her we'd talk soon and I'd explain everything. If I could. The NDA is still in effect, limiting what I can tell people.

The others and I came straight home and fell upon each other like we'd never see each other again. The information about Professor Alan overshadowed the relief from finally being out from under Elizabeth's thumb.

I needed to feel anything but the fear of losing them. As always, my men took very good care of me.

My body hums with satisfaction, even as a shiver passes over me. There's nowhere safer for me than in their arms, but what if being there puts them in danger?

Grabbing my phone off the charger, I leave the bedroom for the kitchen and turn on the electric kettle. I left my phone behind during dinner and we were a little occupied when we got home, so I haven't checked it.

It shouldn't surprise me that the stalker sent Jimi after me. I'm just lucky Patrick was there to stop him. But what if the guys are right about Patrick being the stalker? Wouldn't Jimi have recognized Patrick when he stopped him?

Would I have noticed that?

He's the only one who's received texts from the stalker. None of my guys have. It's just odd.

My brain latches onto those questions and has me spinning out. So tea and doomscrolling until I'm tired again.

After I get a cup down, put an herbal tea bag in it, and fill it with hot water, I open my phone. There are several unread messages. Normally I might have a message or two, but definitely not this many.

I release a breath as a quick scan reveals none of the messages are from Unknown.

MOM:

> Wondering if you're doing okay, call us as
> soon as you get this.

That's so not like my mother. The time stamp is from eight o'clock. I'll have to call her first thing in the morning.

The next one is a group message between Sara, Hope, and I.

HOPE:

> I'm getting strange messages from an
> unknown number about Madison.

SARA:

> Me too

> I don't think Madison had her phone on her
> tonight.

> Shit, my friend Kayla just said she got
> something strange.

> I'm adding her to the chat
>
> KAYLA:
>
> What the fuck is going on?
>
> Who is this asshole?

She included a screenshot of the conversation.

> UNKNOWN:
>
> I'm reaching out as a friend of Madison's
>
> I think she's in trouble
>
> Someone should check on her. I would but she's cut me off.
>
> I'm worried her bosses are taking advantage of her.
>
> KAYLA:
>
> Who the fuck is this?

My hand covers my mouth as I read those texts repeatedly. Who else did Unknown send this to? Is this what my parents are worried about? My bosses taking advantage of me?

I close out of the group chat and look at a message from Hope.

> HOPE:
>
> They sent a pic. I didn't want to share in the group text.
>
> I'm so sorry, Madison

I almost don't want to click on the picture, but I know I need to. I open it and it's a pic of me in the play room, bound upright on the bench with the guys fucking my mouth and pussy. I'm in a satiny nightgown so only the guys are exposed in the picture. Though the picture crops out most of them, including their faces.

It looks hauntingly familiar, and I finally place why it feels like

I've seen this before. It's a still from the video we took. A video I asked them to take. Who has access to it besides the guys and me?

Maybe I'm becoming numb to these invasions of my privacy, or just numb from the constant surveillance, but I'm not shocked that both Kayla and Sara mention pictures to me individually as well.

KAYLA:

Just don't tell me if one of those dicks is my brother's

My tea forgotten, I set my phone on the counter and draw in a breath. My mind is blank. I can't even process what the stalker is doing now. Showing my friends pictures of me having sex with multiple men? Did he send that picture to my parents?

My parents aren't prudes, but no parent wants to see that. At least I have my nightgown on, but it's obvious what's happening.

"You okay, princess?" Seth sits beside me at the island, wearing only his boxers.

I slide my phone over to him and stand to go dump my oversteeped tea out in the sink before preparing a fresh cup. "Do you want some tea?"

Seth glances at me from my phone. Shaking his head, he returns to reading through the messages. I get my tea prepared and sit next to him. Resting my head on his shoulder, I'm glad I don't have to withhold my affection from any of them.

I need them, but what if the stalker takes this further?

"We should wake the others." Seth sets my phone down.

I grab his arm when he tenses to rise. "Not yet. Let them sleep. There's nothing any of us can do about this until the morning."

"That picture . . . How did they get in the play room?" Seth opens the picture, studying it.

"Pretty sure it's a still from the video we took." I sigh and drink my tea.

"Fuck." He's not raging. He's calm about this. I need that right now. I need him.

"How would he have gotten access to the video?" I ask, feeling surprisingly calm given the stalker has pictures of me having sex with multiple men and sent one to my new friends. But it's three in the morning. I'm wiped out but not tired enough to fall asleep.

We've eliminated a few threats to our relationships and livelihoods, but the stalker and the corporate spy are still out there.

"It's possible they got it when we watched it." Seth runs a hand over his hair. His gaze goes to the walls surrounding the TV. "Took a picture of the screen."

Cameras are so small now that it's possible we missed one. "I just want this to be over. I want to get through this rough stuff and start living again."

A tear rolls down my cheek. I'm just done with it.

"I don't want to worry about this guy or girl or group." I lift my head from Seth's shoulder and turn to face him. "Our lives are on hold. I want to say fuck it and move far away from here where no one can ever find us."

Seth captures my face in his hands and smooths the tear over my cheek with his thumb. "If I thought it would stop them, I'd book us a jet. I'd leave all of this behind and start over again as long as we could be together."

I wish I could say *let's do it*. Run away and start over. The five of us.

But that's not realistic. At some point we have to face what's coming. We need to find out who is fucking with our lives.

"Do you think they're the same person? The stalker and the corporate spy?" I search his eyes, hoping he has an answer, even a theory. Somewhere to start.

"I don't know. They may be working together or have something in common, but the spy is trying to take us down, and the stalker wants you, princess. They both were working toward their goals before we even met."

"We just didn't know about either until after we met." I release a frustrated breath. "There's got to be overlap somewhere."

Too many coincidences.

"I'll have Blake give his guy a call in the morning. This is one more thing pointing to the stalker escalating." Seth draws me in for a hug. I rest my head over his heart.

"I need to tell my friends what's going on," I say softly.

"Yes, you should since the stalker sought them out." Seth rubs my back. "Have them over later today. Tell them whatever you want to. I trust your judgment. They're good women."

"What about the NDA?"

"I'll make a note that I gave you permission." Seth waits until I meet his eyes. "But the NDA doesn't really apply anymore. The whole contract was a way to hold us apart. That's done with. You're ours, princess. We aren't going anywhere and neither are you. We should discuss it with the others, but we should nullify both the contract and the NDA."

I tip my head back to look into his eyes, and all I see is his trust and love in me shining back.

Chapter 152

A Meeting of Minds

Madison

Since Kayla is flying in to work here this week, we waited for her flight to arrive in the afternoon to talk. Sara, Hope, and I are sitting in an awkward silence when Blake lets Kayla into my room. Each of these women have a piece of my story, but none of them have the full picture.

As soon as the door closes, Sara stands and hugs Kayla. When they disengage, Kayla eyes me as I sit there. My heart pounds because I don't want to lose the first friends I've had.

"Come on, Madison. We know you aren't that shy. Get over here. You need a hug." Kayla walks over to me, pulls me up, and hugs me tight. "I'm so sorry this is happening to you, honey."

The tension seeps from my muscles and I hug her back, grateful she's here. "Thank you."

"Okay." Kayla releases me and turns to Hope. "Hope?"

Hope smiles and holds up her hand in greeting. "Hi."

Kayla shakes her head. "I'll get a hug from you after we figure this shit out."

She takes a seat and they all turn to me. I swallow hard. I'm wearing jeans and a t-shirt today with a sweatshirt over it. After the pictures they saw, I needed to feel bundled up.

The stalker revealed my life to these women. My mother just wanted to know if I was being safe. My parents didn't receive a picture. Thank god. But they got a warning that I wasn't being careful and that my bosses were taking advantage of me.

"You all know I have a stalker—"

"Who is a major asshole. Seriously, who sends out pics of a girl getting dick?" Kayla shakes her head. "Assholes, that's who."

The others nod, but I continue, "I'm not just dating Coop."

I meet Sara's eyes. "Or just Coop and Noah. We're all together. The four of them and me."

I look down at my hands, waiting for the chastising to begin. Telling me what a whore I am.

"Man." Kayla breaks the silence. "Living the fucking dream. Literally."

Sara snort laughs. I lift my gaze to Kayla and she smiles and winks at me.

"I knew Blake was fucking someone. I'm glad it's you." Kayla crosses her legs. "I get it though. If four really hot dudes were okay with me screwing all of their brains out, I'd be down."

"That explains so much." Hope sits forward. "There've been times I swear you had something going on with Blake or Seth, but I thought you and Noah were just really good friends. Wait, isn't Noah dating Sara?"

Sara holds up her hands. "Nope. Just going out to cover for him dating Madison and to make my mom think I'm dating. Oh, and trying to make my brother's best friend jealous."

"Is it the hot Viking?" Kayla's eyes twinkle as she practically vibrates on the chair in excitement. "Please tell me it's the hot Viking."

Sara blushes. "No, not Dante."

"Then pass him my number, would you, because I could use

some of that hot dominant energy about now." Kayla gives a little shiver.

"What about Bea?" I ask, remembering Kayla's girlfriend.

"We're arguing about where to live. I want to move back here and she doesn't." Kayla pushes her hand through her dark hair. "Honestly, a relationship with one person is hard enough. I don't envy you with four of them."

"We manage." I shrug. It hasn't all been sexy times and rainbows.

"Okay, back to the asshole who's trying to ruin you." Kayla gestures for the conversation to move along.

"He sent those texts to you all and my parents."

"The picture?" Sara looks horrified that my parents might have seen that picture. That would have been my reaction too.

"No. Just more warnings that my bosses are taking advantage of me." I put my hands in my lap. "The stalker was at the benefit. They took a video of me and Coop in a secluded hallway."

"I'm going to need to see that video—"

"Kayla!" Sara chastises.

"For informational purposes only." Kayla arches an eyebrow with a smirk. "So when you were getting spit roasted, was the dick in your mouth Coop's? You can blink twice to let me know."

"Kay-la!" Sara rolls her eyes.

Laughter spills out of me. With all the bullshit happening in my life, Kayla is a breath of fresh air. Hope smiles.

Kayla sits back, satisfied, as Sara shakes her head.

"Okay, so you have a stalker and he knows you're getting busy with your four bosses." Kayla's green eyes meet mine. "He's got access to you. He's either someone with money or on the extra staff for the event."

"He has money. My old roommate—"

"The one that attacked you?" Hope leans forward.

I nod. "She took pictures for him. The police have the phone she used. We think. But it was broken and dead. We're waiting to find out if anything is on it. She told her boyfriend it was her insurance policy."

Sara's mouth is open as she looks at me. "You were attacked before the benefit?"

I release a breath. "It's why I moved in so early with the guys."

"And got freaky." Kayla grins.

"We actually were together that first week." I swallow and cross my legs. "When I was hired, they offered me an arrangement."

Sara's eyes widen. "Like, really?"

"Yes, we have a contract and an NDA, which is why I couldn't share before." I smile apologetically at Hope.

"It's okay. I just don't understand why you said you were dating Coop." Hope tucks her hair behind her ear. "Of all of them, he would be the least likely to date."

"You saw him comforting me. And we were afraid the stalker had footage of Coop and me together in the file room." My cheeks grow warm.

"Why would he—"

"The stalker sent me a video of me in the file room after someone turned out all the lights. But before that, Coop was there. We didn't know how much the stalker might have seen or heard. Then Hope saw us hugging. It made sense for one of them to date me so they could keep me close and watch over me. Noah wanted to be that guy." My heart still tears a little at how that hurt him unintentionally.

"Aw, Noah's such a good guy." Kayla puts her hand on my knee and shakes it. "You two probably look fantastic together. Was he the guy fucking you?"

My lips curve into a smile as my cheeks flush. "Honestly, I'm not sure which guys are in the picture. I haven't really studied it."

"Well, when you get around to it, let me know so if one of those dicks is my brother's, I can put a sticker over it." Kayla winks as she settles back in her chair.

"You could just delete the picture," Hope says.

Kayla laughs.

"Okay, let me see if I have this straight." Sara blows out a breath. "You start work here and the bosses all want to be with you. You get attacked by your roommate and her boyfriend?"

I nod and touch my neck, still feeling the bruises even though they're long gone.

"Then you move in here. You fuck Coop in the file room and someone films you in the dark. Then Hope sees Coop hugging you and the video the stalker took might have included him, so you roll with it and bam, you and Cooper Graham are dating. Wait, engaged."

Reflexively, I twist the ring on my finger. "Coop announced it at the benefit. Pretty sure he was getting back at Leighton."

"Oh, what happened last night at dinner?" Hope looks from Sara to me.

Sara fills them in on all the details. By the end, Kayla is smirking.

"I think you should date Drew Young, Sara," Kayla says.

Sara blushes and looks away. Maybe she should. If that guy she likes is never going to make a move, she should find someone who will.

"We're waiting for the police to look at the evidence. With the videos, the dress, and the texts, we hope they can see he's escalating and move the phone to a higher priority." I sit back and stare at the black TV screen. It could all be over if Valerie kept a picture of the stalker on the phone.

"Wait, aren't you breaking your NDA?" Kayla points out.

"Seth and I talked last night." I look at each of them. "I trust all of you and he trusts me. The whole contract was to prevent us from feeling more for each other, but that failed. I love them and they love me."

"Damn, living the dream." Kayla shakes her head. "So what do we do next?"

"Not much we can do." I tuck my feet under me on the couch. "We make sure the police have screenshots from your phones. They may access your history to see if they can determine where the text came from. Otherwise, we're at a standstill."

"Then I vote wine and a girly movie." Sara heads to my refrigerator.

Hope reaches for the remote. "And not focusing on what must be an amazing sex life. And the fact I'm not getting any."

Heat floods my face.

"Definitely not focusing on amazing sex. I've been dating her boyfriend for the last few weeks." Sara shakes her head. "Pretty sure I could hook up with Drew Young though. He does seem open to fucking."

She laughs and we join her. They're still willing to be my friends. Relief slips through me.

"You know, I could go for a group thing. All girls?" Kayla looks at all of us half hopeful, half trying not to laugh.

"Maybe some other girls. I like dick." Sara blows Kayla a kiss as she passes her a wineglass.

"You just haven't seen my dick." Kayla winks. "I can be as big and thick as you want."

Hope laughs. "Oh shit, are you talking about strap-ons?"

"Strap-ons, dildos, vibrators. I got them all."

"I'm going to have to go with Sara's answer." Hope blushes. "I like a man's body. Hard and solid."

"Whoa." Sara holds up her hand to stop Kayla from talking about hard and solid things. "Wine first. It's way too early in the day to discuss cocks without being a little tipsy."

I relax into the corner of my couch with a glass of white wine and friends surrounding me. This right here is what I've always wanted. My guys are fucking icing on the cake, but friendship is so precious to me.

Hours later, after three bottles of wine, two movies, and laughing until my sides hurt, I'm walking the others across the lobby to let them out. Blake hovers in the background, letting me have this time with my friends but always protecting me.

"Okay, we all have the group text, but I want dinner one night this week." Kayla looks around and then past us to Blake. "No dicks allowed!"

"Except silicone ones." Hope giggles.

Kayla grins. "I'll pull you over to the dark side yet."

"But first," Sara says, "we take over the business world. The four of us could give those guys a run for their money."

"Hey, I like those guys." I fake pout and turn to Blake. He takes a step forward, but I smile and wave him off. A little rush of desire races through me.

"Fine, but we'll find something to conquer." Sara weaves a little as she scrunches up her forehead, thinking. "Maybe I should graduate first."

Kayla laughs. "Come on, let's leave this one to her dicks."

"We should go to my brother's bar." Hope holds up her hand as if remembering something and frowns. "Crap. It's closed until later."

"Then we'll go later." Sara loops her arm in Hope's.

Hope smiles. "I think I'm still going to go check on Jason."

"Want us to come with? I like brothers, just not mine." Kayla flashes Hope a grin.

I don't know about the others, but I'm definitely buzzed.

Hope shakes her head and hugs everyone. "Good luck, Madison. I'll text you later. See you."

She wanders out the door and toward her brother's bar. Maybe someone should go with her?

Sara gives me a hug. "Someday we're going to talk about how that works with all your guys."

My face heats, flustering me. I can't imagine telling anyone what the guys and I do. She pulls back and gives me a wink.

"My turn." Kayla hugs me tight, grabbing my ass. When Blake clears his throat, I laugh.

"Kayla." His deep voice echoes in the lobby.

Kayla giggles and releases me. "Stay strong."

She holds her fist out for me to bump. When I do so, she snuggles up to Sara. "I guess we'll have to stick together."

"Bye, Madison." Sara waves as they walk out the door.

I watch them through the glass and feel Blake move up behind me. He doesn't touch me. He doesn't draw me into his arms. But he's there. Steady, solid.

"We should practice your self-defense moves." He reaches out and tucks a strand of hair behind my ear.

"Okay." I still have a little buzz, but those flutters in my stomach remind me that I really enjoy Blake. We're fucking with the others, but not just us. Yet. I need to hold that line. But I want to know how to defend myself when this stalker comes at me. No more letting my attacker have the upper hand.

"Maybe something to absorb some of the alcohol first?" Blake gives me an indulgent smile.

"That sounds good." I follow him toward the elevator. I swear I'm forgetting something. Turning, I look out the glass front and see nothing on the street. The elevator dings and I step on.

Chapter 153

On the Same Page

Blake

It's almost an hour before we're heading down to the gym. I needed to make sure Madison was sober enough to learn the hold releases. When she meets me at the elevator, she's changed into leggings and a tank top that show off her every curve.

I have on a t-shirt and sweatpants. It's hard to miss her heated eyes as her gaze flows over me, lingering on my bulge. When she wets her lips, my cock twitches.

Reminding myself she's not ready for one-on-one time with me yet, I usher her into the elevator. We're talking, that's the important thing.

"How'd it go with your friends?" I lean against the wall as we head down to the workout room. I know this is important to her, having friends. Even if one of them is my sister.

"Good." She tucks a stray hair that escaped her braid behind her ear. Her blue eyes meet mine and my heart pounds. "They're concerned about me, but I'm glad they know everything. It's like a weight lifted off me."

"It's good that you don't have to hide from them, tiger."

Her gaze jumps to mine and then slides away. Fuck, is she nervous to be alone with me? Does she not trust me to hold back?

"I won't jump you, Madison."

She tips her face toward me, and I smirk.

"Except for training purposes."

A smile comes over her and it's like the world is bright again. I rub my chest where it aches at how much I love this woman.

"I hate how things are between us," she says softly.

"Me too, love." I want to take her into my arms and hold her through the threat of the stalker. Sending those texts to her friends and family definitely upped the stakes. If the two of us weren't in this weird in-between, I would have kept her in my arms as long as I could.

This fear grows every day that we might not figure out who the stalker is before he does something to her. Keeping her locked inside isn't healthy for her or us, but fuck, would it ease my mind if we locked her away with us twenty-four seven.

Bill is doing what he can to move us up the line, but there are always higher priorities in a police station. I hope the evidence we need is on that phone. Madison is right though. The conference room was bugged when we talked about retrieving the phone. The stalker may have known about it as well.

Even if he tampered with it, he'll fuck up. He has to.

I can't lose her.

The elevator doors open and we step into the workout room. I turn on the lights while Madison stretches on the mat. Having Noah down here as a buffer was good before, but now it's just her and me.

Joining her on the mat, I warm up, knowing both of us might have bruises by the end of this. If Madison is alone and attacked, I need to know she can handle herself. I'd rather her not be alone. I plan to haunt her every step until we have the stalker behind bars.

"Okay." I clap my hands. "Escaping a choke hold."

She swallows and straightens, pulling her shoulders back. The determination on her face to work through this fear makes me proud.

"We're going to walk through this step by step. Okay?" I step closer. "We'll do it in slow motion over and over until you have the rhythm down. Then I'll put on some protective gear so we can go full force."

"Let's do this."

"First thing, when my hands touch your throat, take a deep breath to steady yourself. Then tuck your chin so I can't put pressure on the front of your throat." I put my hands on her throat with no pressure.

She inhales and tucks her chin down.

"Next, from the outside, grab the inside of my wrists."

"Like this?" She rests her hands over my wrists.

"Yes, now you're going to pull me toward you and knee or kick me anywhere. If you can aim for the groin or stomach, that would be best, but you can kick my shin too. You want me to bend toward you so you can push me off balance and escape."

She gives me a nod.

"No contact these first few times. We'll walk through it. Ready?"

Her blue eyes sparkle. "Yes."

We go through the motions multiple times. I encourage her to make some adjustments until she's moving through the motions quickly.

"Good. Let's go through the other escape method."

She shakes her hands out in front of her. Her eyes are fierce.

"Same thing. Breathe, tuck your chin. This time you're going to grab my left wrist with your left hand, crossing over both my arms. With your free hand, you're going to aim for my nose with the palm of your hand or pull back and punch me. At the same time, you can knee or kick me."

"Okay." She stands with her feet apart ready.

When I put my hands on her neck, she goes through the motions as I repeat the instructions. Over and over we practice, going in slow motion without any real striking.

Then we move on to a back choke hold.

"As soon as you feel the arm around your neck, tuck your chin and grab their arm with both hands. Step to the left and pull down while you snap your arm back to their groin."

We go through the motions several times before working through a few more hold scenarios.

"Do you want to break for a while?" I hand her a water bottle.

She shakes her head. "No, I want to keep going."

We sit on a stack of matts while we drink. What we've done so far hasn't required much exertion. But the next part would.

"Are you sure you want to go through the actual motions?" I brush a strand of hair away from her face and tuck it behind her ear. She's had issues with hands on her throat. "We could do it tomorrow after work."

She shivers a little. "I'd rather freeze with you than in the actual moment when someone's attacking me."

I blow out a breath. "That's fair."

We drink in silence for a few moments.

"Have you tracked down Andrea yet?" She picks at the label on her water bottle instead of looking at me.

"No, but Courtney returns to work on Monday after her family leave." I finish my bottle of water. "We have a lot to discuss with her. And we have to wait to see if the spy contacts our honey trap."

"Do you think it was a coincidence that Courtney was gone when Robert tried to get to me?" She's really focused on that water bottle now.

"No. I don't believe in coincidences."

Do I think Courtney is involved? Yes. I'm not sure how deeply involved she is. But we believe Peter plays a part in the corporate sabotage, and given his interest in her, I can't believe it's a coincidence that she's tied to both Peter and Andrea. Andrea wants nothing more than to humiliate us the way she believes we humiliated her.

Madison nods and drinks a little more. Her brows pinch as she thinks about something. I wish this all could be easier, especially for her.

Her blue eyes flick to me with a question lingering in them.

"What do you want to know, love?" I draw in a deep breath. "I'll try to be an open book."

She downs the rest of her water and sets the bottle aside. "You're really possessive when it comes to me and other men. It makes me think that maybe someone cheated on you? Or betrayed you in some way?"

I rub my hand down my face. "Before we decided to share women, women would use us to get to someone else. Usually but not always Coop."

"But Coop dated Leighton since high school, right?" She cocks her head.

"They didn't officially date until college. And Coop wasn't faithful to her." I watch her carefully because I don't want her to think I'm trying to blow up Coop. "He's different with you."

She nods thoughtfully. "Have you ever been in love before, Blake?"

I shake my head. "I've dated. Even had a few monogamous relationships. But did I love them? No."

"Why not?" Her blue eyes lock on mine.

"Because they weren't you." I take her hand and weave our fingers together. "I can't tell you why those other women couldn't break through. Maybe I've always guarded my heart. But you broke that wall, making me feel vulnerable."

She puts her leg up on the mat as she turns toward me. "Why vulnerable?"

I cup her cheek and sigh. "You're everything I want, everything I need. You spark something fiercely possessive in me. I want to wrap you in bubble wrap and hide you away, but I also want to watch you soar and become the powerhouse I know you'll be someday."

She leans into my hand.

"It wasn't a line when I said loving you terrifies me, tiger." I swallow and blow out my breath to loosen the grip on my chest. "You make me want things I've never wanted before. Never thought I could have and keep the guys as my family. You hold us together. You make us complete. And if you left us, I'm afraid of what that would do to the bond we've had for years."

I rest my forehead against hers. "You could destroy us, love."

"I don't know what the future holds," she says quietly. "I can't say we won't have rough patches, but I'm in this with you. I thought I was going to have fun fucking my four bosses before I moved on to my career. Have the adventure I skipped in college. I didn't expect to fall for you."

Something settles deep inside me.

"I knew I was falling for you when we went back to my apartment that first time." She lifts her forehead from mine and searches my eyes. "But I think I was always falling for you. It hurt when you held yourself back in the beginning. I didn't understand why you didn't want me."

"I wanted you too much." Leaning in, I press a kiss to her forehead. "I didn't want to get caught up. If you ended up being like the others, you would have hurt me. You had that power from the start. From our first phone call."

"Blake, I love you. I'm never going to stop loving you. I can't imagine being with someone other than you four. You're all I need, all I want, all I love." She smiles with so much love I can feel it reach inside me and squeeze my heart.

"I'll make it up to you, tiger. I'll make this right somehow." Proving that I trust her is nearly an impossible feat, but I'll find a way. "I can't lose you."

She nods. "I know."

"Is it okay for me to hold you? Even when we're alone?" I brush that pesky strand behind her ear again.

"Of course. I love your hugs." Her smile is soft and loving.

For now, I brush a kiss over her lips before standing and offering her my hand to help her up.

"Let me gear up and then we'll go through the motions in real time."

I go get the padding on. We have a self-defense class taught here for employees, so we have the equipment I need. I've helped with the class a few times. I leave the gloves off, but even without them, it will protect my front from her attacks.

When I step back into the room, she laughs.

"You worried I'll take you out?" She pushes her fist against the breast pad.

I grin and shake my head. "It's more so you don't pull your punches. In an actual situation, you can't fake it. We need you to be sharp and react without having to think."

"Let's do this." She stands in the middle of the mat.

"This time I'm going to apply a little pressure, not enough to do any damage, but I want you to feel it. Ready?" I'm worried she's going to freeze and won't ever get past that point. But like she said, better with me than an attacker. If she can trust me, we'll get her past it.

"Ready." Her lips press firm with determination.

When I grab her neck, she takes a deep breath. I squeeze slightly. Her chin tucks. Her hands come up and she knees me in the groin. It doesn't get me, but I feel the force on the cup. I bend over like an attacker would if she got him there. She grins at my bent over figure.

"Good job, tiger, but you forgot to run away. And hit harder and knock me over. Pretend I'm Hunter."

She grimaces. "That's a visual I didn't need."

"You need to be rough, love." I step close to her. "Haven't you wanted to take down that bastard?"

Her eyes spark up at me. That's what I want to see.

"Good. Use that anger and hit me for real."

Chapter 154

Knee Deep

Madison

"I think you have it." Blake opens the door to the apartment. "A few more practice sessions and no one will grab you unless you want them to."

I beam because I feel powerful right now. It took a few false starts before I was confident I wouldn't actually hurt Blake, but imagining Hunter as my assailant definitely spurred me on. I'd love to put him in his place.

"I look forward to kicking your ass."

He smirks and pulls me into his arms. "Anything for you, tiger."

His spicy cologne fills my nose as I press my head against his chest. How I could go a day without touching this man is beyond me. Even though I focused on my moves, touching and being touched by Blake made me long for how he plays with me. I love submitting to him, but that takes trust on both our parts.

He's trying and that helps.

Sparks race through my system at being this close to him. But I need to hold that line.

Coop clears his throat. "When you two are done?"

I lift my head off Blake's chest and look up into his gorgeous green eyes. He presses a sweet kiss to my lips, making me long to capture the back of his head and deepen it. But he turns with his arm around my waist to bring me into the kitchen.

Coop sits at the island, working on his laptop.

"Did you find any security breaches?" Blake becomes all business, and I rest my head against his arm. After our talk, I feel more confident that we can get back to where we were.

I've missed being his.

His thumb strokes over my hip, making lightning chase through me.

"None. Our security measures kept them out of our system, which means there's a bug in this room or they hacked the TV and took a screenshot." Coop runs a hand through his loose, long hair.

I stare at the TV. "Can they do that?"

"It's not typical." Coop leans back against the counter and stares at the black TV. His eyes narrow. "Most hackers are looking for money. There's not a lot of information on our TVs that would be useful for them. I disabled the camera and microphone on the TV after we bought it. I didn't want it to be a security issue. The stalker could have accessed it via the Bluetooth but would have needed to be close to set it up. I've disabled the Bluetooth and any other entry points."

"Did we talk about the video anywhere but in the apartment?" Blake squeezes me against him. They never found any bugs in the apartment with their multiple sweeps.

"I can't remember." Coop shuts his laptop and turns to me. "Do you have the picture, sweetheart?"

"I'll grab my phone." I left it on the charger since I didn't need it. Squeezing Blake one more time, I head into my bedroom. When I return, Blake sits next to Coop.

I hand Coop my phone with the picture open. Blake looks over Coop's shoulder.

"My money is on screen capture." Coop shakes his head. "Given the cropping, it's hard to tell, but there are no artifacts on the shot and it doesn't look off angle."

"And if the stalker had a camera in here, why point it at the TV?" Blake takes the phone and hands it back to me. "He would have gotten more interesting things from us watching it."

I look down at the photo. I loved every minute of making this film. Watching it with the guys made me even wetter. That the stalker had access to it makes me queasy.

Blake reaches out and squeezes my arm. "He'll fuck up. He has to."

I nod. He has to.

Coop stands over me and looks at the picture on my phone. "He should have sent the one with you getting fucked by all of us."

His finger trails along my spine all the way down to my ass.

"All of us stuffing you full of cock."

I turn the phone over and set it on the island. I can't let the stalker control every aspect of my life. Stepping into Coop, I reach up and run my fingers through his hair, letting the silky strands slide over my skin.

"I'd rather make untainted memories." I lift my gaze to his heated blue eyes.

Lust stirs inside me. I kept it tamped down while Blake and I were training, but with Coop here, maybe he'd appreciate some payback for when Blake ruined his playtime. Maybe Coop can take control.

His eyes rake me up and down. "Want to show me your new moves, sweetheart?"

Blake remains motionless at the island, carefully scanning my face.

"I wouldn't want to hurt anything vital." I give Coop the smirk he usually gives me.

He stalks slowly around me. "What do I get if I win?"

"What do you want?" I take measured steps back as he follows my retreat until I'm against Coop's door. My heart beats quickly with his every step.

He closes the distance. "Blake, I'm going to need help with our dirty little whore."

A shiver of anticipation races through me. I'm cornered, trapped, and I really don't want to get away as I search Coop's darkened eyes. The stool scrapes the floor and Blake's steps pulse in time with my thundering heart.

Playing with these two on the same page could be as explosive as when they play opposing each other. I press my thighs together at the growing ache. Blake leans on the wall next to me as Coop's hands come to either side of my head.

Blake lifts my braid and runs his hand down it, leaving it to fall over my shoulder. "I bet she can be a good girl if she tries."

Fuck. Like a devil and an angel on my shoulder. A shiver works through me.

"Maybe I just want to be fucked." I lift my gaze to Coop's. His smile is wicked.

"Then you'll need to follow orders, sweetheart. If you're a good little whore, we'll fuck your ass and pussy until you see stars." Coop leans his head down so his mouth touches my earlobe, sending sparks through me. "How do you want to play, Madison?"

My gaze collides with Blake's lust-filled green eyes on his otherwise stoic face.

"Do you want us to take you or do you want to give in to us?" Coop's words make me soaking wet.

I search Blake's eyes. He wants my submission, and this is the only way I can give it to him.

My lips press against Coop's neck as I whisper, "I'm yours to do with what you please."

His breath is ragged in my ear before he slips an arm around me and opens his door.

"Blake." He gestures for Blake to precede us into the room, then backs me inside until my knees hit the bed.

Blake shuts the door.

"Do we want her showered or sweaty?" Coop tips my chin up to search my face. My insides buzz. My lips part in anticipation.

"I know you prefer a dirty girl." Blake sits in the dark leather chair in the corner.

"Strip." Coop draws me away from the bed and sits on the edge with his legs apart. His eyes never leave me.

I take off my top and sports bra. Aiming for the hamper, I toss them over. Coop leans back on his hands as his hooded eyes take in my breasts. They grow heavy and my nipples tighten at his perusal. After I kick off my shoes and toe off my socks, I slide my thumbs into the waistband of my leggings and panties and draw them both down.

"Gorgeous." Coop doesn't move but jerks his head toward Blake. "Turn so Blake can see you."

I do as he says and watch Blake's hooded eyes as he takes in my naked body. His gaze feels like a heated touch as it strokes along my skin. Every inch of me burns to have them touch me.

"Go help Blake get his cock out." Coop's voice is more authoritative than usual and it's flooding my system with need.

I take a step in Blake's direction.

"Uh-uh, my little whore, on your hands and knees if you want to be our good girl."

His words almost make me moan. Fuck, playing with these two never fails to make me so fucking wet.

I lower down to my knees, then crawl over to Blake, knowing Coop is enjoying the sway of my ass. Kneeling before Blake, I reach for the waistband of his sweats and pull them down. He lifts his hips to help me but keeps his hands on the arms of the chair.

I want to lick his thick thighs as I reveal them, but today, I'm going to be their good girl. I need permission.

His boxers are next. His thick erection bobs against his stomach as I free it. My mouth waters, wanting him to slide his cock into my mouth. He reaches over his shoulder and tugs off his t-shirt with one hand, leaving his sculpted body naked for my viewing pleasure. Blake is ripped and every inch of his hard body is mine.

I want to rub all over him and claim him like he's claimed me so many times before.

For a second, we just breathe as I kneel at his feet. His expression fills with pleasure at my submission even if it's not actually to him. We both know I'm submitting to him through Coop, but it doesn't strip away the joy of it.

"Straddle him, my dirty whore, and take his thick cock into your wet pussy."

Fuck. I stand and then kneel, straddling Blake's hips before sliding his cock's head across my clit to my entrance. I suck in a breath at how good it feels. Slowly I ease down over him, taking him into my pussy and feeling the stretch of his cock against my tight walls.

My eyes lock on Blake's but I don't fuck him. Those weren't my instructions. Coop walks around the bed. I take a few deep breaths as my pussy pulses around Blake's cock. Our bodies are pressed together and his green eyes lock with mine, but he doesn't touch me.

The nightstand drawer slides out and closes. A squirt sounds as Coop closes in behind me. My pulse skips, knowing what comes next.

His naked knee wedges between my thigh and the arm of the chair. His front engulfs my back in his warmth. I keep my eyes on Blake's, drowning in the love and lust reflected there. My breasts skim his chest. Everything slows down. Blake's breath bathes my lips as Coop spreads my ass cheeks and nudges his slick cock against my puckered hole before easing inside.

I suck in a breath as he breaches my sensitive opening and fills me so full. Stuffed with both of them.

Blake holds his thumb up to my mouth. "Suck it like a good girl."

I take his thumb into my mouth as Coop pushes the rest of the way inside my ass. I hum around Blake's thumb. I'm full of cock. My tight pussy and ass flutter around them.

Blake takes his thumb from my mouth and slides his hand between our bodies before rubbing his thumb over my clit. I suck in another breath and put my hands on his shoulders to hold myself upright.

"Rock your hips like a good little whore. Fuck our cocks until you come all over us." Coop's words make me wetter and the fire burning inside rages out of control. I want it so fucking bad.

As I lift a little off Blake's cock, Coop's pushes deeper into my ass. When I take Blake's cock back inside, I slide off Coop's a little. It takes me a few seconds of trial and error before I find a rhythm.

My nipples brush along Blake's chest with every move of my hips. His thumb circles my clit, winding me up until I can't help myself.

"Good girls don't come until told, my dirty whore." Coop's words in my ear make me ache, but I hold off the orgasm as best I can while still rocking against their cocks. Every thrust and pull pushes me closer to tipping over the edge.

"Wait." Coop's hands grab my hips, steadying them. He drags his cock almost all the way out of my ass before thrusting back in. Biting my lip, I moan and try to hold back the orgasm barreling down over me, aching for release. He fucks my ass while Blake flicks my clit with his thumb, and his thick cock makes my ass even tighter and more sensitive to Coop's thrusting.

Blake's other hand cups my breast and my already sensitive nipple. I whimper at the additional stimulation, knowing I won't be able to hold off for much longer. My whole body tingles.

"What do you think, Blake? Should we let her come?" Coop thrusts his cock in deep and I cry out but manage to keep from shattering. I'm hanging by a thread.

My pleading eyes meet Blake's. I'm going to come soon whether or not they want me to. I'm not that strong. I want to be his good girl. I want to be their good girl. He thrusts his hips up and pushes deeper into my pussy while pinching my nipple. Both of them are so deep inside me.

"She's already choking my cock, but she's a good girl." His thumb presses on my clit. "She hasn't come yet."

"Come for us like a good girl." Coop's cock punches in and out of my ass as Blake toys with my nipples and clit.

My release barrels over me. I cry out as I convulse around the two cocks inside me. My pussy squeezes around Blake's cock.

"Ride me, tiger," Blake whispers.

I rock my hips over him as Coop keeps fucking my ass. Another wave crashes over me, drawing Coop into his release. He groans in my ear as he floods me with his warm cum. Kissing my neck, he slides out and backs away from me.

Blake's hands go to my hips as I ride him, desperate for another climax. He thrusts up into my pussy, taking everything I have to give. I cry out as I crest the wave of release one more time. When my core milks his cock, he groans and fills me.

I collapse against his chest, more sweaty than when we began.

"Shower time." The sound of the shower running fills the room as Coop opens the bathroom door.

I straighten and look into Blake's satisfied green eyes. "I love you."

He cups my jaw. "I love you." He draws me in for a kiss that claims every piece of me for this man.

He lifts me off him and stands. When I turn to head to the bathroom, Blake's hand smacks my ass hard.

"Hey, what was that for?" I look over my shoulder at his smirking face and twinkling eyes.

"You forgot to call me Daddy."

Chapter 155

Check

Blake

After verifying Courtney is back from her lunch, I head down to her office. Monday morning got away from me. Small fires kept me busy until noon. But this is important. If anyone knows where Andrea is, Courtney will.

I knock on her open door and she looks up from her computer. I don't miss the slight hint of fear before she carefully makes her face impassive.

"What can I do for you, Blake?" She rocks back in her chair as her eyes track my every move.

I step into her office and close the door. Taking my time, I sit in the chair across from her. We're certain she's involved in the corporate sabotage, but how is she involved with the stalker?

Or are they working separately and the crossover is a coincidence? Not that I believe anything is a coincidence.

I lean back and meet her eyes, waiting to see what she'll offer me. When I clasp my hands in my lap, she sets her keyboard to the side and takes a deep breath.

"My mother—"

"I hope she's doing better, but I'm not here to discuss that."

Her face quickly moves from surprise to fear to that blankness again. "How can I help you, Blake?"

"You worked a Saturday a while ago." I cross my ankle over my knee.

"I work a lot of Saturdays." Not according to Hope or my records of her coming and going.

"This one should be memorable since you found Madison screaming in the file room."

A flash of anger passes over her face. If I wasn't watching her closely, I would have missed it.

"The lights went out on her and she panicked." Courtney shrugs. "Seems like you shouldn't leave her alone if she can't handle it."

I let that remark pass because I don't want her to become too defensive. "What were you working on that day?"

"The Lawson project. We were a little behind because a team member got sick, so I came in that day to help us catch up." Courtney relaxes in her chair.

"You came to help Madison when she screamed, but your office is on the opposite side of the building from where she was."

Her eyes sparkle. She's not stupid. "I was getting more coffee in the break room when I heard her."

I nod like I'm accepting her story because I need her to feel confident that she's getting away with everything. I don't know what she has to do with the stalker, but there's some connection there.

"Did you see anyone else that day?"

"No." She doesn't elaborate.

I don't know whether or not to believe her. So I just nod in acknowledgment and move on. "I need to find someone and you know where they are."

"I don't know what—"

"Andrea."

Her mouth forms an O shape before her lips press together.

I lean forward. "If I have to put a PI on it, I will, but something tells me you know where she is."

"Haven't you done enough to ruin her life?" Courtney can't hide her disdain.

I'm beyond caring about Andrea at this point. "She got her payout and her payback. If you don't know where she is, I can always sic Cross on her."

Everyone here knows about Cross and what he can do. We've needed his help before on a couple of projects. He's smart but brutal.

Courtney's eyes narrow. "What do you want from her?"

"I have some questions." Am I angry at Andrea for making Madison a target? Yes, but I'm not going to tell Courtney that. "There are some things we need to go over for closure."

She looks skeptical, but then she caves. "Fine. I can give you her cell phone number and she can decide if she wants to meet with you or not."

Madison

Monday feels like every other day. There were a few text messages with the girls on Sunday evening about arranging to have dinner together on Thursday. The guys were less than enthused about my plan to go alone with Hope, Sara, and Kayla, but Blake said he'd make sure we were taken care of.

We had a quick lunch at our desks to keep up with work today. When I glance at the time, it's almost four. I stand and stretch. When I glance into Seth's open door, he's on the phone. He lifts an eyebrow at me in question.

I point at my nonexistent watch to indicate the time. When he looks down at his computer, he nods and mouths, *I love you*. A smile spreads across my face.

Last week was rough, but hopefully, we're finding our way back. That no one worries about me going and getting the groceries is a good thing. With my access card in hand, I step into the elevator and press lobby.

When it stops on the sixth floor, I step back as my heart pumps a little harder. It never stops. The doors open, and Blake lifts his head from looking at his phone and sees me. His hard face softens, and he steps into the elevator. At the smell of his spicy cologne, I relax and draw in a breath.

The doors close and we continue down to the lobby.

"Grocery time?" Blake glances at me.

"Yes." I brush my hands over my pencil skirt.

"Need any help?" His green eyes search mine. "I mean with the groceries. I don't want you to think I don't trust you, because I do."

I smile softly. "I've got this, but thank you for the offer. Where are you headed?"

"I need to check on a few things." Blake steps closer. His hand wraps around the back of my neck. "If you need me, call me, love."

His lips collide with mine and my breath leaves me. For a second, it's just him and me and everything is perfect. I never want this to end, but it's just a moment. He steps back as the elevator reaches the lobby, but his heated gaze holds me for another breath.

A jolt of desire rushes through me. I step into the lobby and look for Fox. Blake's fingers graze my hip as he brushes past me and heads to the receptionist. He leans his arms on the reception counter and gives her a smile meant to disarm her.

His gaze flicks to me. I don't feel any jealous stirrings because I know he's mine. Whatever he's doing is for work and that's all I need to know.

Fox comes through the double doors, wheeling in the groceries. His gaze bounces off Blake at the receptionist's desk before it finds me. His smile is genuine as he heads my way.

"We have to stop meeting like this." He gives me a cocky, flirty smile.

I just shake my head and grab a couple bags to load into the elevator. "I really need to introduce you to Hope. She's my friend that works here."

"Trying to pawn me off?" He tsks as he sets the bags next to mine. His eyes settle on my engagement ring, but he doesn't mention it.

"I just think you two might hit it off." I grab a few more bags.

"I'm game." He grabs the last couple bags and sets them in the elevator. "Give me a minute, need to reload."

He wheels the cart out of the building, and I lean against the wall, pulling out my phone.

ME:

Hey, remember when I told you about Fox?

Hope usually responds right away so I wait a minute. When I don't get a response, I glance at the receptionist and Blake. She would know if Hope was in today. Hope didn't mention anything yesterday when we were in the group chat about feeling sick.

Maybe the hangover kicked her butt.

The doors open, and Fox comes in with the next load. As soon as we have the elevator full, we ride up. I try Hope one more time.

ME:

Not sure if you're in a meeting or just busy with work. If you want, I can try to set up a meet with Fox. I'll get his number before he leaves.

I slip my phone back into my pocket, grateful this skirt has a pocket. Fox watches me from the corner with his easy smile. Something he said in the past makes me wonder . . .

"You delivered groceries when Andrea worked here, right?"

He grins. "Yeah, she liked me to stick around for a while."

Okay, let's clarify that before my brain takes us the wrong direction. "To help put away the groceries?"

"That and fuck her." His brown eyes meet mine. "She loved for me to fuck her anywhere the guys would eat. I'm not the kind of guy to say no to that."

Ew. Yeah, not getting his number for Hope.

"Do you keep in touch with her?" The elevator arrives on the floor and I open the door so we can carry the groceries in.

"Nah, I'm more of an opportunity seeker." He gives me a wink as he passes me with the bags. "Andrea just wanted to pull one over on these guys. Maybe they're strict bosses. I didn't need a reason. She was all over me."

From what I know about Andrea, I could see that.

"What about the others?" I ask as he takes in the last of the bags.

"Nah, Rachel was stuck-up. Tiffany flirted a little, but she didn't last long enough for me to hit that." Fox pauses in front of me in the doorway. "I'm discreet and Andrea wanted a little something to tide her over. So if you're looking . . ."

I laugh. "I'm not interested in anything little."

He shrugs. "Your loss."

I shake my head and gesture to the elevator. Fuck, the guy is a flirt, but I didn't think he was like that. We take opposite sides of the elevator as it goes down to the lobby.

"Did you and Andrea . . ." Yeah, I'm not saying it. "The whole time?"

He smirks. "That girl was on me from day one to the last day I saw her. When I came here, I came prepared."

I don't need him to finish that sentiment. But I hope he means a condom.

The elevator stops at the lobby, and he walks off backward. "Anytime."

I roll my eyes, and my gaze stops on the receptionist. She's working, but no one is at her desk. The elevator doors almost close, but I step off and walk over to her.

"Hi." I nearly wave but stop myself.

"How can I help you?" Her tone is formal, like she doesn't know who I am.

"Could you tell me if Hope Williams is in today?"

Her brown eyes blink at me before she sighs and looks down at her computer. Her fingers fly over the keys and then stop. "She's not in."

"Thank you." I head back to the elevator. As the doors open, I glance back and find the receptionist watching me. This time I do wave before I step on the elevator and use my access card to go back up to the apartment.

If I didn't have groceries to put away, I could have stopped at Hope's floor and doublechecked. It's not that I don't trust the receptionist—actually, that's exactly why I want to check. That woman doesn't like me. I shake my head as the elevator comes to a stop and head into the apartment.

The windows let in the sunshine as I move around the kitchen putting the groceries away. I like this time on Mondays. It's away from the hustle and bustle of the office and gives me a little peace as I complete the task at hand.

As I put the last box of pasta in the cabinet, my phone buzzes in my pocket.

Hope! It has to be. I pull my phone out and bring up my messages.

UNKNOWN:

Now!

What the hell? An ear-shattering alarm goes off in the apartment. My heart pounds as I look around. I'm all alone, but the alarm is familiar. I need to remain calm. The guys checked the elevator first.

I grab my access card and slip it into my pocket with my phone. When I get to the door, I open it and someone shoves me back. I glimpse black as I stagger on my heels back into the apartment.

When I straighten, the figure is at the door locking it. They're covered in black from head to toe, but male and taller than me. He turns to face me, and a mask completely covers his face.

A scream locks in my throat. My breath stutters in and out. Adrenaline pumps through my body. My brain screams at me, *run!*

I kick my shoes at the intruder before running to my room, whipping the door open, and slamming it shut. I go to lock it but remember the alarm releases all the locks for emergency personnel to get in. As I glance around for a weapon, my gaze lands on the stairway door. I bolt over to it and open it right as my door bangs on the wall.

Racing through, I pace myself on the stairs to make sure I don't do something stupid like twist an ankle. The guy is right behind me. His breathing is heavy like mine. When I reach a landing, he grabs my arm in a punishing grip and jerks me to a halt.

My blood chills as I tug on my arm, but he tightens his grip. For a second, I give in to panic. Let the icy dread roll through me as I stare at my assailant. Black gloves, black shoes, black shirt, black pants. The mask is black with no holes.

Fuck that noise. Stepping closer, I grab his arm at the pressure point like Blake taught me and kick the guy in the nuts as hard as I can. When his grip falls away, I push his shoulders hoping he goes over, but I don't stick around to find out. I charge down the stairs.

Chapter 156

White Knight

Madison

My heart hurts it's pounding so hard, but I don't hesitate. I don't stop to rest but keep winding down the stairs. The cold concrete hurts my bare feet, but I don't care. I need to escape. The only way out is at the bottom of these stairs. I need to reach the bottom. There's no other way out.

The intruder recovers much quicker than I would have liked. His heavy steps echo mine until they're like a drumbeat in my ears. The only other sound is our breath. My stomach twists. If he gets ahold of me again, he won't be so easy to shake.

My phone vibrates in my pocket, but I can't do anything to lose my lead. One moment of hesitation is all it will take for him to catch me. That's not happening. I'm not going to be this guy's victim. I'm done with that.

One more floor. Tears stream down my face. My heart feels like it's going to explode, my side aches, and my lungs are on fire. As I round the corner, a body collides with mine. I don't think. Just react.

I shove, but it doesn't move the person. I open my mouth to scream.

"Madison, it's me!" Blake's voice drains all the fight out of me. I lift my gaze to his face, closing my mouth. I collapse and wrap my arms around him. My heart still thunders in my ears. I was all alone. I can't catch my breath. But I'm safe.

Blake turns to lead me down the steps, but I tug on his shirt.

"Someone's. Following. Me." Every breath is a struggle.

His green eyes meet mine and we both wait. The footsteps that were steadily following me are gone. The flashing emergency light is the only thing that moves.

"Go outside. I'll look." Blake tries to pry me off him, but I cling tighter and shake my head.

Fuck that. I've found my safety and won't let him go. If I have to, I'll wrap myself around him and he can drag me with.

"Please." I tug him toward the exit. I don't want to be left alone again. Safety is right outside that door, but what if whoever attacked me has someone waiting?

Blake hesitates. He wants to go after the intruder. I can read it in his body language. His green eyes search mine. Whatever he sees is enough to convince him. He takes my hand and we begin down the stairs. Tension unwinds from my heart.

With every step, the adrenaline slowly leaves my body. Everything hurts and my feet begin to ache. When I lag behind, he turns and glances down at my bare feet.

Without a word, he swings me up into his arms, with one under my knees and the other under my shoulders, and carries me down the stairs. I wrap my arms around his neck and rest my chin on his shoulder.

My gaze lingers behind us, waiting for the man in black to make an appearance. But he's not there. Blake pushes on the door and we're out in the sunshine. I blink against the sudden brightness, draw in a ragged breath of fresh air, and release it.

I'm not safe anywhere now, except when I'm in their arms. They'll keep me safe.

Blake

I set Madison on her feet in the grass and she sits on the concrete ledge. Her shirtsleeve is torn. Mascara runs down her cheeks. We have a designated meeting point out front, but I can't take her out there like this. Not without a lot of questions that I don't want to answer.

"Are you okay?" I squat in front of her and search her tired blue eyes. "Are you hurt anywhere?"

She shakes her head. Her eyes remain on the door.

"I'll let the others know where we are."

When I text the others, I ask them to bring the police. There's a possible intruder in our apartment or in the stairwell. This isn't a shadow heading toward the back of the building.

Putting my phone in my pocket, I focus on Madison. I wish I had some water to give her, but right now, it's just me and her. I'm not going anywhere.

"What happened?"

She pulls out her phone and hands it to me. It's open to a message from *Unknown* that says *Now!*

Fuck.

She draws in a breath, steadying herself.

"That came in right before the alarms went off. When I opened the apartment door, a guy dressed head to toe in black pushed into the apartment. I threw my shoes at him and ran to the emergency stairs. He grabbed my arm." She looks at the red marks banded around her arm, drawing her fingers over them. Those will definitely bruise, but she grins. "I grabbed above his elbow, kicked him in the nuts, and ran."

"You got away, tiger." Pride swells in my chest, even as fear knots my stomach. She was alone in there. Again. But this time I protected her, by making sure she knew how to defend herself. "Did you recognize the man? Anything distinguishing about him? Even a scent?"

Her gaze goes to the door that remains shut and her smile falls. "Nothing stood out. He's taller than me, but I don't know by how much. It was all too quick. Definitely a man, but he disguised his features."

"The building is surrounded by the police and emergency personnel. If he tries to leave, they'll find him." I reach out and take her hand. "Are you okay? Do I need to have an EMT check you out?"

She exhales. "No, just catching my breath after running down the stairs. I could hear him behind me."

A shiver runs through her and I wish I had a suit jacket, but mine's on the back of my chair in my office. I sit beside her and put my arms around her, offering her my warmth.

Voices disrupt the quiet around us. Coop, Noah, and Seth come around the corner with a few officers. Seth points out the door and stops to talk with the police.

Noah comes forward and sweeps Madison into his arms. "You okay, kitten?"

She nods and tears slip down her face. Coop wraps his jacket around her shoulders and presses a kiss to her head. Satisfied that she's looked after, I leave them to comfort her and join Seth.

"The stairs lead to our apartment, but that elevator is only accessible by card." Seth's tone has an undercurrent of fury. Someone has access to us when they shouldn't.

"Madison opened the door. That's how the intruder gained access. The only exit on that staircase is our apartment." I turn to the officer. "As far as we know, he's still in there."

"I'll let our leader know." The officer steps back over to his group and I see him on his radio.

"Is she okay?" Seth runs a hand through his hair, his gaze on the one thing that matters: Madison. She has on Coop's jacket. The sleeves fall over her hands and the jacket covers most of her. She looks small and vulnerable.

My chest aches at the thought of losing her.

"He grabbed her arm, but she got away." The pride in my voice is unmistakable. She listened and learned those moves, and when it mattered, she didn't freeze.

Fear and rage fill my chest like a swarm of bees. She shouldn't have had to fight. Our apartment should be safe.

The officer comes back over to us. "We have a team entering the building now. If he's still inside, we'll find him."

"If not, then he's either an employee or blending in with the emergency personnel." Seth grabs my shoulder. "I'll book the hotel for tonight. We need to let the employees back in for their belongings."

"We'll move fast." The officer nods and motions to his men.

Fuck appearances. She's ours and we're hers. I stride over to Madison, draw her into my arms, and hold her for a moment. "I'm glad you're safe."

She snuggles into me. "Thank you for showing me how."

"I'd hoped you'd never need it." I kiss the top of her head and guide her back to Coop's arms. When I meet Coop's eyes, I know he'll keep her safe. "I'll be back."

Seth comes in and gives her a quick hug and a few quiet words before he joins me. We go around to the front and across the plaza where the employees all stand around talking. Seth steps forward to address them.

"We're not sure what set off the alarm yet." Seth's voice rings out over the crowd.

They all quiet and turn their attention to him. My gaze scans for anyone who shouldn't be here. And for the people I know should be out here and aren't on assignment.

"The police are making sure it's safe for us to go back inside. I know it's late and you want to get home to your families. If you don't need to return inside, you can head home and put your hours in tomorrow. Please check in with your manager before leaving. If you need to go into the building to get your belongings, we'll let you know when it's clear to do that."

The crowd murmurs as people find their managers. I've spotted

Peter and Courtney. They stand near Yvonne, the receptionist, but they aren't talking to each other. Peter looks like he always does, not winded or sweating from running back up the stairs to the apartment.

If her stalker gained access, how? Is this just another scare tactic or was it an attempt to grab her?

Seth touches my arm. He nods to a space off to the side where we can talk and not be overheard.

"He might be over there." I nod to the crowd. Someone hurt her again. They could be staring at us right now.

"Any description from Madison?" Seth leans back against the building and his gaze flows over the employees.

"Male, taller than her. Mask. All black." I blow out my breath. "It was fast and she didn't have time to get details. She protected herself and ran."

Seth nods. He squeezes my shoulder. "Thank you for teaching her."

I take out my phone. "I need to let Bill know what's happening."

"I'll check to see when we can have the security footage." Seth walks a few steps away to call.

I text Bill Carr, my friend on the force who's working this case for us.

ME:

He tried to get her. He put his hand on her.

BILL:

At the office?

ME:

Yes

BILL:

I'll be there

The same officer from around back comes over as I return my phone to my pocket. Seth joins us.

"This was on the ground outside of the elevators." He holds up a baggie with a white key card that stays at the receptionist's desk.

Seth talks to the officer but I block it out.

My gaze pivots to where I saw Yvonne earlier. She's still there, talking to Courtney. I'll need to verify that this is that access card and it was used to get up to the apartment level. It doesn't have access to the actual apartment, so the guy had to know Madison would open that door.

Otherwise, I would have seen someone waiting for her at the bottom of the stairs when I went to find her. Unless I spooked someone away. If so, maybe a camera caught them.

"No one was inside. We checked everywhere." The officer hands Seth back his card. Knowing these men were in our apartment, in Madison's apartment, feels like another violation from the stalker. Our rooms were all locked, but not the play room.

Fuck. I'm sure they've seen worse, but I don't like to advertise my kinks.

"Noah, Coop, and Madison are on their way to the hotel. We need to finish up here before we head over there." Seth claps me on the back as we walk into the building.

When we reach the apartment, we check that everything is in order and nothing is missing. I'll have a team sweep it for bugs and I'll check the play room myself. We don't know when he stopped pursuing Madison or how long he was alone in our space.

While Seth packs a bag for us, I go down to the lobby to meet with Bill.

"Sorry I couldn't get this to you sooner." Bill holds out a flash drive after I tell him what happened. "With this attempted kidnapping, we pushed the phone up the line, and I got our techs working on it. Pretty sure your stalker got to it before we did."

I take the flash drive and turn it over in my hand. "What makes you say that?"

"You might want to watch that before you show Ms. Harris." Bill nods to the drive and turns to look over his shoulder, but we're all alone. "Pretty sure that's a message for her from her stalker. Whatever Valerie might have had is long gone. We couldn't recover anything from the memory besides what's on that."

A stone lodges in my stomach. He always seems to be one step ahead of us. "What's next?"

"Keep an eye on her. If she feels threatened, tell her to call 911." Bill clears his throat. "We don't have a suspect to charge. But I can have some guys come by during their patrol."

"Thanks, Bill." I shake his hand. His hands are tied, but if something happens, he'll help us out.

"Wish I could do more." Bill lowers his head. "You staying here tonight?"

"No." Our walls have been breached. I'm not sure any of us would put Madison at risk. "I'll contact a personal security company in the morning."

Bill nods. "That would be wise."

We talk for a few more minutes about his wife and their grandkids before he leaves. The thumb drive burns in the palm of my hand. I'm not sure I want to know what's on it, but I need to know in the same breath. Whatever it is, somehow this guy has to fuck up, and that's how we'll catch him.

Chapter 157

Message Received

Madison

"Water?"

"What?" I stop staring out the window at the twinkling lights of the city to focus on Noah and the glass he's offering me. "Oh, thank you."

I take it and drink. Noah sits in front of me on the ottoman.

"What do you need, kitten?" He runs his hand through his hair and I can see this isn't the first time he's done that. We've been in this suite for a while now. It was light when we arrived and now it's dark outside, but I've been numb.

After the police took my statement and a picture of the red marks on my arm, Coop and Noah handled me. They got me in a car and drove me to the hotel. Coop led me to the shower, bathed me, and then bundled me in a terry cloth robe. They set food in front of me and I ate without tasting it.

I'm sure they talked to me or around me, but it's like my brain just shut down and I gave my care into the hands of the men I love.

The cool droplets on the side of the glass run along my fingers. Noah's concerned brown eyes lock with mine.

"I'm sorry," I whisper and take another drink before setting the glass down. "I guess I checked out for a while."

"We were worried." He tugs on my robe, gently. "I'm glad you're okay."

I give him a small smile. "I'm good."

And I mean it. I feel free in a way I never did before. I didn't wait for someone to rescue me. I saved myself. But my attacker gained access to me when I should have been safe. I keep racking my brain to figure out who my stalker could be and why he's so hell-bent on getting to me.

"What's on your mind, kitten?"

I inhale and exhale. "Who is he? What did I do to make him think I would want any of this? What could I have done differently? Was I too flirty? Did I dress provocatively? Did I reject him in some way without even knowing it?"

Noah's hand slides into mine. "This isn't on you. This is on the guy who thought you owed him something. Not you."

"I know that here." I touch my temple. "But it all feels wrong. I must have done something to get his attention. I just don't understand."

Noah's other hand cups my cheek and I fall into his brown eyes, wishing we could stay in this moment forever and not have to worry about stalkers and spies. It's not realistic or even possible, but I could be happy right here with one of the men I love.

He rests his forehead against mine. "I want to keep you safe."

I close my eyes. "I'm safest in your arms."

The door to the suite opens and we both turn to watch Seth and Blake stride in. Coop comes out from the bedroom. Blake's gaze lands on me and he doesn't pause as he crosses the room. As I stand, he sweeps me into his arms and holds me so fucking tight.

I breathe in his spicy cologne and rest my cheek against his steady heartbeat. I love how he protects me.

"What happened?" Coop asks.

"The police retrieved the data from the phone." Seth's voice doesn't sound hopeful. A shard of ice goes through me.

I lift my head to look into Blake's green eyes, hoping against all hope that the answer is on that phone. Hoping he'll tell me this is over. That we know who is doing this to me.

Blake sighs. "It's a message to you."

"His fucked-up version of a love note." Seth shakes his head. His concerned eyes track me.

My heart pounds almost as hard as it did coming down those stairs, but I have to know. "Can I watch it?"

Seth looks to Blake. I return my focus to the strain around Blake's lips and eyes. Whatever it is, it isn't good. My blood runs cold imagining the things that could be on that phone. What all did Valerie take pictures or videos of? What kind of message could the stalker send me this time?

"She has a right to know," Seth says quietly.

Blake searches my eyes before he releases a breath. "Come on. Let's get this over with."

"Can I get dressed first?" I look at the bag Seth carries. I don't mind being undressed around my guys, but I need all the armor I can get to deal with my stalker.

"Come on, princess." Seth holds out his hand to me. Taking it, I follow him into the bedroom. He places the bag on the bed and pulls out sleep shorts and a camisole. He sets them to the side. A pair of panties and a long robe join them.

"Madison." Seth turns to me and I face him. "May I?"

When I nod, he unties my belt and pushes the robe off my shoulders to pool on the floor. A little shiver works through me. I'm not sure if it's the change in temperature or the heated look in his eyes.

He holds my panties out for me to step into and draws them over my hips. His warm fingers linger on my skin. Awareness of this man flows through me. His hands draw me close to him as his head falls to my bare shoulder.

I rest my hands on the back of his neck and whisper, "I'm okay, boss."

"We need you, princess. We can't lose you." He tips his head and kisses the side of my neck. "I love you."

"I'm yours, boss. I love you so much, Seth."

He pulls me into a hug, pressing me against him. For a second, we stay like that. Him fully dressed, me in just panties, pressed tight together like if we let go, we'll be lost. After a few deep breaths, he steps back and finishes dressing me.

Every touch promises something more. More than sex. We have love and this bond that even the stalker can't shatter. Seth will stand by me no matter what and I love him for it.

He wraps the silky robe around me and pulls me in by the ties. His mouth captures mine. It stirs up my need and is all too brief. But we're just delaying the inevitable.

When he leads me into the living room where the others have a laptop set up, Coop holds out his hand. I take it, letting him draw me down onto his lap. He wraps me in his warmth and I snuggle against him to keep the chills at bay.

I'm not ready to get a sneak peek into my stalker's head, but I don't have a choice. Being ignorant isn't an option. Hiding away hasn't helped. He's found me. He'll find me again and I don't want to be caught unaware.

"I'm ready," I announce to the room even though no one asked.

"Do you want to know what to expect?" Blake asks like I'm some broken fragile thing that will fall apart.

These four men have made me stronger. As long as I have their love, I can survive anything. When I meet Blake's green eyes, he straightens like he sees the strength inside me. There's a proud glint in his eyes.

"No, just play it."

Music fills the room. The screen is black. The song sounds familiar. Where have I heard it before? There's the sound of rain and the screen brightens. My heart skips as I realize that's not rain.

It's the longer version of someone creeping up on me in the shower. The door opens and I'm there, pressed against the wall, chasing after an orgasm after meeting the loves of my life.

Noah takes my hand and I squeeze his. This isn't traumatizing like it was when I first saw it. I already knew this existed. This invasion to my privacy. The picture zooms in. First, on my parted lips. My hand on my breast. My stomach. My other hand thrusting between my legs.

It zooms out and the person backs away, panning across the mirror before shutting the door quietly. There's a flash of black as it crosses the mirror. I freeze. Fuck, that wasn't Valerie.

"It's not the same video, tiger. I checked." Blake's tone is light, but I can feel his anger bristling under it.

Fuck. I mean, I didn't make a habit of masturbating in the shower, but it seemed like a safe place to do it. I shake my head.

"What about the person in the mirror? It wasn't Valerie. Can we get anything from that?" I turn when the screen goes black and the music stops.

A voice sends chills through my bones.

"Oh, little one." His voice is strained but also modified, like there are too many tones to identify what his real voice sounds like. There's this repetitive sound I can't identify. "It's a shame about your dress. The only cum on it should be mine and yours."

The camera turns on and a mannequin is stretched out on a twin bed. Its hands are cuffed to the iron headboard. A torn dress covers its body. My lips tremble when I register it's the dress he sent back to me. My floral sundress.

The camera shakes as he moves closer and sits next to the mannequin. The camera follows his leather-gloved hand as he traces its lips before sliding down its neck. He pushes the fabric off the rounded breast of the mannequin.

"So many questions, little one. Are these sensitive? Do you like it when your nipples are pulled and pinched? Can you come from having your breasts played with?" He hums as that repetitive thwapping sound continues.

He runs his hand down the mannequin's stomach before sliding his gloved fingers between its legs. He strokes there in time with the thwapping.

"How about here, little one?" His voice is even more strained. "Do they even know how to please you? Or do they fumble around, forgetting about your pretty little clit, too busy thrusting their cocks into your tight cunt?"

My eyes narrow as realization of what that sound is hits. Recoiling, I cover my mouth with my hand. "Is he masturbating?"

"Sure sounds like it, sweetheart." Coop draws me in tight against him. "Do we really need to watch this?"

"Just wait." Blake's hands are clenched.

"I'm sure they've taken you everywhere, little one. Your pretty mouth, your tight cunt, your supple ass. I don't mind. You see, they're just warming you up for me. They may have you now, but you and I are end game."

Groaning in that weird multitonal way, he comes on the belly of the mannequin. Before his cum can slide onto the dress, he wipes it with a pair of panties. He must have one of those cameras that you can wear while doing an activity because he's definitely using both of his hands.

"These I'll keep until I have you in the flesh, little one."

He holds up the white panties I wore that night. The ones Noah cut off me.

"They smell like your arousal and now they smell like us. You should smell how good we are together."

The video clicks off. I lurch from Coop's hold as bile burns my throat. I rush to the sink at the bar and throw up. It keeps coming up as the images replay in my head. The piece of the song from the beginning plays through my head like an earworm.

It's familiar but not. Like I should know it. I dry heave a few more times before I realize arms hold me firmly.

"I've got you, kitten." Noah draws me upright. Coop wipes my face with a washcloth, taking his time to clean every inch. He steps away and Blake hands me a glass of water.

"That song." My throat is raw and my voice raspy.

"Hozier." Coop leans against the bar, watching me closely. "Pretty sure it's a song called 'Talk.' It was on his album a few years ago. Does it mean anything to you, sweetheart?"

I drink the water, thinking. "I had that album and listened to it my first year in college. But it doesn't have any significance that I can remember."

"Maybe a dance or something?" Noah brushes my hair out of my face.

Shaking my head, I scrunch my forehead. "I didn't have time to go to dances. I was too busy studying, working, and going to class."

Setting the glass down, I walk into the bathroom and brush my teeth. It's easiest to focus on that song. Not on what my stalker wants me to think about. He was careful with his DNA. None of it touched the dress. Careful to only show his gloved hand.

Was that him in the stairwell or another person sent to do his bidding?

When I walk back into the bedroom, the guys sit on the edge of the bed, waiting. Blake holds out his hand and I go to him, sitting between him and Seth and leaning my head against Blake's shoulder.

"This stalker uses other people to get what he wants. Valerie, Jimi, Robert. What if the guy who attacked me today was just another stand-in?" My chest rises and falls as I draw in their presence, letting their warmth chase away the chill in my bones.

"That makes sense. But who would he use this time? Someone who has access to our building." Blake wraps his arm around my waist and pulls me tighter against him.

My heart flutters.

"It could be an employee. Someone we wouldn't have noticed going in and out of the building." Seth slips his hand into mine, tangling our arms together. "Someone Yvonne would give the key card to."

"Or someone who knew where the key card was." Noah lets out a rough breath.

"Someone like Fox? A guy who's been up to the apartment." I scrunch my nose. "He apparently had sex a lot with Andrea up there. And he was just there."

"I'll check into him." Blake rubs my arm. "There are too many possibilities."

"I vote we just disappear for a few months. We can take my private jet." Coop stands and paces in front of us. "Fuck like bunnies on a tropical island."

"This guy has lain in wait for a while now to get her." Noah shakes his head. "Disappearing will only make him more desperate. The question I can't get past is, he's waited years for her, so why now?"

"She didn't even know she had a stalker until she started working for us." Blake's thumb rubs up and down my side almost absent-mindedly.

"We didn't know someone was working against us until she started working for us either." Seth brings my hand to his lips and presses a kiss there while he thinks. "We know they were probably working separately, but that doesn't mean they don't know about each other now."

"We won't figure it out tonight." Noah stands and takes off his shirt. "We need to rest."

My gaze takes him in as his blond hair falls over his eyes while he slips his pants and socks off until he's only in his boxers. Noah is the leanest of my guys, but he works out. His muscles are clearly defined, but he doesn't work to make his body a masterpiece like Coop. Just enough to stay fit and healthy.

I wet my lips.

He turns his knowing brown eyes on me. "We need to rest and go to work in the morning."

I don't know if I'll sleep tonight with that video running rampant through my brain. That portion of the song stuck on repeat. I don't want to play the full song for fear of what message the lyrics might contain.

Blake lifts me onto his lap, startling me. His green eyes search mine as I feel him harden beneath me. I bite my lip as tingles race through my blood.

"You look like you need a distraction, tiger." He strokes my hair out of my face.

The others move behind me and anticipation trickles down my back. "Yes, Daddy."

Blake smirks as he grips the back of my neck. "Good girl."

Chapter 158

Due and Payable

Madison

Every time the phone rings, I jump. My desk is too exposed. There are so many ways someone can get to me and I can't do anything about it. Even though the guys all have their doors open, I'm still alone out here.

My mind tackles the video. Why that clip? Why that song? Why that dress? I pick up my phone and see it's only a little after eleven. I texted the group chat with the girls this morning about what happened. Kayla and Sara have both responded, but not Hope.

Where is she? When I call her desk, it goes straight to voicemail. Maybe I should call her cell phone. Blowing out a breath, I call her cell and again, right into voicemail. Reluctantly, I call down to the receptionist.

"How can I help you?" Yvonne's dislike for me comes through loud and clear even though her tone is pleasant enough.

"Is Hope Williams in today?" I look at my messages to her yesterday that remain unread.

"No. Is there anything else?" Her eye roll comes through in her voice.

"Thank you. No." I disconnect the call and pull up the number to Hope's brother's bar, McAvoy's. It's early and it won't be open, but maybe I can get her brother. This restlessness makes me feel like I need to move. I walk into the break room as I press Call.

The phone rings and rings. "McAvoy's."

"Jason?" I ask, wondering if I should have called him at all. But it's weird that she's not at work and I haven't heard from her.

"Speaking."

"Um. This is Madison, a friend of Hope's. She hasn't been to work this week. Last I saw her was Sunday evening and she was heading to your bar." It all rolls out of me in almost one long sentence.

"Hope didn't come here Sunday." Jason's voice falters.

Fuck. Fuck. Fuck. "Uh, I don't know where she lives. She was pretty drunk when she left. Maybe she got sick and went home?"

"I'll go check on her." Jason clicks off the line.

I hold my phone away from my face and stare at the blank screen. Where could she be? If Jason doesn't know where she is . . . I feel like such a shit friend for waiting until today to reach out.

"Hey." Coop grabs my elbow and turns me to him. His thumb swipes at a tear on my cheek.

I wipe the others away, surprised to find them there.

"What's wrong?"

"Hope." My lip quivers, but I'm not going to cry because it could be nothing. "She hasn't been into work this week and she didn't go to her brother's bar on Sunday."

"Let me check with HR to see who called her in." Coop rubs my cheek. "I'm sure she's fine, just sick."

I nod. Of course she's fine. The alternative is unthinkable.

We walk back to my desk, and he goes into his office. My stomach clenches thinking about how much time has passed since anyone saw her. My guys would worry if they hadn't seen me in an hour, but no one checked in with Hope.

That's not entirely true. I checked in on her Monday. Wait! The group chat. She'd responded Sunday night when we were figuring out Thursday night plans. I open up the chat window and scroll down to the chat Sunday evening.

Every response was *K* or *no*. That sick twist in my stomach tightens. What if something happened to her? I'd never be able to forgive myself.

"She sent a text in."

I turn at Coop's voice and look at his blank face as he reads whatever is on his tablet.

"Nothing specific. Just taking sick leave." Coop drops it to his side. "I have her address if you want to go check on her tonight or at lunch."

"I called her brother. He'll go check on her." The twist doesn't ease, but at least we're doing something.

"If you want, we can swing by after work and bring her some soup." Coop steps forward and drags his thumb over my bottom lip. "It's not too far from here."

I lift my gaze to his light blue eyes. He would do that for me, help me help my friend. That twinkle of mischief is still in his eyes, but also so much love for me.

"I'll wait and call Jason back to see how she is." If she doesn't want to talk to me while she's sick, I'm not going to force her to see me. Maybe she just really hates being sick.

Blake steps out of his office. His gaze flicks between Coop and me as he shrugs on his suit jacket.

"Are you heading out?" There's nothing on his schedule for lunch today.

"Andrea called. Wants to meet and clear the air." Blake shakes his head and comes over to me. "I couldn't be happier that she was the bitch she is, because if we hadn't gone through her, we wouldn't have you."

His kiss is warm and filled with love. I swear I'm going to get a contact high from all the love these guys are throwing around.

"I love you, Blake." I search his green eyes to make sure he believes what I'm telling him.

He gives me a cocky grin. "I know, love. I'll be back soon."

Coop draws me back to him as Blake walks away. "Need me to facilitate some more time between you two?"

I press my hands to his chest. Pretty sure Blake and I are on the same page again. But I did enjoy our time together.

"Coop." Seth steps out of his office. "Theo has something. He wants us to meet him downstairs. Patrick is already waiting for us."

"To be continued." Coop kisses me until I'm dizzy with desire. He steps away with a smug smile.

I just shake my head and touch my lips, buzzing from his kiss. Seth's dark blue eyes meet mine as he straightens his shirt cuffs.

"We'll be back shortly, princess." He closes in on me and kisses my cheek. The heady scent of sandalwood fills my senses, making my insides soften. "Noah's meeting is done in fifteen. The receptionist doesn't have an access card anymore. You'll be good? You can come down with us if you want."

"I'll be good." I can't follow them around all the time. There's still work to do.

Seth nods and brushes his thumb along my jaw. They make their way to the elevator and disappear inside, leaving me alone. Turning, I look at their office doors, knowing no one is inside them. A little fear trickles down my spine as I step up to Noah's. He had to go down to the main floor for a meeting with his team.

The phone rings and I jump. I laugh at myself because the only way into this area is the elevator or the emergency stairs. Both doors I can clearly see from my desk.

"This is Madison." Sitting at my desk, I stare at the elevator. I'm fine up here on my own. I just need to focus on work.

"You have a package at reception." The receptionist is brief and to the point.

"Okay." I glance around, wondering if I should leave my desk when no one is up here. "I can be down in fifteen minutes."

Noah will be back.

"I need you to come get it now. I can't keep packages at my desk." She clicks off the connection.

Okay, then. I wanted to be where people are, well, this will work. I grab my purse in case I want to stop at the vending machines on the way back. Suddenly, chocolate sounds great. It feels ridiculous, but I should text the guys what I'm doing in case they come back early.

My phone vibrates as I enter the elevator and press the button for the lobby. I glance down and see it's a text from Hope. Relief pours through me. Her brother must have told her I'm worried about her. Thank goodness.

I open it as the elevator descends, but it's an audio file. I press Play.

"Be a good girl." The modulated voice from my nightmares comes out of my phone's speakers. My pulse quickens. "Tell Madison what's going to happen to you if she doesn't come to me."

"Madison? Madison, don't come it's a trap!" A loud slap sounds and Hope cries out. I flinch like he hit me.

"Stupid girl. If you don't want your friend to end up like Valerie, you'll take the box and go to your old apartment. The key is in the box. Further instructions will be provided there."

My hands tremble and my stomach twists.

"Oh, and don't forget to shower, little one. I want every inch of you sparkling clean for me. I'll be watching."

The message ends. I startle when the elevator doors ding and open to the lobby. The chatter of people enters the elevator, but I can't move.

He has her. He's going to hurt her. He might already have hurt her.

The box? I step out of the elevator and see the white box tied with silver ribbon. Just like his other present. My stomach churns. The elevator closes behind me and I wish I'd stepped back on it and ridden it back to safety, back to the guys.

They're busy. They'd want to know, but I don't know how much the stalker has access to. Can he see me right now? Does he know what I text? Fuck.

I can't let Hope get hurt. Not in my place. It's time to unmask this fucker once and for all. I'll play his game, but I'm playing it my way.

"Thank you," I tell the receptionist as I take the box.

"Whatever." She turns back to her computer.

"Can you tell Blake that I need to run an errand?"

She looks at me like I'm insane. "Why don't you just text him?"

I make up an excuse. "I forgot my phone." I don't want to let my stalker know that I'm telling Blake anything.

"Fine." She types up a quick message and sends it.

"Thank you." I swallow and take my package out to the curb. It doesn't take any time to hail a cab and I'm on my way to my old apartment. Fuck.

The box sits on my lap, but it might as well be filled with poisonous snakes the way I hold it. I'm not eager to find out the contents. Why wouldn't he just leave it in the apartment?

Fuck, the locks. Blake changed the locks and I don't have a key, but apparently, one is in this box. Biting my lip, I open the ribbon and lift the lid. Inside on top of some white tissue paper is the key.

I quickly grab it and put the lid back in place, tying it shut. My phone buzzes and it's the group chat with Hope, Sara, and Kayla. He has her phone so I know he'll see whatever message I send to them.

> SARA:
>
> Still on for Thursday dinner? I need some margaritas!
>
> KAYLA:
>
> Yasss!

Biting my lip, I consider what I can say that will make them suspect something is wrong. How much does the stalker really know about me? How many conversations has he listened to?

ME:

We should have daiquiris at McAvoy's. They're the best.

SARA:

Girl, yes. OMG, Kayla, you have to try them.

KAYLA:

No need to twist my arm. I'm down.

ME:

We need to remember to take a selfie. We forgot last time.

Please, Sara, remember the night at McAvoy's. When the stalker sent me pictures of us. The cab stops in front of my apartment and I pay the fare. I swallow down my fear as I enter the building and head straight up the stairs. He could be here waiting for me.

I know it's a trap, but when will the door shut behind me and make it impossible to escape?

The cameras in the apartment are probably back to watch me. After all, he has a key. Bile rises in my throat. Why would he want me to come back here? As I top the stairs, Robert's door comes into view.

We've eliminated him time and again, but what if he is the stalker? I don't trust anyone outside of my small group. My friends and Seth, Blake, Noah, and Coop.

The key fits the lock on my door and I push it open. I choke down a scream because the apartment, which should be empty, now has furniture in it. It's like I never left.

But as I get closer, I can tell it's not *the* furniture we had. The couch isn't dingy or stained. The table isn't scarred from Jeff's knife digging into it. Everything looks the same but new.

Dread pools in my stomach. When I enter my bedroom, sure enough, it looks exactly how I had it. Like I never left. With my heartbeat throbbing in my ears, I glance up at the light. I could climb up and see if there's a new camera in there.

It probably wouldn't be there though. That would be too easy. Underestimating my stalker is dangerous. He's gone to a lot of trouble to set this up. If I don't do what he says, I don't know what he'll do to Hope. Placing the box on the bedspread that looks like my old one, I stop. I need to breathe. I need to scream. I need to run. But I can't.

He has Hope. No one but me knows that. I need to help her. Even if I told someone else, we have no clue who the stalker is. We'd never be able to find her.

I swallow and open the box, pushing the tissue away to uncover the new floral sundress that I loved. When he sent the torn one, he said he'd bought the same dress. My stomach flips and my hands tremble as I lift it out. There's a note beneath it.

In bold script, it reads:

I want our first time to be special.
Take your time getting ready.
Wash thoroughly.
Listen to your favorite song.
Wear your favorite dress.
Tonight is all about you, little one.

The urge to ball the note up and throw it across the room rides me hard, but I resist and let it slip back into the box. There's a small box inside and I open it to find my grandma's bracelet, which was in my jewelry box in the apartment. There's another larger box with a pair of sandals, brand new. They match a pair I wore to death because I loved them.

Nothing about this freaks me out anymore. I just feel empty and numb. Of course he gathered all these things and set this up. I'm sure he had a part in making sure all the guys were busy when he texted me and sent me the box.

I just want this over. If today is my last day, so be it. I've loved enough in the past month for a lifetime. I want my future with my men, but that can't happen with this stalker plaguing my every step.

I'll fight when I can, but I need to make sure Hope is safe first. I can't believe he dragged her into this. But I'll do what he wants to keep her safe. He better not have hurt her.

There's another thing wrapped in tissue paper. It feels like fabric when I pick it up, so I unwrap it, revealing pristine white panties and a bra. In my size.

A shiver creeps down my spine as I try to keep from making a face of disgust. Instead, I pick up all the items and head into the bathroom. Against the wall facing the shower is a flat screen that wasn't there before.

I notice the camera lens at the top, and when I turn on the shower, the light clicks on and the screen comes to life. The same song by Hozier, "Talk," comes on, but this time it starts from the beginning. The screen begins a slideshow of pics and videos of me over the past four years.

Private moments. Candid moments. Even some with me and the guys I brought home during college. I never looked comfortable with those guys. I never felt comfortable with them. Not like Blake, Noah, Coop, and Seth make me feel.

Do they even know I'm gone yet? Ignoring the screen, I strip and step into the shower. Blake and me in this room fills my mind as I wash with soap and hair products that are brand new and the same as mine. The song fills the room with its haunting melody, but my gaze keeps being drawn to the door.

The lyric about being loved by my stalker cuts at some fragile part of me. I might not get out of this. No one will come riding to my rescue. I have to figure out how to save myself.

My gaze flicks back to the door.

What if he comes in? What do I do? How do I fight him off and find out where Hope is?

It all feels so hopeless right now. I finish the shower and dry with the towel hanging where it always did. I let my brain turn off and just go with muscle memory as I get ready like I would before I met my guys. Everything I need is exactly where it should be.

The stalker knows my life. He knows me. But he can't know everything about me. Not my thoughts or feelings. I smooth the brush through my hair before putting on cotton candy pink lipstick.

I haven't worn this brand since freshman year. I'm not even sure if they still make it. When I'm finished, I watch the video for a few moments and listen to the ominous tone of the song. When I leave this bathroom, everything will change.

I'll save Hope and find out who my stalker is. Then I'll figure out how to get away from him by leaving a trail my men can follow to find me. Please let them find me.

Chapter 159

Clock Out

Blake

The bar isn't crowded for midday, and I see Andrea right away. Heads turn when she walks in. She's always attracted attention no matter where she goes. Her dark hair hangs in loose curls down her back. Her blue eyes find me immediately. She's slightly taller than Madison. Her dress clings to her curves.

At one point, she was all I could think about. She consumed me, but now, I can't stand the sight of her. To me, she represents all the women who tried to come between us. Who tried to destroy us.

She played us. That would be bad enough, but she tried to hurt Madison. Luckily Robert isn't a fool except when it comes to Madison. I can't blame him. She gets under my skin like no one else has.

I love her.

Andrea's red lips curve into a familiar smile as she approaches.

"Blake." She holds out her hand. "I'm glad you reached out."

When I shake her hand, she joins me at the bar. She gives me a coy look.

"A handshake?"

"What were you expecting?" I take a sip of my drink and hold my finger up to get the attention of the bartender.

"You always greeted me with kisses." She sighs as she crosses her legs toward me.

The bartender saves me from saying something I might regret. I need her to give me information. She asks for a glass of red wine and he gives her a nod.

"You've stayed in touch with Courtney?" I keep my tone casual.

"Yes, we grew close while we worked together. It shocked her when you asked for my number, but I knew." She's smug.

"What did you know?"

The bartender sets the wine in front of her, and she takes a sip, trying to draw my attention to her lips. She turns to me and gives me this smile that says she's hopeful.

"That your new assistant isn't everything you hoped she'd be, so you're looking to resume our liaison." She purses her lips.

I chuckle. She has no fucking clue. "You'd let go of the past? From the way you left, I figured you were finished with us."

"Definitely finished with the group, but you know I've always been more interested in you." She tips her chin down to look up at me. "You treated me the way I need to be treated."

"Hmm." I take a drink as if contemplating her offer. When compared to Madison, Andrea is severely lacking. "Why do you think our current assistant isn't exactly what I need?"

Laughter spills out of her. "She's barely an adult. She probably gets along best with Noah, does everything Seth tells her to, and Coop . . . He's probably still fucking everything that moves. I don't believe they're engaged for one minute. Maybe he needed someone to get his mother off his back."

I give an acknowledging grunt.

"But you . . ." She smiles and runs her red-nailed fingertip down my sleeve. "You need a woman to give you what you need. Someone who will obey your every command."

"We had a good time." I give her that because she's a narcissist and will eat it up like candy.

"We did." She spins her bar stool toward me. "We can again."

"It was Seth's idea to bring her on." I just need Andrea to feed me information. Prove to me how smart she is.

"He always did like a pretty face." She sips her wine. "I'm sure she's eager to please everyone too, like a little puppy."

My jaw clenches but I smirk. "She doesn't know what it takes to please someone like me."

"I'm not surprised." She sets her hands on the bar. "Courtney says she's naive. You need someone who will be cunning and cutthroat."

"And you're that woman?" I tip my glass, watching the fluid shift, waiting for her to give me what I want.

"I'm the best you've ever had. As a lover. As an assistant. As a partner." She leans back and slides her foot against my calf. "I could run circles around that little girl."

"Hmm, I don't know if I'll be able to get out of the contract." I give her an assessing look. "We agreed to exclusivity this time around."

"I don't think she'll be a problem for long." She smiles.

"What makes you say that?"

"I've heard she's got someone who will do anything to make her his." She slides her hand over mine. "Which means you'll be free to choose whoever you want."

"Do you know who it is? If anyone could figure out the mystery, it would be you." I turn my hand over to hold hers and raise her knuckles to press a kiss on the back of them. I meet her heated eyes. She thinks she's got me. Fuck this bitch.

"I wish. He didn't seem in a hurry to get her away from you guys." She shrugs delicately and rubs my hand with her thumb. "I got a little too eager."

"How so?" My skin crawls from her touch.

Her eyes narrow on me and I give her a cocky grin.

"You'll be mad." She blows out a breath and pouts. "It'll be just like before. You'll choose those guys over me."

"Maybe I'm done being second best. Maybe I'm ready to go out on my own so I can be with the best I ever had." This is almost too easy.

"I was pretty angry at the way you guys treated me." She meets my eyes.

"We had to make a statement, especially when you tried to blackmail us." When her hand tenses in mine, I run my thumb over hers. "We couldn't let you sell our story."

"I tired of waiting for you to figure out I was the one." She sighs. "You didn't seem to want to be away from your friends, even though they just weigh you down."

I nod like I agree with her. "So you helped Courtney try to ruin our reputation so you'd force me to go out on my own."

Her eyes widen briefly before she nods.

"Only because I knew that's what would be best for you. I started collecting your clients, knowing you'd want to help me make my company the best. I just need you to make it complete. The only problem in our way was the girl, but that guy is definitely taking care of her." Her smile is wicked. "We'll be able to be together."

I have to stop myself from squeezing her hand. From forcing her to tell me what the fuck that's supposed to mean. My heart pounds, and the need to check on Madison rides me hard, but she's safe in the building with the others. "What do you mean he's 'taking care of her'?"

"He's taking her now." She smiles and bats her eyes at me. "So you'll be free to come to me. And we can tell all the clients I liberated that they'll have the best of the best, because it will just be me and you."

He's taking her now. Fuck.

"Who is he?"

"Who cares?" Andrea runs her hand down my tie. "You and I have a lot of making up to do, but I forgive you for being cruel to me."

"How do you know about him?"

She straightens at my tone a little. I need to calm the fuck down and get what I need from her.

"I'm just amazed you know. It's not common knowledge that she has a stalker." I lift my other hand to push her hair behind her ear. "You always kept me guessing."

She smiles. "Yvonne. She told Courtney. She's been helping us a little with our plans, too, since she knows your schedule."

My blood turns to ice. I release her. "So you admit to compromising our business and that you were the one who talked to Robert."

She seems a little confused as I draw away, but she nods. "Robert was a mistake. He couldn't follow through, but he definitely seemed like the kind to kidnap the girl. I did it all for you and me." She sets her hand on my thigh and looks at me like I'm the prize. "I wanted to make sure you knew I cared about you. That I wanted you to be number one. You don't deserve to be Seth's lackey. You should be the boss and I'll stand beside you. We can do it together."

"You'll hear from our lawyers soon. Potentially the police." I stand and nod to the bartender to close my tab.

"The police? What?" Her blue eyes blink up at me.

"That's what happens when you break the law, Andrea. And I want to thank you for proving that Madison is the only woman for me."

She laughs. "This is a one-time deal, Blake. You can take me now or join your friends as your business crumbles around you."

I shake my head and walk out of the bar, pulling up my text messages. I need to check on Madison. There are no new text messages.

ME:

Where are you?

MADISON:

. . .

I get in the car and Tim heads in the direction of the office. All the while those three dots appear and disappear and then stop. My pulse races. My hands are clammy. When I text the others, I don't get any responses. I pull up the app I installed on Madison's phone to track her location.

I've never needed to use it, but it's standard on our corporate phones in case someone loses it. It's at her old apartment. I open up the group chat with Seth, Coop, and Noah.

ME:

Does anyone have their eyes on Madison?

Turning to Tim, I say, "Change of plans."

I give him the address for Madison's apartment, and he turns the car around. There's no way I'm letting anyone else get their hands on the love of my life.

Noah

The meeting drags on. I tap my pen against the conference table and think about Madison. Every night with her is amazing. Last night was no exception.

This meeting should have been over twenty minutes ago.

Adam keeps talking about the differences between last year's numbers and this year's. I should take notes. Instead, I've been worried about what happened yesterday. The stalker almost had her. His bruises formed on her skin this morning.

More fucking bruises.

If he can get to her here at work, he can get to her anywhere. Though I'm all for making it as hard as possible for him. The problem is, we still have too many suspects. I know the guys are focused on the stalker being a man, but there's still a slim chance it could be a woman. Or multiple people.

A dangerous obsession with Madison could drive anyone mad.

But she's my obsession, ours. I keep going over conversations in my mind, trying to figure out who the stalker could be.

"Mr. Burns?"

I wince at the name, but Phoebe is new. "Just call me Noah. What can I help you with?"

Phoebe blushes and glances over at Adam. "Um, we don't have anything more to report."

I rise and close my laptop. "Good. Meeting adjourned."

Before the others even gather their materials, I'm out the door and opening my phone.

BLAKE:

Does anyone have their eyes on Madison?

I get in the elevator and tap my key card. What the fuck is that supposed to mean? Everyone is supposed to be on the office floor, but maybe they went to lunch early.

ME:

Heading up now. Are we at lunch? Should I go to our apartment instead?

The elevator arrives at the top floor and I step out into the office. Her desk is empty. That's not surprising. I walk over to the other offices. All empty.

I go over the entire floor, but no one else is here.

ME:

Where is everyone?

BLAKE:

Seth, Coop, and Madison were in the office when I left.

Andrea said the stalker is taking her now

Her phone shows her at her old apartment

I'm already at the elevator and the doors open. I step in and press the button for the apartment floor. What the hell is going on? Why would she be at her old apartment?

ME:

I'll check here.

BLAKE:

Yvonne might know more

Yvonne? The receptionist? Fuck.

As I step into our apartment, it's clear she's not here. I know it, but I continue my search with panic rising up to strangle me. How the hell did he get her?

Yesterday he had to use the fire alarm. Today she was upstairs working. Everything seemed like a normal day. She even gave me that smile when I left for my meeting.

Fuck, I need to check the main floor. Maybe she went to see Hope. Why the fuck aren't Seth and Coop responding?

Chapter 160

Unraveling

Seth

Coop and I ride the elevator down to the sixth floor.

"Should we have left her there on her own?" Coop glances at his phone.

"Noah's meeting is over in fifteen minutes." Worry trickles through my blood, but we need to finish this. It's only a few minutes. She'll be fine.

When the elevator opens, Patrick nods to greet us. "Gentlemen."

"Patrick." Coop narrows his eyes on Patrick. We've all suspected him to be the stalker, but there are too many other possibilities.

"Theo is in the conference room and security is on their way." Patrick leads us down the hallway. I study him for any sign that would prove he's Madison's stalker. She hit her stalker yesterday, but nowhere that would be visible.

"We didn't see you yesterday," I casually point out.

"Worked at the office in the morning and I spent all afternoon at the police station. I got mugged at lunch." Patrick opens the door and we step inside. "I'm just glad the guy only wanted my wallet."

"Sorry that happened to you," I say. "I hope they get the guy."

He couldn't have been here chasing Madison yesterday afternoon then, but that doesn't mean he couldn't have hired someone.

"Hey." Theo looks up from his computer with a smile. "We got them."

Coop grins. "Finally, something goes our way."

I nod and take a seat next to Theo.

"Security will escort them out." Patrick sits at the end. "But we have time if you have some questions to ask them."

I get my head in the game. "Sounds good."

A knock sounds on the door. Then our security team walks in with Courtney and Peter.

"Please have a seat." I gesture to the open chairs in front of me.

Courtney presses her lips thin and narrows her eyes but sits down. Peter looks like he's sweating bullets.

"You two have been busy." I take the paper with all the clients they contacted from my folder and slide it across the table.

Peter pales, but Courtney barely glances at it. She crosses her arms.

"This is your official exit interview. We'll determine litigation soon." Coop reclines like this is beneath him. "But there are a few things we'd like to know."

Peter will be the weakest link. He already looks like he's going to vomit.

"Tortious interference, defamation, potentially criminal charges if you used our information to create a new business."

Peter swallows, but Courtney smiles.

"Defamation only works if what we said wasn't true. If we said anything." She leans back in her chair and crosses her legs.

"Do you have anything of use to add, Courtney?" I ask.

"Not without my lawyer." She turns her nose up and I gesture to Matt who steps forward.

"Matt will take you to your office to gather your personal effects. You'll need to give him all your access cards and keys for your office." I gesture and Matt pulls her chair back.

She nods and leaves with Matt.

"Peter, do you understand what's happening?" I study him. He's still pale.

"I . . ." He stops and looks at Patrick and then Coop and finally me. He sighs like he knows he's got no recourse at this point. "She asked me if I could help her. I knew what she was doing was shady as fuck, but . . ."

"You wanted to fuck her." Coop sits forward with his elbows on the table. "I bet she made it worth your while."

He swallows. "Yeah, but it was only smaller companies. Ones that wouldn't make a huge impact. It was all good until Courtney told me to go after Madison. I've got nothing against you guys. Honest. But fuck, Madison kicked me in the balls and I worried I'd be pissing blood. I wouldn't have hurt her. Courtney just wanted me to take her somewhere."

Fuck. He was the man on the stairs. "You bruised her."

"What?" Peter looks over at me. "Oh, sorry, man. The adrenaline was pumping through me so fucking hard."

Patrick leans in. "You just admitted to attacking a fellow employee. I've already texted my contact at the police department and they're sending a car to take you down to book you for assault."

"Fuck. Fuck. Fuck." Peter pushes his hands into his hair and pulls. "It wasn't my idea. It was those bitches."

"Bitches?" I ask, as in more than one.

"Courtney and Andrea. They have this whole plan to take you guys down. If they weren't so hot, it wouldn't have been worth it. Fuck, it wasn't worth it. They keep saying you guys are morally corrupt, but I don't want to go to jail because these bitches didn't get the job they wanted. They wanted me to pretend to be the stalker so Madison would leave."

"Alex." I motion to the other security officer.

"Come on. I'll tell you anything you want to know. Just don't charge me. I can't make it in prison." Peter looks as panicked as he sounds. "Yvonne. Fuck, Yvonne is in on it. She tells us your schedule so we can go after new clients after doing research. She gave me the key card to get up into your apartment. Fuck, she had the black outfit all ready—"

"That's enough." Patrick stands and gestures to Alex. "Save it for the police."

Alex looks to me and I nod, wondering what the hell was wrong with Patrick. When the door closes behind them, Patrick sits.

"He's obviously making shit up to save his own ass." Patrick straightens the stack of papers in front of him. "He probably took that card himself. But none of this interview is admissible in court, so better to save it for the police."

Maybe. But Peter was talking. We could have gotten more from him. Even if they were lies, it's information to look into.

"The assault charge will stick while we gather more evidence to support our other claims." Patrick sighs. "You'll tell your assistant that we've got the guy?"

"Yes. It will take a load off her mind to know at least this guy's been caught." My eyes never leave Patrick. But Peter's not the stalker. I had Cross look into him. He didn't ever have contact with Madison before she started working here. There's no intersection. Why did Patrick cut him off? What more did Peter know?

Coop clears his throat. "We should probably head back upstairs."

When my gaze meets his, he gives me a subtle nod to come on. "Right. Thank you, Theo, for all your work."

He dips his head at the praise as he grabs his stuff. "I'd do it again in a heartbeat. That was fun."

"Thank you, Patrick. Do you want me to walk you out?"

Patrick looks down at his phone. "No, I can find my own way out. I'll head to the police station to give them the evidence. As always, if you need me, you know how to reach me."

Patrick packs up his things and follows Theo. The door shuts, leaving Coop and I alone.

"Let's review that tape again." Coop stands. The tape of the security footage from yesterday at the receptionist station. We were trying to figure out who got the card and when. But now that we know who to watch out for, we might have better luck.

It doesn't take us long to find Peter at the receptionist desk as Yvonne passes him the card, so subtly that had I not known that's what was happening, I would have never realized it.

My phone has been going off, but we were too intent on the video.

Finally, I pick it up and look at the texts. Oh, shit.

"Coop, we have a problem."

The door opens and Noah steps through the doorway. His hair is messier than usual. His eyes are wild and panicked. My heart plummets into my stomach.

"He's got her."

Coop

We head down to Yvonne's desk. The elevator is so fucking slow, I think I'm going to lose my mind. My heart feels suspended, waiting to see what the fuck is up and what's down.

We don't know he's got her, but she's gone, and Blake said her phone is at her apartment. There's no reason for her to leave us. We love her and she loves us. I can't let my fear take over. I can't let myself believe she left us willingly.

But if the stalker has her, that means Peter and Patrick are off the hook. They were both with us.

The doors open, and Yvonne sits there like all is right with the world. I should have guessed she was in on this. She always flirts with me like I'm her ticket out from behind that desk.

I stop the other two. "Let me talk to her."

Seth looks like he wants to protest.

"If we all gang up on her, she's going to balk. Let me charm her." The idea makes my stomach churn, but I've got to know what she knows.

"Okay."

"Let me know what Blake finds." I run a hand over my hair to make sure it's all in place.

Blake's stuck in traffic. Every second is precious, but in this case, we have to wait. Madison isn't responding to any of our calls or texts. But I can't focus on that. Not right now.

The last time I talked to Yvonne, she'd let my mother up to the offices unannounced. Now this. If she's somehow involved, I'm not sure I can control myself.

When I stop in front of Yvonne's desk, she lifts her gaze to mine. There's wariness in her eyes, but she pastes on a smile.

"Good morning, Mr. Graham. How may I help you?"

"Yvonne." I give her a slight nod. "I just wanted to see if you might have seen Madison leaving the building."

We watched the exchange on the video before coming down. Madison talked to her for a few minutes. Yvonne typed something on her phone and then sent it. Madison left with a box under her arm and went out the front doors. She didn't come back in.

She didn't leave a message. Nothing. She's just gone.

"I think she left a while ago. I rarely keep track of people's lunch breaks." Her brown eyes meet mine with no hesitation. She didn't mention the package.

I lean down and give her my best smile. "Did she leave a message for someone?"

Yvonne gives that fake look like she's thinking before she shakes her head. "I don't remember her leaving a message."

"We don't have time for this." Seth stops behind Yvonne and she stiffens. "Give me your corporate phone."

She sets it in his hand. Seth scrolls through it.

"Fuck." He holds up the phone so I can see the screen.

YVONNE:

Your bird is in the wind. She thinks I'm messaging one of them.

HIM:

Good

"I'll collect my things and go." Yvonne grabs her purse and gives me a smile. "There's nothing you can hold me back for. It's been real fun working for you guys, but I've got someone willing to take care of me."

When she stands, Seth moves out of her way. There's not a lot we can do here. She has every right to leave, and if we detain her, they could charge us with unlawful imprisonment.

We don't need her, anyway. The video showed her giving Madison a white box with a silver ribbon. Just like the one her torn dress came to her in. Madison took it and left. We know she went to her apartment.

I blow out a breath. "Time to follow the breadcrumbs."

Chapter 161

Trapped

Madison

Part of me expects to open the bathroom door and be attacked. But when I open the door, nothing happens. I return to the bedroom, put on my jewelry and shoes, and pick up my phone. It buzzes in my hand and I scream a little.

> **BLAKE:**
> Where are you?

I automatically begin to type *My apartment for now*, but my phone buzzes again.

> **UNKNOWN:**
> Don't tell him or I'll kill your little friend.

Fuck. I type a little more on Blake's message. *I'm saving Hope*, but I don't send it. Then I flip to the other conversation.

> **ME:**
> What next?

UNKNOWN:

Leave your phone on the bed and go to the kitchen.

On the counter are instructions

ME:

Okay

On the message to Blake I type, *Leaving phone and following instructions in kitchen. I don't know where I'm going, but I will make it back to you.*

Leaving it unsent, I swallow and set my phone on the bed beside the box, flipping it over so if they text, the stalker won't see that I wrote something. Blake, Noah, Coop, and Seth. I hope they all know how much I love them.

All I want is to get back to them, but not at the cost of Hope's life.

I leave my room hesitantly. Fearful he might be here, ready to pounce like all the others before him. When nothing happens, I walk to the kitchen. On the counter is a small box I didn't notice before. I open it and inside is a folded note and a cell phone.

Somewhere in this room is a camera watching me. Maybe multiple. I unfold the note and read it.

Downstairs a car waits for you, get in the back seat.
They'll bring you to me

Fuck, this is where I could call the police and let them know what's happening. Or run back to my guys and be safe.

Let Coop hold me while we all discuss how to get out of this. Seth would tell me to be smart. Think things through. Blake would tell me to be strong. Even when fear takes the lead, I can hold my own. Coop would say something to break the tension and then hold me and tell me I'm fierce and beautiful.

And Noah . . . A tear slips from my eye to trail down my cheek.

Noah would be my rock. He would stand beside me and support me in whatever I chose to do.

They all love me and I ache to return to their arms. But I also know they'll understand why I'm doing this.

I leave the note behind.

The TV turns on. An image of Hope tied to a twin bed fills the screen. She wears the same outfit as Sunday with a blindfold over her eyes.

"Just let me go," she whispers. Her voice hoarse like she's either screamed too much or hasn't had anything to drink. Maybe both. My stomach twists into knots. My pulse quickens with the need to help her.

"When my little one arrives, I'll free you." The modulated voice sounds from off to the side. "If she doesn't . . ."

A gloved hand with a knife appears near Hope. I cover my mouth as it slides across her upper arm. She screams as blood runs down her skin from the opening wound.

"So much skin to cut, so much blood to lose. Too bad you're so small. Get here quick, little one, or I'll have to grab one of your other friends when this one doesn't make it."

Blood streaks down Hope's arm as she makes little gasping noises. Tears track down my face. I can't let him hurt her more. I pick up the phone from the counter.

When I rush out the door, I slam into Robert. He grabs my arms to steady me.

"Madison?" He releases me. "What's going on?"

I shake my head. "I need to go. Now."

"Are you okay?" His concern makes the tears flow harder. The guys know my number on the other phone, but not this one.

"Tell Blake that I'm following the instructions. I don't know where they'll lead, but I have to go."

"Madison. How can I help?" His brown eyes hold mine. This guy has watched out for me since day one. He may have liked me more than I liked him, but I know he isn't the stalker.

"Do you have your phone?" My whisper is barely more than a breath. I don't have a lot of time. After opening the new phone, I find the contact page with the phone's number, then cover the little camera on the front. I don't know what the stalker has set up, maybe he can see and hear everything through this phone.

I hold the phone against my side and lean in to whisper. "Take a picture of the screen and show it to Blake."

Robert nods and I hold out the phone, covering the camera. When he takes the picture, I mouth, *Thank you.*

I don't know how much time I have, but hopefully knowing this number will help them find me. I hurry down the steps to the first floor and cross the lobby. A car waits on the curb, but I hesitate.

I could keep running until I'm back in their arms.

The front window on the car rolls down slightly. "Ms. Harris?"

I draw in a deep breath and step closer. "Yes?"

"Get in the back."

I glance back at the building that was my home for years. Movement in the glass on the door captures my attention and I see Robert. He's taking pictures. I exhale.

Good. Maybe he'll tell Blake or he'll call the police. Either way, it's better than nothing. My gaze returns to the car idling at the curb.

Fuck. This is it. Once I get in, I'm in *his* hands.

I open the door and slide onto the leather seats. The partition is up and I can't see the driver or outside. The windows are practically blacked out.

The phone buzzes in my hand and I'm afraid to look.

UNKNOWN:

Good, little one

When a shiver works through me, I straighten the sundress over my knees. There's nothing I can do while the driver winds down streets. Time passes, but I can't even tell if we're still in the city. Trying to keep track of all the turns he makes is impossible. For all I know, we're driving in circles.

The phone rests on the seat beside me. It could be my lifeline or only the stalker's connection to me. It could be both. I don't know what the guys can do with the number if they get it.

Maybe there's a way to track it, but don't you need to use it to be trackable? The only number I can communicate with is the stalker's. This phone is his. He'll know if I reach out to anyone else. Besides, I don't have anyone's number memorized.

There is one thing I want to know.

> **ME:**
>
> Is Hope okay?

UNKNOWN:

She'll be fine as long as you do what you're told.

> **ME:**
>
> You'll let her go when you have me?

UNKNOWN:

When I know you'll behave.

> **ME:**
>
> Send me a pic so I know she's okay.

I blow out a breath even as fear creeps up my spine. Coldness settles over me and I shiver. He doesn't send the picture, but I'm not sure I would have trusted it was new and not something he took days ago.

Setting the phone aside again, I rest my head on the seat. I'm not letting my mind dwell on this being a fool's errand. I have no proof that Hope is still alive, but I have to have faith that she is. Because her dying at the hands of my stalker would be unimaginable. I don't think I could recover from something like that.

The driver doesn't pause long at any point along the way, but I don't try the doors to escape. I'd rather not confirm I'm locked in.

After about an hour, the car comes to a stop. The phone buzzes.

> UNKNOWN:
>
> You've reached your destination, little one.
>
> Get comfortable
>
> I'll be there soon

Picking up the phone, I open the car door. When I step out, all I see is green and a little white house. It's too fucking serene to be the end. It's beautiful and peaceful and at complete odds with the anxiety flooding my body. The surrounding trees block my view so I can't tell which way the city is from here. Which way is home?

When I close the door to the car, it rolls away, crunching gravel as it goes.

I stare after it, half wishing I'd jumped back in, but Hope is counting on me.

Straightening, I walk up the sidewalk and pause at the door. Am I supposed to knock? Just go in?

The door lock snicks. The phone buzzes in my hand.

> UNKNOWN:
>
> Wait inside, little one

Fan-fucking-tastic. I walk into what looks like a vacation home. The alarm beeps to alert me the door is open. The house is beautifully decorated with nothing that would identify its owner. No personal pictures hang on the wall next to the basic artwork. The living room has cream-colored furniture with blue accents. There's a fireplace that looks like it's actually wood burning. Little blue vases sit on the mantel.

It looks so normal. But nothing about this situation is normal.

"Hello?" My voice is small. When no one answers, I say it louder. "Hello?"

Still no one.

I relax a little. I'd rather be alone in this strange place than sharing the space with my stalker.

Okay, I shake off the shivers of dread and focus. Take in my surroundings. Figure out if there's anything I can use to protect myself. I'm not defenseless here. He doesn't have me tied up, just Hope. And until I find her, he might as well have me trapped.

While the house is small, the kitchen is large with marble counters and beautiful chef-worthy appliances. No knives or stabby things. I check every drawer. Not even a pair of scissors.

I move on to the next room. A crystal chandelier hangs over a dining room table with seating for six. Down the hall, I find a primary bedroom with an en suite bathroom.

All my bath products are in it alongside masculine ones I've never seen. I spend as little time as possible in that room. I don't want to think about what he wants from me or how I'm going to overpower him here.

I'm checking out the bedroom drawers when I hear the beep of the door opening. Cold sweat coats my body as I shut the drawer as quietly as possible. I sink down behind the bed. Unfortunately, another mattress is under it or I'd slide beneath to hide better.

Heeled footsteps click on the wood floors outside the room I'm in. Heeled? Not the typical sound of male steps. I freeze as doors open and close.

Then the footsteps stop outside my door. I hold my breath, too afraid to move.

The door opens, and Anna Beck stands there looking around. She walks in and stops at the end of the bed, seeing me there. I can't move.

Holy fuck, what is she doing here? Is she my stalker? Has she been in front of me all along? Her excitement to see me at the benefit? The weird lunch date? The odd bathroom conversation? She's known me forever. How hard would it have been for her to figure out everything? She has money and power.

"Madison?" She glances over her shoulder and then steps toward me.

When I flinch away, she holds her hands down in front of her to calm me. There's nowhere to go. I've cornered myself.

"What are you doing here?" She keeps looking over her shoulder like she expects someone to pop up behind her. It's unnerving. Is she working with someone else?

"A car brought me here." I don't know what game she's playing, but I'm not buying into anything right now. I straighten and wait for her explanation.

"Is Patrick with you?" She glances again.

"No." My brow furrows. Why would Patrick be here? Why doesn't she end this game?

Her eyes narrow. "Look, I don't know what he promised you, but he's not leaving me for anyone. We have a prenup. He'll get nothing, and he's used to money. Trust me. This is fruitless."

I tip my head to the side in confusion. Leave her for me? What is she trying to get me to say? How will she use that against me? "I'm sorry, but what?"

"He's made promises to women before. God knows, the man can't keep it in his pants. But he always comes back to me." Sighing, she gestures for me to follow her. "I didn't figure you'd be one of them. After all, you have Cooper Graham, but Patrick can be persuasive."

"I'm not here for your husband." I'm barely holding back my shock. If this is a game she's playing, I'm buying into it. She thinks I'm sleeping with her husband? Fuck.

What if this *is* all a game?

I follow her back into the living room. She heads over to the bar and opens it with a key.

"Do you want a glass of red?" She raises her eyebrow as she holds up a bottle.

I shake my head. I'm so confused. "Where are we?"

"No? Shame, but more for me." She uncorks a bottle and pours herself a glass. "One of my family's homes. How did you even get out here? I didn't see a car. Though it shouldn't surprise me. He tries to keep it secret, but I always know. This is the first time he's used this particular house."

She sets the bottle down and lifts the glass to her lips, meeting my eyes over the rim. "I found pictures of you and figured you were his latest obsession, but then you and I talked. And Coop. Well, why would you want my husband when you have Cooper Graham?" She laughs and takes a drink. "Fuck, I'd leave my husband for Cooper Graham."

Maybe she's telling the truth. I don't know what to think, but she's not being aggressive. Maybe I can get more information if I share. Besides, if she's the stalker, she already knows all this. I won't be telling her anything new.

"I don't want your husband. A car brought me out here and dropped me off. Someone's been stalking me." I lift the phone and bring it over to her. "They gave me this phone."

Her brow furrows as she reads the opened text conversation. "I've gotten notifications of my family's vacation home being accessed for the last month. I figured it was Patrick and his latest whore, but it's possible someone else could have been using it. With my client load, I haven't been able to get out here, but today there was an accident and my client canceled."

Her eyes widen as she looks up at me. As our situation finally registers. We're alone in the middle of nowhere with a stalker on his way.

"We should go." She sets down her wineglass and takes my hand.

When she tugs, I don't move. I shake my head. It's not that easy. I haven't found Hope. "The stalker has my friend. I can't leave."

"What are you going to do? Just give yourself to whoever this psychopath is?" She drops my hand, goes to her purse, and digs through it. "Fuck. I mean, there's a list of people who have access to this house, some with questionable morals. But I never imagined they'd bring someone here to be victimized."

"Maybe my friend is here somewhere? An attic? The basement?" I ask hopefully, wrapping my arms around my waist. I didn't find either when I was looking. "If I knew she was safe, we could leave and get the police."

She holds up her phone, squinting at the screen. "There's a basement. A false cabinet hides the door in the kitchen on the right. Fuck."

Staring at her phone, she moves it around like she's searching for a signal.

"What's wrong?" My stomach twists.

"I'm not getting a signal. Usually I have to go up the drive a little." She looks from her phone to me. "Do you want to go with me or see if your friend is in the basement?"

My heart is pounding so hard. If Hope is here and we can get her out, I don't have to face my stalker. I'm only here to save Hope. I want to be gone from here as quickly as possible, before the stalker comes for me.

"I'll check the basement." I straighten.

She nods. "Okay, give me five minutes."

She walks out the door, and I head to where she said the basement door is hidden. I open the cabinet and see stairs leading down into the darkness. When I flip the switch, a dim light comes on down there.

Fuck, this feels like a stupid move. What if she's just trying to lure me into the basement without having to drag me there? I glance over my shoulder, but Anna is still outside. What if this is all a trap? *Yes, Madison, go into the basement where all my torture devices are waiting.*

A noise rises from the basement. A muffled thump. Fuck. I creep down the steps slowly and turn on the flashlight function on the phone. The thumping gets louder the closer I get to the bottom.

My heart feels like it's going to burst out of my chest as I reach the floor and turn the corner. Hope's blue eyes meet mine. She's muttering something behind the gag tied around her mouth. Her foot stops kicking at the footboard.

I rush to her side. The cut on her arm is cleaned and bandaged. I lift her head to untie the cloth across her mouth. I have so many questions, but all I can do is focus on freeing her.

We can talk as soon as we're both safe.

A beep sounds as the front door opens and closes.

"She's down here," I yell. I frantically work at the knot with my fingernails. To Hope, I say, "Don't worry. Anna is here and she's going to get us to safety. We're going to be okay. Everything's going to be okay."

Heavy footsteps walk across the floor overhead, making me pause and look back to the stairs. Ice trickles down my spine as Hope makes noises behind the gag. My pulse stutters as the door to the basement slams shut.

Chapter 162

Informed Decision

Blake

Traffic has tied me up for too long. My foot taps on the floorboard as my fingers twitch on my knees. *He's taking her now* keeps running through my mind. I can't be too late. When Tim pulls up to the curb, I throw open the door and get out. The car engine stops and another door opens and closes.

"I'm not letting you go in there alone." Tim straightens his suit as he walks up the sidewalk to join me. "You can't just rush in."

He's right, but if she's in danger . . .

"Let's go." I nod to the door that's ajar. I hate that she lived here. Sure, she was a broke college student, but all the times she might have been in danger because of where she lived and who she lived with, it makes me angry.

We climb the stairs quickly. Both of our drivers are physically fit, retired military, and able to handle themselves if we need bodyguards. It's the reason we hired them. As soon as Tim and I top the stairs, Robert's door opens.

"Hey!" He steps out into the hallway. "Madison left thirty minutes ago."

I look him up and down. He runs a hand through his already messy hair.

"She was in a hurry, but she gave me this." He holds out his phone with a screenshot of a phone. Madison's bracelet can be seen in the shot. "She said she was following instructions."

I go to her door and turn the knob. It's unlocked. As I open the door, I hiss out a breath and stare at the furniture. Fuck, it looks like her apartment before we cleared it out. What the fuck is the point of this?

Tim brushes past me as he walks through the door and carefully checks every room.

In the kitchen, there's an open box and a note. I read the note. He sent a car for her. I check her phone's location and it's still here.

"All clear. Blake, you're going to want to see this." Tim's voice carries through the apartment.

Discarding the note, I head to Madison's bedroom. It's just like it was when she lived here. A box similar to the one the torn dress came in sits on the bed. A note lies inside.

As I read each line, hot rage pours through me. He wanted her to get ready for him. I crumple up the note and toss it in the box. I want to destroy everything in this room because she's not here.

I was too late again. This time I might lose her forever.

"Her phone, sir." Tim points out the cell phone I tracked here.

I pick it up and enter the code. Her conversation with me is on the screen.

> *My apartment for now. I'm saving Hope.*
> *Leaving phone and following instructions in kitchen. I don't know*
> *where I'm going, but I will make it back to you.*

My heart squeezes. "He has Hope. Tim, can you call McAvoy's and find Jason Williams? I'll call Bill Carr."

Nodding, Tim heads into the other room with his phone in his hand.

I press Bill's contact and it rings.

"This is Carr."

"Bill, it's Blake. He's got her." Something inside me breaks and my words crack. My breath shudders in and out. Fuck, I need to hold it together.

"What do we know?" Bill's tone is clear and authoritative.

I fill him in while examining the box. When I enter the bathroom, I find Madison's clothes from today. The shower is still wet and her soft floral scent fills the room. The only major difference is the screen on the wall.

Curious, I press buttons but nothing happens. I turn on the shower and the screen flares to life. A song streams out. The same one that was with the message the other day. Images flash on the screen. A younger Madison with other guys. Guys that didn't matter to her then and don't matter to her now.

"There's got to be fingerprints somewhere in here, Bill."

"Maybe. He's been careful. I don't see him slipping up now when he almost has her." Bill's walking somewhere. "How long did you say Hope Williams has been missing?"

"Last we saw her was Sunday. Two days ago." I run my hand through my hair and turn off the shower. The music continues. It must be on a timer.

"I'll get that phone number to tracking."

When I walk into the living room, Robert steps forward.

"I took pictures of the car that drove her too."

Something concrete. Thank fuck Robert is a nosey guy. I stride over to him and tell Bill, "I'm sending you some pictures of the car that drove her. It's likely a service, but maybe we can find out where it dropped her off."

This might give us the most information. I clap Robert on the shoulder and give him a grateful smile. "Thank you."

"Anything to help Madison." He steps away, and I give him my number to forward the pictures to me.

I rattle off the plate number to Bill before sending the pictures to him. She's wearing that floral sundress and her makeup isn't what she normally does. What sick fantasy is this guy playing out?

Bill says he'll get back to me as soon as he knows something. He's sending a car to the apartment to process everything.

I need to tell the others and find out what they know. We'll have to wait for Bill to work his magic. With two potential victims currently and an active crime in progress, they'll be moved to the front of the line.

The stalker could have them anywhere. He has a thirty-minute lead on us and we have no direction yet. Even though we have clues to where he's taking her, we still don't know who he is.

Madison

I finish untying the knot holding the gag in Hope's mouth. What happened to Anna? Those weren't her footsteps. Did she get away? What if the stalker got her too? She has children at home waiting for her.

What if Anna was a distraction to get me down here? She seemed sincere in her confusion, but can I trust her? Should I trust anyone? But if she's a victim like me . . .

Anna should have left and gotten help, not waited for me. Who knows what the stalker would do with her? I should have insisted, but what if Hope needs medical attention?

I pull the gag out of Hope's mouth.

"You shouldn't be here." Hope's voice is hoarse and low. "He knew you'd come for me."

"I wouldn't leave you here by yourself." I reach for the rope binding her wrist. "Yesterday I was worried about you, but I got attacked and forgot to follow up. I'm so sorry."

She shakes her head. "He has my phone. He made it look like I texted in sick. I live alone, so anything could happen and no one would have known. Jason would check, if I didn't show up after a few days."

"I called him earlier. He said he would check on you." I release one wrist and move to the next. "Do you know who the stalker is?"

Hope shakes her head. "No. He disguises his voice and wears all black. For all I know it could be a different guy every time he comes down. I'm not even sure where we are. He releases me to use the bathroom, but that's it."

If there's more than one of them, we're screwed. I might be able to get away from one guy, but for how long? When he chased me down the stairwell, he still had plenty of energy and I was burning mine out. And this time I'll need to make sure Hope gets away too.

When I move down to her ankle, she sits up to rub her wrist. Footsteps walk overhead and we both pause and look up. My breath catches as fear grips my heart tight.

It sounds like he's dragging something across the floor. Fuck, could that be Anna? My hands shake. A door opens and closes. Everything inside me freezes, waiting, worrying that his next trip will be down those stairs. The steps walk back across.

"Hurry," Hope whispers and leans forward to untie her other ankle.

My phone buzzes and my heart clatters to a halt.

UNKNOWN:

You're not supposed to be trapped, little one.

Anger pours through me, hot and heavy.

ME:

You're the one that trapped me.

UNKNOWN:

I saved you, little one.

You weren't safe at that company anymore.

ME:

The only threat to me is you

UNKNOWN:

Poor little one. I'm not the one that chased you.

I don't play those types of games

Not like your beloved Coop

He wasn't the one chasing me? More lies?

At the mention of Coop, ice swirls with the anger coursing through me. He can't get to them. Can he? Are the guys safe?

My heart aches with how fast it beats. With me here, the guys should be out of danger.

The footsteps recede again. Determination floods me as I work on the knot in the rope binding Hope's ankle. The front door beeps as it opens and shuts. I blow out a breath. For now, he's leaving us.

A car starts outside as I free Hope's ankle. This is our chance. Maybe the stalker left, maybe Anna got away. Either way, we have an opening.

"Can you stand?"

She nods and we both look up as the car heads off. With bated breath, we wait for a few minutes, listening to find out if he's still here. When nothing happens, I help her to her feet, and we walk to the bathroom first. It's pretty sparse compared to the one upstairs.

There's a cup and I fill it with water for her.

"Has he fed you at all?"

She nods while she swallows down more water. "Once a day."

Fuck, that's not enough. Even though she's small, that's not enough food. She lowers herself onto the closed toilet with shaky legs and leans forward, obviously exhausted just from walking in here. She's not in good shape. If we have to fight, it will just be me fighting for us.

"Are you ready to climb the stairs?" Because I'm not leaving her down here alone. Fuck no. I hope Anna got a call out to the police before the guy arrived. If she's really on our side.

Nodding, Hope sets the cup on the counter. She gives me a steady look. Holding her hand, I let her use me to help her walk. We go slowly. I doubt the door is unlocked anyway and I don't know how much time we'll have before he returns.

We get to the stairs and need to pause to let Hope rest for a moment.

I glance up at the door and the light that edges in around it. "Why don't you stay here and I'll check to see if it's locked."

I don't want her to waste her energy. She nods and sits on the steps.

Creeping up the stairs, I get to the top and wait a moment to listen. No movement still, but what if there really is more than one of him? We heard the car drive away, but what if that was Anna, escaping?

The other option is that sound of something being dragged was Anna. A shiver races down my spine. It feels futile. Like he knows my every move before I do it and I still know nothing about him.

Even as hopeless as I feel, a little light shines deep inside me.

Blake will find me. He always does. He has to.

Closing my eyes and hoping, I twist the knob. It doesn't move. I shine my phone light on it and it's smooth on this side. Studying the door, I know it swings out into the kitchen so I check the hinges. They're on my side.

I could potentially pull the pins out with the right tools, or the right makeshift tools. I glance at my phone screen. The flashlight is draining the power, but the phone has no service here. It does however have wifi, which is how the stalker is sending me messages.

During the car ride, I checked and the phone has limited capabilities. Everything is password protected except the messaging. I can't even check to see if he blocked numbers.

I press my head to the door. Even if I could get a message out, the stalker would know, and I don't even know where I am or how to tell them how to find me.

Returning to Hope, I sit down next to her on the steps. "I have wifi, but there's a lock on the administrative tasks like adding additional apps. I don't know the guys' numbers, but even if I did, all I know is this is Anna's family vacation home."

"Can I try?" Hope holds out her hand. "I know Jason's number by heart."

"This is the stalker's phone. He can probably see anything we send."

"Good." Her blue eyes harden. Her strength is still there even after days of captivity. The stalker never should have dragged her into this.

I place the phone in her hand. She sends her message and hands it back to me. The basement is almost as stark as the upstairs. Definitely no weapons, but maybe something got left in the corners.

I can't just sit here and let this happen to me. We can prepare.

"I need to look for something to knock those hinge pins out. Like a nail and a rock would work. Do you want to help or do you need to rest?" I run my eyes over Hope. Besides a few bruises and the bandage, she seems fine, but two days without much food or water has to be making her weak.

"I'm all in on finding a way out of here. I'm not staring at the ceiling for another two days."

When I offer her my hand, she stands with my help. We go around the perimeter of the basement together, because we only have the one flashlight. The few times it caught on something reflective, I got excited, but it turned out to be Christmas tinsel.

Time seems to pass differently down here. We don't know if Jason received our text. If the cops know we're missing. If Robert was able to get to Blake and give him this number. No texts come through as we finish searching the bathroom.

We both turn to the bed. It's obviously held together with something. But we don't have any tools to take it apart. There are a couple of tiny windows. Neither of us could fit through them. With no neighbors, breaking them and yelling would only piss off the stalker.

We sink down on the bed with our hands interlaced. I'm exhausted. The level of fear racing through me is just too much.

"I'm sorry you're here because of me." This all feels really fucking disheartening right now.

Hope squeezes my hand. "At least we're not alone."

The hours she must have spent down here. Alone. Not knowing what would happen next. I squeeze her hand back. She rests her head against my shoulder. Exhaling, I glance up at the door. Someone should find us.

The front door beeps as it opens and slams shut.

"Anna?" A worried masculine voice fills the upstairs. "Anna, where are you?"

My mind registers Patrick's voice. Hope smiles. "We're saved."

I want to believe we are, but how many times did we think Patrick might be the stalker? He isn't creepy toward me, and he saved me from Jimi, but was that because he knew Jimi would be attacking me? He also got those texts from the stalker.

Indecision paralyzes me. Am I walking into another trap? Or is this our ticket to freedom?

Chapter 163

Business Bombshell

Seth

We're all gathered in the police station with Bill Carr and his team. Blake stands against the wall with his arms crossed, intently following Bill with his gaze. Coop sits next to Theo toward the back corner of the room.

Theo types furiously to help figure out where the text to Jason came from. We've tried calling the phone and messaging it, but it's either out of range or our numbers are blocked.

Jason Williams stands next to Blake, a permanent scowl etched on his face. We listened to the voice message the stalker left about Hope. Madison went to protect her. To give her a chance. As frustrated as I am about Madison putting herself in harm's way, I'm proud of her devotion to her friend.

Noah sits next to Coop with his hair a mess. He's paying attention to both Bill and Theo. His fingers work on a small section of rope, tying knots and fraying the end. Just like my raw nerves.

We're all tense and just waiting to find out where she is. Bill gathered us all with his team to make sure we're caught up and so we can add anything we can think of.

"We've pulled a listing of all of Anna Beck's family's properties." Bill pulls up the list and shows where they are on the projected map. Right now, we assume Anna Beck is also a hostage, held against her will, according to Hope's message.

But no one is sure. They called Patrick Beck, but it went straight to voicemail. He left the station hours ago after making sure they had the evidence on the spy. He should be here too. His wife could be in danger.

Or he could be the danger. It keeps running through my mind. The access to us and to Madison he's had. This past week especially. And what the fuck was up with him sending Andrew Faust our way? Yes, he was the perfect bait for Courtney and Andrea, but Patrick had to know Madison and Andrew's history.

"The couple of texts that went through to the cell phone Madison has were most likely en route to the vacation home." Bill takes off the homes that aren't in the direction the phone was moving. "We aren't able to ping it for a location, so either it's off or out of range."

That leaves three properties where Madison could be.

"Thanks to Mr. Addler, we have the plates of the town car that drove Madison to the cabin. We're working now to get an emergency court order to find out where it dropped her off and who hired the car, so it will be admissible in court."

When Theo leans close to Coop, I walk over to them in the back corner of the staff room.

"It was sent via wifi. I've got the IP address," Theo quietly explains. "I can find out where it originated, but not legally."

I glance over my shoulder at Bill who's assigning tasks to groups. We could pull him over and ask, but this is Madison and Hope. I'd rather get them alive and not be able to prosecute their abductor than sit through a murder trial.

Fear pulses through me. It's been hours since I've seen her. We might already be too late, but if we keep doing things through the "proper channels," we might lose her entirely.

Theo, Coop, and Noah look up at me, waiting for my decision. "Do it."

I turn to Coop. He runs his hand through his hair and nods.

"I'll call my guy." Coop stands and takes out his phone. Wherever we're going, we need to get there fast.

We're all feeling the stress. She's by herself. Even if we get the right address, if we rely on the police, it might take a while to actually get to the location. Who knows how much more trauma our girl would endure in that time?

We have the means to get to her and to go around the normal red tape. We'll do what it takes and worry about the consequences later.

Madison

Hope stands and tugs on my hand. "Come on."

"What if it's a trick?" I can't just walk into my stalker's hands. That's what I've been doing all day. Giving in to what he wants me to do. He has the power to hurt the people I love. And they won't see him coming.

Hope and I aren't safe here, but we're also not giving in.

"We're stuck here, Madison. We have no way out. At least up there, we might have a chance. There are two of us. We could overpower him and get out. He has to have a car, right?"

"It's too far away from the city for him not to have a car." Standing, I nod. "Okay, let's do this."

I stop her as we reach the stairs. "If you have an opening, run. Don't worry about me. If he has you, he can control me. But if you escape, I can fight. Promise me."

Her blue eyes search mine and tears well in them. "If it's our only chance, I promise."

When she hugs me, I wrap my arms around her tight. I don't know what's going to happen once we get upstairs, but I want to get us both out of here alive and whole.

We climb the steps and I pound on the door. "We're in here! Help!"

Footsteps hurry our way. The door is yanked open. The brightness of the kitchen blinds me momentarily. But then Patrick is there in his suit and running a hand through his blond hair.

"What are you two doing in the basement?" He seems genuinely surprised as he steps back to let us out.

I put myself between him and Hope. I can't trust anyone. "Someone kidnapped Hope and then threatened me to get me out here."

To this house, that you know about. Fuck, am I talking to my stalker? He's no longer paying attention to me. Anna did say that she tracked his phone out here multiple times, right? Or did she just notice the door to the place alerting her that someone was here? Fuck, why can't I remember?

"Have you seen Anna? The last place her phone was located was around here." He looks at his phone and presses on a few things. He holds it angled so I can't get a good look at the screen. "It doesn't make sense. Why would she come to this place?"

"She was here and went outside to get a signal. But when I went into the basement, someone locked me down there." I shift with Hope behind me toward the back door. We can make a run for it. Even without a car, we're better off hiding in the woods than fighting off this man.

"I didn't see her car outside." Turning his back to me, he walks toward the living room.

"Now's our chance," I whisper to Hope.

Patrick curses low.

"Patrick?" Anna's confused voice reaches us. "What are you doing here? Someone hit me on the head."

"I've got you now, dear."

I step toward the doorway to the living room. Patrick kneels next to Anna, who's half in a closet. He lifts Anna into his arms and lowers her gently onto the couch.

"I was worried you were having another affair." She presses her fingers to her bleeding temple.

Hope rushes over to the sink, grabs a washcloth, and wets it. She walks past me into the living room and I follow, wrapping my arms around my waist, waiting for the next shoe to drop.

"Here." Hope holds the cloth out to Patrick.

He smiles and takes it. "Thank you."

Anna's gaze finds mine as she smiles. "You found your friend." Her face crumples and her hand clenches onto Patrick's sleeve. "Your stalker is still out there."

"We heard him drive away." Hope steps back beside me. I edge in front of her slightly. I didn't protect her before and the stalker took her.

The seconds tick down around me. I can feel the door slamming shut on our opportunity to get out of here. It's like this ticking clock in my chest that gets quicker and quicker until it's practically strangling me.

"We should all leave," I blurt out. "We can get in Patrick's car and drive to the police station or the hospital. The authorities can come out and make sure everything's safe. Maybe they can figure out who the stalker is. But we should leave now!"

Patrick plays the doting husband perfectly, tenderly wiping at his wife's head injury. Even flinching when she hisses in pain. "I don't know if we should move her."

"Fine. Give me your keys and I'll go get help." I step forward and hold out my hand. "If she needs an ambulance, I'll call as soon as I get a signal on my phone. Hope needs to be evaluated by a doctor. She's probably dehydrated."

I wiggle my fingers. *Please. Please be the good guy you're pretending to be.* Please let me be wrong that this is just another trap.

"Honey, she's right." Anna grabs Patrick's wrist and pleads with him. "We can all go. I'll be fine. We need to get to a hospital. We need to leave before that guy comes back."

He brushes the hair away from the nasty cut on her forehead. "If you think you can make it."

"I do." She gives him this tender smile that makes me feel bad for even considering her husband was my stalker. He has two kids. Sure, he might be a cheater, but that doesn't make him a creepy stalker masturbating on a mannequin tied to a bed in my old dress.

A little shiver trails over me. My phone buzzes in my hand.

UNKNOWN:

Time's up, little one

"No, no, no, no, no." I grab Hope's hand and tug her back with me. We need to get to the back door. We need to escape.

"What's wrong, Madison?"

"We have to go." I turn as the door beeps and opens. A man all in black is in the doorway.

My heart aches as it tries to pry its way out of my chest. Hope gasps behind me and I back into her until the wall stops us. Her hand clings to me so tight it will leave a mark, but I don't feel any pain. All my focus is on my stalker.

"What are you doing here?" Patrick stands like he's going to defend us. Fuck, more people my stalker can use against me.

The man in black chuckles. "Claiming what's mine."

There's no voice changer on this time. His voice sounds hauntingly familiar, but my mind won't place it right now. All I feel is fear breaking me out in a cold sweat. Every instinct is telling me to run, but my feet remain frozen to this spot.

He's just standing there looking at me, waiting for something. Sweat trickles down the middle of my back as we all just stare at each other.

Fuck this. I jolt out of my fear and shove Hope through the kitchen door and block it, putting my hands on either side. "Run."

Her footsteps hurry away from me and the door opens and closes.

The man in black tilts his head as he studies me. "You aren't going to run?"

I shake my head because if I follow, he might catch Hope and use her against me again. I can't let that happen. My fingers dig into the doorframe. He won't get past me, not without a struggle.

Breathe, Blake's voice says in my head.

A realization hits me. I didn't hear a car come up the drive before Patrick arrived. My eyes narrow as I really look at Patrick, still hovering over Anna but not doing anything to actually protect any of us. Everyone stands in their positions, waiting.

Waiting for what?

What the fuck is going on?

How the hell do I buy myself time? The basement locks from the outside, so if I get there, I'm cornered, trapped. The bathroom didn't have a lock. Have I given Hope enough time to escape so I can run for it? Go out the back door and run to where?

At least I'm buying time for Hope.

The man in black stalks forward and I brace myself for his attack. The moves I've learned flow through my mind on repeat, just waiting for him to grab me.

"Aren't you scared of me, little bird?"

I gasp. My body shakes as cold floods me. He didn't say *little one*. The stalker always calls me that. Only one person calls me *little bird*. I step back, needing distance. Needing to get away.

He yanks off his gloves and reaches for me. I knock his hands away, but my motions are slow, like I'm cutting through molasses.

I can't.

No.

This isn't happening.

Tears well in my eyes. But I fight against letting them fall.

"Come on, little bird. You don't think I'd let you fly away from me that easily." He laughs as he tugs off his ski mask.

As soon as he reaches for it, I race to the bar and grab the almost full bottle of wine and hold it like a bat. Hunter Adams chuckles darkly as he turns his blue eyes on me. His grin chills me to the bone.

"I love it when we play, Maddy."

Chapter 164

Help Needed

Madison

My hands shake, but my grip on the bottle is solid. Hope got away, that's what matters. I'll deal with whatever this is.

I'm prepared to fuck someone up. Except I don't know who's friend and who's foe, but I do know I'm getting out of this without anything fucked-up happening to me. I'm done with that shit. The bottle shifts in my hand as the liquid swishes inside.

"Do something, Patrick." Anna pushes on his arm. He remains sitting by her side on the couch.

"Yeah, Patrick." Hunter's smile is pure evil as he turns his gaze to Patrick. "Do something to protect Maddy and your wife. Isn't this the moment you've been waiting for? To play the hero?"

Patrick drops his head and shakes it like he's disappointed. I focus on him. He's relaxed and not worried at all. Spiders crawl up my scalp.

I dismissed Hunter as the stalker because it isn't the way he works. He doesn't hide in the shadows. He just takes what he wants. But Patrick blends in. He becomes part of the shadows until you don't even realize he's there.

My breath catches. Hope said it could have been completely different guys checking on her. Maybe it was.

Patrick laughs lightly. My hair stands on end as fear ripples through me. There's no way out of this. Only through. All I can do is fight through the horror before me.

"This!" Patrick thrusts his hand toward Hunter.

I jump at his loud voice. My tremors increase.

"This is your problem. No pizzazz. No sense of style. You just plod your way through until you either get caught or get what you want."

"What the hell are you talking about, Patrick?" Anna shrinks away from him like he suddenly grew horns and a tail.

"Like this." When Patrick lifts his head, he's completely calm and rational looking. Too calm for a guy trying to protect his wife.

My heart pounds so hard it feels like it's trying to get out of my chest.

He gestures to Anna. "You hit her over the head and dumped her in a closet. You could have tied her to the bed and done anything to her. Used your blade to make sure she bled out, but no, let's just hope she bleeds to death in the closet from a minor wound."

Hunter strokes his chin as I watch them in quiet horror. Then he shrugs.

"You have goals and so do I. You want your wife dead and Maddy to be so fucking grateful that she stays in this creepy ass scenario with you. Hiding away from the world. Fuck, dude. Maddy might be a whore, but that would be a strong ask for anyone." Hunter chuckles. "But I'm more than willing to break my little bird until she doesn't care who's fucking her as long as something is inside her cunt."

My gaze hops between Patrick and Hunter. Hunter isn't the mastermind stalker because Patrick is right. Hunter is like a bull in a china shop, all brute force and no finesse. But I never imagined the two of them would team up.

How the hell did that happen?

Patrick's face remains calm as he stands and wipes his hands on the washcloth Hope gave him for his wife. His movements are slow and methodical. "I knew you'd be a terrible partner. But I didn't take you for a fool. I'm giving you what you want. Revenge on Madison for revealing your depravity to your father. A chance to finally take what you want. But what do you do? You try to blow me up so we have an even bigger mess on our hands."

Hunter shrugs and turns his hungry blue eyes on me. Fuck no. I take a step back behind the bar, needing more between us.

"I just think Maddy should know who she's dealing with." Hunter draws his knife out of the sheath at his side and uses the tip to pick at his fingernails. "I'm not afraid of her knowing my truth. I've never hidden from her and watched her without her knowing. Didn't follow her for years."

He leans against a table as his gaze rakes me up and down. The knife flashes in the light and I swallow. He sliced that knife down Hope's arm. It makes me ill thinking of the lengths they went to get me here. And if he did that to Hope, what will he do to me with the knife?

How will his revenge on me play out? I really don't want to find out.

"What's going on?" Anna tries to lift herself up on her elbows.

"You don't want to hide, Hunter? So you'll tell her you're the one who talked to her professor at the benefit? Told him she wanted it rough? That she *owed* him? And that if I hadn't overheard you, she would have been all alone dealing with that drunken mess?" Patrick sets the washcloth down and moves toward the bookcase behind the couch. His every move is purposeful, but nonthreatening.

Anna's mouth is open as she tries to make sense of this. I shift a little farther behind the bar to put something between me and them. Their focus isn't only on each other though. Both watch me. It's like they're hunting me but fighting the other predator for their prey.

My hands still shake and they ache with how tightly I'm gripping the bottle. With them talking, no one is attacking me.

"You told my professor to attack me?" I capture Hunter's attention. The longer they talk, the more time Hope has to escape. It gives my guys time to find me. It gives me time to figure out how to get out of this unscathed.

"You should see the creepy shit this guy has on you." Hunter thrusts his knife to point to Patrick and takes a step in my direction. My foot runs into the wall as I back up. "He has everything on you. Medical records. Pictures. Schedules. He's obsessed, and not in a friendly way. In an *I'll murder your family and fuck you in their blood way.*"

"Why are you telling me this?" It doesn't make sense. If they've been working together, why the sudden change in plans?

"I wasn't crazy about the murdering his wife part of the plan. It's not really my thing." Hunter pins me in place with his cold, soulless eyes. "You have two options, little bird. You can be my toy and we'll forget all about this kidnapping business. I'll use you until I'm finished and then you can get on with your life. Or you can become whatever sick fantasy Patrick wants you to fulfill. With his wife dead that leaves a spot open in his life. You want to be a mommy to his two brats? Or maybe I'll just put babies in that sleek body of yours."

"Pretty sure you're leaving out a third option." I glance at Patrick who's obviously going for something, but Hunter's focus is on me now. Who am I more afraid of? It's really a toss-up. Fuck.

"No, little bird. You can be mine or his. Those are your options. I'm not into sharing like your bosses." Hunter chuckles at my flinch. "Of course, this asshole knows all about it. He wrote up the documents. Showed them to me to prove how big of a whore you are. I was afraid you'd hired an attorney when he showed up at my house after the benefit. You should see his video collection of you taking them. I have to admit, Maddy, I knew you were a whore, but fuck. I can't wait to bury my cock inside you and see if you're as good as you look."

The blood drains from my face. My skin crawls. The realization that these two men watched me and my guys makes my blood pound in my ears.

Hunter continues to close in on me, but I'm ready.

"You want me dead, Patrick?" Anna's voice shakes. "What about our life? The kids?"

"Yeah, Patrick." Hunter turns to him and smirks. "What about the kids?"

"They love Madison. She was more of a mother to them than you ever were." Patrick's eyes are cold as he meets his wife's stunned gaze. It's like every ounce of humanity drained out of him, leaving him filled with only evil. "I knew from the moment she stepped into our lives that I had to have her. That she would be everything you weren't."

Patrick leans casually against the bookcase like he has all day and we're discussing the weather. "I let her finish school. Her drive, her ambition would have driven a wedge between us, so I needed her to do what she set out to accomplish. But then she ran into you."

His eyes flash with anger as he pins Hunter with them. "You made her skittish and almost broke her confidence. When she was at the point of having to leave or take a job with you, I moved her resume to the top of the stack at Morrigan Technology."

"You did?" I can't breathe. How entangled in my life was this asshole?

"I figured it would be a good test." Patrick chuckles. "They'd offer you the job with the option to fuck all of them. You'd hold onto your integrity and tell them to fuck off. Then you'd need me to step in and help you."

Hunter laughs. "You didn't know how much of a whore Maddy is? Even after following her for years?"

I shake my head. "I'm not a whore."

"No, but you became their whore." When Patrick lifts his hand, it takes me a moment to recognize the black thing he's holding as a gun. Oh, shit! The world slows down suddenly. The air sizzles with tension.

Hunter makes a noise, but then a crack fills the room. Anna screams. I jump back against the wall. I hold my breath. Hunter staggers, bending over but not falling to the ground.

"I had plans. Hunter would have killed Anna and I would have killed Hunter. The guy who stalked you and killed my wife. You would have been grateful and realized what you really needed was me. I needed someone to save you from. But I didn't realize how incompetent Hunter would be." Patrick steps forward and I move. The wine bottle is heavy, but I keep it raised to strike.

Blood pours over Hunter's hand where he grips his shoulder, but he's still standing.

"You're fucking mental." Hunter lunges, but he's too far away. Another crack fills the room along with the acrid scent of smoke. I scream and duck this time.

Anna cries out as Hunter hits the ground.

"Now, I didn't want to be the one to do this, Anna." Patrick swings the gun her way.

"What are you doing?" she whispers. Her eyes are wide as she stares at the gun in her husband's hands, pointed at her. My pulse thunders in my ears.

He's going to kill her.

He killed Hunter.

But Patrick doesn't show any emotion as he looks at the woman he married and had kids with. Chills shake me. I can see the monster that stalked me. He hid it well, but now it's out and I'll never be able to forget it.

"What Hunter was supposed to do, dear. Don't worry. I'll tell the kids you were a hero who tried to save Madison from her stalker, but he shot you."

"Wait!" I yell, finally finding my way out of my paralysis. I can't let him kill Anna. "Wait, please. You don't have to do this."

I set the bottle on the bar and hold my shaking hands up in surrender. Anna is pale and trembling. I can get us out of this.

"Yes, I do. She'll ruin everything." His eyes narrow on her, but I'm the one he's obsessed with. I'm the one that can talk him down. Maybe?

"Patrick, please. Let's talk about this. I don't want you to have to kill your wife." Fuck, I step out from behind the bar and walk around Hunter's prone body. My stomach turns, but I swallow back the bile that wants to rise. "You want it to be you and me, right?"

"That's all I've ever wanted." His brown eyes lift to mine. I force a smile.

"I was worried you would be like Hunter." I try not to think of his body on the floor and the pool of blood beneath him. My heart is working triple time. I can't let him kill Anna. I just need time. "Why don't we let Anna lie down in the guest bedroom while we talk?"

"This won't work with her alive. She'll take my children from me." His finger inches toward the trigger.

"I'm sure she'll be more reasonable once she's slept some. Head injuries." I glance at her face. Tears stream down her cheeks and she seems frozen in fear, staring down the barrel of the gun. "You can always deal with her later if you have to, but . . ." Oh, god, I don't want to do this. "I dressed especially for you."

Goosebumps rise on my skin thinking of all the times he watched me. The lengths he went to follow me and keep me under his thumb. The terror he reigned on my life.

"Morrigan was supposed to be a test." The gun lowers a little, but he still has it aimed at Anna. "You would have needed my help."

I nod like I understand. "I'm sorry I failed."

He gives me the smile that must have made Anna fall in love with this psychopath. "You're perfect in every other way. Everyone has flaws."

He should know. He's a fucking psychopath, but I nod again. Like I accept my fate.

"Anna looks a little queasy. Why don't I help her lie down and then you and I can be alone?" I step even closer to her and put my hand on her shoulder. *Please, just do this one thing.*

His gaze drops to Anna and she sucks in a breath.

"Fine. For now." He drops the gun to his side.

I breathe a little easier. I help Anna rise and walk her to the guest bedroom. As we cross the threshold, she grips my arm.

"We have to get out of here," she whispers.

"I know. Lock the door. Hide in the bathroom if you need to. I'll try to keep him away from you as long as possible." I'm hoping to give everyone time. Anna more time to live. Hope time to find help. The guys time to find me.

She grabs my arm and her wide brown eyes meet mine. "Madison, I've never seen him like this. He killed Hunter without a second thought. He wants to kill me."

I draw in a breath. Part of me wants to check out and not deal with this at all. To let my fear overwhelm me. But I won't.

"And I'm going to do everything I can to keep him from killing you." I help her sit on the bed. "Try to rest and get some strength."

"Be careful," she whispers and lies down, curling away from me.

I draw in a shaky breath. I don't want to go back out there. Face my stalker and all his issues. I don't have much choice though. If he comes in here, I can't guarantee he won't kill Anna before I have a chance to stop him.

I brush my hands down the sundress. Everything he's done has been to get to this point. Where he's in control of me. Where he's set up the perfect scenario to make me fall for him. In his mind, this will work out.

I have to feed into that fantasy. Fuck, I don't want to. I want to be back in my lovers' arms. For a moment, I bask in the world where I'm safe with Seth, Noah, Blake, and Coop. They love me and I love them.

I'll do whatever it takes to get back to them.

Stiffening my resolve, I walk out of the room.

Hope

My knees feel like rubber as I run. I found a car a little down the lane, but it was locked and I didn't have the keys. If I had more time, I could have tried to get into it, but the masked man was in the house. I wanted to put as much distance between him and me as possible.

That left running for help. I'm free, but Madison is stuck there with two other hostages and the sick bastard who took me off the street. She came to save me, but I'm going to save her if it takes everything I have left.

My breath wheezes in and out of my lungs. A stitch forms in my side and my leg cramps. Tears stream down my face. I slow to a stop and look around with my hands on my hips as I gulp in air like it's water.

How long have I been running?

This gravel road must lead somewhere, but trees surround me, blocking my view. This is the East Coast. We can't be far from civilization.

Bending at the waist, I take a few deep breaths, trying to settle my pounding heart. If I had any food in my stomach, it wouldn't have stayed there. Two days of captivity plus two years at a desk have made me weak.

If I get out of this, I'm working out more. I'll make Jason train me. He'll love that.

I'm just glad the bastard grabbed me on the way from Madison's. At least I have sneakers and comfy clothes on instead of work clothes and work shoes.

If that's anything to be glad about.

Fuck, this is messed up.

Glancing back, I can't see the house anymore, but I can't see anything beyond the trees either. I don't know what's happening to Madison now, but she gave me this chance and I'm taking it. Okay, I've got to move. I've got to keep going forward. I need to save them if I'm not already too late.

My breath catches and I swipe at the tears on my cheeks. No time to think like that.

A humming fills the air, and for a moment, I'm afraid it's a car coming after me. I freeze in the road. But as the noise gets louder, I realize it's coming from the sky.

A black helicopter comes my way, flying low enough they might be able to see me. Relief pours through me.

"Hey, down here!" I wave my arms. I don't care who's in that helicopter, as long as they help me and Madison.

Chapter 165

A Proxy Fight

Madison

When I step into the living room, Hunter's body grabs my attention. His body. He's dead.

I swallow back the bile rising in my throat. While Hunter was an asshole, I never wanted him dead. I wanted him to deal with the consequences of his actions. I wanted him to leave me alone and respect my wishes.

"Little one, come here." Patrick's voice sends icy cold fingers of dread down my spine. My stalker. The phantom in the night who terrorized me for longer than I even knew. My feet are glued to the floor.

The door is right there. Outside is right there. It's not locked. I could just run, lose myself in the forest until help comes. Tears press against the back of my eyes. But then Anna will end up like Hunter.

A body on the floor in a puddle of her own blood.

Elijah and Lily will be motherless.

I don't care if she's a crap mother like Patrick says, she's still their mother. They'll need her, especially if their father ends up in jail where he belongs.

He murdered Hunter. William's only son.

I need to protect Anna while I can.

I take a step toward the kitchen. Every inch of me screams to run and hide, but I keep my feet moving forward, giving Hunter's body a wide berth.

When Patrick sees me, he smiles like he's so glad I'm here, like it's voluntary. This man ignored me at every turn. My insides twist. I want to scream. I want to fight. But he'll just pull Anna out and use her like he used Hope to get me here.

"Don't be shy. I'll make you something to eat and we can talk."

He gestures me forward and holds out a chair. Everything in me says to run. To get to the door and just run like the hounds of hell are on my heels. I want to. Fuck, do I want to.

But I'm trapped. So, I walk over and sit in the chair like a good girl.

My heart clenches. Blake calls me his good girl. Yvonne sent him that message. He'll know I wouldn't go anywhere alone willingly. My men can do anything, including find me. I believe that with all my heart. My only goal is to survive until they make it to me.

I smile softly at the thought of them here, rescuing me.

"I hope you still like peanut butter and jelly sandwiches." Patrick pulls me from my fantasy and crashes me back into this reality. "We need to stock up on groceries. But don't worry, I'll do it until you feel better."

My eyes widen. *Feel better?* "I'm okay."

"I'm sure you're in shock, little one. Today was stressful. But it's almost over." He sets a plate down in front of me and puts his hand on my shoulder.

I flinch away. I can't help it. I don't want his hands on me.

Tsking, he squeezes my shoulder hard.

"Now, little one, is that any way to treat the man who saved you?" He releases me and takes the chair next to me, setting another plate on the table for himself.

"Saved me?" The words come out incredulously. What does

that even mean? He didn't save me. He coerced me into coming here. God knows what else he has planned. I can't put it into words or I'll break down. Lose myself in a hole I won't want to climb out of.

I look at the sandwich. Do I trust anything this man gives me? He could have drugged or poisoned it.

"You were headed down a dark path, little one. But I got to you in time." He takes a bite and gestures to mine. "Eat."

I lift the sandwich half and bring it to my mouth. A brick falls in my stomach at the thought of eating anything made by his hands. I bite a small bit of bread off and chew.

That pleases him. Good. "I found out about Courtney and Andrea's plan to slowly dismantle Morrigan and used them to distract the guys. Yvonne was only too happy to help me out. That one has a devious mind."

Yvonne, the receptionist. Fuck. She was working with him? Why did I think she would ever help me? She hated me from the moment we met.

"She'll be here soon. She needs to get away so no one can question her. I'll take care of her."

I swallow hard. Take care of her? Will he kill her too?

"Those other two though. Courtney and Andrea." He shakes his head. "They wanted you out of the way. They got impatient for your stalker to take you."

His brow furrows as he sets his sandwich down. My breath catches. What did I do wrong?

"We need water," he says.

I breathe out as he leaves the table.

He grabs glasses out of the cabinet before filling them with water from the refrigerator. My mind is slow to work right now, but not because of any drugs. At least I don't think so.

There's this fog of everything running through my mind. Hunter's body, in the next room. Anna, relying on me. Hope, some-where outside looking for help.

Seth. Noah. Blake. Coop. Do they know I'm gone? Do they know something's wrong? Are they on their way?

My thoughts are scattered every which way, and I need to be present and aware of this man at all times.

Setting the glass in front of me, Patrick resumes his seat.

"They got impatient?" I need to keep him talking. Talking will keep him from doing whatever he intends to do to me. Andrea and Courtney.

"Yes, they tried to pretend they were me. But they were amateurs." He sips his water and smiles. "They were useful though. And Yvonne kept me informed of their plans, so I could use them to my benefit and plant other ideas when it suited me. It was beautiful really. The only problem is they got impatient."

His fingers touch the bruises on my arm. I still but don't pull away. "He never should have touched you. Yvonne told me what they were going to do so I could warn you."

That text before the alarm. It didn't make sense. Why warn me? But if it was someone else . . .

"The girls were better accomplices than Val though. But she had access and she gave it all to me." He stops talking for a moment. His eyes taking on a far-off look. "I did it to keep you protected, of course. I knew you needed to spread your wings before I could cage you."

He stares off into space for a moment with a creepy smile. His gaze drops to my plate and he pushes it toward me. "Eat, little one. You need food for energy. We have a long few weeks ahead of us."

Weeks sends shudders through me. I pick off the corner of the bread and put it in my mouth, chewing as slow as I can. If drugs are in the sandwich, hopefully the bread is fine.

"I knew you were sexually adventurous during college. Those guys used you to get off, but you did the same. You didn't want any of them. Because I know you. You're like me. You just want a family surrounding you. You want what Anna has."

I swallow hard around the dry bread. He has it so wrong. I have a family. I have my guys, and they're everything I've ever wanted.

"A stable husband, children, a home. I'll give it all to you." He finishes his sandwich and moves his plate away.

His full attention turns to me. A hive of bees stirs within me as he reaches out and tucks my hair behind my ear. I freeze since I won't run away.

"Such a prize. I should have realized you hadn't finished sowing your wild oats. That you needed a man and not a college boy to help fulfill your needs. I enjoyed watching them fuck you, little one."

While his finger glides down my neck, my hands clench in my dress to keep from knocking his hand away or running.

"You enjoy sex, Madison. It's part of your appeal." He grips my chin and turns my face in his direction. His dark eyes flare with heat.

My heart stops. Panic fills me.

I thought I could do this. Just hold him off for a little longer. I can't. My fear locks me in place.

His thumb traces beneath my lip and his gaze burns there. "I've read your consent forms, little one. It took me a few days to find them in their office, but I did. There's not much you won't do, is there?"

He drops his hand. His eyes cold as they meet mine, like I've disappointed him. "Eat."

It's a command, and I'm not about to find out what he'll do for punishment. He may have read my consent forms, but that doesn't mean he'll abide by them. They were never for him.

I lift the sandwich to my lips and take a bite.

"Good girl." He smirks as he takes his plate to the sink.

I'm tempted to spit it back out on the plate, but he moves around behind me. So I chew and swallow. Something sticks me in the arm.

"Ow." Turning, I watch in horror as he pushes the plunger on the needle. *No, no, no.*

"I'm not stupid, little one. I know it'll take time to convince you that you belong here. That you'll be safe here. You may want to run away now, but soon you won't."

I stare at the needle as he draws it out. Horror fills me. "What did you put in me?"

"Nothing bad. Just something to make you relax and not worry so much about things that don't matter." He takes the needle over to the counter.

"Like I won't worry about Anna?" What he plans to do to her? Or what he plans to do to me? Oh, god, I have to get away before the drug takes effect. Before I can push back from the table, rope bands below my breasts and around arms, pulling me tight into the chair.

"What are you doing?" I whisper as the ropes get tighter.

"Anna will keep." Patrick sits in the chair next to me and turns me to face him.

I struggle against the rope, but it's tied tight.

He brushes my hair out of my face. "I want to trust you, little one, but our situation isn't exactly straightforward."

"I'll do what you want, just release me," I plead, but his eyes are so cold.

He chuckles. "I know Noah likes to bind you." His hand falls on my bare knee and bile rises in my throat. His fingers toy with the hem of my dress. "They take good home videos. That nightgown was perfect. You're perfect. So submissive and needy. You like being used, little one. I can't wait to use you."

There's heat behind his words as he pushes my skirt up.

"No." I jerk at the rope, but he just smiles and drags my skirt up higher.

"I may only have one cock, little one, but I have plenty of toys to help you feel that fullness you crave." He pushes my skirt higher until my panties are visible.

"Stop, please." I try to jerk back, but I don't dare kick him. I have to keep my head. If he ties up my feet, I'll be completely helpless.

"I wish they had video of whatever you did to rip your dress, little one." His finger trails up and down my inner thigh. "I would have loved to see you like that. Maybe we'll recreate it when you're more in the mood."

I want to scream, but it would be pointless. There's no one to hear.

"The police assured me there were only two samples on the dress." He lifts his darkened eyes to mine and smirks. "Who was it, little one?"

I press my lips together.

"Maybe I'll invite them to recreate it, so I can watch. Maybe I'll kill them for touching what's mine."

Oh, god, they trust him. They suspect him a little, but they trust him. He could get to them. They could end up like Hunter. Tears choke me and my lip trembles.

"Come now, Madison. Don't act the prude. Tell me which two fucked you in your dress." His hand stops on my thigh. "That audio clip I sent? It was video too. I didn't want them to remove my camera."

His thumb rubs the inside of my thigh and I want to vomit. "We can watch it together. Would you like that? Watching those four fuck you. One after the other. Taking turns in your pussy and then your ass."

He digs his fingers into my skin and I whimper.

"Answer me, little one. We could recreate it right now. I can strip off those panties and fuck you on the table with your hands bound." When his fingers ease like he's going to move his hand to my panties, I can't take it anymore.

"Why?" The word lurches out of me and tears flow down my cheeks. "Why are you doing this to me?"

He grins and sits back. "There she is. Don't play me, little one. I know you inside and out. Every inch of you is mine now. I'm not going to rape you like Hunter would. The drugs will work their magic until you want it. Need it. Crave it. Then I'll give it to you."

Standing, he rubs his hand down my hair. His eyes are soft and fond as he studies my face. "Sweet little one, I don't want to leave you, but I have to take care of the trash. The things I do for you."

He turns and walks away. A sob escapes me.

I have to focus while I can.

How much time do I have? I strain against the rope, but there's no give.

I hear him moving around in the other room, then the sound of dragging. Turning my head, I can't see through the doorway. I've got to keep trying, so I lift my arms and feel the rope shift up. A little bit of hope jolts through me.

Okay, I can work with that.

The dragging continues along with grunts from Patrick. Hunter was not a small man, so I imagine it will take Patrick some time to do whatever he plans to do with the body.

I shrug and scoot down while pulling my arms up against the rope. Little by little, the rope slides up until it reaches my breasts.

The front door opens. My breath catches and I wait as the beep fills the house. I lift my arms and feel the rope, hoping to find the knot. The door slams shut. After a few minutes, a car starts up and drives away.

Okay, I need to get Anna and me out of this. We can go hide in the woods until someone finds us. I don't know what he injected me with. For all I know, it will paralyze me or put me to sleep.

Fuck, I'm running out of time. "Anna! Anna!"

Please hear me. My pulse races.

"Madison! I can't get out of the room."

My head slumps. Of course, he locked the room or blocked the door. That asshole thinks of everything. Dammit, there has to be something I can do besides wait for the drugs to kick in.

My legs! The chair I'm on is wood, maybe I can break the chair if it falls on the ground. I could also knock myself out. I blow out a breath.

I can't give up. I have to try something. Anything. How long do we have before he returns?

Fuck it. I scoot the chair back slightly so I can get my legs up. Putting my feet on the edge of the table, I take in a breath, tuck my chin, and push back quickly. The chair tips and I brace for impact.

The fall knocks the wind out of me. For a second, I lie there before I gasp in a breath. I try to shift to see if that loosened the rope or broke some part of the chair.

Hope flares in my chest. But then it dies. It's not any looser. Fuck.

I glance toward the living room and see the blood streaked across the floor. Yeah, not staying here with a killer determined to rape me. No matter what he says or what drugs he puts in me, it will still be rape.

I wiggle up and slide higher on the chairback some. Okay, if I can't get the rope off me, maybe I can get it off the chair.

Millimeter by millimeter I work myself up the chair. A distant whop-whop sound comes closer and then stops some distance away.

"That sounded like a helicopter," Anna yells. "Madison? Are you still there?"

"Yeah," I strain out as I shimmy on the floor. My blood is pounding. "I'm almost free."

Well, sort of free. I roll onto my side off the chair and my vision blurs, making my head spin. I stay still for a moment while it passes. Fuck, I don't have time for this. Without my hands, it's hard to sit up and it takes me a few minutes.

My head swims more and my muscles tense. I feel like I drank an espresso or five.

I get my knees beneath me and struggle to my feet. With my arms tied, I lurch to the doorway. I just have to get to Anna. She can help me if she's free. Then I can let my body do what it wants.

My heart is pounding so hard as I push off the doorway and sway my way across the living room. My foot slips on something and I look down at the streak of shiny red. My stomach lurches. The color is mesmerizing. Can't think about that now. My vision blurs and my hands shake.

I move, because I need to move. When I get to the hallway, I pull the chair out of the way of the door and lean against the wall.

"Anna." My heart races and I feel sick to my stomach and sweaty.

Anna opens the door and glances around me.

"Madison? Are you okay? Where's Patrick?" Anna turns me and works on the rope.

"He drugged me. We should go." I press my face against the cool wall. Fuck, that feels good.

"We need to get out of here and fast."

The rope falls to the ground, and I watch as it coils softly on the dark wood. It's so pretty.

The door bursts open. Anna shrinks behind me, but I step toward it, ready to take on the world.

Chapter 166

Going Concern

Anna

When the door bursts open with a crack, I flash back to Patrick killing that man. Then he stared at me with dead eyes and pointed the gun at my face. I shrink away from whatever the new threat is as Madison moves in front of me.

"Little one, who let you go free?" Patrick's voice is pleasant, almost sweet. Fear trickles down my spine. He's between us and the door.

Madison sways in front of me. Maybe we can barricade ourselves in a bedroom. I grab her arm to pull her back, but she collapses. I catch her before she drops, but instead of holding us both up, I fall with her to the floor, careful to protect her head.

"What a mess." Patrick squats down in front of me and smiles. A smile I fell for a thousand times before. Back when I thought he was a great guy with some issues. The cheating wasn't awesome, but he went to work every day. He was good with the kids. We even had a decent sex life. But underneath the veneer, he was always a monster.

He kept it hidden well.

When he reaches out to touch Madison, I pull her away from his hand.

His dark eyes lift to mine. The emptiness in them sends warning flares to my brain. Every instinct tells me to run from the predator cornering me.

Whitleys don't cower. I can hear my grandfather's voice in my head.

"What did you hope would happen here, Patrick?" I meet those emotionless eyes of his. He doesn't even bother to wear the mask he showed me for years. How could I fall for this guy? How could I stay with him? I even helped him seek counseling for his sex addiction, which was his excuse for cheating.

"See, you were supposed to be dead now. You always think too small, Anna." His lips smile, but his eyes remain lifeless. "I saw something I wanted, and I did everything in my power to have it. First you and now Madison."

I fell in love with a charming man. A liar, a cheater, and a murderer.

My lips press together to keep from saying anything that could make him explode. Or worse, go get the gun and finish what he started. I've got to keep him talking. "Why her?"

His eyes soften when he looks down at Madison's face. He used to look at me like that. Ice rolls down my spine.

He sits back and stares at her like we have all the time in the world. "The nights I drove her home. There weren't many. She was so young and carefree. She'd ask if she could play songs on my radio."

I put my hand on Madison's wrist to check her pulse. It's strong. Good. She needs to wake up, but what if she doesn't? I swallow hard.

"The song. It's like she wanted me to hear what she wasn't saying. That she wanted me to love her. Such passion. Teasing me in those pretty sundresses. Lily talked about her constantly. Madison did this. Madison says that. I could tell our children loved her. She didn't worry if wearing last year's fashion to the benefit would be tragic." He reaches out and rubs the fabric of Madison's sundress between his fingers.

"This cost thirty dollars. She wore it all the time. She's real and full of life. She doesn't care what other people think of her. And the filthy things she lets those men do to her." His eyes darken as he takes her in. "She can keep up with me."

I want to drag her away from this monster I married.

Yes, I worry about things like how we'll be seen in public. In my life, they're important. People judge us on everything. He never understood that.

He sighs. "The roommate was a miscalculation, but she was effective. Pictures, video, audio. It satisfied me while Madison pursued her education. I knew our children would need more time with you to realize how lucky they were to have her."

That stings, but I don't say anything. He's calm. He's not waving a gun in my face. We're just here talking, almost like normal people. Besides the fact he drugged Madison and she's lying limp half on me.

I don't need to ask him if he would have pulled the trigger and ended my life. I saw it in his eyes. He's prepared to do what he thinks will fix his life. At least the children are in his plan.

I'm on borrowed time now because of this woman, so I'll do my best to distract him while she fights whatever drug is in her system. To give her the best chance of escaping him.

He planned to have Hunter kill me, but one thing bothers me.

"How did you know I'd come out here today?"

He grins that evil smile. "You track me, I track you. I came out here to help with Hope and figured you'd be suspicious. I made sure you'd have time today to get here."

My skin crawls. I had a client cancel earlier because they'd been in a car accident. Is he saying he caused it? The Patrick I loved would never. He'd have an affair with a woman like Madison, but he wouldn't hurt someone to get me to do what he wanted. I can't believe I worried she was having an affair with him.

His eyes lift to mine. "We should move her somewhere more comfortable."

"No!" The word bursts out of me as I pull her in tight. I can't let him touch her. At his dark look, I soften my tone. "She might have hit her head in the fall. It could be dangerous to move her. I'll look after her."

I stare at my would-be murderer. Will he call my bluff? Will he decide I'm just in the way?

He glances over his shoulder and rubs the back of his neck. "I should clean up the blood. I don't think she likes it."

When he turns back to me, I nod. "She'd appreciate that."

He puts his hands on his knees and stands. His gaze rakes over me. "That was always her major flaw. She likes people who are bad for her. I'll cure her of that."

He walks away into the kitchen. The front door is open. I could get away. I glance down at Madison's relaxed face. Borrowed time. But what if I could help her by escaping?

Hope is out there somewhere. Maybe she found help. But what if she's just lost? This property has been in my family for generations. If anyone can find help, I can.

I shake her, but she's completely still. I pinch her arm hard enough to bruise, but still nothing. Whatever he gave her is effective.

The sound of running water reaches me. I slowly ease Madison onto the floor. I can be back before she wakes. Before whatever he plans to do to her. I flinch, knowing what guys do to women on this type of drug.

I hesitate as I rise. I don't want to leave her here but I can't carry her. My head still swims and the nausea rises again. I touch my forehead and wince at the swelling there.

If I can get her into a room . . . I grab her shoulders and try to drag her. She doesn't budge.

The water still runs. If I stay, he'll kill me and do whatever it is he wants to her anyway.

Damn it. I'll be quick. I leave her on the ground. Alone and vulnerable. But I'll find help.

Sounds come from the kitchen as I place each step quietly on my way to the door. One squeaky floorboard will give me away. My heart pounds in my chest. My pulse is erratic.

I'm coming back for her. He doesn't want to hurt her.

My brain stalls. Then why did he drug her? Why did he want her here? In the middle of nowhere with nowhere to run to? Patrick has always been calculating and precise. But I never thought he could murder a man in cold blood and then turn the gun on the mother of his children.

If he needs to hurt Madison, he won't hesitate.

The water is still running as I creep around the front door and onto the porch. My foot hits the gravel drive when I hear a roar behind me. I run. It's all I can do.

Get to cover.

A shot rings out and I scream, but I don't stop and nothing hits me.

I'm over the hill from the house when I look over my shoulder to see if he's following me. Someone grabs me and covers my mouth before I can scream again. My gaze jerks up and I almost cry.

Coop

When a gunshot went off, we were done waiting for the police to arrive. Hope told us the situation. That she'd left Madison with the stalker along with Patrick and Anna. Anna was hurt, Patrick had freed Hope and Madison from the basement, and the stalker showed up.

After letting the police know, we left Hope and Jason at the helicopter while Seth, Noah, Blake, and I headed back to assess the situation. All we know is the stalker has Madison. The local police are en route but we don't know how long it will take them.

As Anna comes over the hill, I grab her to pull her to safety.

"Anna." I shake her shoulders as she sobs against me. I need her to tell me what's happening, especially with Madison. I lift my gaze to Seth and he presses his lips together.

"Where's Madison?" Seth rubs Anna's back soothingly.

Anna turns her brown eyes up to me. There's a nasty cut on her forehead. "He's insane. He's got her drugged . . . He's saying all these things . . . He tried to kill me."

"Do you know who the stalker is?" I ask.

She brings her fist to her mouth as her tears spill over. "It's Patrick."

I step back like she hit me. I had my suspicions, but I never truly thought he was the stalker. All those messages. All that fear. And he sat beside me and worked like it was nothing.

Anna steps forward and grabs my shirtsleeve. "You have to go. He has her. She's unconscious. I don't know what he'll do to her."

"What about the other man?"

Anna's lip trembles. "Patrick shot him."

I lift my gaze to Seth. Waiting to know what to do with Anna. We can't leave her here alone. Noah steps forward.

"Go get our girl." Noah wraps his arm around Anna's shoulders.

"Wait," Anna says and grabs my hand. "The house has two doors. The front and in the kitchen on the other side of the house. Two bedrooms on the side closest to us. I left Madison in the hallway leading to the bedrooms. Please, get to her before he does something."

I squeeze her hand. "We will."

We have to or I'll kill Patrick myself. Noah nods and leads Anna toward the helicopter.

"Fuck, Blake's gone." Seth turns to me, but we both know where he is.

Blake

As soon as Anna said *he's got her drugged*, I saw red. I couldn't wait. I couldn't be too late. Not this time. I can't lose her.

The house is small and quaint. I approach it low and slow, trying to aim for an area where there are no windows. I know there's a man. And that he has Madison.

I flatten my back against the side of the house and listen for anything. Patrick and the stalker are all that's left in there. For all I know, that gunshot killed Patrick.

"We may not have much time, little one. Unlike Hope, Anna knows this area." Patrick's voice comes through an open window. Fuck. Dread flows through me at his use of *little one*. That means Patrick is the stalker.

I edge closer to the window. If Patrick is the stalker, who is the other man? And where is he? Are they working together?

"She ruins everything."

I look in the window and Patrick sits on the bed next to Madison, stroking her hair. She's completely still with her arms down beside her.

"I need to pack and we'll leave. I wanted this to be our home, but Anna ruined that too." Patrick leans down and brushes a kiss over Madison's lips. "Soon, little one."

A hot brand sinks into my chest. Patrick rises and heads to the left. She lies there, still and unmoving. Her chest gently rises and falls.

A hand touches my arm and I jerk around, prepared to deck whoever is behind me.

Coop holds up his hands. Seth stands behind him. I gesture with my head to move away from the window.

When it's safe, we squat against the side of the building.

"Patrick's the stalker. The other is dead," Coop says barely louder than a breath. "Is she okay?"

"She's clothed on the bed. Patrick is in there with her. He's leaving with her."

He could have done anything to her. The message he sent her

with the mannequin races through my mind. She's wearing the same dress. Fuck.

"Plan?" Coop turns to Seth.

"He has a gun and he's planning to run." Seth sighs. "He's killed before. We need to ambush him before he can shoot any of us."

"He's in the bathroom. If we can get him into the kitchen, we could surround him." I want to rush in, but I also don't want to get any of us killed. "Coop can get in through the open window when Patrick goes past."

"I'll go to the kitchen. Blake, you come in through the front door. Keep an eye out, Coop, and give us the bird whistle if he changes locations." It's the bird whistle we came up with as kids to not alert the other team in capture the flag. Seth looks us both in the eyes before he nods. "Let's go get our girl."

We ease back toward the window. Coop stops and gives us a thumbs up. Seth and I continue to the front door. I stop and Seth grabs my shoulder.

"Wait until he passes you."

I nod and watch Seth move around the corner. My heart thunders in my ears but I know what I have to do. We're in this together. We'll get her out of this together.

Water runs in the kitchen. Footsteps come down the hall. Coop lifts himself into the bedroom. I watch through the window next to the door until I see Patrick pass. The gun is in his hand. I swallow and open the door quietly.

He's at the entrance to the kitchen when I step in and a floorboard creaks. He spins at the same time I charge. A gunshot rings in my ears and something tears at my arm. But the adrenaline keeps me going.

Seth grabs Patrick from behind and they struggle. I grab Patrick's arm that holds the gun, pushing it out to the side, but he fights me for it. The gun goes off again, but Seth wraps his arm around Patrick's neck. He gasps for air, but Seth cuts it off. Patrick slowly stops struggling.

I take the gun from his hand and set it on the table. Seth lowers Patrick to the floor and checks his pulse.

"We need rope," Seth says.

I glance around. Coop sits against the wall in the hallway. Blood smears the wall behind him. His hand holds some rope.

"Coop!" Fuck, I rush over to him and lift his chin.

"Is he . . . ?" Seth doesn't say it.

Coop opens his glassy eyes. His chest shakily moves with each breath. His hand grips his side.

"I found some rope." He holds up his other hand. "But I got shot."

I take the rope and chuck it over to Seth. Seth's face is pale, but he takes the rope and ties up Patrick. We just need to control this situation and make sure we're safe before calling in reinforcements.

"Hold on." I rush into the room with Madison, who is still but breathing. Grabbing a towel from the bathroom, I hurry back to Coop. My arm hurts, but I ignore it.

"Move your hand." I kneel beside him and quickly replace his hand with the towel, applying pressure. Blood pools a little below him. A bullet is lodged in the wall behind us. But I'm not sure if that's the one that hit me or him.

"Fuck, no signal." Seth runs out the door.

"Just hang on, Coop. The police should be here soon." I wrap the towel around his back and press against the wound there too. At least it went through him and isn't inside still. I need to keep him alert while we wait.

"She's safe?" He grabs my arm weakly. His eyelids droop.

"Yeah, but she needs you."

His smile is weak. "I'm going to marry her."

"We'll see about that." I don't know what to do besides apply pressure and keep him talking.

"Nah, I put a ring on her first. I got dibs." He's pale. Fuck.

I shake my head. "She didn't know she was agreeing to marry you, you pompous asshole."

"Yeah, but she will. You watch. Don't worry. I know what my

wife wants and needs, so you all will live with us." He takes in a deep breath and groans. "She likes that big cock of yours."

"How gracious of you." I roll my eyes. I should have known Coop would be like this when he's hurt.

"I am a Graham." His voice fades and his head falls to his chest.

"Coop? Coop, come on. Stay with me. Damn you, wake up." The world around me is silent, but I can hear his breath. I can't lose any of them.

Fuck, I should have controlled the gun sooner. I should have figured out Patrick was the stalker sooner. I should have protected them all.

"Come on, Coop. Stay with me. Fight this. Madison needs you." I rest my forehead against his and try to give him all my strength. "I need you. We all need you."

Chapter 167

Taking Inventory

Seth

I'm winded as my cell phone finally finds a signal. Fuck. Fuck. Fuck.

I call Bill Carr and take deep breaths while waiting for him to answer. I'm not as far as the helicopter, but still some distance from the house. I can't leave them alone for long.

"This is Carr."

"We couldn't wait for the police. There were shots fired and Anna Beck ran straight to us. She said Madison was unconscious."

"Fuck. The police are on their way. They should be there any second."

"We went in. Patrick Beck is the stalker. He's tied up, but he managed to shoot Coop in the struggle. You can tell the police to come straight to the house and we'll need that ambulance too."

"Yeah, let me radio them. Make sure you put pressure on that gunshot wound and we'll take care of the rest." He hangs up.

"Fuck!" I shout into the still afternoon air. Coop can't die. I saw the blood and ran to get help. Now I need to head back to see how I can keep him alive until the EMTs get there.

Before I return to the cottage, I text Noah with shaking hands, letting him know what's going on. We don't know what Patrick gave Madison. We knew going in that something could go wrong. But Coop was unexpected.

He has to make it. There's no alternative. No reality where him not being here makes sense.

"Hey. I was coming to join you guys." Noah raises his hand as he jogs toward me. "You okay? What's happening? Is Madison okay?"

"Come on, I'll explain on the way." I gesture toward the house and we hurry back. "Coop's hurt. Patrick's neutralized. Madison's unconscious."

"Fuck." Noah picks up his pace and so do I.

When we enter the house, Patrick stirs on the ground. I've never hated anyone the way I hate him. We trusted him and then he pulls this shit. If I had nothing to lose, he wouldn't be breathing.

But he's not worth my freedom.

"Will you check his ropes?" I nod to Noah because I still don't trust myself. Patrick hurt Madison. He hurt Coop. I hope he rots in jail. But if he even tries to talk to me, I might lose it.

I'm hanging on by a thread here.

But they need me. I walk to the hallway and squat next to Blake. His face is pale, but he's doing everything he can to apply pressure and stop Coop's bleeding. His hands are bloody and there's blood running down his arm. The source is a fairly large gash from a bullet.

"Fuck." I dart into a bathroom and grab a towel. I kneel beside Blake and grab his arm.

"No. I can't let up on the pressure." He jerks away.

"Your wound needs attention too." I press against it and he hisses in pain. "I'm not losing you either."

Blake's eyes meet mine. "We're not losing anyone today."

Sirens sound in the background, heading our way, maybe a minute out. Relief pours through me. These guys are my family. I can't lose any of them. I won't.

Noah

Glancing over at Coop and Blake as Seth moves toward them, I kneel next to Patrick and check the knots in the ropes.

"She'll never be yours." His voice is hoarse. "You wouldn't even have her if it weren't for me. I made sure you interviewed her. I picked her for you."

His eyes are cold as they meet mine. I tighten some of the ropes, maybe a little more than necessary if his grunt of pain is any indication. Good. All the pain he inflicted on Madison over the past month, he deserves to feel every minute of it for the rest of his life.

I glance over to Blake holding Coop's wound while Seth holds Blake's. We're friends, but we're family. Madison holds us together. We would have always found her because she's ours.

"You're wrong." I look Patrick dead in the eye. "She's been mine since the moment I saw her. She was ours before she even knew you were in the equation. You may have known her first, but she never wanted you."

"She was made to love me." Patrick truly believes that. I see it in his eyes. "I'll find my way back to her. You can keep her warm for me, but I won't go down for this. You watch, I'll find the loophole. I always do. I'll find her again."

"Maybe." I sit back on my heels. He made a severe miscalculation. "Or maybe you shouldn't have shot the sole heir of the Graham family. Or pointed a gun in the face of the favored daughter of the Whitley family. Both have money and influence that you can never contend with. You want to know what I think will happen?"

I don't wait for his answer. "I think the police will take you into custody today, but my guess is you won't walk out of that jail. You'll leave it in a body bag."

His eyes narrow on mine, but I don't care about this man. He's never been my friend. He was a guy who worked for us. I just need to make sure he can't hurt the people I love anymore.

I stand and walk away from him without a backward glance. He's not going anywhere. Coop is passed out. His face pale against his dark hair that falls in a curtain. Blake doesn't look much better, to be honest.

"Hang in there." I touch Blake's shoulder and nod to Seth before continuing into the bedroom.

My breath leaves me as the tightness in my chest releases. Madison. She remains completely still, like some sleeping fairy-tale princess. She wears an identical dress to the one I ripped off her. When I sit next to her on the bed, I brush my hand over her blond hair.

"You're ours, kitten. I don't want anyone else but you. No one else can have you."

She's been out of communication for hours. Who knows what's happened to her? What new nightmares she'll have to deal with? The temptation to go back and beat Patrick is only stifled by the sirens fast approaching.

"I don't know what he's done to you, but we'll heal. This will all be a terrible memory someday." I lift her hand to my lips. "I promise to fill your life with so much joy that this day has no room in your mind. Patrick will just be a bad memory that we've washed away."

The sirens stop as they park out front.

"In here," Seth yells. "We need an EMT."

I wish she'd open those blue eyes. "You'll see, kitten. Everything will be okay."

Madison

Darkness holds me down as I struggle to surface from the endless night. There's this steady beeping in my ear, pulling at me, leading me, calling me home.

"Come on, kitten. I know you can hear me."

Noah. A smile pulls at my lips and I turn my head toward his voice like a flower following the sun. His hand touches my cheek and warmth floods my chest. My eyes open and he smiles from his seat beside my bed.

"There you are." His smiling brown eyes hold mine.

"Where are we?" My eyes clear and realization sets in. A curtain surrounds the hospital bed I'm on. I lift my hand with an IV on the side of my wrist. I don't know how I got here. "What happened?"

"What do you remember?" Noah moves to sit beside me on the bed.

I focus on what I remember last. "The stalker. My old apartment. The car. The house. Hope! How's Hope?"

"Hope is good. She's a few rooms down getting fluids and being monitored. Do you remember anything else?" Noah strokes his hand over my hair. There are worry lines around Noah's eyes. Are they for me?

"It's fuzzy. Why can't I remember?" It's like the day is there, but someone smudged oil on the lens, making it hard to see.

"Patrick gave you a drug cocktail, hoping to make you more susceptible to suggestion. And more easily coerced into what he wanted from you. He was trying to speed along Stockholm syndrome from the sounds of it." Noah looks down as he takes my hand.

"What happened, Noah?" I try to sit up, but he holds my shoulder down.

"You need to stay in bed." Noah sighs. "After you passed out, Anna escaped from Patrick. She found us on our way to rescue you. I took Anna back to the helicopter while Coop, Seth, and Blake went to get you."

I swallow because they aren't here. Oh my god, why aren't they here? Tears choke my throat at the possibilities. But maybe they're in a waiting room, maybe it's only one visitor at a time. My voice shakes when I ask, "Where are they?"

"Patrick had a gun."

A shot rings in my memory, followed by another. I cover my mouth, remembering. "He shot Hunter. Hunter's dead."

Noah nods. "Blake and Coop got hurt."

I grab onto Noah's hand to steady myself as my world tips on its axis. "What?"

"When they came for you, Blake got shot in the arm. He's getting stitches now. But Coop got shot in the side." Noah quickly continues. "It went through and he just got out of surgery, which went well. Seth is with him in the recovery room."

"I have to go to them." I try to rise, but Noah pushes me back down.

"You need to wait for the doctor. Some of those drugs are still in your system. We don't need you to get hurt. They're being taken care of. I'm here to take care of you. I just left Blake, who waited until Coop was out of surgery before he got his stitches. Coop is still not awake yet from anesthesia." Noah brings my hand to his lips and presses a kiss there. "Everyone is safe. Everyone is taken care of. You can rest and recover."

I blow out a breath. I still want to see for myself, but I sit back. They were hurt and I wasn't there for them. Everyone was hurt because of Patrick. "What happened to Patrick?"

"The police arrested him. Anna got treated for her head wound and insisted on giving her statement. She went home to her kids. The police picked Yvonne up on her way to the house. They blocked off the road. She was more than willing to talk when she found out Patrick killed Hunter."

"Good." I rub at my head, trying to get the details out of my memory from before I passed out.

"I'm fine. It's just a little blood." Blake's voice comes through a moment before he bursts through my door, followed by a nurse with a bandage.

"I need to put this on you, sir."

Blake stops beside my bed. His green eyes rake over me probably the same way mine rake over him. Besides the fresh stitches, nothing looks wrong with him. His shirt has dried blood on it and I think of

Coop. The nurse presses the bandage to Blake's arm and shakes her head before leaving.

Noah stands and moves out of the way. Blake takes his place, curves his hand behind my neck and pulls me into his chest.

"Fuck, tiger," he whispers as he rests his head down against mine. "You scared at least ten years off my life."

I wrap my arm without the IV around his back, wanting to climb onto his lap and let him hold me, but this is good. The fear flows through me like I'm back there in the apartment, back in that basement, back in that house. Tears run down my cheeks as I cling to him.

"You found me," I whisper. "I knew you would."

"Always, love. Always."

Chapter 168

Pieces of Me

Madison

I'm in a freaking wheelchair when my feet work perfectly fine, but it was the only way the doctor would allow me to go see Coop. And that was only after Blake threatened to carry me, which would have been bad on his arm.

I'm nervous as Noah wheels me down the hall to the recovery room. I don't know what to expect. Patrick shot Coop. Coop could have died. All because of me.

The guilt settles like a lump in my stomach. I know this is Patrick's fault. I know he's to blame for everything. He manipulated this situation to his liking, and that's how this ended with Coop recovering from surgery.

But what if I had talked to the guys before running off? What if I hadn't trusted Yvonne to deliver that message to Blake? What if I'd been the reason Hope died?

My stomach twists.

"What is *she* doing here?" Victoria Graham's disdain carries to me.

"She's Coop's fiancée." Seth's blue eyes meet mine and hold. "He needs to see her."

Fuck, I missed Seth. I want to run into his arms and let him hold me, but that wouldn't be appropriate in front of Coop's mother. That and I'm in this frustrating wheelchair.

Victoria presses her lips together and turns her back on me before walking into what I assume is Coop's room. It's bad enough I already feel responsible for what happened, but dealing with the vitriol from his mother might be too much after everything that's happened. But it won't stop me from seeing Coop.

Then Seth is next to me. He leans down and presses a kiss to my head. "Princess."

I grab his hand and squeeze it, needing that connection, our connection. "I'm sorry, boss."

"You were trying to protect your friend." He squats down next to me and rests his forehead against our joined hands. "You're safe. We're safe. That's all that matters."

His blue eyes capture me again, and all I want to do is sink into his arms and cry like I did with Blake. Seth cups my cheek. "When do you get discharged?"

"Doctor wants to monitor her overnight." Noah rests his hand on my shoulder, and I draw in a breath. None of us should be in this hospital.

"Madison?" A tall man with gray eyes steps out of Coop's room. His hair is white, but aside from coloring, he's an older version of Coop. My heart skips.

"This is Madison." Seth stands. "Madison, this is Carter Graham, Coop's father."

When I move to stand, Carter steps forward, waves me down, and offers me his hand.

"Pleasure to meet you. Coop's asking for you." Carter shakes my hand and steps out of the way so Noah can push me in.

Carter follows us.

As soon as we enter the room with all the machines hooked up to

Coop, tears fall down my cheeks. His eyes are closed and his brow pinched like he's in pain. Noah stops the wheelchair. I stand before anyone can stop me and take Coop's hand.

"Coop?" I try to brush my tears away, but they keep coming.

His hand squeezes around mine as his light blue eyes open. "Ah, there's my goddess."

"You got shot." The words tumble out of my mouth.

"Yeah, but you got drugged." He blinks a little.

Someone moves a chair over for me. I sink into it and when I look up, Coop's dad smiles at me. He gives me a small nod before moving over to Victoria who has tears in her eyes and her hand covering her mouth. He draws her into his arms and she leans against him.

"How are you doing?" I clutch at Coop's hand. Now that I'm close to him, all I want to do is climb into bed next to him and hold him until he's okay.

Noah moves to talk to Coop's parents. After a few nods, Carter leads Victoria out of the room, leaving the five of us alone.

"Well, I got shot." He gives me an arrogant smile. "Figured I'd be the only one with a nifty scar proving how much I love you and want to protect you."

The tears won't stop coming. They're here. They're alive. I'm fine, but Coop is in this hospital bed.

"But then Blake had to get stitches too." Coop glares at Blake. "Cocky bastard."

"You're lucky you didn't bleed to death." Blake puts his hand on my shoulder and squeezes. "Madison would have never forgiven me if I'd let you die."

"I am her favorite." Coop lifts my hands to his lips. His eyes sparkle mischievously. "Next time you visit, come dressed as a nurse. I'll order you a little white dress and we can play doctor."

Fuck, he's out of it. Must be the pain meds. "How about we do that when we get you home?"

"I might be bedridden for a while, sweetheart." He winks.

A laugh slips out of me. His smile fades.

"I'm just glad we got to you in time." His tone turns serious and the tears press against my eyes again. "I don't know what we would have done if—" He cuts himself off and tugs on my arm. "Come here, sweetheart, please."

I stand and sit on the edge of his bed. He draws me closer. I try to be gentle but he holds me against him like he just found me again. The steady beat of his heart pounds in my ear and I soak it in. Every beat confirms he's alive.

"You're mine, Madison. Ours. No one else's. No more games. We'll figure out how to make this work." He kisses my head. "We're in this together. All of us."

I hold him carefully, trying not to hurt him. "That's all I want."

He holds me like that for a while before both of us need to rest.

When Noah wheels me out, Carter stops us.

"Victoria is upset that Cooper was shot. It's not about you, dear." He glances at Noah before returning his gaze to me. "We know Cooper loves you and we'll do what it takes to support you two in whatever decision you make for the future."

"Thank you. I love him too." Tears choke my throat, but I swallow them down.

We stop in Hope's room. Jason sits in the corner while Hope and I talk for a few minutes. The doctors say she'll be good to go home tomorrow too. The police took her statement earlier. I can't stay for long, but I'm glad I could see her and we're both free of that place now.

———

"I'm fine to walk," I argue as we step off the elevator to our apartment.

"You can lean on me if you need to." Blake keeps trying to pick me up, but I'm not the one with the gunshot wound.

Noah opens the door and we walk in. I draw in a breath and look around at the space. Last night they both stayed in my room, while

Seth stayed with Coop. I can't wait to have them all with me again. Here. Where we belong.

It will be four more days before they reevaluate Coop to see if he can come home. Fear of infection. We'll be taking shifts to go sit with Coop in the hospital.

The apartment is warm and inviting like it always has been. But it feels different now, not worse or better, just different. I'm free to enjoy this apartment and what this relationship has become without the specter of Val and her boyfriend or the faceless stalker.

When Noah touches the small of my back, I turn to face him. His brown eyes smile down at me. "Come on, let's get you settled."

I let him guide me to his bedroom. Blake stands in the doorway.

"My team is doublechecking everything, including your room." Blake rubs the back of his neck. "We're not sure what Patrick had access to and what Andrea and Courtney may have managed."

I sit on the edge of Noah's bed. "I'm fine sleeping in your beds."

They both stand there awkwardly. Do they think I'm that damaged by this whole thing?

"Do we need to go to work?" I look at Noah and then Blake.

"Not today."

I nod. The hospital didn't clear me until almost two in the afternoon. I stand and take off the blouse they brought me to wear home.

"What are you doing?" Blake asks.

"Taking a shower." I drop the blouse on the floor and shimmy out of my skirt. "I'd love company."

I stand in my bra and panties, looking at two of my loves. We've all had a long couple of days. I just want to be close to them. I'm wet just thinking about being with them, but I long for our connection more than just getting off.

Noah takes his shirt off and heads into the bathroom to start the shower.

I walk up to Blake and undo the buttons on his shirt. "How's your arm?"

"Good enough." His green eyes watch me intently. "How are you?"

"Drug free. Stalker free." Smiling, I ease the shirt off his bandaged arm. "All I need is my men back in working order and life will be perfect."

Blake lifts his hand and threads it into my hair, tipping my head back. "We still have things to resolve, tiger."

I sigh. Holding his gaze, I work on his belt and pants. "I know, but in here, we can just be us. We can forget about the press and the speculation. The trial that will take months. We can just be with each other. Love each other."

Noah walks up behind me and undoes my bra, sliding the straps down my arms, while Blake finishes undressing. Noah slips my panties off me and draws me back against his naked body. Sighing at the feel of his skin against mine, I want to stay in this moment forever.

His hands smooth over my hips as his cock rests against my ass. "How do you feel, kitten?"

"Alive. Grateful. Horny." I glance over my shoulder to catch his smile.

His hand slides between my legs and dips into my entrance. "We can help with that last one."

Blake takes my hand as Noah draws his hand away, sucking his finger into his mouth. My eyes heat as they meet his. I can see the need in him and it stirs the fire hotter inside me.

Once we're in the bathroom, Blake draws me into the shower, careful to keep his bandage out of the water. I press up against his chest and rise on my toes while pulling his head down to me.

Our lips collide in a tangle of tongues. I reach for his hard, thick cock and stroke my hand over him. His hand cups my breast, stroking the nipple into a hardened peak.

Noah closes in behind me, surrounding me with their hard flesh. His hands grip my hips. His lips trace down my neck before sucking on my skin, making wetness leak out of me.

Blake and I break our kiss, both breathing heavily. Blake's green eyes search mine.

Noah passes something to Blake before spinning me to face him. "We almost lost you."

Fuck. I take his face in my hands and search his brown eyes.

"I couldn't live if she died. What kind of person would that make me?" I admit.

Noah rests his forehead against mine. "I know, kitten, but who would I be without you?"

He lifts me against him and kisses me. I wrap my arms and legs around him tight, knowing I'll never let go again. He shifts my hips and the tip of his cock presses against my entrance before thrusting deep inside me.

"Noah." I gasp against his lips.

"You're mine, kitten. That means you don't put yourself in danger." His hips thrust into me almost punishingly. Claiming me over and over again. Pushing me higher and higher.

I want it. I need it. Kissing him, I whisper, "I won't."

Blake's hand rubs between my ass cheeks, thrusting his lubed fingers into my asshole. I break away from Noah's lips to look over my shoulder, meeting Blake's eyes as the head of his cock slides over my puckered hole.

Noah keeps fucking me as Blake breaches my ass and slides in. My body tightens around both of them, feeling them slide against each other deep inside.

It's too much and not enough at the same time. My body tightens and then explodes as I come around their cocks buried deep inside me. They both fuck me through it. A discordant rhythm that has me throbbing around them, ready to shatter again.

Blake smacks my ass with his good palm. "Fuck, tiger."

I'm building up to another orgasm as they handle me rougher than usual. I crave it. I put us all in jeopardy. Long before I knew any of them. Without even knowing I was doing so. I still don't know why.

Why me? Will it ever make sense? Will I ever be able to forget about what happened? Or will the scars my men carry because of me finally break me?

I'm not sure when I started crying, but Noah tips my face up to his.

"Color, kitten?"

"Green, Noah. Please don't stop fucking me." I wrap around him tighter, feeling them claiming my body, knowing it belongs to them, knowing I'm safe in their arms.

I shatter, coming all over Noah's cock and squeezing like a vise around Blake's, drawing them into their releases. Their warm cum fills me, making me whole again.

But as they draw away, I'm missing my other two loves. The other pieces of my heart.

Noah washes me while I wash Blake. When we finish and dry off, we lie naked in Noah's bed. I rest my head against Blake's chest while Noah spoons me from behind.

Their hands stroke over me, gently, soothing.

"Coop's going to be fine, tiger." Blake kisses the top of my head.

"I know," I whisper, not sure I believe myself. Still afraid Patrick can take one more thing away from me.

Alleged Kidnapper of Graham's Fiancée Exclusive

Patrick Beck, husband of Anna (Whitley) Beck, breaks his silence from jail. Not about his kidnapping or stalking charges, but about his work with Morrigan Technology Group. Specifically, the owners, Seth Hart, Blake Wagner, Noah Burns, and Cooper Graham, and their secret arrangement with their assistant and Graham's fiancée, Madison Harris.

While Ms. Harris works for them, she also lives with them and, according to Beck, was coerced into entering an arrangement to have sex with all four men. Beck offered a contract as proof of his allegations. The owners were not available for comment.

Chapter 169

PR Crisis

Madison

I stand next to the floor-to-ceiling windows, looking down at the circus in front of our building. The media have been camped out there all day, making it impossible for me to leave to have dinner and drinks with my friends like we planned.

"They'll be here soon, princess." Seth comes up behind me and draws me into his arms.

I lean against him. "How's Coop?"

"Being moved to his private room as we speak." Seth brushes my hair over my shoulder.

A shiver works down my spine. I have on jeans and a sweater. This need to be covered is new for me and may be temporary, but I can't stomach putting on a sundress. Or any dress. Around my guys, I feel comfortable being completely naked, but otherwise, I need more protection.

I was looking forward to actually going out. Without an escort, though I'm sure Blake would be there just in case. But I was going to be free to enjoy my life. Finally.

But just when I got my freedom back, Patrick found a way to take it away again. Our arrangement hit the tabloids. It's a small article, but it made some waves. Four powerful men asked their broke assistant to sign a sex contract.

Turning in Seth's arms, I wrap mine around his waist, resting my head against his chest. His heart beats steady in my ear. I draw in a deep breath, loving the smell of him. It may have started as an arrangement, but it turned into so much more.

Tonight we'll sleep in my room. Blake, Noah, Seth, and me. It feels wrong without Coop, but I need them with me.

"He misses you." Seth kisses the top of my head.

"I miss him too." We decided it would be better if I didn't go to the hospital right now. The media should die down after a few days and maybe then I can go. But I'm attached to Coop as his fiancée, which makes them clamor more for the story.

Noah leads Sara into the apartment. The temporary receptionist doesn't have a key card for our elevator anymore. It will take some time to find someone we trust.

"Oh my god, Madison!" She hurries across the apartment as Seth releases me. She throws her arms around me, hugging me tight.

"I'm so sorry I didn't figure out you were asking for help in your text." Her chin hooks on my shoulder. I'm not wearing shoes and she has on boots with heels.

"I didn't know what to say to let you know." Hugging her back, I breathe in her citrus scent. I've never had friends like these women.

"And now this media frenzy." Sara pulls away. Her pale green eyes search mine. "It felt like a red-carpet event as I came inside."

"Yeah." I haven't been downstairs yet.

"We need to figure out a code, just us girls. So we'll know when someone is sending a secret SOS." Sara steps back. "Oh, and a passcode so we'll know if someone else is using your phone like Hope. God, Hope. Is she coming?"

"Yes." I head to the couch and gesture. "Do you want to sit down?"

"Patrick Beck." She joins me on the couch. "What a dick. I mean it's bad enough to try to make you his love slave, but to shame you for your relationship with these guys . . ."

She shakes her head. I don't like thinking about what's to come. The trial. What's his game now? Was this just to hurt us? Or is it a strategy?

"Holy crap." Kayla walks in after Blake. Her green eyes find me. She strides across the apartment and sits next to me, pulling me into her arms. "If I had money, that prick would be dead."

I hug Kayla back. Not sure what to say to that. Do I hate what he did to me? Yes. Am I mad that he shot Coop and Blake? Also yes. Do I wish him dead? That's complicated. He has children who love him. I definitely want him locked away and for them to throw away the key.

Hunter didn't deserve to die, and Patrick deserves to pay for that with his freedom.

"Are you okay?" Kayla holds me at arm's length and studies me. "And Coop, please tell me he's just as beautiful as ever."

"I'm good. Coop will recover." I glance at Blake who rubs my shoulders.

He smiles and I'm grateful that both he and Coop made it through. I hate that they were in danger because of me.

Noah comes in the apartment door, this time with Hope.

On seeing Hope, I stand with tears in my eyes and we collide in the middle of the entryway. We hug each other tight. What we went through together was unimaginable. The fear and the terror made it hard for me to sleep, even surrounded by my men. I can't imagine what Hope is going through even now. Sara and Kayla come and join us in one big hug.

"I'm feeling a little squished," Hope admits and we all back away a step. She smiles. "So we're only allowed to drink at my brother's bar from now on."

"That's fair." Kayla wraps her arm around Hope's shoulders. "We definitely won't let you go off alone any more. How are you sleeping?"

"With the lights on. At Jason's." Hope shrugs. I'm glad she has her brother. "I start therapy next week."

"What's on the agenda for tonight?" Sara sits on the couch and we all join her.

"How about a *Magic Mike* marathon and pizza?" Kayla offers. "Man candy and carbs."

I draw in a breath and realize this can be my new normal. These girls as my friends. My men as my lovers. Now, if we could figure out how to do this without the media circus, that would be perfect.

Coop

"You could come home with us." Mother stands next to the window, looking down upon the peasants. I keep expecting her to wave like a princess to them. "Your room is always clean and waiting for you whenever you need it."

It's been three days and I'm ready to explode if I can't get out of here. Patrick fucking Beck got in another hit. The fucker. Media is staged around the hospital entrance and outside our building.

My mother keeps nagging me to come to their house instead of back to my life. She doesn't understand how I could want to be with a woman who's also with my friends. I don't try to explain it.

The guys and Madison are basically on lockdown and haven't been in to see me. Seth has, but the others are busy with damage control and keeping an eye on Madison.

"When I get out of the hospital, I'll be returning to my apartment." I poke at the food they brought me for lunch. My father hasn't come in yet. I set the fork down and look at my phone.

> MADISON:
>
> Video chat later?

This is the worst part. I can't see Madison. She's once again locked in the tower because of Patrick Beck. There's nothing we can do to stop this. My publicist tried. It's out there and too saturated in the media to pull back.

We've talked about releasing a statement, but we can't decide on what to say. Besides the coercion, there's nothing wrong in his statement. We did enter into a sexual arrangement with Madison. It grew into something more.

"Hey." Seth walks into my room with a white bag.

My mother glares at him like she's done every day since the news got out. In her mind, these guys corrupted me, but honestly, sharing a woman was my idea in the first place.

I straighten on the bed. "Hey."

My gaze goes behind him, hoping he brought Madison, because fuck, I need to touch her and know that she's okay. I miss her.

Seth shakes his head to tell me she's not here. He pulls out a container from the bag and sets it in front of me. I open it to find his homemade chicken parmesan, still warm.

"I love you, man." I push the hospital food to the side and dig in.

"I'll get a coffee." My mother sweeps out of the room.

As soon as the door closes, Seth sits in the chair next to my bed and pulls his computer out of his laptop bag. While it turns on, he lifts his gaze to me.

"How's today?" His blue eyes take me in. He's been at my side the most and usually working while he's here. I appreciate it.

"It would be better if Madison were here." I take a bite. Fuck, I miss good food. "How is she doing?"

He releases a breath. "Missing you. Going crazy not being able to come and see you."

It's Saturday. But the week has been weird. Real fucking weird, the fire alarm on Monday, staying at the hotel, then Tuesday and all the fuckery that came with that, getting shot. The last time I got to see Madison in person was Wednesday before she went home.

After eating while Seth worked, I finally ask, "Have we lost clients yet?"

Seth blows out a breath. "No. Andrea probably did us a favor because only people willing to work with us even after someone shit talked us stayed."

"Maybe our relationship getting out isn't a bad thing. The contract getting out there sucks." I say it because I've been for going public with our relationship for some time. Our company's reputation is secure. "We don't have to pretend anymore. We can just own it. We can just be fools in love with a gorgeous woman."

Seth closes his laptop. Since we missed a few days of work, he uses the time here to make up for it. He leans back and meets my eyes.

"I don't think we have much choice. The genie is already out of the bottle." He runs a hand through his hair. "Even if we contained it, Madison will always carry this reputation with her."

"So what?" I sit up and wince at the pain in my side. I use the bed controls to raise my back more. "None of us are going anywhere. She's ours and we're hers. I love her. I'd marry her tomorrow if I thought she'd be down with that. We're not some temporary fuckfest. We're in love."

"We just need to focus on getting you back on your feet. We can deal with this as it comes at us." Seth rubs his eyes. Probably thinking of all the stuff we did to keep this from tarnishing Madison's reputation.

"Fuck that. Let's get ahead of it. Take her out to dinner. Ignore the media. With everything happening, most of us haven't been on a date with the woman we love. So we take her out. Individually. All together." I give Seth a look. "I know it's a fucking zoo out there, but if we show them there's nothing sensational about it, it should die down."

Seth's look turns contemplative.

"And bring her here. Find a way, because I need her."

"I'm here," Madison says from the doorway. My dad stands behind her and moves her inside as he closes the door.

My heart thumps hard in my chest. It feels like forever since I saw her last. She moves gracefully to my bedside. I reach out my hand and she takes it. Her eyes shine with unshed tears and she wears the most beautiful smile I've ever seen.

"I figured you could use some time to talk." My dad slides his hands into his pockets and looks at Seth. "Want to walk with me?"

Seth rises and kisses the top of Madison's head. "See you soon, princess."

She doesn't shift her gaze from me. When the door closes behind them, I push my food tray out of the way. She helps me. When I tug her toward me, she carefully sits on the edge of the bed.

"Sweetheart, I got shot trying to save you. I need you a hell of a lot closer." I reach up and tuck her blond hair behind her ear.

"I don't want to hurt you." She looks at my bandaged side and a tear slips free.

"I need you next to me. I want to hold you and kiss you and reassure myself that you're whole and safe. Fucking is not possible yet, so climb up and snuggle with me."

She bites her lip and slips her shoes off. I lower the head of the bed some. It takes some coordinated effort, but finally, she's curled up against me on the bed. Her warmth presses into my good side.

With her head resting on my shoulder, I toy with her fingers on my chest. "How are you doing?"

She sighs. "I miss you."

"I miss you too. What about the other stuff?"

She shrugs.

"No comment?" I chuckle but stop because it hurts to laugh.

"Are you okay?" She lifts up and looks down at me. Her blue eyes search mine.

I cup her cheek and lead her down until our mouths are almost touching. "Better now that you're here."

She presses her lips to mine, softly, delicately, like she's afraid I'll break. I part my lips and pull her closer as I take over the kiss. If I thought I'd have enough time, I'd have her suck me off or ride me. Pretty sure neither is on my list of approved activities.

Her hand clutches my t-shirt. At least I'm able to wear a t-shirt and sweats instead of the hospital gown.

"I've ordered you that nurse uniform. It should arrive today." I thread my fingers into her hair and just look into her gorgeous blue eyes.

"What are we going to play?" Her devious smile makes my pulse skip.

"Someone has to be naughty. Either I can be the naughty patient, or you can be the naughty nurse, or we can be naughty together. But this time, Blake doesn't get to take over." I bring her lips to mine for another taste.

"We can have some alone time. I'd like that."

I lower her head back to my chest. "We may need a dirty doctor too, but that's a role best played by Noah."

She chuckles and settles against me. With her in my arms, it feels like everything will be okay. There's still this fiasco to take care of, but we can deal with that when I get home.

"I love you, Madison. This media frenzy might get nasty for a while, but we all love you." I blow out a breath.

"I love you, Coop."

My heart kicks up a notch. I never thought anyone would love me for me, but then Madison happened. I'll do whatever it takes to protect her and help her succeed in life. Because I plan to share in hers however she'll let me.

Chapter 170

Personnel Changes

Madison

Monday afternoon, I'm working at my desk like nothing happened last week. Like I wasn't almost robbed of all this. The grocery order is in and Coop should be home any minute. Seth left an hour ago to pick him up from the hospital. I wanted to go, but work has been crazy. One thing after another.

We're behind from missing work a few days last week, but we're almost caught up.

It finally feels like we're back in the flow, except Coop isn't here.

Theo is filling in for Coop until he recovers enough to work, but Seth took Coop a laptop. He needed something to do or he threatened to check himself out early.

I glance at the time. My foot taps under my desk. Just a little longer and I can go down to get the groceries and see Coop.

"Settle, kitten." Noah rubs my shoulders. I tense at his touch, not expecting it. Hyperawareness of my surroundings is like a shadow I can't just shrug off, even though I know I'm safe now.

I release my breath and lean my head back against him. "It's been a week since we've been completely alone. He's still healing."

"You want me to help?" Noah's fingers slide up my throat, leaving tingles in their wake.

Coop texted me this morning. The nurse outfit came in and he wants his own personal nurse to take care of him this afternoon, but I'm so scared of hurting him or making him have to go back to the hospital.

"Maybe?" I don't want to disappoint Coop by having someone else there, but at the same time, they can help me make sure I don't reinjure him.

Noah tips my head back and kisses me upside down. "Maybe I'll come down later, kitten."

His dark eyes hold mine for a moment. A whole fucking fireworks display goes off inside, thinking of Noah and Coop playing with me. Fuck, these guys have direct access to my buttons and know just how to press them. It doesn't take much. Will it always be that way?

"Go down and get ready for him." Noah steps back and winks. "After you get the groceries."

I laugh. Showing up in the lobby in the slutty nurse's uniform Coop bought me probably wouldn't go over well. The media have calmed down some, but there's still a few every day, waiting outside. Tonight over dinner, we're supposed to discuss our next moves.

Fuck it. I'm not getting anything done here. As I close down my computer, my phone buzzes with a message that the groceries have arrived.

When I step on the elevator, I'm nervous. I haven't seen Fox since he told me about Andrea. He was nice early on. A little flirty, but last time he was a lot more bold. I just don't want to deal with him if he's going to be that way. Hopefully, we can be professional.

By the time I arrive at the lobby, I've taken a few deep breaths. If he starts in on any of his stuff with past assistants, I'm just going to tell him I'm not interested.

The elevator doors open. I lock them open and head to the receptionist's desk. Fox is nowhere to be seen.

The temporary receptionist smiles at me. "She had to go grab the cart."

She? I nod and wait to see what the hell the woman means.

When the doors open, an older woman, maybe in her fifties, rolls the cart across the marble floor. When she reaches me, she gives me a toothy grin.

"Hi, I'm Agnes. I'm your new delivery gal."

A hand touches my waist from behind. It's soft enough not to alarm me. I turn to look up at Blake.

"Fox doesn't deliver here anymore." Blake smirks as his hand curves around my hip. "They shifted our route after I notified the company that he was doing extra deliveries on the job and was making my girlfriend uncomfortable."

"Girlfriend?" My cheeks turn rosy as my heart pounds a little harder.

He shrugs. "That's what you call someone who's yours. Now hurry and get those groceries put away so you can be there for your fiancé."

I grin. The receptionist blushes and tries to appear nonchalant. I turn to Agnes. "Welcome, Agnes. The elevator is right over there. I'll be there in a minute."

Agnes wheels the cart to the elevator. Blake's green eyes sparkle.

I grab Blake's tie and pull him down to say in his ear.

"Thank you, Daddy." I press a kiss to his cheek as he chuckles.

"Anytime, tiger." He swats my ass as I head to the elevator.

I love that we don't have to hide anymore, but I'm definitely not calling him *Daddy* in public. That's just for us.

I run my hands over the slacks Seth picked for me this morning. I still have on high heels, and he finished the outfit with the softest, lightest sweater. At breakfast, he pulled me down on his lap while we ate. I love those quiet times with my guys.

As I step on the elevator, I sigh and use my card to access the apartment level.

"I read that article," Agnes says.

I stiffen, worried about what else she'll say. "Oh, yeah?"

"It wouldn't have taken coercion to get me to sign a contract with a hunk like that." She laughs. "If I were thirty years younger, I'd be all over that man. And I've seen the pictures of the others. You're a very lucky girl."

Her blue eyes sparkle as I meet them.

"The luckiest," I admit.

"My kids are already married or attached. They got lucky and found the loves of their lives. I say if you love those men, you hold on to them tight."

The elevator stops.

"I do." I walk out to the door and use the card. "And I will hold on to them."

Coop

"Do you need anything else?" Seth sets my bag on the chair in my room.

I sit on the edge of the bed and hold my side as it aches. I'm not on the good stuff for pain relief anymore and I'm definitely feeling it.

"Probably just going to rest for a while." I kick off my shoes and swing my legs into the bed. Every move seems to hurt right now, but I'm so done with lying down and doing nothing.

Nodding, Seth brings my tablet and laptop to the nightstand. I take my phone out of my pocket and set it on the bed.

"If you need anything, call or text us." Seth holds out a couple pills and a glass of water. "Madison will unload the groceries soon and she'll take the rest of the day off."

Which is why I need to nap while I can. I need my energy for my naughty nurse.

"Thanks." I take the pills with water and lie down, thankful to be in my own bed.

I wake to the doorknob turning. Confused, I look down at my

phone and see it's been an hour since I arrived. I scrub my hand down my face and glance at the door. My room is empty and the door is shut.

Fuck, did I miss Madison? I sit up and groan. Fuck, an automatic bed is my next purchase. I stay still as a wave of pain sweeps through me. The doctor offered a prescription for the strong stuff, but I want to be clearheaded.

The door opens and Madison rushes in. "What are you doing? You shouldn't be trying to get up."

"Too late." I smirk.

Fuck. My goddess has her blond hair piled sexily on her head. Red lipstick stains her luscious lips. The white dress hugs her curves, pushing her breasts up and together to give her deep cleavage. It ends at the top of her thighs. White garters hold up the silk stockings I ordered for her. The red heels match the piping on the dress.

She's beside me and I forget what I wanted to do because all my blood flow has journeyed south. She presses me back down. I notice she even painted her nails red. Nice touch.

"Do you need something? Seth said he gave you your pills. Do you need help to the bathroom?" She sits on the edge of the bed. Wrinkles crease her forehead.

"You worried about me, sweetheart?" I brush her hair behind her ear.

She sucks in a breath. Her gaze drops to my side. "You got shot less than a week ago."

Her eyes widen as she notices the tenting in my pants.

I drag my fingers down her neck to tease her neckline. "Tell me, nurse, what kind of underwear do you wear with an outfit like that?"

My eyes lift to hers and she releases a breath.

"Are you okay?" she asks.

"Better now that you're here." I drop my hand to her thigh. "I think I'm ready for my sponge bath, nurse."

My hand creeps up to the junction of her legs. No panties, just hot, wet flesh. My cock jerks.

She bites her lip as I stroke my fingers over her pussy.

"I have an ache that you can fix." I smile.

She arches her eyebrow, but her eyes darken as I ease a finger into her slick heat.

"Fuck, I missed your pussy, sweetheart."

Her legs part as I thrust in and out of her. She reaches over to stroke my cock through my pants.

"I want those red lips on my cock." I lick my lips. "You can sit on my face so I can taste every inch of this pussy while you choke on my thick cock like a good little whore."

"I'll have to check with the doctor to see if you're allowed to eat." Her blue eyes are hot with lust as I continue to finger fuck her.

I draw my finger out of her tight cunt and raise it to my lips, sucking her sweet taste off my skin.

"No strenuous activity for a few weeks while I heal, but I can eat or drink anything I want." I take the pillow out from beneath my head and toss it to the side. "Be a good little whore and ride my face."

She stands and bends over at the waist to undo her shoes, flashing me her pussy and ass.

"Damn, I need to fuck you, baby. You're making me so fucking hard, flashing that pussy at me like I don't know you need my thick cock splitting you in half."

Still bent over, she drops her shoes and spreads her legs for me. She's so pink and glistening. Precum leaks out of my dick in anticipation.

"Is this what you want?" She glances over her shoulder. Her blue eyes meet mine. She reaches between her legs and uses two fingers to spread her pussy open for me. "Is this what you need?"

I slide my pants down to free my cock and stroke it while I look at her. "I've dreamed of you every night. Of that sweet pussy riding my cock. I woke up hard and couldn't do anything about it."

She straightens and turns to me. "You need to remain still."

"I'll do anything you want as long as you give me your pussy, nurse." I wink.

She climbs on the bed next to me, kneeling. Her gaze falls on the edge of my dressing beneath my shirt. When she reaches out to lift my shirt, her hands shake. Her fingers ghost over the white gauze covering my wound.

Her brow furrows and her eyes glaze over.

"Hey, sweetheart. I'm here. The worst is over. We're together and he can't get to either of us ever again." I lift my hand to cup her cheek.

Her blue eyes swim with unshed tears. Fuck. I can wait to fuck her.

"Come here, baby. Let's get the emotional stuff out so the only crying you do is in need." I draw her down to me and she curls into my side. We didn't talk about everything in the hospital. I just wanted to hold her then.

"Are you okay?" I ask, stroking my hand down her back. "I know you're not completely okay. This isn't something we'll just get over. The scars will last a long time, but we'll heal, sweetheart."

Her fingers clutch at my shirt. "I wasn't there. You could have died and I wouldn't have been there."

Her tears fall on my t-shirt. "When I saw you unconscious on that bed, I saw red. I didn't know what he'd done to you. Had no idea if you were hurt. Not immediately going after you when we found Hope nearly destroyed me."

"The only thing that kept me going was knowing I needed to get back to you guys." She draws in a ragged breath. "I love you, Coop. I don't know what my life would be like if you weren't in it. I can't even think about it."

"You'd still have the others—"

"But I wouldn't have you." She props herself up to look down at me. "We don't work because I need four dicks. Though I enjoy that part. We work because I need each and every one of you. And you guys need each other. We all love and care for each other. Neither you nor I had family like this growing up. We show our love. We hold each other accountable for our actions. You make us whole. Without you, there is no us."

"You're the missing piece, Madison." I catch her hand in mine. "You make us whole. You make us better. You keep us sane. I didn't know I could love before you. I knew I loved my friends, my brothers, my partners, but that's because they're my family. But without you, we could scatter to the winds and live separate lives. We can't lose you, sweetheart. I love you too much to let you go."

"Then don't. Never let me go, Coop."

I catch the back of her neck and draw her mouth down to mine. This right here is what I missed in the middle of the night. Her in my arms. Her kissing me. Her loving me with every piece of her being as much as she loves the men that are my family.

The door opens but I ignore it.

"Are you sure you're into role-play?" Noah's voice is light. "Because Madison's pussy is right there, begging to be fucked, and you're making out? I thought you were better at this, Coop."

"We needed a moment for the emotional shit." I lift her face from mine and brush away the tears. "We good, baby?"

She nods and smiles. "Give me a second to wash my face."

She slips off the bed and gives Noah a heated glance before disappearing into the bathroom and shutting the door. I exhale and stare at the ceiling.

"How do you want to play this? Because she's worried about hurting you." Noah sits on the edge of the bed.

Putting my hands behind my head, I turn to look at him. "I was just going to let her do all the work. Make her smother me with her pussy while she chokes on my dick."

"I've got an idea. If you're game?" Noah smirks. I love this guy's wicked mind.

Chapter 171

Putting Out the Fire

Madison

I can't believe I cried. I use a washcloth to wipe the tears away. But seeing his bandage made it real for me. Coop could have died, and I'm not sure how we would have gone on without him. How could I go on missing a piece of my heart?

It was easier to forget while he was in the hospital because I worried about the press and how I was going to see him. But here and seeing the bandage, the reality hit me. Patrick could have killed Coop.

But he didn't.

Coop is alive and needs me. I shake out the fears of what could have been and focus.

That's my man out there and I need to take care of him. All of him.

I reapply my lipstick and take a deep breath. That pulse of desire I feel for him is strong. He'll tell me if he needs to stop. If anything I do is too much. I trust him.

When I open the bedroom door, Coop has a blanket over him but his chest is bare. The arm on his uninjured side is behind his head.

Noah stands to the side with a white doctor's coat on and his slacks from work, holding a clipboard.

I smirk and raise an eyebrow. Was he hiding that costume somewhere? Or did Coop have other plans for nurse and doctor scenarios?

"There you are, nurse." Noah glances up from his clipboard. He's not wearing a shirt or shoes, just his pants and the coat. Fuck, these two gorgeous men are all mine.

Biting my lip, I can't wait to find out how they're going to play with me this time. I press my thighs together against the aching need between them.

"Doctor." I move into the room and straighten Coop's blanket a little. His gaze follows me as I move around the room.

"I need you to clean the patient's cock." Noah arches his brow.

"But I don't have a sponge." Fuck, this is cheesy, but Coop's grin is worth it. The whole thing is cheesy. This costume is ridiculous. I thought about wearing panties, but that defeats the purpose of the incredibly short skirt.

No one but my men will see me now. There are no more cameras or anyone to spy on us.

"Use your mouth, nurse." Noah adjusts the hardened bulge in his pants.

I draw the blanket down to reveal Coop's hard cock and wet my lips. He spreads his legs and I crawl onto the bed between them. It may be a cheesy porn scenario, but I'm so aroused right now my pussy aches.

Kneeling on the bed, I lower my mouth, parting my lips to take his cock inside. He slides in deep and groans as I gag slightly around him before relaxing my throat. My eyes lift to find him watching me.

His fingers brush my cheek as I suck hard around him.

The bed shifts behind me and Noah's cock sinks deep into my pussy, making me moan around Coop's cock. My eyes close at the intrusion. I'm already so wet and ready for more.

"Take him deep." Noah thrusts into me, shoving me down farther on Coop's cock.

Whimpering, I slide up and down on Coop's cock while Noah fucks my pussy. My insides boil with heat, ready to explode. Just as my climax is within reach, Noah withdraws and smacks my ass.

"Now, now, kitten, you know what the patient needs."

What Coop wanted from the beginning? My toes curl just thinking of his mouth on me.

I rise off Coop's cock and meet his darkened eyes. "Are you hungry?"

"Starving." Coop licks his lips and my pussy throbs in anticipation.

Noah offers me a hand and helps me off the bed before walking me to the side and helping me straddle Coop's face. I'm afraid to lower myself onto him, but Noah pushes me down.

"You need to finish your job and clean him thoroughly, nurse." Noah strokes his cock lazily.

Leaning over, I take Coop's cock back into my mouth, sucking and licking. His hand wraps around my hip and draws me down tighter against his mouth. His tongue flicks out and runs along my clit to my entrance. Sparks flood my system, and I moan around his cock.

Noah's hand threads into my hair, caressing the back of my head gently. "He needs a deep cleaning."

Noah pushes my head down to take all of Coop's cock. I swallow around his tip in the back of my throat. Coop's fingers thrust into my pussy as he pulls me down and latches his mouth onto my clit, sucking hard.

I shatter, pulsing and coming around his fingers as Noah lifts me so I can breathe. I gasp around Coop's cock before Noah pushes me down again. Coop groans against my pussy, pushing me into another orgasm as he fills my throat with his cum.

After I swallow, Noah lifts me up. My breathing is ragged as I meet Noah's dark eyes. Coop's fingers trail back to my ass and slide inside. He fucks me with his fingers while his tongue lazily sweeps over my clit.

When I gasp, Coop's tongue thrusts into my pussy over and over until I cry out as another release pulses through me. I try to lift away from his devilish tongue, needing a break, but he holds me down on his face as he pushes me right back over the edge.

My whole body trembles, and my breath saws in and out of my lungs. My heart races.

When Noah lifts me off Coop, I'm liquid in his hands. He stands behind me beside the bed.

"Want some more, kitten?" he whispers in my ear.

"I want to feel that slick heat around my cock." Coop doesn't sit up. His cock is erect and my pussy aches for him. I want him so badly.

Noah shrugs out of his coat and pushes his pants down, leaving him and Coop naked with me still in the nurse uniform.

Even covered, I've never felt more exposed with these men. They know me so well. They're so in tune with each other they almost act as one.

"Nurse, grab the lube," Noah orders.

I grab the bottle of lube off the nightstand, handing it to Noah.

He squirts some on his hand and rubs it on his cock. Each stroke of his hand sends a pulse of need through my core. That fire inside me bursts back into flames. His eyes meet mine.

"This is a very delicate operation." Noah grins wickedly. "We need to make sure we handle the patient with care."

"Of course, doctor." I nod.

He hands the lube back to me and I return it to the nightstand. Coop groans slightly, but in pain. When I turn, Noah has tugged him down on the bed with his legs over the edge.

"You good?" Noah asks Coop.

"Green." Coop's hand covers his bandage. My brow furrows as Coop's light blue eyes meet mine. Is he hurt? Will he tell us if he is? Fuck, maybe this is too much, too soon.

Noah grabs my hips and thrusts his lubed fingers into my ass. Oh, fuck. That definitely clears the brain.

"No worrying. He'll tell us if he needs to quit, kitten." Noah presses on the walls of my ass, stretching me.

When he's satisfied, he draws his fingers out and goes into the bathroom to wash his hands. I stand between Coop's legs dangling off the edge of the bed, and stroke his cock, paying careful attention to his face for any signs of pain.

"I'm good, sweetheart." Coop strains against my hand.

"Let's give the patient something to watch, kitten." Noah comes up behind me and unzips the front of my dress until my breasts spill out. He holds my hand as I climb onto the bed to straddle Coop. My knees are next to his hips, while my feet hang off the edge of the bed behind me.

I slide Coop's cock against my pussy before slowly lowering myself down. My pussy flutters around his cock as I sink onto him.

"I love the way you feel inside me," I whisper when I'm fully seated on him.

Noah holds me upright, his hands on my hips, spreading my ass cheeks as his cock presses against my puckered hole. Coop meets my eyes as he reaches out and takes my hands, letting me balance some weight on him, but I don't give him much.

Holding my waist, Noah eases inside my ass. I'm so full everywhere. Both of them inside me. My heart feels like I've found home again between these two. I draw in a breath, ready for what comes next.

"I'll do all the work, kitten." Noah kisses my neck. "I'll fuck this ass and you'll come so hard that you'll milk his cock until he comes for you."

Coop's gaze falls to my exposed breasts and he licks his lips. "When I'm back to full activity, I'll fuck you until you can't sit, sweetheart."

My breath catches as Noah eases out before thrusting in deep.

"Fuck," Coop whispers. "I can feel you inside her, brother. Making her so fucking tight."

Noah's arm tightens around my waist as he thrusts his cock in and out of my ass, pushing me so close to the edge. "I'm always willing to give our whore what she needs."

His hand clutches my breast and pinches my hardened nipple. I let out a cry at the sudden pain and pleasure that streaks through me.

"Especially when you can't do it yourself." Noah bites where my neck and shoulder meet and I buck my hips against Coop.

"When I'm better, I'm tying you up and fucking her in front of you." Coop's gaze follows Noah's fingers on my breast. I suck in a breath as he continues to fuck my ass, pushing me higher until I'm teetering on the edge. My toes curl. I'm so ready to explode.

Noah's hand slides down my hip to lift my skirt. "I prefer to participate." His finger glides over my clit. "But I'm more than willing to let you do all the work."

When he pinches my clit, I arch against him. My world shatters all around me as I tip over the edge, crying out as I convulse around the two cocks inside me.

"Good girl, kitten." Noah doesn't let up. Circling my clit with his finger while fucking my ass through my orgasm, making it last longer, drawing it out. Coop's gaze holds mine the entire time.

When Noah thrusts in deep and groans his release in my ear, I shatter again, pulsing around Coop's cock. His hips buck up into me as he comes, but Noah holds both of us down so Coop doesn't strain his injury.

As we all come down, Noah holds me against him. Our heavy breaths fill the air. Their cocks pulse inside me as my pussy and ass flutter around them in aftershocks.

Finally, Noah lifts me and lays me down beside Coop on the bed. Coop gathers his cum that leaks out of my pussy and thrusts his fingers deep inside me.

"We need to talk babies, sweetheart. Because I want to put one inside you." Coop thrusts his fingers again. I arch into his touch as a small aftershock shudders through me.

"Maybe in a few years." I brush his hair behind his ear and kiss his cheek. I'm not ready for a baby yet, but the thought of having his child warms my heart.

Noah comes back with a washcloth. After cleaning me, he helps Coop move up on the pillows.

"He needs to sleep. You should stay with him." Noah caresses my cheek and I turn to press a kiss into his palm.

There's nothing I'd rather do than be with Coop right now. Nodding, I curl into Coop's good side and he kisses my forehead. The door closes as Noah steps out.

"You're going to marry me someday, sweetheart." Coop's fingers link with mine on his chest.

"You still haven't asked me." I yawn. Now that he's finally safe in my arms, I'm exhausted.

"I don't need to ask you to know your answer." He chuckles and tightens his arm around me as we fall asleep.

Seth

We decided to have dinner in the living room so Coop can join us. He's not quite up to sitting at the table yet. Madison wears pajama shorts and a camisole, while Coop wears pajama pants. They sit close to each other as he leans into the corner of the couch.

I gave him another dose of pain meds with dinner, but he seems well.

The tension that rode my shoulders for the past few weeks eases at seeing everyone I love in one spot. All together and safe at last.

"We should talk about the press release." Blake sits on the other side of Madison. His hand rubs her thigh like he needs to touch her, to know she's here.

"Tell them all to fuck off." Coop raises his fork. "Seriously, it's none of their business how we conduct our personal lives."

"If we don't say anything, they'll make up whatever they want." Noah sits back and observes us all.

"Which is why we need to do a press release." Blake circles it back around.

"We need to control the narrative as much as possible, but we also can't just put anything out there." I rub at the back of my neck, feeling the tension rise again. "Patrick backed us into a fucking corner by saying we coerced Madison into the contract."

"Not coerced." Madison holds up her hand with a smile. "Happily agreed."

"We could have Madison deliver the statement." Noah puts his plate on the coffee table. "Honestly, anything we say will come back to bite us in the ass." He holds up his hand as Coop opens his mouth. "Including fuck off."

"Then do we want to just say no comment?" I try to relax into the chair.

Madison sets her plate down and walks over to sit beside me. Her hands go to the back of my neck and rub at the tense muscles. "What matters is we're all here together. We can just live our lives. No need to hide what we are to each other. Maybe, in a way, Patrick freed us to just be ourselves."

I pull Madison onto my lap so she straddles me. Her blue eyes meet mine. "I want to take you out on a proper date, princess."

"I'd like that, boss." She kisses me briefly before returning to rubbing my shoulders. "I'm happy staying in, but I do need to live my life a little more. Maybe see the outside now that my stalker is neutralized."

"We still want to protect you." I breathe out a sigh. "But you're right. We need to get back to living our lives for us. Which means dates and romantic evenings. Time in the play room. Being all together and having our time to play with you alone."

"Work in there somewhere too." Madison smiles and leans in to kiss me. She sighs softly. "I love all of you. I want to make this work. I want to have a future together."

"That's what we all want, princess." That's what we all need.

Graham Fiancée Exclusive

Tonight Madison Harris opens up about her fiancé, her stalker, and the contract that changed her life.

Madison

"You've got this, princess." Seth straightens my blouse in the greenroom.

I touch my nervous stomach. This isn't like getting up in front of a class and giving a presentation.

A woman ducks her head into the room and says, "Five minutes to go on air." Then she wanders off.

I drag in a breath. I'm about to discuss my sex life on television.

"You'll do amazing." Seth slides his hand up my neck and searches my eyes. "You've been through so much already. This is just one more hurdle to jump. Just remember everything we went over."

I smile and arch an eyebrow. "Maybe I shouldn't have been naked while we went over the interview questions?"

"It's the best way for you to forget yourself and just be." His thumb skates along my jaw. "I'd kiss you, but I don't want to mess up your makeup."

I glance over my shoulder. "Do you really think I can do this?"

It will just be me and the interviewer. Well, and the crew and Seth watching.

"Yes. I believe in you, princess." He presses his forehead to mine. "Now go kick that hornet's nest."

I laugh, but it doesn't put me at ease.

"Just pretend you're talking to me." His blue eyes capture my attention and hold it. I could lose myself in them so easily.

"It's time, Ms. Harris."

Seth smiles and takes my hand as we follow the woman in black onto the set. They stop me and fit me with a mic. Seth steps back and smiles. Fuck, I fought so hard for that smile and it warms my heart every time.

The production assistant leads me over to two chairs next to each other. We decided to go with Mary Striker for the interview. She's fair and generally a good interviewer.

"Mary will be in in a moment." The assistant walks away leaving me alone on the soundstage.

I straighten my skirt and cross my ankles, tucking them under the chair. Seth decided on what to dress me in. We discussed pants, but I didn't want to hide anymore. Not now.

Mary walks onto the set and takes a seat. A flurry of activity circles her as they put her mic on and touch up her makeup and hair. When they finish, Mary smiles at me.

"Thank you so much for agreeing to this interview, Madison."

I return. "We just want to tell our story and clear up any confusion."

"Good. Good." She looks down at her notes and then over at the cameras and probably the director. "So, what's going to happen is I'm going to introduce you and then I'll ask you some questions, so you can get your side of the story out there. Are you ready?"

I glance over at Seth standing off to the side. I think about Coop, Noah, and Blake waiting at home for me. Our home. I'm so ready for this.

"Yes, I'm ready."

Chapter 172

Opportunity

Madison

It's been eight weeks since Patrick lured me to save Hope. Seven weeks since Coop came home and we told our side of the story. After my interview, there was still some interest in our story, but eventually, the news cycle moved on.

We went out on dates, separately. Friday nights became date nights. Seth took me to dinner, followed by a night of playing with different toys.

Noah and I did a book date. We went to a bookstore and bought each other books. When we got home, Noah tied me to his bed and read my dirty story to me until I begged him to fuck me.

Blake and I went axe throwing. I was surprisingly good at it. We also worked on what it meant for me to submit to him and what I needed from him. I fully trust Blake with every piece of me now and he does the same.

Coop and I went to a charity event. Though he found every darkened corner to lure me into and make me come. When we got home, since he was still recovering, I rode him until we both came and then he stayed inside me while we slept.

Sara, Hope, Kayla, and I get together at least once a week. Usually at McAvoy's. We're making our plans for business domination. And enjoying life.

Both Hope and I go to therapy. She's lost some more weight, and sometimes I can see the hyperawareness in her when we're sitting at the bar with our backs to everyone.

I feel it too sometimes. That feeling of being watched or worrying that I'm not seeing someone watching me. But I can't let it control my life and she's trying not to let it control hers.

But tonight is a big night.

I'm putting my earrings in when Seth comes into my closet. He laid out my dress and jewelry for me. The red dress has a halter neckline and pearls that cascade down the open back to brush the top of my ass. The skirt flares out and ends at my knees, and he didn't give me anything to wear under it.

"You ready, princess?" Seth's blond hair has gotten a little longer on top. He likes it when I tug on it. His dark blue shirt highlights his captivating blue eyes. His gray suit fits him perfectly. My man is fine.

"Almost." I put in the other earring and pick up the clutch he chose for me. He still picks out my clothes and I love that he does. I've added a few new items to my closet. Sometimes he likes to dress me too. Which makes me late for work, which means Blake punishes me.

Which I'm always down for.

When I hold out my hand to him, he takes it, leading me out of my room and into the living room. My guys stand as I enter. Noah's unruly blond hair falls over his dark eyes. His dark suit and white shirt make him look edible.

Blake's suit jacket strains on his large arms, but his green eyes take me in, every inch, until I feel hot from just his look.

Coop steps forward. His dark hair hangs loose around his shoulders as his pale blue eyes meet mine. "Fuck, sweetheart, we can just skip to dessert."

When he reaches for me, I dance away, knowing if he touches

me, we won't make our reservation and he'll get exactly what he wants.

"We agreed to go out to dinner together," I remind him, holding my hand up to stop him. He's all healed and allowed full activities again. They promised me a night in the play room, but I want to go out together as a group. Our first date all together.

"Fine, but you have to wear my ring." Coop reaches for my left hand.

The ring he gave me is on it. I don't take it off much, though it's still way too extravagant. Technically, we're no longer fake engaged, but he hasn't asked for it back. He brings my hand to his lips and kisses my knuckles softly.

Anticipation buzzes through me at the look in his eyes. He wants to ravage me tonight and I'm looking forward to letting him.

"The limo is here." Seth pockets his phone and holds out his arm for me. I slip my hand through his arm and he leads us out into the hallway and calls the elevator.

When it opens, we step on and Seth presses the garage level. Blake draws me back against his chest and Coop closes in on my front.

"How many times do you think we can make her come before we get to the ground floor?" Coop's eyes sparkle with mischief. My hands rest against Coop's chest.

Blake slides his hands over my breasts, making my nipples harden against the silk.

Seth raises my skirt out of the way and holds my leg up as Coop runs his fingers up my thigh. I lean my head back on Blake's chest and just watch them.

Coop sinks his fingers into my wet pussy and thrusts them in and out. "So fucking wet for us, sweetheart."

"Fuck, Coop." The sound of his fingers and our breathing fills the elevator.

Noah's fingers join Coop's stretching me open. I moan as they work me together. Blake massages my breasts and tweaks my nipples. When Seth's fingers stroke my clit, I'm done for.

Crying out, I shatter in their arms. They all withdraw. Coop, Seth, and Noah lick their fingers clean of my wetness, making my pussy throb in need.

"Just an appetizer before dinner, love." Blake slides three fingers into my pussy, thrusting them in and out. My breath catches as they all watch him push me over the edge. I explode one more time before the elevator reaches the garage.

I'm catching my breath as Seth leads me out and stops in the bathroom to let me freshen up. When I join the others, Noah holds his hand out to help me into the limo. The last time most of us were in a limo was after the benefit.

Seth wasn't with us because he had to take Elizabeth home. When my gaze lifts to his beautiful blue eyes, he smiles, settling my heart because that part of our story is just history. It's what helped us become us.

He takes the seat next to me as the driver takes us to the restaurant.

"We have a busy week next week." Seth holds my hand on his lap. "But we have this weekend off to play."

I bite my lip thinking of all the things I want to do with my men. All together. I rest my head on Seth's shoulder as they discuss the next week. Business is booming even after the article and the interview of us coming out as being together. We don't know what long-term effects it will have on my career. But I'm not worried.

Blake's phone rings. He takes it out and apologizes with his eyes to me as he answers it. "Blake Wagner."

We all wait quietly as he asks after a minute, "When?"

My hand tightens on Seth's. Phones aren't exactly my favorite things. I still have issues with texts I'm not expecting. I'm working through it in therapy.

"Okay, I'll let them know."

"I understand."

"Talk soon." Blake disconnects the call and slides his ringer to quiet before slipping it into his inner breast pocket.

I'm still staring at him, waiting for the other shoe to drop.

He clears his throat. "That was Bill Carr. They were supposed to set Patrick's trial date today, but this morning, they found him dead in his cell."

Seth wraps his arm around me as the news hits me. I'm not sure what to feel.

"What happened?" Coop asks.

"He hanged himself," Blake says.

What? I'm stunned. Patrick was a lot of things, but to take his own life? It seems unthinkable.

Blake rubs my knee. "Madison, it's over. There won't be a trial now. You don't have to worry about testifying."

Blake and I have spent days working through my fear of seeing Patrick in court. Of bringing up everything that happened. Of remembering everything he did to me, everything I witnessed, and not breaking down.

"Anna?" I ask. We've had lunch a few times, but mostly we just sit in silence. Anna and I survived something that could have been tragic, but we helped each other through it. She and her kids moved back in with her parents. Her divorce would have been final next week.

"She's been at the station. It sounds like she's taking the news well." Blake squeezes my knee. "What are you feeling?"

I don't know what to say. "He's dead, but that's not what I hoped for. I wanted him to go to prison for killing Hunter, threatening Anna, kidnapping and torturing Hope, shooting you and Coop, and stalking and drugging me." I draw in a breath and blink back the tears. Not everything would have stuck, but with that many charges, something would have gotten him. "But I worried it wouldn't happen. That he'd get out on a technicality. That he'd be free and I'd live in fear again."

I breathe in and exhale, meeting each of their eyes. "I didn't want him dead. He's a coward for taking that route. For doing that to his children, but I'm relieved I don't need to relive everything during the trial. I never have to see him again."

"It's over, kitten." Noah's dark eyes capture mine. "You're free. He's gone."

The limo stops at the restaurant and I look at the door, suddenly nervous about what may wait for me on the other side. As soon as this hits the news, I'll need to stay in for probably a week. People will want to talk to me again.

"Is the news out yet?" I ask Blake.

Blake shakes his head. His green eyes search mine. "No, the family has asked to keep it under wraps until they explain it to the children."

Relief flows through me. "Then it's done. He lived rent free in my head for months and I'm done with it. I'm not happy he's dead, but I'm glad to be free of the burden of him. I'm glad to finally escape him."

"Do you still want to go out to dinner, princess?" Seth tips my chin his way.

"Yes, boss. I want one night where I don't have to worry about the man that terrorized me. I want to celebrate that Coop is whole again and only a scar remains of his bullet wound. I want to enjoy all my men. But first I want to go out with the men I love."

Seth rubs his thumb along my jaw. "Anything for you."

When we walk into the restaurant, eyes turn to us. My four handsome men and me. Each of them touches me in some small way as we make our way to our table. There's a slight delay as they determine who gets to sit where.

I just shake my head as Noah and Seth sit beside me. We order our food and talk about work for a few minutes. It's not uncommon. Work is kind of the center of our world.

"This is a date. Not a business meal," Seth finally interrupts. "We're more than Morrigan Technology Group."

Blake chuckles. "Work has consumed us since college. It's hard to shift gears, especially when the woman we love works with us."

"That's something I want to talk about." I clear my throat as they all look at me with questioning eyes. I've been hesitating to bring this up, but now seems like a good time.

"You're not allowed to quit, tiger." Blake leans back in his chair as his green eyes lock on me.

"No, I'm not quitting, but we need to discuss the future. This job was always supposed to be a stepping stone. A leg up in the business world. I love you and will always stay with you as your girlfriend, but to achieve what I want to in my career, I will eventually need to move on from Morrigan Technology."

Seth nods. We've talked about this in our weekly meetings. He likes to touch base on where I'm at, what I'm learning, where I think I need to learn more. He also has me stripped naked while doing it, but it works for us.

"I want to run a business."

"You can help us run Morrigan." Blake arches an eyebrow.

I smile softly and shake my head. "Morrigan is your dream and baby. Not mine."

"What do you want to do, kitten?" Noah takes my hand on the table and squeezes it.

"I don't know yet, but I want to explore some. I'm not leaving tomorrow, but a year or two at Morrigan will be enough to launch me into the next phase of my career." I focus on Blake because he seems determined to keep me there.

"Whatever you want to do, we'll support you. If you want, I'll buy you a business." Coop flashes me a grin.

"And I appreciate that, but I think I want to do it on my own." I blush. "Well, not entirely on my own. I have friends who will help me. Maybe we'll find an established business or start one from scratch. But we want it to be ours."

"I can appreciate that." Blake blows out a breath. "I just hate having to train a new assistant."

My eyebrow rises. "About that."

Blake clears his throat. "I'm not talking about *training* my assistant. You're our girl. We're not replacing you for that."

"I know." I cross my legs. "But maybe you guys hire a guy assistant when the time comes?"

I look around at them. Coop smirks.

"Probably. We wouldn't want anyone to assume we have a contract with the new assistant as well." Coop leans on his elbows. "You know, sweetheart, if you'd sat next to me, I would have made you come at least twice by now."

My body heats. Coop loves to play in public. I like it too. That risk of getting caught fires something naughty in my brain. Coop is usually very discreet, and I know he'll take care of whatever comes of it if we get caught.

Before they caught my stalker, I worried about being recorded.

Thinking about those videos makes me think of Anna and how she's dealing with Patrick's death. She obviously didn't love him anymore, but they built a family and life together. He threw that all away. Now his children don't even have a father in prison to visit.

"What's going on in your mind, kitten?"

I meet Noah's dark eyes. "Thinking about Anna."

He nods and squeezes my hand. "She'll be okay."

He's right. She has a support system in place now. She had to. Either way, Patrick was no longer part of her life.

When our food arrives, I focus on eating and enjoying my men.

They've made it a point to watch movies on Sundays with me. We're playing catch up since I didn't watch TV during high school or college. So we talk about movies and they usually all have opinions on what I should watch next.

But I decide based on their recommendations.

"It's a classic," Noah says.

"So is mine." Coop gestures with his fork. "I just can't believe you've never seen it before."

I shake my head, trying not to laugh.

"You can't compare *Casablanca* to *Die Hard*." Noah lets out a frustrated sigh.

Seth chuckles and takes my hand on the table. "This one might go on for a while."

I smile and lean in to brush a kiss on his cheek. "If you'll excuse me."

When I rise, Blake begins to push his chair back but I hold up my hand.

"It's a crowded restaurant, Blake. I'll be fine to go alone." I smile because he wants to protect me. "There's nothing to protect me from anymore. And if someone tries something, you know I can handle myself."

Blake returns my smile. We've kept up with self-defense training. I've actually taken him down multiple times now. Things usually get heated during our sparring matches though. Sometimes I don't want to get away.

I move through the tables to the restroom. Awareness of my surroundings seeps into my conscious mind. Some women lean close to each other and whisper as I pass. Some men watch me walk. I'm aware of everything, but I'm determined to not let it make me cower or run to get Blake to walk with me.

The bathroom is empty when I enter it. I breathe a sigh of relief. When I'm washing my hands, the door opens and Deidre Byrne walks in. She's dressed up tonight and her silver hair is pulled into a beautiful bun with diamond clips.

Her sharp brown eyes focus on me. "Madison Harris, how have you been?"

I'm surprised she remembers me. "Good. I've been meaning to call you about a mentorship."

I dry my hands and she smiles.

"We definitely should talk." She glances at the door. "Are you here with your men?"

My cheeks grow hot. It's still odd that everyone knows about us, but I'm getting more used to it. "Yes."

"I thought there was something more between you when we had lunch. I've never seen four men so smitten with one woman. You must be exhausted all the time." Deidre gives me a knowing smile.

"They keep me busy at work and at play." I gesture to the couch in the bathroom. "Would you like to talk for a minute?"

She nods and we both sit.

"I'm not looking to leave Morrigan Technology yet, but in a year or so, I want to explore my options and figure out what I want to do. I'd love if you would mentor me and help me navigate a career similar to yours."

She smiles and arches an eyebrow. "How about a career just like mine?"

"What do you mean?"

"I mean, would you consider coming to work under me to take over my business in five years? We can wait to transition you in after you're finished learning at Morrigan Technology, but Seth and I have been talking."

"You have?" Seth hasn't mentioned it to me.

"I've been interested in you since our meeting. You're intelligent and the way you absorb everything is something special. There aren't many people who can go into an interview and talk about their private lives with the same poise you showed. Especially something as scandalous as having a sex contract with your bosses. But you went out there and clarified the important parts while ignoring the interviewer's tactics to get you to admit to anything more. That's a good skill to have when you work in an industry focused on feminine pleasure."

I draw in a breath. That interview was hard but necessary.

"You're looking to level up. You're ambitious and driven. I need that quality in whoever takes over Cliodhna. We need someone who will make sure this business keeps growing." Deidre tilts her head. "I think that someone is you, but you'll need training."

"I'm honored, and a little speechless to be honest." I swallow as my brain spins on the details. "If it doesn't work out . . ."

"You work with me for five years and then you move on if it's not a fit." Deidre's shrewd eyes search mine. "It'll pay you enough to have a nest egg to start your own business, but I think you'll find it's the right place for you. If not, you'll learn more about starting your own business and what it takes to run one. Those men were smart to hire you. I believe I have additional knowledge that will help you move into something else or take over Cliodhna."

I take a deep breath like I'm about to plunge into an icy cold lake. This might be just the opportunity I've been looking for.

"But first, let's start with that mentorship." Deidre pats my hand. "I just wanted you to know where my head is at because even during the mentorship, I'll be picking at your brain to figure out if you're a good fit. Does that worry you?"

"Not at all." I smile. "Should I call you on Monday to figure out a schedule?"

"Absolutely. Do you still have my card?"

"Yes. I can't wait to get started." I stand and smooth down my skirt.

Deidre rises and holds out her hand to shake mine. "We'll make a fantastic team."

Chapter 173

Filing

Blake

Madison is taking too long. I scoot my chair back.

"Blake." Seth's tone is a warning. "She needs this."

Fuck that. She needs to be wrapped in Bubble Wrap and strapped to one of our beds.

"Seth's right. She's still getting over the incident." Noah glances toward the bathrooms. "She needs to do things on her own to find her legs again."

"Fuck." I move my chair back farther. "I know, but—"

"But she's a capable woman and she'll always find her way back to us." Coop nods in the bathroom's direction as Madison works her way through the tables.

I take in every inch of her, looking for anything out of place. She wasn't the only one traumatized by the stalker. We're all a little more wary. A little more on guard.

When she joins us, we all stand. She flushes with a smile as Noah holds her chair out for her. After she sits, we all lower into our chairs.

"Ran into Deidre Byrne in the bathroom." Madison glances at

Seth. "She wants to mentor me and then have me come work with her to see if I'm a good fit to take over Cliodhna."

Seth grins and leans in to kiss her. "That sounds like something to celebrate."

He catches the attention of our server.

"What do you think?" Her blue eyes search mine.

"I think she'd be insane to pass you up." I smirk. As much as I want to keep her locked away in the tower, I know she needs to fly on her own too. "Seth's just excited about the toys."

"Fuck Seth. I'm excited about the toys." Coop rubs his hands together. Madison blushes a deep red, but her arousal is obvious in the darkening of her eyes and the catch of her breath.

The server brings champagne and flutes to the table. The sound of the cork makes Madison pale. Noah takes her hand and rubs it, whispering in her ear. Loud noises still take her back to that house.

I'm glad I'm not the only one who can help her through this. We've all been diligent. She's not fragile, but there are times she needs to be distracted from her thoughts. Distracted from being back in that house or her apartment. From that terror.

I'm actually glad Patrick is dead. We never have to see him again.

I didn't tell Madison that Bill suspects it wasn't suicide. The cameras stopped working that night. Patrick should have never threatened to kill his wife. Her family wouldn't want to deal with him potentially getting out or pleading to a lesser charge. They wouldn't want him to have any rights to his children.

No one will investigate his death. It's a closed case. Suicide is the official statement.

Patrick terrorized all of us for months. He almost broke Madison multiple times, but we held her together.

Now he's gone and we're still here. He can't hurt us anymore. She doesn't have to face him during a trial. He doesn't have a chance to see her again. Maybe I should send a thank you note to Anna and her family for taking care of the problem.

The server hands me a champagne flute and fills it.

"To Madison." Seth raises his glass and watches her as he speaks. "To a future filled with opportunity and good fortune. To the woman I love with all my heart and soul. To being the glue that holds us all together and for bringing joy into our lives."

We all clink our glasses and drink. Madison's eyes sparkle as she meets each of ours. She's not divided among us, but shared. Her heart is big enough to hold all of us. And all our hearts belong to her, fully.

Madison

I may have had a few too many glasses of champagne with dessert. The chocolate cake was divine. But as we head back to the limo, I'm not as stable on my feet.

When I stumble, Blake catches me against his side as we step outside. I'm not sure if it's the effects of the champagne or the feel of his hard body pressed against mine, but I'm ready for more dessert.

His green eyes shine down on me, and his smirk makes my heart flip over in my chest. "You ready for tonight, tiger?"

"Yes, Daddy."

Smiling, he shakes his head. "Are you going to be a brat tonight?"

I shrug. Maybe I'll be a brat or maybe I'll obey. Smirking at Blake, I take Seth's hand as he draws me into the limo. I don't sit on the seat beside him but straddle his lap. "What's the plan, boss?"

The divider is up between us and the driver. Traffic is a little heavier on Friday nights. I'm ready to play. I thread my hands in Seth's hair as Blake closes the door.

Seth's hands slide up the outside of my thighs under my skirt to cup my bare ass. Sparks scatter throughout me.

"We want you to beg for it, princess." He slips his hands lower but doesn't touch my aching pussy.

"What am I begging for, boss?" I'm ready to squirm on his lap to get his hands where I need them most.

"To take all of us into that divine body of yours."

Those words make my pussy so fucking wet. "How are you going to do that?"

He slides his hands under my thighs and strokes his fingers along my groin. I almost whimper, but I hold it back and wait for him to explain.

"You're going to take Coop and Noah into your tight little cunt. I'm going to take your mouth."

My eyes widen.

"And Blake is going to take your ass."

My mouth drops open as my pussy and ass clench at the thought. It was a lot with Seth in my ass. He's big, but Blake is bigger.

"You can take it, princess." Seth's confidence is hopefully right. "But first, why don't you get us all primed? Do you think you can make us all come with your mouth before we get home?"

I lift an eyebrow. It's not that long of a drive, but I'm up to the challenge. I slide off Seth's lap onto the floor of the car and undo his belt while looking into his dark blue eyes. When his cock is free, I don't waste any time, taking him deep into my throat, gagging slightly but relaxing to take him farther. I swallow around his tip.

"Fuck, princess." Seth slouches a little as I suck and lick and work his cock. I add my hands to stroke what isn't in my mouth and to gently squeeze his balls. I lift my ass into the air and pull my skirt up so the others can see my bare pussy glistening for them.

Coop groans. "Fuck. Me next, sweetheart."

When I hollow out my cheeks, sucking Seth so hard, he curses as he thrusts into my mouth a few times before coming. I swallow around his jerking cock, taking all of his cum.

Sitting back, I meet his eyes. He smiles softly, knowing I'm waiting for his command.

"Blake next, princess."

I crawl over to Blake and tug his belt open. Anticipation makes me so fucking wet. I lick my lips when I pull his cock out. I tease his tip with my tongue the way he likes before taking him into my mouth and meeting his eyes.

His green eyes burn into me as I stroke him and suck on him. I'm so into what I'm doing and focused on Blake's breathing that I gasp when a cock slides into my pussy.

"Don't worry, goddess, I'm shortening your work." Coop draws out before thrusting back in deep. "Got to get this pussy ready."

Fuck, just thinking about later and how much they'll stretch me is enough to trigger my release. I moan around Blake and take him in deep as Coop pushes me over the edge. Blake holds my head down as he comes with a groan. I'm still coming around Coop's cock when Blake lifts my head off him. Blake wipes his thumb along the corner of my lip and presses it inside my mouth. I suck the cum off his thumb while meeting his eyes.

"Perfect, tiger."

"Noah next," Seth says.

Coop pulls out while I crawl to Noah's lap. I spread my legs wide to ready for Coop to fuck me more as I draw Noah's cock out. Our eyes lock and I remember the first time I did this with Noah. My first day of work. He cups my cheek.

"I love you, kitten."

When I take his cock into my mouth, Coop thrusts back into my pussy. I moan as I take them both, falling into a rhythm with Coop's thrusts until I'm tumbling over the edge and taking them both with me. I swallow Noah's cum while Coop groans, but he doesn't come inside me.

I lift my mouth off Noah's cock.

"One more, princess."

Coop's eyes meet mine and he draws his cock out of me, still hard, practically weeping precum, glistening from my wetness.

He kneels on the floor with me. I turn and take him deep into my mouth, humming at the taste of myself on him. I suck him hard, knowing he's right there.

"Fuck, sweetheart." Coop grabs the back of my head and thrusts into my mouth before he groans his release. When I finish swallowing his cum, he lifts me up and takes my mouth in a carnal kiss. His fingers thrust into my pussy and his thumb rubs my clit until I can't think anymore as the flames engulf me.

My pussy convulses around his fingers as I moan into his mouth.

He rests his forehead against mine as he slowly fucks me with his fingers, sending little aftershocks through my system.

I thread my fingers through his hair and hold him back so I can search his light blue eyes. "Pain?"

"No, sweetheart. I'm ready for everything," he whispers.

My pussy throbs around his fingers. "Me too."

The car pulls into the garage as Seth helps me straighten myself. When we step onto the elevator, Blake backs me into the wall.

"We need to get you opened up, tiger." His green eyes glitter as he unzips his pants.

"Whatever you want, Daddy." I wink.

His chuckle is the only warning I have before he lifts my legs and impales me with his thick cock.

Gasping in a breath, I struggle to get used to the stretch of his hard cock buried inside me.

"I want your pussy wrapped around my cock, love, because later, I'll fuck that ass until you beg me for mercy."

I clasp my hands behind his head and cock my head. "What is it with you guys and begging tonight?"

"We love when you say please, princess."

The sound of a squirt bottle fills the otherwise quiet elevator. My pussy flutters like a Pavlovian response to the sound.

When Blake lifts me off the wall, Seth steps up behind me. His slick fingers slide inside my puckered hole and I shiver against Blake. Seth works his fingers in and out of my ass while Blake holds me still.

"We want to experiment tonight and see if you being filled with cum is better than us holding back," Blake murmurs in my ear. "I'm for the holding back."

Seth pulls his fingers out and thrusts his lubed cock into my asshole, all the way to the hilt.

"Fuck." My whole body tightens around the two of them before shuddering through a release.

"I like the idea of you being filled with our cum." Seth kisses me behind my ear.

I'm on board with whatever my men need.

Seth and Blake have a rhythm of their own as they fuck me together. All I can do is cling to them as they use my body. Their cocks sliding against each other with only thin walls separating them. When they speed up, I shatter around them on a cry, drawing them both into their release.

Warm cum fills me as they both thrust in deep. With every jerk of their cocks inside me, an aftershock floods me with endorphins. The elevator dings its arrival at our floor, but when the guys set me down, it's not our floor.

It opens to the downstairs office.

"What are we doing here?" I ask. It's dark and even the camera lights are out. A shiver races through me.

Coop takes my hand as he leads me into the dark. "It's my turn to play, my little whore. You remember the file room?"

I shiver. "Not exactly a fond memory."

"That hint of fear while I fucked you?"

Heat flows through me. "That was good. It's just what happened after . . ."

"I want to do what I promised you." Coop opens a door and backs me into the file room until the cold metal of the cabinet is against my back. My breathing is chaotic as the fear paralyzes me. That breath that haunted my steps coming closer and closer.

I can't see my hand in front of my face. It's so dark it's suffocating. My head is shaking before I even say anything.

"Coop, I don't think I can—"

"Yes, you can, goddess. Because you're amazing, and we need to fill that head with beautiful memories to overshadow the bad ones." He leans against me and kisses my neck. Awareness ripples through me. "Do you hear that rustling?"

I hold my breath and listen. I nod.

"That's everyone else getting naked."

My pussy aches at the thought of them naked, surrounding me.

Coop's hand goes to my neck but doesn't close around it. His other hand massages my breast.

"You're going to stay in that fabulous dress. Slip off your shoes, my little whore."

I take them off and sink a few inches. My heart pounds like a frightened rabbit's. I'm sure they can all hear it.

"Here's what's going to happen. You get to the count of ten and then we're coming after you. The only cover you have is darkness." His mouth brushes my ear. "We will find you. And when we find you, we'll take you. Any way we want."

<h1 style="text-align:center">Chapter 174</h1>

<h2 style="text-align:center">The Grind</h2>

Madison

"How do you stop this, kitten?" Noah's voice is close. Fuck, it's dark. But I trust these men to take care of me.

"Red. Yellow if I need to pause for any reason." I bite my lip. "What if we run into something?"

"I went over this room with a fine-tooth comb, tiger. There's nothing that can hurt any of us besides bumping of elbows and knees into file cabinets. I disabled the cameras." Blake's voice is calm. "You're safe. We're safe."

"We won't tell you who we are if we grab you. You can fight us off if you want, but we will fuck you, my little whore." Coop licks the side of my neck and I moan.

This shouldn't turn me on, but fuck. Everything in me is hyped up after the champagne. It's so dark, and with my heart racing, I'm more than eager to have more.

Coop steps back and I shiver as the cold rushes in.

"One."

Shit. I hurry to move around the file cabinet, trying to remember the layout of the room. It's large. I remember that. I work my way around the filing cabinets with my fingers dragging along them. Coop counts slowly.

"Ten."

My breath catches at the lack of noise. I hold perfectly still. My heartbeat is too loud in my ears. I hold my breath, trying to hear them, but there's nothing. I shiver. Where are they? Will I be able to tell who grabs me first? Will I fight?

That's the question. Am I going to freeze, or will Blake's training kick in and I'm going to accidentally hurt one of them?

There are a lot of moves that have me kicking balls. I really don't want to damage that.

A breath comes closer and I slide along the cabinet, but the pearls on my back clink against it, sounding like thunder in the quiet room.

Fuck. I push off and hold my hands out in front of me to find the filing cabinets on the other side. Cold metal meets my fingertips and I press flat against it.

Someone whistles, sending chills through my body. Then they all whistle. Fuck, these are the men I love, but that's spooky. It's like they're checking their locations, which also helps me because none of them are close to me.

I find a corner and sink down into a crouch, waiting to see what happens next. My hand holds my heart to keep it from beating out of my chest. But my body is heated and the anticipation of being caught actually makes me throb.

The one time Coop and Noah played something like this with me I could see them coming, but this is a whole different level. It's cool enough in here that I'm not sweating, but my skin feels tight as I hide in plain sight.

The sound of footsteps comes close to me. I press back into my corner as the footsteps draw near before they move away. The anticipation I felt slips away too. Fuck, maybe I want to get caught.

I stand, careful not to brush my pearls against the metal, and circle around. Maybe I can find the light and we can be done with this. Hands grab me, and before I can shriek, a hand covers my mouth.

A hard body presses against me from behind. His breath is heavy in my ear. I grab his arm that holds my mouth. I tug fruitlessly on it. His other hand lifts my skirt between us. He leans us both over and thrusts his cock into my pussy.

Fuck, that feels good.

I moan into the hand holding my mouth. Barely any sound escapes as he fucks me fast. I grip his hand holding my hip and try to pull his arm away, but he holds fast.

"Touch yourself." His almost nothing whisper makes it hard to distinguish who it is. "Make yourself come."

I stroke my fingers over my clit instead of fighting. As soon as I tighten around him, he comes with me. Before I'm even done with my orgasm, he pulls out and whispers low, "Next time I'm fucking your ass, sweetheart."

Coop disappears, leaving me standing there with his cum between my legs and my pussy still throbbing from my rushed orgasm. I need to move. We were quiet but not that quiet.

When I slide along the file cabinet, a whistle sounds, followed by the others. Fuck, someone is close and in front of me. I back away, but someone grabs me.

A surprised cry escapes before he clamps a hand over my mouth and pushes my back against the filing cabinet. His hard body presses against mine and that smell of the outdoors fills my nose.

Noah.

He lifts my leg, and his cock rams into my pussy. I moan into his hand. When I try to shove him away, he chuckles darkly and releases my mouth to grab my hands. He drags them over my head.

"Careful, kitten. If you cry out, the wolves will descend on you."

I bite my lip, but fuck, I think I want that. Noah's cock thrusts in and out of me quickly. His mouth captures mine. I know he wants a fight, but damn, I love to give in to this man. I struggle a little but also lift my legs to wrap around his waist.

His hold on my wrists tightens as his tongue plunders my mouth. My hips rock with his and I forget about the noise as the pearls on my back clink against the metal like a fucking dinner bell.

A hand skims down my side, startling me from the kiss and fucking Noah. That's not his hand.

"I warned you, my little whore."

Noah lifts me against him and turns me. Coop grabs my ass cheeks and his cock presses against my puckered hole before easing in. I cry out into Noah's mouth as Coop fills me with his cock.

They rub against each other inside me, filling me so fucking full. My body trembles between them. Noah leads my hands around his neck and I hold on as they fuck me between them. Every inch of their invasion into my body makes my blood sing.

We've taken it easy when we play together while Coop was healing, but now he's back to taking me hard and fast. I shatter between them, crying out into Noah's mouth as I drag both of them into their release.

Their hot seed fills me before Coop pulls out. Noah lowers me to the floor and steps away. I'm still panting and catching my breath as they vanish into the darkness. My dress slips down around my legs.

The inside of my thighs are wet. But I'm still turned on and want more. I'll never get enough with these men. The others have to know where I am. Should I just wait for them to find me or try to hide again?

I slide to my left and the scent of sandalwood alerts me before my hand runs into hot male flesh. My breath catches. My adrenaline spikes again. Seth.

He catches me against him and his mouth finds mine. I pretend to struggle a little, pushing against his chest as he holds me close. He lifts both my legs and pushes me back against the filing cabinet.

His cock slides inside me and I whimper into his mouth at how sensitive I am. My pussy flutters around him, clinging to him as he drives his hips into mine, grinding against my clit while spreading my legs wide.

Crying out into his mouth, I shake as my orgasm takes me under. His strokes quicken as he thrusts deep inside me. Holding his jaw between my hands, I deepen the kiss. He groans into my mouth as he fills me with his cum.

"Had enough, princess?" Seth whispers against my lips.

"No, boss." I haven't had Blake yet. I want them all. I want to feel their cum dripping from my pussy before they all take me.

Seth pulls out of me and smacks my ass. The sound is loud in the quiet room. Then he whistles as he walks away.

The whistles this time are close, practically surrounding me. My heart skips as I leave the file cabinets to cross to the other side, but instead of cool metal, I run into hot flesh. I yelp and back into someone else.

When I try to move to the side, there's someone else there. Fuck. I'm surrounded and trapped. Anticipation fills me with flames of need.

"Last chance to use your words, tiger." Blake is in front of me. His hand threads through my hair, sending sparks all down me. The tie on my halter top loosens. Someone else slides my zipper down.

"See, she can be a good little whore," Coop says.

I shiver as my dress flutters to the ground, leaving me bare with all my men surrounding me. It's dark but their heat is overwhelming.

Someone pushes on my shoulder, forcing me down to my knees, but Blake helps me so they don't slam onto the carpet. Blake lowers with me. They're all with me on the floor. The sound of their breath is loud in the room and my body is on fire.

I'm not sure who's where, except Blake. My body trembles.

Blake lifts me against him and his cock slides between my legs. I part my legs around his hips and he thrusts up into me, bringing me down on his lap. Someone parts my ass cheeks and presses against my asshole.

I wrap my arms around Blake and bite his shoulder as someone pushes into my ass. I'm so full of cock. Someone grabs my hair, lifting my head and turns my face to the side. A cock presses against my lips and I open.

He thrusts in deep before fucking my mouth. Tears well in my eyes from how deep he goes. Blake and the cock in my ass fall into rhythm. Blake pulls out while the man behind me pushes in. They work in tandem while the guy holding my hair fucks my mouth.

I relax into their hold, letting them use me. Another hand plucks at my nipple, pinching and squeezing my breast. Someone groans as his cum fills my throat and I swallow quickly around him.

He pulls out and another hand grips my hair. The hand turns my head the other way and I part my lips, ready for his cock. I take a deep breath before he thrusts in, pushing all the way into my mouth, making me gag.

Coop curses behind me as my body clenches around everyone. The cock in my mouth draws back and I gasp in a breath around his cock before he fucks my throat.

Blake and Coop keep up their rhythm of thrusting in and out of my pussy and ass until I'm just a mass of sensation between them all. I moan around the cock in my mouth as I gush my release all over Blake's cock.

"Such a good girl," Blake whispers in my ear.

"My good little whore," Coop whispers in my other ear as he fucks my ass harder, extending my release until I can't think. I'm just part of this all. We're all one as we strive to come together.

The guy in my mouth groans as his release fills my throat. I tighten around Blake and Coop, still climaxing or coming again. They both groan as they come with me.

Their cocks pulse as they spill their cum within me.

This time they don't withdraw right away. I'm sandwiched between the men who took bullets for me as we all breathe harshly together, coming down. I rest my head on Blake's shoulder.

Someone turns on a cell phone to add some light without blinding us all.

I release a breath, knowing our night isn't over, but feeling so content with them all right here with me. I can't imagine anything other than what I have with them. I didn't know my life could be like this. To be so loved by these men.

My future is carved with them as part of it.

When we finally rise to our feet, Blake swings me into his arms and carries me to the elevator. In our apartment, he doesn't set me down as he takes me into my bathroom instead of the play room.

"We're not done, are we?" I lift my head and meet Seth's eyes. I don't want our night to end with anything other than the play room.

"No, princess, but a quick shower and a bath to help relax you seems like a good break." Seth runs his hand over my back, sending shivers through me.

Noah turns on the shower and we all step in. When Blake lowers me to stand, they all wash me. Hands slide over me and I close my eyes, loving this feeling. The slight overwhelm when they all touch me, all caress me.

Hands glide over my pussy and ass, my breasts, my neck, my legs. I don't try to figure out who is where, just enjoy the stimulation. When I'm clean enough, Noah lifts me against him and we exit the shower. He releases me and steps into the bathtub. After he lowers into the bath, he holds his hand out for me.

I join him in the warm water, smelling the Epsom salts with eucalyptus. He draws me back against him and bends his knees on either side of me. I love when they take care of me. I rest my head back against his chest and my arms on his legs.

"This is heaven," I whisper.

"It is." Noah slides his hands around my waist and holds me.

The others are in the shower washing themselves. When we finish in here, we'll go into the play room. Anticipation buzzes hot and heavy through my veins.

But this right here, being held by Noah and seeing all the men I love, I'm at peace. We have each other and a future together. I close my eyes for just a minute, absorbing this moment.

Chapter 175

One More Time Forever

Madison

"Madison." Seth's voice is gentle. "We don't want you to prune up."

I wake and the guys are all out of the shower with their boxers on. Noah's hand gently strokes my stomach. I draw in a breath. I must have fallen asleep.

Seth smiles and takes my hands while Noah helps me stand. The water courses off my body and Blake holds open a towel for me. When I'm out, Coop offers Noah his hand to help him out and they clasp arms.

After Blake pats me down, Seth slides a silky slip of a nightgown over my head. I brush my teeth while Coop brushes my hair and then quickly braids it before tying it off. He drops a kiss to my shoulder before he backs away.

I've never felt more loved than I do with these four men. They are my forever.

Blake takes my hand and we all head into the kitchen. "Have a seat, love."

He walks around to the refrigerator and passes out bottles of water. I open mine and drink, not realizing how thirsty I'd been.

"How are you feeling?" Seth asks.

"Good. I'm ready for more." My cheeks flush with heat, but I'm not embarrassed. I want this. I want them. I want what only they can give me. "Please, boss."

"You can beg better than that." He quirks an eyebrow.

Coop stands and lifts me from my chair. I grab his shoulders as he sets me on the island. His heated blue eyes dance with mischief.

"Since we're going to come this time, maybe she shouldn't." Coop rubs his cheek against mine as he steps between my legs. "Seems fair to me."

"You want to edge her?" Noah sounds way too interested.

I swallow because I'm not good at denying myself pleasure, especially around them. "What if I can't hold it back?"

Coop drops his boxers to the floor. I bite my lip. Precum pools on his hard cock.

"We'll stop and go to bed." Seth's smile isn't what I was hoping for. "You need to learn control if you're going to be good in business."

I shake my head at his twisted logic. "Maybe we can build up that control over time?"

Coop slides his cock against my bare pussy. I hiss at the sparks lighting me up. "You remember when you tortured me, my little whore? When you tried to make me come knowing I shouldn't?"

He thrusts his cock deep into me, stretching me. I gasp.

"Fuck," I breathe out. My pussy flutters around the invasion.

"If you're going to fuck her, let's get her into the play room." Blake tugs on my braid. "That way I can bury my cock in her mouth."

I throb around Coop's cock as he lifts me against him and carries me into the play room. The lights are dim. The bed and the bench with the raised ends are readied for us. Coop lifts me off him and drapes me over the high end of the bench with my knees on the flat surface, my chest hanging over the end.

Blake takes hold of my hair. "Open, tiger."

I meet his green eyes and part my lips. He guides his cock into my mouth, sinking in deep. Coop thrusts his cock back into my pussy and I moan around Blake's cock. They fuck me fast and hard.

Probably so I don't come, but it's like a race to see which of us comes first. Even though I'm not supposed to win, I get closer and closer to the finish line.

Just as I'm about to come, Coop groans and fills me with his cum before pulling out. I throb with need, aching for release. But it slowly fades. Blake holds still with just his tip in my mouth. I lick and suck on him slowly, trying not to push myself too much but getting wetter with every stroke of my tongue.

Coop's hands grab my ass and spread my ass cheeks. "I've missed your ass, my little whore. I'm tempted to trade places with Blake and have him fuck your pussy while I . . ."

He thrusts his lubed cock deep into my ass. Fuck, that feels good. I moan around Blake's cock.

" . . . fuck this ass. You're so fucking tight still. We need to open you up, lube you up, and stretch you to hold all of us."

I draw in deep breaths through my nose, trying to calm down the sparks that are ricocheting on my insides. One stroke and I could come. My gaze finds Seth's eyes. He smirks like he doesn't think I can control my release.

He'd be right because I really like to come, but I'm determined.

Blake fucks my mouth again, pushing so deep he goes past my gag reflex and into my throat. I tighten around Coop's cock in my ass, but I don't come. Dammit. I'm going to win this time.

Groaning, Blake comes down my throat and I swallow every drop. He pulls out of my mouth and tips my chin up. His green eyes search mine.

"I love you." He leans down and kisses me. "You are my everything. I will never let you down again."

"I love you," I whisper.

Blake steps away. Coop draws out slowly before thrusting in deep again. I whimper at the need to come welling inside me. He does it over and over, slowly out and then thrusting in deep.

"I could do this all night, my little whore." He wraps his hand around my hip and thrusts three fingers into my dripping wet pussy.

I bite my lip as my insides tremble around him. He chuckles darkly in my ear.

"Wouldn't it feel so good to come around my cock?" he whispers as he draws out and thrusts back in. His fingers curl to press against my G-spot, making me ache.

It would be so easy to give in. But coming would end the night and would let Coop win.

"You two shouldn't ever play a board game." Seth's voice brings me back from the edge. "One of you would end up throwing the board in the air and nobody would win."

Coop chuckles again before smacking my ass. I yelp and he draws away from me. "Next time, baby, I'm taking you and me for a ride to see who can make the other come first."

I take a few deep breaths before Seth moves behind me. I look over my shoulder when he doesn't touch me as he sits. He rubs lube on a butt plug, but he also has a larger than normal dildo next to him too.

Swallowing, I stay where I am. "What's the plan, boss?"

"These will help stretch you out." He finishes with the butt plug and meets my eyes. "You ready, princess?"

I nod and he slides his lubed hand over my ass before slipping his fingers inside.

"Fuck." I bite my lip to hold back the moan wanting to escape as his fingers slide the lube inside me and press on the muscles to release. I glance over at Noah and Coop sitting on the bed's edge. Blake stands on the other side watching me.

I could come just from them watching me. My nipples are so hard they ache.

Seth pulls his hand back and takes the plug, easing the tip into my hole. "Breathe, princess."

I take a breath as he eases it inside until it's all the way in, filling me. I draw in another breath as he takes a towel and wipes his hands. He uses a wipe on his hand before he picks up the dildo and lubes it up.

I'm already dripping wet, but this should help with taking two cocks. Seth slides two fingers into my pussy and presses them down. The blunt tip of the dildo pushes against my entrance. I'm already so full. I suck in a breath as he pushes it in with his fingers inside me.

"Breathe, princess." Seth strokes his fingers in and out with barely the tip of the dildo inside me with them. "You can take this."

Maybe. Without the butt plug making everything tighter? Definitely. But damn, this is a lot. But I've had both Coop and Noah inside me as well as Seth and Blake. I groan as he pushes the dildo a little deeper, stretching me so wide.

"Need something to bite on, tiger." Blake echoes my thoughts.

"Maybe something to distract me?" I admit.

A vibrator turns on and I whip my head back to look at Seth. He holds a bullet in his hand.

"I'll come," I warn him. A hot breath on my pussy would make me come at this point.

His blue eyes spark with heat. "Then come, princess."

He holds the vibrator to my clit and presses the dildo in at the same time. I cry out as my release pulls me under. He works the dildo in and out of my pussy as the vibrator continues to push me over the edge.

Noah tips my chin up and I pant as my pussy convulses around the toys inside me.

"Need something to suck on, kitten?" His dark eyes lock with mine. Wetness drips out of my pussy.

I lick my lips and open my mouth for him.

"Good kitty." He holds the back of my head and thrusts into my mouth in rhythm with Seth fucking me with the toy. I suck when I can as I come down a little between peaks. Noah's fingers massage my jaw as his hand tightens in my hair to control his thrusts.

Seth takes the vibrator from my clit and I release a breath before Noah slides his cock deep into my throat.

I'm still stuffed full and Seth thrusts the dildo in and out while his fingers rub against my walls. Noah pulls back and I suck and lick along the underside of his cock. My gaze lifts to his dark eyes as he watches Seth fuck me with the toy.

The toy slides out and I whimper a little at the loss, but Seth drives his cock into my pussy in one stroke. It flutters around the invasion. He pulls almost all the way out and then presses his cock in with the dildo, stretching me almost to the point of pain.

Pleasure bursts inside me. My release screams through me as I moan around Noah's cock. His cum fills my throat as he groans his release.

"Good girl." Noah caresses my face as he steps away.

Seth pulls out both the toys, an aftershock rippling through me. Noah pulls out of my mouth and I struggle to catch my breath.

"So much for edging her." Coop slides his hand over my ass. I shiver beneath his touch. Every inch of me is sensitive and on the cusp of coming again already.

Seth shrugs. "She needed it."

Coop slides his hard cock into my pussy and I groan at how good he feels. Holding my hips, he pulls me back until I'm sitting on his lap with his dick inside me. He rests on the opposite rise of the bench and pulls me to lie on him, my back to his front.

"Put your feet up, sweetheart."

I lift my feet and put them up on the bench, squeezing him tighter inside me. He slides my nightgown up a little, but then skims his fingers over my breasts over the satin, using the silk to slip over my nipples.

My breath catches as Noah lifts my legs and parts them as he sits down between them.

"Help Noah get hard again, baby," Coop whispers in my ear as he tweaks my nipple through the silk.

I reach for Noah's already hardening cock and stroke my hand down to his balls. Noah slides his hands up my thighs slowly.

"Have I ever told you how much I love your pussy, kitten?" His hands stop at the top of my thighs and he studies my pussy with Coop's cock buried inside it. His thumb slips over my clit.

I draw in a sharp breath as my hand squeezes his hard cock.

"Such a pretty pussy you have." He leans over me and takes my mouth with his, taking everything I have as he thoroughly wrecks my mouth. His forehead rests on mine as we breathe each other. "It's a shame I'm going to ruin it."

He takes hold of his cock and slides it back and forth over my clit, sending pulses of need through me. Our eyes lock on each other as he slides his cock down against Coop's. Coop lifts my legs, opening me up more to the pressure of Noah's cock filling me too full.

My mouth parts on a silent scream at the exquisite pressure.

"You feel that, baby?" Coop whispers in my ear. "How tight you are with both of us inside you? How stretched you are to take us this fucking deep?"

I can't say anything. I can barely breathe. Noah sinks all the way inside me and wraps his arms around me to draw me against him as he lies back.

Blake's hands caress my hips. His presence looms over me as he straddles Coop's waist. I'm not sure I can take more. I suck in a breath, knowing what's going to happen next and wanting it even if it feels like it will tear me apart. His cock presses against my asshole and he eases in steadily.

I cry out as he fills me, settling in deep. Panting unevenly, I can feel them all inside me. Blake's cock rubbing against the others.

"Breathe, kitten." Noah trails his finger from the side of my eye down to my lips.

I suck in a breath and try to keep from shattering around them all.

Seth turns my chin his way and rubs my lower lip with his thumb. My body trembles between them and my pussy pulses around them.

"One more, princess."

Noah glides his finger over my clit and my lips part for Seth. Our gazes collide. Seth strokes his cock into my mouth. Sucking on Seth's cock, I shatter into a million pieces, clenching around Noah, Blake, and Coop as my orgasm tears through me.

As it eases, my body goes limp on Noah's. Blake wraps his arms under my knees and around me, practically folding my loose body in half.

"Want to make Coop come, love?" Blake whispers in my ear.

Seth grins, drawing out of my mouth and stepping back, stroking his cock. I take a trembling breath. He winks at me. He likes to watch almost as much as he likes to take part.

With his cock buried in my ass and his arms wrapped around me, Blake lifts me, fucking me up and down on Coop's and Noah's cocks.

"Fuck, fuck, fuck," I whisper as my orgasm runs me over like a freight train, squeezing around all three of their cocks like a vise. I scream as Noah circles my clit in almost lazy strokes.

"Fuck," Coop groans. His cock jerks inside me as he fills me with his cum and triggers Noah's release. They're pressed so tight together, rubbing against each other as they stroke inside me.

Noah moans his release. His cock fills me. My whole body trembles in Blake's arms as I can't seem to stop rolling into another orgasm. Seth steps forward and holds his cock to my lips. Moaning, I open for him.

Cradling my jaw, he slides his cock into my mouth and comes on my tongue. Humming around him, I swallow every drop.

Blake lowers me on Coop's and Noah's still-hard cocks and pushes me down on Noah. My legs fall on either side of the bench. Blake draws his cock out and thrusts back in.

"You want more, tiger?"

"Yes, Daddy," I cry out.

"Good girl." Growling, he fucks my ass. I cling to Noah as another wave of my orgasm takes me under. When Blake roars and his cum fills my ass, I black out for a moment as bliss surrounds me.

I suck in air as our heavy breaths fill the room. Their cocks twitch inside me as my pussy pulses around them.

"Fuck, I love you all so fucking much." I blow out a breath.

"That time was on purpose?" Coop strokes his hand over my hip as Blake pulls out. "Not because you were stuffed so full of cock?"

I chuckle softly and run my finger around Noah's nipple as I rest against his chest. "I love you, Noah."

He lifts my chin. His brown eyes glow with the love he has for me. Never for a moment did I doubt Noah loved me. We are meant for each other. "I love you, kitten."

Pressing up on Noah's chest, I turn to Seth. His dark blue eyes make my heart beat a little harder. We've had a few rough patches, but there's no one else in this world I'd rather spend the rest of my life with. "I love you, boss."

"I love you, princess."

Blake walks in, drying his hands. His green eyes take in every inch of me. Of all of us, our love story was the rockiest. Distrust is hard to get over, but he's always been my protector. He's always saved me, and I hope in some way, I've saved him.

"I love you, Blake."

He grins. "I love you more, tiger."

My heart feels like it's glowing as I lie back against Coop's chest. I lift my hands to caress the scruff on his jawline. My dark prince. I let out a content sigh. The guy I didn't think could love me but I couldn't help falling in love with.

"And? My little whore? My goddess? My future wife? Do you love me?"

"How could I not love you, Coop? You make my life complete. All of you. I didn't know I was missing you until I met you. I could never let any of you go. I love you, Coop."

"Good." His hands stroke up my sides. "Because I love you more than anything else in this world. We all do."

Chapter 176

Epilogue

Three Months later

Madison

"No, no more shots." I shake my head as Sara beams from across the table. Hope and Kayla smirk as they try to flag down our server in the busy bar.

"I'm celebrating my internship." Sara preens and grins. Her pale green eyes sparkle. "One internship and a semester and I'm officially done with college. And we're one step closer to world domination."

Kayla hands me a shot glass. "To world domination. You have to drink."

I shake my head and take the shot. "Seriously, no more. If I come back drunk, Blake will spank me."

"So more drinks?" Hope raises an eyebrow.

Fuck, they know me too well. I love it when Blake punishes me. But if I'm too sloppy drunk, I won't remember it and I'll just wake up with a headache and a stinging ass.

"Fine, no more drinks." Sara leans in and whispers, well whisper shouts to be heard in the busy bar, "I have a date with Drew Young next Saturday."

My mouth drops open. "Seriously? After he fucked two women behind each other's backs?"

"Only one was behind the other's back." Sara shrugs. "I'm moving on and he's funny. I'm done waiting for Wyatt to come to his senses. To realize we're perfect for each other. I'm done waiting. Period. After everything you two went through, waiting for something that will never happen is ridiculous. Wyatt's not going to notice me, so instead of pretending to be with someone else, it's time to actually *be* with someone else."

She wiggles her eyebrows and Kayla laughs.

"Gonna get some vitamin D. Nice." Kayla lifts her soda glass and clinks it on Sara's water. "See if he has a hot sister to set me up with."

"Is Bea still not coming with you?" Hope's wide blue eyes meet Kayla's.

Kayla's smile falters. She swirls her straw in her drink and shakes her head. "I'm trying to convince her, but she says she can't."

Hope rubs Kayla's back. We're all excited about Kayla moving here. The choice is her career or her girlfriend, which sucks.

"What about you, Hope? Are you dating anyone?" I ask, hoping to keep Kayla from sinking into too many drinks.

Hope's cheeks flush red, but she shakes her head. "After the last few blind dates, I'm taking some time off. It's just so pointless." She sighs. "If I need to get off, my BOB is better than anyone else I've been with."

Kayla pats Hope on the back. "Since I'll be a free agent when I get here, I'm willing to help with that anytime you need it. I got any size dick you could want."

Sara, Hope, and I bust out a laugh. Kayla is still trying to convert us. Sara is the first to stop laughing.

"Okay, it's been months since you came out as dating four guys, so what's with the ring still?" Sara raises an eyebrow as she holds my hand up to the light. The diamonds sparkle and warmth floods me.

I shrug. "Coop likes that I wear it. His parents feel that if he's going to be with me and the guys, then he should at least consider marrying me so our children will have their name."

"Seriously?" Hope's mouth drops open.

I smile and run my finger over the ring. "It's not like I can legally marry them all, but Seth has been working on figuring out a way to bind us legally together and Noah's been looking into ceremonies."

"For real?" Sara beams. "This calls for a toast."

I laugh and wave off the toast. "Not for a while yet. They're just preparing for the future."

Sara is already talking to the server though.

"Good, because I want it to be official that you're my sister-in-law." Kayla squeezes my hand. "And all those cute little babies you have with Coop are my nieces and nephews."

"Mine too." Hope grins. "I'm going to be the best aunt."

Sara passes out the four shots. "To being aunties."

Fuck it. I take my shot, knowing Blake's picking me up and the ride home is going to be awesome. The punishment is always worth it.

A year after that

Madison

"Dammit." I suck my throbbing finger after crushing it in the drawer.

Coop steps up behind me in the mirror and draws my finger out of my mouth to examine it. "Calm down, sweetheart."

His hands guide my hips back against his. I'm wearing my bra and a half-slip, while he's in his boxers. His erection presses against my ass.

"This is my first day at a new job." I glare at my reddened finger. "It has to go perfectly."

"You always have a job with us." He lowers his chin to my

shoulder and meets my gaze in the mirror. "I'm not sure how we'll do with Trevor."

Trevor is an older man who is a professional assistant. He knows what he's doing and the week I spent with him to get him up to speed on our processes flew by. He'll be an amazing asset to my guys. Plus, he's happily married to Adam.

"Besides, Dee already loves you." Coop inches my slip up.

"And she'll love me more if you don't make me late." I put my hand over his and meet his eyes in the mirror. This game of making me late was fine while I worked for them, but it's not going to fly with my new job.

He kisses my shoulder, sending sparks skittering through me. "You just need a release to calm you down, sweetheart."

It doesn't matter that we've been together for a year and a half. They all still key me up, and I know it's useless to resist him. He sucks on my shoulder as he lowers my panties. They flutter to my ankles. I thread my fingers into his silky hair. He hasn't tied it back yet, so it's loose.

I tug on it hard, and his light blue eyes flash to mine. He smirks.

"You want to play rough, my little whore?" He bites my shoulder and I moan.

He wraps his arms around my waist and lifts me, leaving my panties behind on the bathroom floor. I love when he manhandles me. I grab at his arms, but his grip is tight.

He drops me on the bed and when I try to scramble away, he grabs my ankle.

"Uh-uh, little whore. You're mine now."

I flip onto my back as he lowers his boxers. He's still ripped and the slight scar on his side is all that remains of his wound. He crawls over me while dragging me under him.

Biting my lip, I try to wiggle out of his hold. I'm not trying that hard though. When he lifts my hips to his mouth, he thrusts his tongue into my pussy.

"Fuck." I grab his hair with one hand and the bedspread with the other as he lashes my clit with his tongue before spearing it in and out of my pussy. Moaning, I arch as pleasure sizzles through me.

"If you're going to fuck our little slut, you could have at least woken me up." Noah moves down the bed to me. "Good morning, kitten. Getting ready for work?"

I meet his brown eyes and nod, not able to breathe let alone talk right now. Noah kisses me deeply as Coop fucks my pussy with his tongue. Noah releases my bra before tossing it away. I shatter, coming in waves as Coop drags me to the edge of the bed.

Coop parts my legs, holding them wide open for him. "We need to be quick though."

"That shouldn't be a problem." Noah grabs my hands and holds them above my head. "Open your mouth, kitten. Get my cock nice and wet."

I part my lips as Noah kneels over me. Coop thrusts deep into my pussy, making me moan. Noah feeds his cock into my mouth, pushing in deep. I hum around him as they fuck me.

"That's my good girl." Noah pulls out of my mouth and spreads my saliva between my breasts. He slots his cock between my breasts and thrusts between them while rubbing my nipples with his thumbs.

Coop pulls out of my pussy and pushes my knees up to Noah's back before sliding into my asshole.

"Fuck," I breathe as they work my body expertly, taking what they want from me and giving me everything in return.

"Open your mouth, kitten."

I part my lips and Noah holds my neck to thrust his cock through my breasts and into my mouth. Coop rubs my clit. My insides are waiting to burst.

"Come all over my cock, my little whore."

I suck on Noah's cock while Coop fucks my ass and pushes me over the edge, gushing my release. I strain between them as I come, sucking greedily on Noah. Groaning, Noah comes in my mouth. Coop thrusts a few more times before he curses and comes deep in my ass.

My head falls back on the bed as my breathing returns to normal.

"Princess, you need to get ready for work." Seth walks through the bedroom in his suit for the day. His blue eyes lock with mine and he smiles.

"Coming, boss."

"Yeah, you did." Coop smacks my ass before he pulls out. Noah rolls onto the bed beside me.

"Have a good day at work, kitten." Noah presses a kiss to my lips.

When Coop drags me down the bed, I shriek a little. He lifts me into his arms and carries me into the already running shower. Seth probably turned it on, knowing we'd need it.

"Don't get my hair wet." I warn him. "You've already used up a lot of my time."

"You loved every minute of it." He kisses me and sets me down in the shower. After he washes himself, he helps me rinse off. "Fuck, Madison, how am I going to get through the day without fucking you?"

His light blue eyes sparkle with mischief.

"You haven't," I point out and turn off the shower. Grabbing the back of his neck, I drag his mouth down to mine for a thorough kiss. "I'll take care of you when I get home."

He smirks. "You better."

I dry off and hurry into the dressing room where Seth waits for me with fresh panties and bra. "Sorry."

He shrugs. "I expected it. It's not like we didn't take advantage of the fact you worked with us this past year and a half."

I smile, too delighted in being theirs to be ashamed. "Are you sure I'm ready?"

He works on the buttons on my shirt. "You're ready."

I bite my lip and he leans down to kiss it.

"You're going to kill it, princess."

I hug him tight before hurrying out of the closet because that man makes me want to misbehave too. I grab the to-go mug of coffee Noah made me and give him a final kiss as I hurry out the door, taking the elevator down.

When I reach the garage, Blake shakes his head. "You're late."

"I'll be on time." I stretch up to give him a kiss.

His hand wraps around my waist as he leads me to the car. He opens the door, and after I get in, he walks around and joins me.

"Aren't you going to be late?" I arch an eyebrow as the driver puts the car in drive.

"Come here and take your punishment." He pats his lap.

My panties dampen as I lie across his lap.

"Count them, tiger."

I blow out a breath.

"You'll get an extra one for that. Count." His hand lands on my ass cheek.

"One."

By the time he gets to five, I'm squirming on his lap, hoping for relief.

"Six."

He straightens me on the seat next to him. My cheeks feel warm as I squirm to get comfortable. Not only is my ass cheek sore but also I'm turned on.

"Do you think it's wise to send me to work turned on, Daddy?" I arch an eyebrow at him. "After all, there will be all those toys there."

"Behave, tiger, or I'll have you on your knees for dinner."

I press my thighs together and let out a sigh. But it's not like I don't like being on my knees. As if he can read my thoughts, Blake chuckles.

"No toys today, tiger. Otherwise, that's all you'll get tonight." His green eyes hold me.

The car rolls to a stop outside my new office building. "Fine, but I think Coop should be in charge tonight."

They still sometimes try to dominate me between the two of them. I'm all for it personally.

Before Blake can say anything, I kiss him and slide out with my coffee. I'm happy to let Blake be in charge of me, as long as he lets me come.

I draw in a breath and stare up at the glass-and-metal building. It's a new chapter in my life. I'm excited to see if this could be my future. But whatever the future holds, I have four men that will be with me every step of the way.

Chapter 177

The Final Epilogue

The Future
Seth

It's chaos when I open the door to our townhouse. I'm the last to arrive home because I had a call I had to make that kept me late at work.

"Papa's home!" A little blond terror runs past me in the foyer.

"No running, Oliver!" I say after him, though I know it won't make a difference.

"Hi, Papa!" His other half slams into my leg, hugging it.

I brush Olivia's curls out of her blue eyes and she gives me a huge grin. "Where's Mommy?"

"Upstairs, getting ready." She squeals as Oliver flies past and she takes off after him.

"Oliver, Olivia, bath time!" Blake yells from the top of the stairs.

"Papa!"

At the little voice, I look up to find one of our toddlers descending the stairs with a bright smile on his face. His dark hair falls into his eyes as he takes one step at a time while holding onto the railing. His green eyes sparkle as he gets to the second to the last stair and launches himself at me.

I scoop him up on instinct. He giggles and kisses my cheek.

"Miss you." His pudgy toddler hands hold my face still as he very seriously looks into my eyes.

"I missed you too, Liam." I shift him to my side. "Shall we go find the others?"

He nods and his fingers play with the back of my hair. If anyone had told me I'd thrive with this chaos in my life, I would have told them to check themselves into a mental hospital.

After Madison went to work at Cliodhna, our business was still booming. A few of those years we barely saw each other, catching time together whenever and wherever we could. We made sure to keep Sundays as our day to play. No one worked on Sundays, that became our rule.

Eventually, Coop actually proposed to Madison, but at the same time that we all did. Our relationship has never been conventional, but it's ours. We found a way to make our lives one with the help of a lawyer and a wedding service that satisfied all of our families.

A few years after that, the twins were born. They favor Madison, but it doesn't matter who the biological father technically is, because they're ours. Just like Madison has always been ours.

A year later came James, our first dark-haired child with bright blue eyes. Then came Liam, and while the green eyes could be Blake's, there's a probability that he could be any of ours. Xander followed a year later with dark hair and blue eyes. And last is baby Sophie with her blond hair and brown eyes.

While Madison has all our help, she finally said no more for a while. It might have become almost a competition to impregnate her. None of us had that on our kink list, but something about seeing her with a swollen belly made us all a little insane.

I walk into the kitchen with Liam and he struggles to get down. When I release him, he runs over to join Xander and James on the floor with blocks and toys. Noah has Sophie in a high chair with some finger foods as she watches her brothers play.

Her brown eyes find me and she grins. I release my breath. The chaos is worth every minute.

Noah nods toward the sink. "Grab me a washcloth, please?"

I grab the washcloth and hand it to him. He wipes Sophie's face and then her little hands. Yawning, she watches him and then me and then the boys. When she's all cleaned up, Noah lifts her and puts her on the floor.

She stands for a minute before dropping to her butt and crawling over to her brothers. Walking is still new to her and she prefers to get there faster. It won't be long until she's running after the rest.

Noah rubs the back of his head. "When's our reservation?"

"Eight."

"Can you watch them so I can change?" He smiles as Xander comes over, babbling about his block and showing Noah.

"Dada." Xander puts his hand on Noah's leg to steady himself. "Up."

Noah stoops and picks up Xander who shows him the sides of the blocks with all the seriousness a toddler can have. Noah makes the appropriate noises and asks questions.

I feel a tug at my pants and look down to baby Sophie. She holds her arms up for me. She's a quiet one, relying on her brothers to do the talking, or Olivia when her and Oliver slow down for a few minutes.

When I reach down and lift her into my arms, she snuggles against my chest.

"Dada needs to go change, Xander. Play with your brothers." Noah sets Xander down to toddle over to the others and sit on the kitchen floor.

Noah touches Sophie's soft hair before heading out to get ready. She doesn't lift her head. She fights so hard against sleep every night. Tries to stay up to be with the others, but she never makes it.

Coop walks in, dressed and ready to go. "Bags are packed and in the car."

James turns and runs over to Coop. "Pop Pop."

Coop squats down and looks at the others to make sure they aren't looking. "We had a deal, right?"

James nods, solemnly. "I made sure they stayed quiet while Sophie ate."

Coop narrows his eyes at him and then produces a chocolate. James's eyes light up and he shoves it into his mouth. He wraps his arms around Coop's neck and then runs back to the others.

I wait for it, because no one can put any food in their mouth without everyone figuring it out. Xander and Liam stand and wobble over to Coop.

"What's up, guys?" Coop smirks at the two of them.

"Pop Pop, can we have one?" Liam asks, holding out his hand. Xander mimics him, holding out his hand as they both put on their best *please* faces.

"What's the magic word?" Coop asks.

"Please," they say together.

He grins and fishes out two more chocolates, putting one in each of their hands. They grin and stuff them in their mouths before saying, "Thank you."

He straightens and tugs his suit jacket into place. His smile softens when he looks at Sophie's face. Her little fist is in her mouth as she sleeps against me.

"She'll get drool on your shirt," Coop warns. He originally wanted to be called Pops, but Oliver and Olivia kept saying Pop Pop until it stuck.

"Worth it." I sigh and cradle her against my chest, loving her soft scent. "They're going to be mad at you for giving the boys sugar."

"I'm not going to tell them." Coop laughs and the doorbell rings.

Before we can move that way, we hear the door open.

"Hey," Blake says. His voice carries into the kitchen from the foyer.

"Who are these little angels?" Kayla says.

"It's us, Auntie Kayla." Olivia sounds exasperated.

"Olivia? Oliver? That can't be right. Those kids are always covered in dirt."

They giggle.

"We had a bath," Olivia states. "Hi, Auntie Nan."

Olivia and Oliver run into the kitchen and claim the table and a stack of paper and crayons.

"You guys are sure you're good for tonight?" Blake asks as he comes in the kitchen with Kayla and her wife, Nan.

Kayla coos as soon as she sees Sophie asleep in my arms. She grins up at me. "Somehow that makes you look sexier than Coop. Though you're all still sexy. Madison is so lucky."

"I'll take it." I'm sure she'd willingly take Sophie off my hands. But it's so rare that I get a moment to hold a sleeping child, I'm not ready to let her go yet.

"How'd the call go?" Blake asks.

"No, Daddy." Olivia turns and glares at Blake. "No work talk at home. Mommy's rules."

Coop snorts and Blake whacks him on the back with a fake concerned look.

"You choking again, Pop Pop?" Blake lifts an eyebrow.

"No, Daddy." Coop is barely holding it together.

"Mommy said you can't call Daddy that, Pop Pop." Olivia rolls her eyes and tries to focus on her drawing.

Coop walks over and scoops Olivia into his arms. "Are you going to tell on me, Liv?"

She giggles and shakes her head. "No, Pop Pop. Put me down."

"Magic word?"

"Please," she says while giggling.

He puts her back in her chair.

"All right," I say quietly to get their attention but not wake the baby. Our children look up at me and my heart just can't stop growing. Having this family has really made my life complete. "Mommy

443

and your daddies are going to be gone all night. That means Aunt Kayla and Aunt Nan are in charge."

The older two nod and the younger ones are fighting over their blocks again.

I lift my gaze to Kayla. "Good luck."

"Are you taking the baby with you?" Nan asks. She wiggles her fingers to take Sophie.

I sigh and kiss the top of Sophie's head, taking a second to breathe in her scent before passing her off to Nan's arms.

Sophie wakes for a second before settling against Nan's chest. Everyone releases a collective breath. Noah comes into the kitchen.

"Hey, Kayla. Nan. Madison isn't down yet?" He glances over his shoulder.

"She wasn't up there when you changed?" I move toward the doorway. Blake puts his hand on my shoulder.

"She wouldn't let any of us in the bedroom to change." Blake smirks. "She was afraid she'd never get ready."

Kayla chuckles and Nan smiles.

"Go on. Have a good night. You guys deserve it." Kayla makes a shooing motion.

But that just begins the long train of good night kisses. After another ten minutes, we're standing at the foot of our stairs waiting for our wife.

"I can go knock," Noah offers.

"No need." Her voice floats down to us. Six babies and years of being with her and I'm still caught off guard by this beautiful woman who I call mine as she comes down the stairs. She's lost most of the baby weight. She says she still has more to lose, but to me, she's just as stunning nine months pregnant as the day she first walked into our lives.

Her red dress dips in at the waist, showing off her hourglass figure. This woman is everything I need, everything I want. She stops on the landing and looks down over her dress.

"I should change." She turns but I catch her hand. Her blue eyes are wide and uncertain.

"You look perfect, princess." It's taken me years to convince her that it doesn't matter what flaws she thinks she has, to me she'll always be perfect.

She softens and nods. "I do love the dress. Thank you, boss."

She closes the distance and kisses me on the cheek. "I love you, Seth."

"I love you." I capture her chin and hold her close, dropping a kiss on her lips. Her smile is soft and that's all I need. This life is exactly what I need. Having her and my friends and sharing our children. Her blue eyes sparkle up at me.

"Do you want to say good night to the kids?" I ask.

We can all hear the kids chatting away at Nan and Kayla.

Madison smiles. "Give me five minutes."

It never takes five minutes, but I humor her.

Madison

It took fifteen, but we made our reservation. Dinner was amazing as always. We love what Chef Matthews creates. We celebrated my promotion to CEO and Deidre's retirement with champagne and chocolate cake.

When we get into the limo to head to the hotel, Noah takes my hand in the car and lays a blindfold across my palm.

I arch an eyebrow. "Now?"

"It's a surprise, kitten." He smiles.

Turning my back to him, I hold the blindfold up to my eyes so he can tie it behind my head. This whole night has been planned meticulously by the guys. Blake and Noah made sure the kids would be taken care of. Seth picked out my fabulous dress. And Coop was in charge of picking our hotel for our first night out in a while.

Our first complete night off since the twins were born. Fortunately with five parents, we've been able to find time to spend with each other, but not all together. There's always a baby that needs changed, or a diaper, or a nightmare. I've missed being able to be with my guys all together. I miss our Sunday afternoons and stolen moments in the middle of the night.

Tonight is about us. Not being Mommy, Daddy, Dada, Papa, and Pop Pop.

But being just us.

The limo comes to a stop and I move to take off the blindfold, but Coop grabs my hand to stop me.

"Not yet, sweetheart."

I smile a little uncertainly, but I trust them to get me wherever we're going. Even if it looks odd. They help me stand and guide me across the sidewalk. A snick of a lock fills the silence before we're inside. My heels click against the floor and there's no sound beyond their softer footsteps. Wherever we are, there aren't other people.

"Where are we?" I ask softly. "I thought we were going to a hotel."

"Patience, tiger." Blake chuckles.

They guide me into an elevator and something smells familiar. We haven't been to a lot of hotels, especially recently. The goal tonight is to reconnect and not make another baby. I love my children, but six is definitely enough.

Though the guys seem to want more. As much as I love being pregnant, I'd just like to get my figure back for a while.

Coop draws me back against him and murmurs in my hair, "I love you, sweetheart."

"I love you." I lean my head back against his chest and place my hands over his around my waist.

The elevator stops and they lead me forward. Another click of a door unlocking, and then we're inside a darkened space. Someone turns on some lights and Noah takes my blindfold off.

I blink and focus on the floor-to-ceiling windows overlooking the night skyline. The sectional couch. The library. The kitchen with its marble island. Nothing has changed too much in this space, except us.

And Seth changed his room to a nursery for when the guys needed to care for the kids.

Without a thought, I step forward. It's been a few years since I've been here. We lived here for years before we decided to start a family and get a house. Seth maintained the apartment for nights when someone had to work late, but those have been few and far between.

Now, their focus has been more on the children and being home to spend time with them than on business. It was easy to lighten their loads once the company became the number one cybersecurity firm, even with our relationship in the open. They've really stepped up and let me have my career. And Deidre has been fantastic about the children and maternity leave. I even have a nursery set up in my office for when the kids were little and I was nursing.

Years ago, when I first stepped into this apartment, I was in awe of these men and this job and what it could mean to me. I could have never guessed then that we'd be here. In love, married, with a houseful of kids.

Seth steps up behind me and wraps his arms around my waist. "What are you thinking about?"

"Everything. The opportunity you gave me and what I've gained from it."

"You deserved everything, Madison." He draws me toward the play room door.

My thighs clench and I grow wet just thinking of what's behind this door. Even after all these years, I'm turned on by these men and what they can do to me. We talked about moving some of the furniture over, but after deciding to all share a bedroom and have a couple offices in the house, plus six children . . . It became less of a priority to move it.

Coop turns on the lights, revealing the massage table setup. He smiles. "I snuck down earlier today to prepare. It's been a while since we pampered you, goddess."

My pulse picks up. Seth steps up behind me and unzips my dress. His warmth penetrates my back and sparks light within. His breath moves the hairs on the back of my neck, so they tickle against my skin. A shiver runs through me.

"Do you want to give yourself to us, princess?" He kisses the nape of my neck as his hands slide into my dress over my shoulder blades.

"Yes, sir." My breath catches as he pushes the dress off my shoulders. So fucking much.

My body has changed over the years, but I don't see it when they look at me with those hungry eyes. They strip down to their boxers. Every one of them firm and tight still. Their health is important to all of us, because we all want to be around for a long time and our jobs keep us fairly inactive otherwise.

A home gym instead of a home play room we decided would be better in the long run.

"Come on, kitten." Noah holds out his hand. When I take it, he draws me into his arms and releases my bra before lowering my panties to the floor. "What's your safe word?"

"Red." I could never find another word that I liked after the incident in the file room. In all these years, I've never had to use my safe word, but Noah always checks to make sure we all know it. Even now.

"Lie down. Let us worship you." Blake claims me from Noah and leads me to the bed, helping me to lie face down.

Their hands work my tired muscles. My legs and my arms, then my back and legs.

I'm on the edge of total relaxation when hands move to my inner thighs, climbing higher, spreading me wide. My breath catches and my insides boil as those fingers work closer and closer to my pussy.

Hands knead my butt before sliding between my cheeks. I bite my lip, fuck how long has it been since I've had their full attention on me, all at the same time. It's intoxicating and heady.

A finger teases my clit as another circles my asshole. Their hands are slick from the massage oil and I'm wet for them, aching with need. Fingers slide into my asshole and pussy at the same time.

Fuck, I moan. It's been so long and yet, they've taken care of me in other ways, but not with their full attention.

"So fucking wet, kitten." Noah kisses my calf. Other kisses rain down on my body as they work their fingers in and out of me, all at once. The pleasure builds up slowly until I can't hold back. Crying out, I tumble into ecstasy, clutching at their still thrusting fingers, shivering under their kisses.

"Do you want us to bind you and use you, princess?"

"Yes, please," I cry as they push me over the edge again. My breathing is fast and my body trembles.

Their hands disappear and then Noah helps me sit up. He runs a rope through his hands and my pussy clenches, knowing what comes next.

"Arms across your chest in an X."

I put my hands on my shoulders. He takes his time binding my upper body. Every brush of his skin against mine stokes the fire hotter inside me. The tightness of the rope releases me from everything. His heated eyes meet mine and I can't help but feel this burst of love. There's something special about what Noah and I have.

We can sit for hours and not say a word. As long as we're touching each other, it's good. We made an impression on each other from the beginning and that feeling of being connected has never stopped. Never once did I doubt Noah's love for me.

"I love you, Noah." It's practically oozing out of my pores and I can't hold it in any longer.

He leans forward and kisses my lips. "I love you, kitten."

He helps me down off the table and leads me over to the bondage horse. Blake and Coop lift me onto it, so Noah can bind me face up, tying my ankles wide. When he finishes, they all step back and turn to Seth. I follow their gazes.

Seth sits in a chair watching us. The anticipation of his orders has me soaked and I almost moan at how much I need this. He smirks.

"Blake, fuck her mouth. Noah, her pussy, but leave room so Coop can work her ass." Seth holds up a large butt plug, glistening with lube.

My breathing is heavy as Blake takes my head in his hand. But he doesn't just take my mouth with his cock. He lowers his head and presses an upside-down kiss to my lips.

"I love you, tiger," he breathes out. We had a rough start and a few bumps along the road. Our trust has only grown more deep and respectful over the years.

"I love you, Blake." I meet his green eyes, so filled with love.

"You know you wanted to say it." Coop laughs. While Coop finds it humorous that our kids call Blake Daddy, I've actually stopped calling him that when we're playing. I'm still a brat for him occasionally, but not by calling him *Daddy*.

"Okay, Pop Pop." Blake smirks.

I giggle. Seth shakes his head.

"You guys are ruining the mood." Seth blows out a breath.

"I'm good," I say. When Seth arches an eyebrow at me, I smile. "I'll take whatever you can give me."

Each of them is looking at me. Coop still has a smirk. I haven't lost any of my desire for them. They haven't lost interest either if their hard cocks are any indication.

I release my breath. "I want to give up my control to all of you, but I'm glad we've grown together. That we have this huge life together and that this is just a part of us now."

"Very moving, my little whore. Now can I shove something up your ass or not?" Coop winks at me and I give him a smile back.

My gaze lands on Seth.

"Our goal tonight is subspace, so let's try to remember that objective." Seth rolls his neck and cracks it. "So, if we've got all the ribbing out of the way?"

"Yes, boss." I meet his eyes and see the flare of heat in them. I want what he can give me. What they all can give me.

Coop's wet fingers glide over my ass as Blake takes my head.

"Open, tiger."

I open my mouth and he slides his cock inside. He keeps it shallow while Coop works on my ass. All the humor dissolves as the tension winds inside me. When the tip of the toy slides inside my asshole, Noah thrusts his cock deep inside my pussy, making me moan on Blake's cock.

He fucks my mouth a little deeper with every thrust while Coop works the plug in and out, sinking in a little more each time. Noah's cock pulses inside me, but he doesn't fuck me yet. His fingers begin to toy with my clit, softly enough that I strain against the touch, trying to get him to press firmer.

When Coop seats the toy all the way to the flange, Noah drags his cock out before slamming back into me. I gasp around Blake's cock and he thrusts it deep inside my throat. Sparks collide beneath my skin as they take me higher and higher. Until I forget where they end and I begin.

This is all I need. Them and me, boiled down to our core. I love our friends and family and our children, but having them like this makes me feel so much more than I ever thought I could.

I'm so glad for everything that happened to make us a family, to bind us so solidly together. I know going into the future that nothing will tear what we have apart.

Coop takes my nipple into his mouth as the others alternate fucking into me. My eyes lock onto Seth's. Bright white heat overwhelms me as I shatter around them.

"That's it, tiger," Blake groans as he comes in my mouth. I swallow every last drop as Noah keeps fucking my pussy. Coop shifts in front of my mouth and slides into my throat, deep.

My love for these men knows no bounds. They'll take care of me tonight as I give in to them. And in the morning, we'll fuck more before returning home.

Meet C.S. Berry

C.S. Berry is a combination of my love for writing and my love for reading. She began as an experiment and took off into something I absolutely adore. It's not often you can do what you love and it works as a career. As for me, I love reading and romance and heroines seriously getting railed. I assume since you've read my books that you do too.

If you want to discuss books or anything with me, come join my Facebook group, C.S. Berry's Spicy Executive Suite. And you can always catch me on Instagram @csberry.

Oh and me, I have a lovely family who aren't allowed to read my books. But are so proud, they keep leaking my pen name. My dog and cats don't care about my writing as long as I sit still long enough for them to snuggle. For more of my books and to join my newsletter, visit my website csberry.com.

XOXOXO,

C.S. Berry

For more stories and updates:
csberry.com
Join my Newsletter

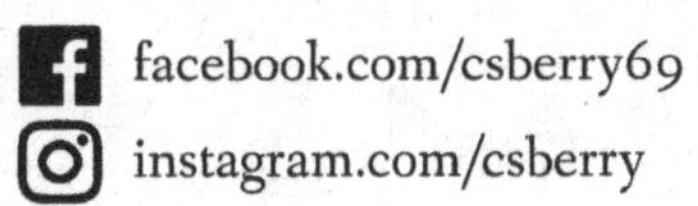

facebook.com/csberry69
instagram.com/csberry